Books by V. S. Anderson!

Among the Bones

Readers say:

"If you love mystery and suspense you must read this book."

"Great book very suspenseful. I plan to read book 2 in this series also."

"This is a tale of psychological suspense and intrigue, making it a page-turner like all of Anderson's books. Enjoy."

Three Strides Out

Readers say:

"Finally. A book about horse shows and jumping by somebody who knows about it, really knows."

"Fantastic read. Taut and chilling. Excellent plot."

"Craftily leads readers to an epic ending."

"Once I started this book, I did not stop until I finished. I stayed up until dawn to finish it. Great read and details about the horse show world are spot on."

King of the Roses

"An impressive debut by a superb writer."
—*Publishers Weekly*

"The Derby is run in less time than it takes to describe it—but the description itself is one of the most exciting whodunit chapters you're ever likely to come across."
—*San Diego Magazine*

". . .No racing novel since the advent of Dick Francis's series of mysteries has captured my admiration like this book.

". . . I have always felt that Dick has no peer. Now I am not so certain. . . ."
—*The Maryland Horse*

Readers say:

"Believable characters and dialogue, a complicated plot with many scary twists, beautiful descriptions of setting and race horses, and tense and exciting action scenes."

"The characters are complex and three-dimensional, all with blatant flaws and redeeming qualities, making it difficult to guess early on who the real heroes and villains are."

"It is great to read a book using horses and the racetrack that is so very real to actual situations! I thoroughly enjoyed this story and give it 5 STARS as a great read."

Blood Lies

"Another welcome find is Virginia Anderson, whose hefty BLOOD LIES (Bantam Crime Line) borders on Dick Francis' turf, the world of thoroughbred breeding and training in Kentucky . . . Action abounds, and it all centers on characters, the boy especially, who have dimension, including depth. A real winner, this one."

—-Charles Champlin, *Los Angeles Times*

"The plot is complex, the character development is detailed and the style is eminently readable. . . . The climactic scene will keep you on the edge of your seat. Altogether, I would call *Blood Lies* an extremely good read."

—-St. Petersburg Times

Readers say:

"Great read. Could not put it down till it was finished. I would definitely recommend this book. Plot twists galore."

"This book has it all and at such a fast catch me if you can pace, I found it really hard to put down."

"Really enjoyed this book very much. Definitely got my horse fix and a good mystery. The story was solid, tough and well written. The plot was intriguing. The characters were complex and believable."

AMONG THE LIES

Book 2

The Sarah Crockett Mysteries

AMONG THE LOST CHILDREN

By

V. S. Anderson

AMONG THE LIES

By V. S. Anderson

ISBN 978-0-9975768-9-4

The story, all names, characters, and incidents portrayed in this production are fictitious. No identification with actual persons (living or deceased), places, buildings, and products is intended or should be inferred.

Cover Design by 100Covers

Also by V. S. Anderson

KING OF THE ROSES[1]

BLOOD LIES[2]

THREE STRIDES OUT[3]

AMONG THE BONES[4]

Visit the author at https://www.virginiasanderson.com

For publication updates and news on promotions, sign up with Virginia's Books[5]

---

1. https://www.amazon.com/gp/product/B010QWR6DA
2. https://www.amazon.com/gp/product/B010QYDY3Y
3. https://www.amazon.com/dp/B0BRQZDXCS
4. https://www.amazon.com/dp/B0D8XL6S3J
5. https://virginiasanderson.com/newsletter-sign-up/

AMONG THE LIES

1

The buzzer goes off downstairs. That will be Kendra, for her standing appointment. It amazes me how regular, how punctual, she is. I expected resistance, seventeen-year-old sullenness, even finally rejection. She gives me snippets of these in plenty, yet twice a week, on schedule, she returns.

I am a professor of English—really, of writing; there is a difference—at Cresthill University, a small four-year school outside of Austin, Texas. Kendra and I are partners in an academic research study on reluctant writers approaching college. Her contract calls for her to produce writing, and she produces it. My contract calls for me to read her writing, and I read it. I don't know exactly what she comes for, or, really, what she gets. But there is something in me beyond my role as a college writing teacher, beyond my role as the carefully staid woman she has agreed to report to: something that bleeds. By rights that part of me should terrify young people like Kendra, but often they seem gentled, even drawn to me. Sometimes I wonder whether they respond to a need in me they are coming to understand as the pain of my unspent love.

I long ago quit asking her "How are you?" No need to; she'll tell me regardless how "it"—whatever it is that has happened—sucks. Instead I consult my bank of questions she might really answer. "What did you do last night?"

"Slept." She plunks down her notebook.

"I'm glad to hear that. Want tea?"

She works her mouth as if she's going to spit. "When do I ever?" She scrapes out her usual chair at our small kitchen table, flops hard into it as if it has tried to escape her, and sprawls.

She is made up today, thick dark lashes and a deliberate red mouth, her ash-brown hair wound into a knot on her head. Beside her I am a dull brown dog. I draw out my own chair. I am always aware, when she comes, of underplaying myself. I instinctively tone myself down working one-on-one with students, disguising an ever-present part of me I don't dare show. I'm not sure it's a virtue hiding my true nature so carefully, or any kind of best practice. But dissembling that way lets me give them what I owe them as their writing teacher, a reassuring space where together we can confront the misery writing inevitably gives us. "So what did you write for me today?"

Again I'm pleasantly surprised, though there's no reason, by now, that I shouldn't expect it: she did write, and she will let me read it, and she will endure whatever I have to say about it, and she will come back for more.

And she will unwittingly bring me a gift that is not in our contract. For those brief hours together, I will be able to offer this young woman the kind of nurture I cannot give to my own daughter, whose fumbles toward eloquence I will never read.

———————-

It was on just such a day, after I had seen Kendra off after a routine session, that the police came. They arrived in the form of a short, solidly built man in a scruffy but not quite ill-fitting suit that I have come to think of as whimsical in its carelessness. His thinning hair always reminds me of silk plucked off a corn ear harvested too late. His face is always a bit flushed, but that may be because I am one of the few people capable of unsettling him. His name is Sander Clauson, and he is a detective lieutenant in Austin, where I live.

We unsettle each other. Our history is full of seismic lurches and swells and occasional peaceful interludes. That day it had been a while since we last interacted: he'd had no reason to contact me, and I hadn't pursued my long-standing grievance with him. So that afternoon, when I looked over my balcony railing at the sound of the downstairs buzzer and saw him on the small porch below me,

I took a moment before I crossed to the door of my third-floor flat and pressed the button that let him come up. It wasn't an idle premonition that sharpened my breath. It was logic. We had parted amicably enough at our last encounter, but we were not friends. He did not do social calls. Something had happened. Whenever I thought, *something has happened*, there was only one place my mind flew.

I had to wipe my hands on my jeans before I opened the door.

"Good afternoon, Dr. Crockett," he said.

Not like him, pleasantries. "Good afternoon, Lieutenant," I retorted. He never played games, but for the moment it was easier on me to pretend I was playing one.

"Mind if I come in?"

I swung the door wide and stepped back. He had never before been to my home. I am not a naturally tidy woman, but to my relief, he looked around indifferently, as if he'd seen this kind of domestic chaos a thousand times before. He tugged nonchalantly on the lapels of his unbuttoned jacket, as if an interaction like this between us were a familiar habit. His only concession to the weirdness was to bounce on the balls of his feet a little, maybe to assure me he was in motion and would soon be leaving. "Something odd's come up. Something you might know something about."

I settled on the sofa. "Odd" removed enough possibilities that I felt able to gesture toward the chair beside me. For a second he hovered, then found his way into the chair the way somebody unused to boats might lower himself into one. I arranged my hands on my knee in what I meant to be neutral body language, looking for the rhythm of a casual conversation. "I know something about a lot of things a lot of people would call odd."

"Well, let's try one." He took a plain legal envelope from his inside jacket pocket and offered it. "Take a look."

I slid out four pictures. Of the house in which we now sat. The house where I live.

"Goodness," I said after a second. "I hope you didn't get these off a real-estate listing. If anyone here is selling, I hope they'll let me know."

"Not off a real estate listing," he said. "A corpse."

That was like Clauson. Clauson did not know any euphemisms. And if you ever suggested he might try being a little more subtle, he would think you were speaking French.

"A girl," he said. "A suicide."

In our experience together, I could count about six times I had wanted to punch him. This made seven. Seven times he'd dropped something on me that he had to know would land on raw bone.

I said, "I don't know any girls who would commit suicide."

"Maybe you don't know you know any."

I offered the pictures back. He didn't take them. I set them on the coffee table. "Sorry to seem uncooperative, but no, I don't know any such girls." If any of the students in my university writing classes were suicidal, none had confided in me. From my insulated distance on the sofa, I eyed the shots. Front views, from the sidewalk beyond the gate, one from the other side of the street, of the late 19th-century mansion where I owned the top-floor suite. "Why do you assume I'm the one this photographer was interested in? Three sets of people live here. Why me?"

"This is why," he said.

The second envelope held just one photo. He laid it on the table on top of the others, as if granting me the right to decide to pick it up.

I didn't. I could see it clearly. It pictured me, opening the gate at the sidewalk. Implanted clumsily with some sort of photo-editing program was a large silver-handled dagger extending out of my upper back.

I said nothing, though I expect he saw my eyes widen. Into that devil's pocket he reached again. Out came a third envelope. This one he thrust toward me, unopened. So I still had a choice. But I had never refused anything that had come between us in the past. The photo I pulled out looked like a selfie, a crowd of girls' faces all squeezed into the rectangular panel, alabaster teeth and whirls of hair, brown to strawberry and gold. The whole crew mugging up at the invisible overhead phone. Above a girl on the periphery, dark-haired, with a wide, upturned mouth and deep-set dark eyes, hung that same photo-edited dagger, smaller but more detailed, aimed at the crown of her head.

"You know any of these girls?" he said.

I searched among the clustered faces. I counted five. Soft, I thought. Plush. Downy dolls with perfect smiles. Were the fangs retracted for such images? "Did you get this photo with the others? Off a girl's corpse?"

"Yes." He shrugged. "Not a homicide, so not my case really. But since you were in the middle of it—"

I let myself laugh. "So you got talked into asking your good friend Sarah about it."

"Since I knew you."

No, not friends. "And that's the girl?"

He nodded. I studied her. Alongside the princesses in the photos, she was marginally the scullery maid. Her face was a little too narrow, her smile a little too cramped, her eyes a little too turned down at the corners, for beauty. "She was being cyberbullied?" After all, that's the story you hear on the morning talk shows. From cyberbullying to suicide.

"Sure she was," he said matter-of-factly. "By at least one of these sweet little ladies. Which one is the one?"

"You don't expect me to pick out the bully by looking at this picture, do you?" I set the photos down with the others. "From a bunch of strangers?"

"But from the looks of those other pictures, you're not a stranger to one of them."

This man was stuffed as always with secrets he knew I cared about but that he had no intention of divulging. I understood he couldn't shower me willy-nilly with information, even about crimes that concerned me. But this wasn't the first time he'd left me hanging because he had a use for me. Not long ago, I'd learned things he hadn't about a murder because my need to know was more desperate than his.

"I gather this girl's death is public knowledge," I said. "Maybe I could be of more help if you told me who she is."

"Was," he corrected. "Corinne Miller." He waved toward the pictures. "She had these printouts from her laptop stuffed in a pocket on her blouse."

"Corrine?" I asked. "Two 'r's'?"

"No, one 'r,' two 'n's.'"

I fiddled with a pile of papers on the coffee table before I answered. "I suppose a sensible person would be afraid."

"You're not."

"Not exactly." I was a target, yes, but not in the way Clauson thought. When my daughter Anna disappeared six years ago, when she was eleven, something arrived in her place. Something that sometimes spoke in her voice, slipped into her clothes—her jeans shorts, her halter tops, the neon-sequined shoes she liked—something that knew me, sought me out. For the first few years following her disappearance, this presence, hers, had sniffed through the rooms of my mind, querying, waiting: *Where are you? Why are you taking so long?* But last year my daughter's spirit had brought me a troubled child and said, *What you can't do for me, do here*. I had obeyed. Now here it was again, another child, someone else's child, on my doorstep. *You can't save me*, said my daughter's pushy presence, aiming its unforgiving emotional weapon, *but another one is reaching toward you. What you can't do for me, do here.*

Clauson's metallic blue gaze fixed on me, scissoring me apart even as I tried to decide how I felt. For the most part, I had always been honest with him, and I saw no reason not to be now. "I've had my fill of getting involved with other people's children. But someone is apparently so troubled by me that she—assuming it is one of these girls—would create this . . . message. Corinne and I must share something besides the message. We've both done something that matters a lot to someone."

His mouth pursed, a pinched wound in his rosy frown. Part of me wanted to give him a reassuring pat on the knee just to see how much alarm I could cause. But I continued mildly, "Let's put it this way. This time around, I'd rather be saving my own child instead of someone else's. But this is a threat to *me*." I said what I knew he would take as a warning. "If I know you're taking it seriously, I won't have to deal with it on my own."

He sat up with a lurch, grabbed the pile of pictures, crammed them into that inner pocket. "Here's the thing, Dr. Crockett. I'm going to email you some pictures. The girls we're checking out. Maybe one of them won't be a stranger. But you recognize one of these kids, you find out something about them, don't sit on it trying to save her like you tried to save the Pierce girl. You spit it out."

I met his outburst with a glare that seemed to make him sag. So he felt what I did: the pull of our history, a chain weighted with an implacable anger. He had to know he had just added a link. My actions last summer did save the Pierce girl. To his chagrin at the time, they also saved her father Russell, who had been accused of his wife's murder. I didn't remind him. He leaped up, the old hardwood floor thudding a little at the sudden pressure. "I'm just saying be careful," he said.

If I had been careful last summer, I wouldn't have saved Russell Pierce or his daughter. But it would take Clauson and me all afternoon to agree on what we meant by "be careful." "Absolutely," I said.

He made a hasty but amicable escape—almost. I followed him down to the porch and let him get down the steps before I called, "By the way . . ."

He must have known that my long-pending business with him would eventually surface. A new flush bloomed in his jaws. I said, "Speaking of your cases, do we know any more about Celia Monahan?"

"I haven't gotten a report. I'll check on it."

"I would appreciate it."

He took a step but turned back with a grim little smile. "You're a little too polite, Dr. Crockett. I know you better than that."

"I'm not going to stalk her."

"Yeah, let's don't."

Then he did go. But I hadn't made the promise he thought I had.

2

Celia Monahan.

I should never have browbeaten Lieutenant Clauson with that name.

I shouldn't have forced him to confess his sins of omission, all the tasks on my behalf he had promised but hadn't done. Then I wouldn't have been propelled back along the downstairs hallway toward the staircase by a fresh surge of my ever-present anger.

I haven't gotten a report.

Hah.

In such moments, in the past, the bleeding part of me, the unreconciled angry part I think of as Raging Sarah, had driven me to take what some would call unconscionable risks. Some of those risks accomplished nothing, but then there were those last summer that had saved those lives. Maybe some new lives needed saving, but I didn't yet know whose. Was I in danger? Had Clauson not been truthful about the threat to me from his collection of mean girls? But that evasion, if it was one, wasn't what set me stomping down that hall hard enough to set the old floor boards creaking. No, it was that set of promises Clauson had reneged on, promises he'd hoped would keep Raging Sarah quiet. I'd managed to keep her stuffed in a mental dungeon where she couldn't blow up any bridges. But tonight she was rattling her chains.

Two things helped me keep the walls up around her. One, it was late, dusk on the April evening. Two, Adela, whom I heard rustling in her downstairs kitchen as I passed.

I peered in to find her sitting on the floor, her spidery legs, in the stretch-waist tights she favored, extended in a V. She was hunched over something vaguely metallic between her knees.

Adela grew up in this house; she had owned it long before I bought the top flat and Larry and Wallace bought the middle floor.

Now in her seventies, she lived in all the downstairs rooms, leaving the stair-climbing to us. She considered me a nice lady who paid my share of the water bill on time and who sometimes stirred up ruckuses that so far hadn't involved property damage or any bloodshed she personally had to mop up. She cocked her head my way when I asked, "Can I help?"

She ripped off a pair of cheaters, then flung down a much-mangled piece of paper. "This damn garbage disposal. 'Easy installation' bullshit. With damn instructions I can't read."

Oh.

Repairs to her co-owners' share of the house got done professionally and promptly. But anything of her own, for some reason, she felt compelled to tackle herself. More than once she had succeeded at projects that amazed me: redoing her bathroom, installing an electric wall heater, replacing her car's headlights. In my view, she just hated to be bested by inanimate objects. But now it looked like the inanimate object had won.

I picked up the sheet and saw why she'd lost patience with it. It was written in a font for ants.

"Give me the glasses," I said.

She offered them up, not shifting her position. "You want to do the yelling at some poor customer service flunky? You'll be nicer. You're not as mad as me."

"Someone's going to yell at customer service?" Larry entered from the back screen porch on his way in from work, his monogrammed leather satchel over his shoulder. "Oh, please! Let me!"

Not that he would have done much yelling; he was the mildest of creatures. He couldn't make out the directions, either. Neither could Wallace, his partner, when he entered a few minutes later. I don't know who decided our collective vision would become more acute over a bottle—or two—of wine. I do know that we got the damn thing installed and that it deftly ground up a whole eggplant skin Larry fished out of his and Wallace's compost pail. We cheered and I went back upstairs thinking I should at least wait until I was sober to plan how to do what Clauson wouldn't about Celia Monahan.

———————

I sobered up painfully when I opened the door of my flat and Alice said "Corinne."

Surely she didn't say that. Maybe she said, "Cornflakes." With an African Gray parrot, even when your hearing isn't wine-muddled, you can't always tell.

Alice hadn't been invited to participate in Kendra's and Clauson's visits; letting her out in company invited lawsuits. But as captive birds go, she had little room to complain. I had converted an entire corner of the main room to her "jungle," replete with all things parrot, from real branches and cloth fronds she could rip up and things to make noise with and organize in piles and places to swing upside down. I had pulled drapes across the jungle that day, but as always, she listened. She could have heard Clauson say "Corinne."

My wine haze resurrected my ever-latent anger. *She said Corinne's name. She has never said my child's.*

She never knew Anna. Clauson never knew Anna. Her school friends and her teachers never really knew her. No one ever really knew her. Except, of course, me, and my ex-husband Eric, her father.

And his lover, Celia Monahan.

3

Celia Monahan.

On my computer, front and center, lived one of those folders I never lost track of, never let get crowded in with other icons, buried among pdfs, lost in ranks of jpegs and video files. It held pictures of my ex-husband Eric Wyles and Celia Monahan.

Eric alone, Celia alone, Eric and Celia together. Two exotic storks. Eric blinding bright, Celia dark, feral, and sharp. They strutted before me in these photos as if they owned a universe I was not allowed to know. In it they raced their expensive cars up precarious Alpine highways, flung themselves down raging rivers in boats as delicate as blossoms, crashed their expensive bikes down boulder-strewn cliff faces, and flew. Eric designed and built hang-gliders and ultralights. In them Eric and Celia sailed off to distant moons.

Most people would think I was jealous. Why not? Celia stole the high-wire husband I had so miraculously netted—"miraculously" because in comparison to him a college writing teacher was a lowborn clod, even one with a high-paying tenured position at a respected school. Such earthbound creatures brought home paychecks so that others could sprout wings and step off mountains. So of course I should be jealous, not to mention resentful. But I was not.

No, the reason for my obsession with Celia and Eric lay in this fact: One day six years ago my eleven-year-old daughter went to play soccer at a local church playground where her Girls' Club met. When Eric went to pick her up that evening, she was not there.

She was not anywhere.

I knew some things about Eric because when we became lovers, Russell Pierce found them out for me. He had established an investigative team during his murder trial and he had left it in place as a gift for me. He had the pictures taken; he had them sent to me via text or emails. Here were some things he helped me know.

Eric was seeing Celia before the collapse of our marriage. Eric took Anna to see Celia. Eric ejaculated in a car Celia owned at the time, a car mysteriously stolen the day Anna disappeared. At some point prior to that day, Anna had been in that car.

A wild leap, the police told me. Of course your daughter could have been in that car. That's a long way from what you're accusing him of.

A long way in their minds, but stitched together for me in so much my daughter almost told me so many times. What did you do today with Daddy? A silence. Then: we played. Played what, darling? A game on your tablet? A longer silence. Just a game he showed me. In the car. In the car? But instead of answering, she took the phone he had bought her and went in another room.

I should have followed, that day and so many others. To do what? Those were the days she had begun to shriek that she hated me, wished she had another mother. Oh, she's just becoming a tweener, people told me. It was nothing. A nothing that made her scream at me and cry.

So I, deep in the fantasy I could salvage my marriage, shrank from confrontations with this "nothing" and with Eric over all the ways my unwonted solicitousness was smothering our child. Talked myself out of starting a battle one time too many, until I waited a few days too long.

How many times had Clauson promised that he would intrude just a little on the mirage of this perfect couple, find ways to expose the truths that I saw beyond their ethereal fairy-tales? *Do something if he won't!* my intractable alter-ego, Raging Sarah, shrieked. Bu I had been called hysterical the first time around and I feared a repeat of that disabling label even though I knew the day might come when Raging Sarah incurred it. If she did, it would be because she and I knew, even if the police didn't, that if they ever pursued those truths about my ex-husband and his lover, they would slam into a fact no one could say I had imagined: at some point the two of them, Eric and Celia together, had let something happen, had caused something to happen, to my child.

4

That night, as I did far too often, I opened that special folder, the one packed with pictures of Eric and Celia, this time to stoke my anger at Clauson for doing nothing and also to mentally flail at myself. It had been nearly a year since I first heard Celia's name, and still she stalked across my imagination, free as an angel. She deserved an inquisition. Why had I sat around waiting for Clauson to give her one?

"Fuck and damn," I said aloud, pushing away from the computer and disrupting Alice, who had been picking loose threads out of my sweater. No, creating loose threads in my sweater. She said, "Rattlesnakes." Or maybe she said, "Raffle tickets." I should have found time for her in the many gaps between Kendra and Clauson and the garbage disposal: you could not neglect parrots. They would mutilate themselves out of boredom. Maybe a game of parrot solitaire (she actually knew the suits!) would ease me past nightmares of Celia so I could salvage a night's sleep from the fading wine haze.

"Okay, let me get the cards," I told Alice. She said perfectly clearly, "Fuck and damn."

Oh, dear. Soon she'd regale Kendra with this new evidence of her misguided education. I was dealing cards under her beady suspicious gaze when to my surprise, Russell called.

——————

Russell and I came together last year because he was also searching for his lost daughter, not lost quite like mine was, but lost enough that when he found her, it took him a while to come to terms with all that had changed. There had come a moment when he wanted to marry me but decided he should not. Quite simply, he did not want to marry the fractured part of me that was all that Raging Sarah would let him have.

We had ended, that day, with an understanding that had guided us for nearly a year. He had been recruited to New Mexico to do scary defense stuff with computers, and I was in Austin, still the respectable academic when I was not mentally stalking my daughter's abductor, whoever that turned out to be. My first duty to Russell was to resolve the issues that plagued me so that I could commit to the life we both imagined. He would help when he could and with what I asked for. He might have his own opinions about the steps I was taking, but he promised not to impose those opinions on me.

I had to admit that one reason our pact had worked so well was that I hadn't really taken any meaningful steps. I never asked how much he knew of what I had and hadn't done, whether and how much his team (One person? Ten?) watched over me. He had certainly never objected to my feeble efforts to "stalk" Celia. But then, there was no danger in driving on public streets behind Celia in her red Audi to the warehouse where Eric honed his creations. No jeopardy, not even legal, in sitting and sipping coffee from a thermos while I waited and watched. I always let her drive off unmolested; I settled for screen-grabs of her edgy professional portrait on LinkedIn, on Tik Tok, Facebook, and Instagram; I copied, pasted and filed her cool sales pitch to consult, develop, promote, publicize. That was the extent of my risky behavior. My daughter did not need to come home to find me in jail.

But both Raging Sarah and that ghostly presence of my daughter living in my imagination had recently been grumbling quite a bit. Staring at the pictures Russell had sent me was increasingly not enough. I was no closer to answers that would free me to a different life.

But oh, how I had relished the glimpses of that promised life in those months of quiet joy with Russell, so different from the five years before. Those years had been empty, lonely, without touch, without another body against mine, no breath in the air around me but my own. Russell had taught me a love I had never learned from my ex-husband Eric. Love with Eric had been a whirl through a firecracker spray of light and sparks. But this new love was completely different: I wanted Russell, the sight of him, his voice, his forthright presence, as a kind of inundation, a slow sweet wash that expanded forever. He'd laughed when I shared this image. "You make me sound fucking boring."

"Well, the fucking part usually isn't boring," I had said.

So that night after Clauson's visit and my home-repair collaboration I was pleased to see his number. But I was also surprised. We had talked just yesterday about the New Mexico trip we were planning for me the following month. He wanted to show me petroglyphs. I wanted to bask in the idyllic future I guiltily thought of as "after Anna" as if my commitment to finding her was some passing phase. That night I assumed we'd talk as we usually did of the happy nothings in which my plans about Anna didn't figure: what little he could share about his work, Alice's latest brilliance and curse words, his daughter Tommy and her new major in mathematics and whether she would find AI less worrisome than he did, how the weather in Santa Fe was so much better than in Austin and how I should come there more often, about . . . about . . . never really about us. "After Anna" always seemed far distant. I needed some plan to bring it closer, but nothing had suggested itself.

I curled on my screechy old glider on my balcony and opened FaceTime. The street three stories down was quiet as always, the April night stirring the sheltering trees. On the small screen Russell came to life, brought to me by Pure Fucking Magic, his home office behind him, a lamp at his elbow: a solid, square-shouldered man with direct blue-gray eyes that always saw more of me than I meant to give away. I was happy to have escaped thoughts of Celia. I hadn't seen that day for what it was, beginning with Clauson's visit: a quiet shifting of the ground under me in which doors to the future creaked open, letting in unexpected slivers of light. I hadn't seen Russell's surprise call as part of that seismic shifting. But it turned out he hadn't called to noodle over trip details or Alice's achievements. He had called to tell me that Celia Monahan had become a person of interest to the FBI.

That news didn't land quite the way he might have expected. It called up my memory of my own interaction with the FBI. *Oh, that FBI? The one that shrugged off my theories about Eric and wanted to investigate my college boyfriends, for goodness' sake!* They had taken a lot of notes, those FBI people. I would hear back, they told me. I never did. But Russell wouldn't have called if he hadn't considered this information important. My mind zoomed where it always did, to Anna. The FBI investigated missing children. Celia was connected to at least one child who was missing. "Wow, that's interesting. Does it have anything to do with Anna, do you think?"

"Not so far. At least as far as we know."

It was his sharp tone that made me look twice at his expression on the tiny screen. Russell was one of those people with a smile always just below the surface, as if even the grimmest situations were mere speed bumps we would all muddle past. But now the ever-present smile-in-waiting had tangled up with lines of concern.

"I'm not in any danger, am I?" I asked.

The frown lines didn't lighten. "I hope not. I don't know."

"But why should I be? I haven't been anywhere near Celia." Surely my episodes of distant surveillance didn't count. "Is this man she was spotted talking to someone I should know about?"

There was an unfamiliar heaviness in the way he leaned on an elbow; he rubbed his eyes. "The alias we know is George Franklin. We don't know a lot about him. But you're in Celia's orbit via Eric. People interested in her might be interested in you."

This new apprehension didn't suit him. Did he think I should be afraid? In fact, my pulse thumped with excitement. "Is there something I can do?"

"Yes," he said, still sharp, as if he'd brought me a knot that needed cutting. "Pay attention. To your surroundings. Unexpected things happening around you. Odd things."

Odd things. Clauson's word. But the teenage prank Clauson had described didn't merit this kind of worry. I took a breath to tell him about it, but stopped. The whole day seemed to want to be taken away somewhere and looked at, as if its secrets were swathed in brown paper that I wanted to peel off by myself. I found myself wanting to shift us to one of our usual mellow conversations. "Of course. If anything happens, I'll tell you. I was hoping you had something new to tell me about petroglyphs."

Maybe I sounded flippant; his silence felt heavy. But the smile lines came back, I thought a little forced. "You'll probably be sick of petroglyphs before I'm finished. I found a whole new site to go exploring."

"That's terrific. Send me the GPS."

We did talk then about Santa Fe and all the wonders I would find there, along with other reassuringly mundane bits of our separated lives. It was nearly midnight his time when we hung up. I went in to face an affronted parrot, who was not mollified by the cardboard paper-towel innards with which I tricked her into her cage. As I thanked the prescience that had made me spring for shriek-proof insulation when I bought my apartment, I decided to blame my obstreperous alter-ego Raging Sarah for stifling the news about Clauson and pushing the conversation about Celia and the FBI to such a hurried end. She was the one who wanted to paw through these things that had happened, as if she thought she was the only one who would know what they meant.

Well, if anything came of the day's events, there'd be plenty of time to tell Russell. Up to now I hadn't had anything to tell him that would alarm him, but I didn't like the way the possibility of alarming him made me feel. Raging Sarah had nagged me from the day Russell and I had agreed not to marry that one day he might regret his promises to let me make my own decisions about how best to find my child. It was hard not to listen to Raging Sarah. Sanity and logic, foremost among Russell's many virtues, had had six long, futile years to find Anna. But was I going to start hiding things from him so he wouldn't worry?

You may have to, Raging Sarah said.

Damn. I took a moment from picking up food Alice had apparently used for volleyball practice to talk back to Raging Sarah: "I didn't hide anything. I'll tell him when there's something worth telling."

She might have followed me, still poking, if I hadn't had to make one last detour for a nightly duty to perform.

5

That duty was my nightly NamUs search.

NamUs was a website started by empathetic law-enforcement officials who realized one day that they had all these unclaimed and unidentified bodies, and that out there in the world, hunting for exactly these bodies, were the families and loved ones of people gone missing and never found—searchers like me, come to NamUs to dig for answers among the digitized records of the bones. Those blessed by NamUs found their loved ones embodied in the sterile data, where they could virtually finger precious traces: scraps of clothing, rusted watches, trinkets, sometimes hair tendrils, sometimes dry snippets of text that spoke of DNA.

The site is maintained by the National Institute of Justice, part of the federal government. I had long since entered the dry data that was all I still owned of my child. Height, weight, hair, eyes, age last seen, date last seen, dental records. I had her dental X-rays; she'd had no fillings, just a couple of idiosyncrasies we'd been preparing to correct with that teenage torment, braces. She'd once fractured a bone in her foot playing soccer. I had those X-rays, too.

NamUs laid my entered data alongside the thousands of files of unknown victims (tens of thousands since the site's 2007 inception). And each time a new case was delivered—from police, coroners, courts—the site ran its impersonal checks: Yes, this data point matches, yes, maybe, yes, no . . . no, this isn't your daughter. Not this time.

The number of possible matches expanded each year. At first I cared only for the bodies of eleven-year-old girls with the right time-elapsed-since-death found within a few days or months of her last day with me. Then girls with the right time-elapsed-since-death who had been eleven at death but who had been found within the last year, the last two years, the last three, four, five. Add to that those twelve-year-olds, thirteen-year-olds, fourteen-year-olds, God, now seventeen-year-olds . . . After all, I had no way of knowing whether she'd been killed instantly, killed after a month, after a year, two years—or whether she'd even been killed at all.

And they didn't always find the jaw, with the slightly crooked incisors my X-rays would have matched. They didn't always find the right foot that might have shown me the scratch mark of a healed fracture. They might not even find the pelvis that would have verified sex; they might not have DNA. So I couldn't surrender my judgment to electrons that wanted to filter out the less likely cases. I had to probe even the outliers, just to be sure. More than once, I'd hung there frozen, too terrified to tremble, until some small, anomalous trait or feature I dug out from the details—*this is not Anna*—gave me leave to breathe and stumble on.

More than once, I'd met other mothers in person. For sometimes you simply had to go there, wherever the fragments were held, to go there and see. Once I even sat in a drab municipal office in a distant city and listened as a man and a woman laid claim to a child about whom I'd been so sure . . .

Not every woman in my place would have tormented herself with nightly trips to a place like NamUs, which by definition could never supply good news. Yet I kept going back. Every failed search on NamUs gave me one more scrap of hope Anna was still alive. And not just hope: a rush of relief like the precious hit from an addiction. I craved that dose of hope from each NamUs failure the way some people cling to a drug they know can kill.

But since I had known Russell, the nature of my searches had changed. When I first met him, he'd told me that I didn't really want to know the truth. *You crave this game, the answer always one more chase around one more corner. But that's no kind of life*. Eric, damn him, had echoed: *Kids gone this long don't come back, but you can't accept that. As long as you can hound me, you don't have to move on.*

So every keystroke into NamUs was an act of defiant denial. *I can face it. Bring it on*. Yet every keystroke rang with a supplication: *Don't let me find her here*.

But now I was less sure of what to pray for. In Russell's rare unguarded moments he betrayed what he was thinking: that once Anna was dead, my search would be over and we could get on with our new life. Sarah could begin her sad but necessary work of acceptance. She would mend herself into the whole, restored woman he had been waiting for.

Sadly for *his* hopes, he could envision futures for me without Anna but I could not. In every future I could imagine, she was there, alive and treasured, part of the whole he planned for us.

It had grown so hard watching him tap square pegs into the round holes of what might be an impossible future that I had begun to think, perversely, that the hope I *should* be holding on to was the one that would free us at last to confront "after Anna." I should hope to find her here in the bytes of NamUs, among these scavenged bones.

——————

At least tonight NamUs did not mock me. It did not hand me my daughter's body. The path ahead was still open. I logged out wearily, thinking that at least Corinne's parents would not have to search NamUs for her. A gesture for poor Corinne felt like a true last duty. I looked up her obit.

She was seventeen, a junior in high school. She had a younger sister. She died. No mention of a service. No flowers; donations to a local children's hospital, please.

My memory wrote her parents' missing sentiments into the bleak obit language: *our beloved daughter, how could we lose her? How could we have saved her? What did we do wrong?*

My fingers wanted to crawl to the search box for them, to tell them the one thing I knew for certain, in case someone else did not.

They'll say grief can be accepted, your time with what you've lost remembered as a gift. They'll say memory will live on as a sweet burden, the pain finally fading.

I laid my hands down on either side of the keyboard. I sweated into the wood of my desk so profusely I was amazed I hadn't marked it.

All lies.

6

I slept after all, woke to a spring morning free of wine haze but swimming in dreams of Celia and strange men and little girls chittering around me like imps. I staggered out to attend to Alice, who did not understand the concept of having to go to work.

I arrived on the Cresthill campus in a foggy April rain, in good time for my appointment with Taneesha Carrington, who had temporarily replaced me in the university's writing program administration during my two semesters of research leave. Along with tenure came a good parking spot, so I had only a short sprint to my office on the ground floor of Tremaine Hall. I wasn't all that sorry for the diversion; a lot of my best self lived on this clean and well-ordered if not elegant little campus on the northeast edge of Austin, to which I had been lured from the University of Texas by an offer I couldn't refuse. In the familiar space I let myself into, I became, with a surprisingly welcome sense of letdown, an ordered partner to the bland filing cabinets and the books on the shelves.

Taneesha and I had scheduled a working session and then an escape to an indulgent lunch. I'd been looking forward to the emotional lift I'd get from serious work on clear goals with Taneesha; time with her had a way of reassuring me that lives could still rest on solid ground. I'd recommended her for the position because I knew her virtues: a wide theoretical grounding in writing theory and pedagogy coupled with a respect for day-to-day practice, and above all the priceless ability to distance herself from the constant and pointed provocations that students would sling at her door. More than once, when a disgruntled student sat in my office with her fingers on all my buttons, I'd cut the power to those buttons by asking, what would Taneesha do?

Maybe I should consider unburdening myself to her a little, looking for stable guidance and maybe a reprieve from the loneliness that had plagued me these six years. I talked to almost no one about my daughter; mistakes I'd made last year reminded me that it was wisest to steer clear of my pain and share only my jaunty upsides. Taneesha didn't know my history, but she had the kind of capacious soul that might be able to take it in. True, she would probably echo the common-sense warnings I expected from Russell, and maybe she would counsel me to give Clauson more time. And meanwhile, out there somewhere, Raging Sarah and I were both certain, waited a terrified, assaulted, bleeding, girl . . .

I shook myself. I was a tenured professor of English, come in to confer on professional program matters. Exactly the mother my daughter needed to find waiting: active, financially stable, *sane*.

I had come into the office early because I wanted to take home a couple of books for the research study and I wasn't sure where they were. My shelves had long ago run out of space; since then, books both read and unread had piled up on anything that could be construed as a level surface. Hunting through three layers on a little table tucked into one corner, I felt a presence in the open door behind me. I turned, expecting Taneesha. Instead, I found myself facing a small, pale woman raising her hand to knock. She wore a gray skirt, a cream-colored blouse with a floppy bow at the neckline, and a dark blue blazer. At her throat hung a simple silver chain, and cautious silver studs winked in her ears. Her medium-length brown hair curled obediently around a white, worried face.

Russell had said to watch for odd things happening around me, but there was nothing especially odd about this woman; I thought *parent* and my reaction was routine. Couldn't be a bad grade, I hadn't given any grades this semester, and besides, federal privacy rules said even administrators like Taneesha and I couldn't talk to a parent about a student's work. I summoned a polite-but-not-too-inviting smile from my collection of professional expressions. "Can I help you?"

She looked around the office, her small mouth pursing in something like bewilderment, probably wondering how the clutter in a working office could have run so amok. She shifted a tidy black handbag from her arm to clutch its strap in both hands. "Are you Sarah Crockett?" she asked.

Not Dr. Crockett, like a parent asking after a child's professor. No, Sarah. And that difference told me in a cold flash who she was.

I didn't want a single ounce of her burden but beneath that reluctance came a gut-deep flutter. A piece of Clauson's odd thing that had happened was standing right here. I worried for a tenth of a second about the ethics of pushing through her grief to see whether anything I needed to know about photo-edited daggers lay beyond it. "Yes, I'm Dr. Crockett." I gestured toward one of the few clear chairs.

She lowered herself a little gingerly, probably thinking that the chair hadn't been dusted in quite a while. "I'm Rebecca Miller. My daughter . . . Corinne . . ." She positioned the handbag on her lap. "They said in the office you'd be in today. I imagine you know why I'm here."

I settled in my own chair before my computer. "Yes, the police spoke with me about what happened. Did they show you a picture of me?"

"Yes, with that . . . you can imagine . . ."

That seemed to be the way it took her, the inability to finish what she'd started to say. She looked out the big, heavy-paned window. Tommy Pierce had gone out that window into the small courtyard the night I met her; the window was latched now, no escape. I had ten minutes before my meeting with Taneesha. What could this woman and I tell each other in such a fragment of time?

"Did you know my daughter?" she asked.

"No. Not at all. I don't know where that picture of me came from or what it means." I braced my hands on the knees of my jeans, pushing away from the scent of her anguish so I could think. What did she know about those pictures, those girls, or that dagger? "The police officer who showed it to me showed me pictures of some other girls, but I didn't know any of them either. I assume he showed them to you, to find out if they were Corinne's friends."

"Friends!" She made a terse sound, more a bark than a laugh. "They . . ." She found the end of this sentence. "Killed her. They accused her, called her names . . . called her . . ." But this she couldn't manage. "We took down all her Facebook, all the places she posted, it was just too awful. The police took copies of everything. But they act like they aren't even sure a crime has been committed. They have to be so sure who sent what, who said what . . . They even act like Corinne did those things."

"What things?"

But she waved me off. "I just thought surely, if one of the girls was threatening you, you must know her and you would have some idea of how to make the police do something about this . . . awful thing."

She apparently didn't know that she was talking to someone who had failed to make the police do something for six years.

"May I make a suggestion?" I ventured. "Would you consider sending me pictures of Corinne's acquaintances, the ones who might have been involved, with their names?"

Her brows came together in small checkmarks. "The police told us not to do anything like that, accuse anybody, and our lawyer agrees. He said we might be liable for slander if we suggest that the wrong girls had anything to do with it." She glanced over her shoulder at the door, guiltily, I thought. "My husband doesn't know I'm here. He thinks we should let the police handle everything."

"But you do have copies of messages that the other girls sent your daughter? Don't those constitute evidence, proof, that they're involved?"

She faced me bleakly. "We have another daughter. My husband thinks that if we don't leave it to the police, someone will come after her next."

"I just . . ." No, I couldn't say what I thought, that her silence would bring on whatever evil was out there faster. Her fear was too raw, my words too much like blame. "I just feel that if I knew some of the girls' names, I might be able to help more. Make a connection of some kind."

She shook her head. The brown curls shivered. "I just hoped you would know which one of them was the ringleader. That wouldn't be a false accusation, if you knew. *I* want to know." She fluttered in the chair. "I think the police think they used each others' accounts, so it's not really possible to tell who sent what or did what." Her hands tightened around each other. "I can't believe you don't know anything."

"Seriously, Ms. Miller, I don't. I'm really sorry about Corinne and I hoped you—"

"I know about *your* daughter, of course."

I stiffened, startled. From what depths did she drag up Anna? "Well, yes, that was in the papers. It doesn't have anything to do with—"

Now I was the one whose sentences couldn't reach endings, because she didn't let them. "Corinne knew her," she said.

I fumbled for moment, counting the years backwards. Yes, at seventeen, Corinne was the same age my daughter would be now. "She did? Did they go to school together?" Low inside me not just a shivering but a pounding. "Do the police know?"

She had pulled her feet under her as if preparing to stand. "You know who did this," she told me. "But you won't tell me. If Corinne was alive, she could tell you a few things about your daughter." Her face spasmed, her mouth twisting as her voice rose. "She could tell you what's happening to your daughter but she can't, because she's *dead*."

She probably never knew how close I came to leaping up and shaking her by her frail shoulders. "Ms. Miller!" Professionalism vanished. "What do you know about Anna?" I shouted. "You have to tell me! What could Corinne have said?"

She stared at me, suddenly blinking, tears bleeding down her cheeks.

"What did I say?" she said, the wail now a whimper.

"That Corinne knew what's happening to my daughter. What could she have told me?"

"I didn't say that."

"Yes, you did."

She pushed up fast. I did, too. "I was just . . ." She backed away, stumbling over the chair behind her. "Don't you dare tell anyone I said that. I shouldn't have. Don't you dare cheapen my daughter's memory by insinuating she was involved in something that has nothing to do with her."

Her bitterness ran deep and I struggled to wade through it. "I can't keep this from Lieutenant Clauson."

"We will sue you," she said, stalwart now in her indignation. "For lying. Corinne didn't even know her. I made that up."

We faced each other, both panting, me with fury, Ms. Miller with anger, surely, but also fear, guilt, regret?

My voice shook now. "I am very sorry about Corinne. I know about this loss. But if you know something about Anna, it's only right that you tell me."

But she edged through the office clutter. "I hoped you would help."

"I can't—"

"But I see you don't care to. Bruce and the lawyer are right. No one will help."

I made another move toward her. "Corinne knew things that can help me find my daughter, you said so."

She made a kind of spring for the door that still stood open. The look she gave me as she reached it was so ravaged I could not meet it. "Unfortunately," she said, her voice now low but solid, "I don't need *your* help to find *my* daughter. I know exactly where she is."

———

I sat down, staring at the open door.

Oh my God.

But I needed a stronger god than the one that well-worn phrase summoned. One strong enough to answer the prayer I sent it, *take this woman's gibberish and make it real.*

After forever I found my office phone and tapped the button for Taneesha. I was thankful to get her voicemail; that gave me more seconds to still the quake in my throat. "Running late. Be there in fifteen."

You disappointed the woman and she wanted to hurt you. You can't trust a word she said.

Oh, yes, Sane Sarah, ever the convincing one.

That was exactly what all the sane people around me would tell me. The police would get nothing from Ms. Miller but denial. Only I had heard her say it. Only I was desperate enough to believe.

And I could no more jump her in the street and slap her around than I could Celia. I wanted to grab my own phone and call Russell. Could his team find a connection between Anna and Corinne? Could there be a link after all between the girls in Clauson's puzzle and Anna, Celia, and me? But this all felt so new and ragged, and I had to get used to feeling it around me. Besides, if I called Russell, he would tell me to do exactly what I was doing: breathe and think.

Yes, now was the time for thinking. Think, for example, of what I could do with this insane possibility on my own this very afternoon. The Internet would be much more obliging than Ms. Miller. What school had Corinne gone to? What Girls' Club or Brownies unit had she belonged to? Ms. Miller said they had taken down Corinne's social-media sites, but could there be some other thread, trace, whisper, she had left and that I could find? Clauson had said he would send me more pictures. Among them might be some hint, some opening. Maybe even a face I knew. Some chance however tenuous that Corinne had known Anna, befriended her, talked with her in those crucial weeks, might even have heard since—any chance at all!

I put my hands to my face, felt my pulse still pumping. If I didn't cool my heart rate, Taneesha would want to call 911. I took out a wipe and swabbed off the heat. No better place for ideas to incubate than our meeting. If I could remember what Sane Sarah looked like, how she acted. After several long breaths, I stood and found I could walk. I even remembered to shoulder my satchel with my program files.

On my way down the hall to the stairwell, I found a strange lightness in my steps. Yesterday had been quietly seismic; today the earthquake had delivered. Even the damn woman's retraction, clumsy and desperate, had given me new hope. A universe of new doors opening before me. I'd wanted to get off my butt and do something. Finally I could.

7

By the time I reached the second floor I didn't need the comfort I'd imagined finding with Taneesha; I needed a war council. But the peaceful hour ahead could let me catch my breath. After the tedium of scheduling a semester's classes we'd have lunch, like two normal people. Then I could go home and begin.

I found Taneesha's door wide open: she almost always kept the door open in case students came for appointments or just dropped by. God, how I admired that office. Taneesha had found ways to tame the wild busyness that can overwhelm an academic, especially a teacher of writing, whose very nature conjures piles and piles of texts. (And no, computers haven't made a serious dent.) Taneesha was one of the few people I knew who could file something and then remember exactly where she'd put it, a rare skill that meant she could enjoy a clean, gleaming desk, welcoming upholstered chairs, and a windowsill space where a plum-pink orchid curled toward the Texas sun.

But instead of her usual welcome, she faced me with brows drawn and tight commas of concern ringing her mouth. As I sank into one of the plush chairs, she crossed and closed the door.

I wasn't unduly alarmed; administrators on university campuses fielded a barrage of knotty problems and no doubt one had turned up that she felt she needed to discuss. I matched my expression to hers. "That looks like a frown."

She settled into her own chair, even lowering her voice a little. "I started to email but I decided it would be better to wait until you got here. I don't know exactly what to do with it. Whether it falls into one of the categories we're legally obligated to report."

My long university background told me which bin her news would likely fall into. "A student told you something."

"Yes, a young woman in my first-year comp class. A seventeen-year-old, so she's a minor. She came to me about a girl named Corinne Miller. Have you heard of her?"

Well, yes, I had heard of her. "A local high-school girl. Who killed herself."

Taneesha's brows rose. "I didn't think the news had it. How did you know?"

"The police told me," I said.

Her brows rose higher. So much for my plans not to burden colleagues with tales of troublesome young women and AI-embellished daggers, let alone Ms. Miller's hints. But if Corinne's case was going to seep into the Cresthill population, Taneesha would need the gist. I did some rapid mental editing, briefing her on Clauson's visit and the pictures. "Corinne's mother came to ask me if I knew anything about any of the girls. I think she was disappointed that I didn't." No one slandered, no lawsuit triggered. "Clauson seems to think that if I can figure out why I've been threatened, the people investigating cyberbullying might be able to use that information to develop leads."

"But you didn't know Corinne, did you?"

"I don't know any of the girls in the pictures he showed me, as far as I can tell."

"My student apparently knew her. From church, I think. This student told me she'd seen a post—on one of these local chat boards—from a girl named Simone claiming that Corinne was a slut."

If Taneesha noticed that her news had made my breath hitch, she didn't show it. "Is your student sure this Simone girl sent the post?" I asked.

"No, she made it clear that she didn't know Simone and didn't want to get involved. She just thought that because of what happened with Corinne, someone should know it was being said."

"And she didn't save a copy of the post?"

"No, more's the pity. You know, some of these sites can be set to delete messages automatically, so even if we did know the source we might not be able to recover it. And the way kids leave their phones lying around—" she grimaced; she had a teenaged daughter, "—it would be hard to prove who sent what."

"We-e-ll . . ." I drew out my response, stealing time to think. "Did the student say why *she* got the message? Is this Simone part of a group?"

"She said a lot of girls from her high school and church post messages and she doesn't know all of them well." She shook her head, the lines around her mouth deepening. "I think she felt ambivalent about coming to me. Look, I know I'm the administrator of record right now, but I hope you won't mind if we work this out together. The immediate question is whether I report this or not."

Yes, any hint of abuse or suicidal impulse required reporting, regardless of the student's wishes. It wasn't clear so far this was that kind of case. But I wanted this to be Taneesha's decision, not just because the choice was hers by rights as acting program director, but because for me there was a worrisome line. If we reported, we'd hand the police control over the doors I wanted to go through in search of Anna, and I hated giving them that power, above all not now. Not that I couldn't make an ethical decision, but I couldn't pretend I wouldn't have seen it as a sacrifice. I worked on making my voice neutral. "What do you think? Should this be confidential for now?"

To my relief, she nodded. "It's possible that this young woman knows more than she told me, but I didn't get that impression. My sense is that to find out more, we'd have to interrogate her pretty aggressively. Or end up letting the police do it. And that just doesn't seem appropriate if most of what she has to tell us is what the police already know."

"There's the name. Simone."

"Yes. An unproven accusation."

I worked my way to the answer I hoped we both wanted. "If your student were reporting harm to another university student or to a minor, we'd have a clear duty to report. But she's not saying that someone new is in danger. I could tell the lieutenant, but I'd want the student's permission first."

"Actually, I think she'd be upset if it came out that she was the one who'd told about the post." She leaned back, the weight in her expression lifting. "I told her that if anything continued to concern her, to feel free to come see me. And that we had people on campus she could talk to if she wanted. But she just said it was okay, no big deal." On her desk she spread out the stacks of papers. "Thanks for talking all this out with me. It's just one of those gray areas."

"Yes," I said. "It is."

———————

That afternoon, true to his word, Clauson sent me more pictures.

One of the girls in the pictures was someone I knew. And her name was Simone.

8

Saturday morning I sat in the Cactus Café on the University of Texas campus, sipping my coffee so slowly it might have been a rare brandy. On my mind: how to tell my ex-English-Department colleague Diana Cleveland something she was not going to want to hear.

Diana and I had been colleagues during my years at the University of Texas at Austin, but not friends. She studied straight rhetoric, what Aristotle called the "art" of persuasion. She taught theory to graduate students, never stooping to the dreaded "freshman comp." She wasn't loud or obnoxious, but at faculty meetings back when I taught at UT, her wide and energetic knowledge of current events, her ready supply of advice and opinion, always made her the most noticed person in the room.

Coming up with the language I needed for this talk should have been easy. I, too, am by training a rhetorician. A rhetorician is supposed to be adept at choosing tracks of communication so as to produce desired results. Unfortunately, my most immediate desired result had complications not unlike those I'd encountered with Taneesha: I would be digging for information that people had every right not to give me, information that would lead me places they might not want me to go.

Luckily Taneesha hadn't picked up on my reaction to the mention of Diana's daughter Simone, one of Corinne's companions—not to be confused, as Ms. Miller had said, with her child's friends. The less I burdened Taneesha with my ethically dubious use of what she'd told me, the better. I'd gone home from our lunch to start clumsy online probes for connections between the two girls and Anna. Neither Corinne nor Simone appeared on any of Anna's class rosters. The Girls' Club had sometimes fielded soccer and track teams and had entered swimming competitions at the Y where Anna took lessons; archived newspaper pages reporting those events yielded no results.

Well, I was just getting started. Simone was the first step down a path littered with the lives of a lot of other people's children. I told myself that Diana needed to know what I had learned from Taneesha, but that didn't mean she would welcome the information. Hence the sticky moments ahead.

I had considered turning the whole business over to Russell, including what Ms. Miller had said. But it seemed early to hem myself in with sage recommendations until I had looked past the smoke to see if anything was burning, and way too early to make Diana's daughter the object of surveillance without even giving Diana a chance to ask Simone what she knew.

Now when she made her entrance into the Cactus, she didn't give me a quick "Hiya, you" the way she used to at UT when we passed in the halls. Instead I got silence as she slung her book bag over the back of the chair opposite me and looked around. I'd chosen this time in hopes the place might be relatively empty, and so it was. She lowered herself restlessly, adjusting her trademark black skirt and lightweight beige blazer. "This is kind of odd, Sarah. What's up?"

I was getting used to that word "odd." Now I used it to ease us into the conversation. "It's kind of an odd situation."

"We have to define 'odd,' I guess."

Spoken like a true rhetorician. Rhetorical theory older than the Romans says you have to define your terms before you can decide whether what you're dealing with is good or bad. In this case, the best bet was "bad." "Maybe 'odd' isn't the best word," I said, deliberately mildly. "I've found myself in a situation that might more correctly be called bizarre or worrisome or frightening rather than odd."

"Frightening?" She looked over her shoulder at the coffee menu on the wall at the front of the room, a reaction to my words that I actually would define as odd. I'd have been riveted by the word "frightening," not trying to choose between a mocha and an espresso. Still twisted toward the menu, she pushed her well-disciplined blonde bob behind an ear. "I hope I haven't done anything to frighten you."

"You haven't that I know of. But someone you know may have. Your daughter Simone."

I expected her to tighten up, go still, grope for something concrete on the table to anchor her surprise. At least I expected her attention. Instead, she shoved her chair back and headed for the counter, as if she hadn't heard what I'd said. I caught the corner of her purposeful smile as she negotiated with the barista. She came back to the table balancing a cup steaming with the deep burnt notes of the darkest of dark roasts.

Busily she settled again, her smile never wavering. "You certainly know how to start a conversation with a bang, Sarah. What in the world has Simone done?"

Exactly what I was here to find out. "So far, I hope, nothing. And if she has done something, I hope it's just an intemperate social-media post."

She managed to make her quick sip of the coffee dismissive. "That *is* odd. I see all her Facebook posts." Her bright blue eyes crinkled at the corners. "You're sure you have the right Simone?"

I hid a flare of indignation. Simone might have done something to threaten me and all I got was that condescending smile? "'Simone' is a fairly unusual name. I don't have a copy of the message in question because on many of the sites popular with teenaged girls they can delete their posts. The police may have some of these messages." I had planned to hold off mentioning the police but damn it, I was doing her a favor. I could be reporting all this to Clauson. "What I mean is, I have to decide whether to tell them. If Simone is involved, I wanted to talk to you first."

"O-o-oh, that's it!" She set the cup down, centered precisely between us. "The Miller girl! Yes, Simone knew her." She adjusted the cup a micro-inch, started to pick it up, then stopped. "You're not suggesting Simone had anything to do with that poor girl's death?" She shook her head. "I'd know."

How soon could I manufacture a turn to Anna? I counseled myself to be patient. Or maybe *cunning*, I thought. A good word for the care I'd have to take if I wanted to worm my way past parents' defenses to the memories and secrets of their kids. "Kids online can use each other's phones and accounts. Simone might not even know someone posted in her name."

"What exactly did this post say?"

"That Corinne was a slut."

"And you saw it?"

Questions she had a right to ask. "No, a student reported seeing it."

"Reported it to you?"

I wasn't about to expose Taneesha's student to Diana's examination. "It seems that before her death Corinne was targeted by threatening images and messages like this. I'm involved because whoever did that is also threatening me."

That revelation did make her blue eyes widen. "You? But why?"

I threw in a helpless shrug. "I hope someone can tell me. The police have an image of me with a dagger sticking out of my back. Apparently they don't know who produced it. They're trying to find out."

She raised her brows coldly. "And you think Simone did this?"

"I have no idea." Not only did I have to court Diana's goodwill, I had to dodge the legal dangers of unproved accusations that Ms. Miller had schooled me in. "There could be a whole secret online conversation going on out there." It was time now, no more putting off the move that mattered. "For example, you may remember I lost my daughter six years ago, and there could even be . . ." I waved a hand, just offering a suggestion, ". . . conversations online about what happened to her."

She gave a little snort that ruffled the surface of her coffee. "Seriously, Sarah? Among Simone and her friends? None of them would have known her." She set the cup down and leaned back, drawing away from me, but not fully in dismissal this time. She refocused, stroking the cup handle, as if searching it for an invisible flaw. I, too, waited for something to crack. I knew Diana as an analytical scholar, self-possessed and clear-headed. But she was a mother whose child I was indirectly accusing. After a moment she pushed her cup away firmly. "Even if they did, that wouldn't answer the question, why this attack on *you*?"

Had she even known about Anna's disappearance? Maybe not. "I was hoping you might talk to Simone." I aimed for tentative, even humble. "I'd like to know the names of Corinne's other . . . friends. So I can see if any of them are connected to me."

"You don't know any names?"

"No, I've just been shown pictures. Other than Simone, I didn't recognize anyone."

"Shown pictures?" Her firm jaw tightened. "By the police?"

I stayed humble. "I did promise the officer who showed me the pictures that if I learned anything about these threats to me and to Corinne, I'd tell him." I jumped in ahead of a breath she took to speak. "Maybe it's just girls being girls. Nothing would make me happier than for you to talk to Simone and find out there's nothing for me to pass on."

Finally she raised her cup and drained it, slowly, meticulously. She leaned forward. Her voice dropped to a new register, lower, even intimate. "You know, Sarah, I'm sensing just a bit of a threat from you."

I didn't blink. Fair enough. I wouldn't have reacted kindly in her place. "No one needs to do anything without more information. But I can't settle into victimhood."

Her smile flashed on, off, too bright for the reassurance I hoped she wanted to convey. "Of course not. Absolutely I will talk to Simone. Obviously she's also in danger."

"Of course."

She swiveled to hitch her heavy bag off the chair back. "Well, thank you for telling me about this, Sarah." She stood, shouldering the bag, smoothing her blazer. "I wouldn't have known a word of it otherwise. Who knows, if you're right, it might have been the police who told me. That *would* have been alarming."

I stood, too. My gut said she wasn't lying: my news had disturbed her.

She pushed her chair in. "I'll call you."

"Thank you."

Another smile as she turned to leave me, this one less bright than glassy. "Until a better 'next time.'"

9

Kendra had a make-up session that Saturday afternoon. Thank goodness. An hour's diversion might let the tumult of what Ms. Miller had told me connect with what Taneesha had said and what Diana had not. That whirl of emotion wanted so much to become a plan.

As I gathered my notes, I toyed with taking what I had learned about Simone straight to Clauson. That might scare up some facts. But he would be riveted to the cyberbullying case, not Anna's, and he wouldn't know what questions to ask. He could hardly quiz Simone on Ms. Miller's garbled intimations, and if I shared those with him, he'd label them "Crockett hysteria" and file them away.

Besides, I had agreed that finding out what Simone knew was her mother's job, at least for now. Diana might come back with facts that could make the whole question moot.

That settled, I let Alice out of her jungle corner. "Hi there, sweetie," she said. She knows many endearments I did not teach her. "Hi, you little sycophant," I said back, confident she'd never master such a term without serious coaching (though I'd been wrong before). She climbed claw over claw to the top of her lattice, from which she cocked her head as I removed her feed dish to clean and refill.

Checking the clock, I saw that I was looking forward to Kendra's arrival. Teaching was always hard, but with Kendra, the protocol of the study meant I wasn't strictly teaching. More nearly, I was a living being immersed with another in the flower field of language, waiting to see what bloomed. Sometimes, with patience and listening, I could lead her to like what she had written; for that moment I could see her transported, and her happiness heartened me. Today I could do with some heartening, so I was glad when the buzzer went off downstairs.

Her session that day turned out to require patience and listening in spades. She stomped up the stairs, slapping down her notebooks and folders as always. But her face flamed with simmering agitation. We floundered through our usual routine, with me prompting, "Tell me about what you brought today," and her giving her usual peevish answer, "Just junk." "Why do you think it's junk?" "It just is." And then we got to it: "They say my writing is dumb."

Every now and then, "they" joined us at our table. "Who said that? Your mom?"

"Mostly my dad."

Okay. We'd met with parents at the start of the study, clarifying their roles as explicitly as we could. Kendra's dad was a tall, slightly overweight man with a soft chin and watery hazel eyes who'd talked a good bit more than he'd listened. I'd left our orientation meeting fairly certain he didn't quite understand his instructions. It seemed I was right.

Discussing it over lunch on Friday, Taneesha and I had agreed that the study was problematic in a lot of ways, not least in our inability to control for a lot of variables like parental adherence to our rules. I'd signed on because the director, a close colleague, had begged me to, and I did wonder if we might not learn a few things. We had a reasonably large sample, nearly a hundred students, all "reluctant writers," from a range of socioeconomic ranks, both applicants to Cresthill and provisionally admitted UT students, all of whom planned to start college in the fall. Each had been assigned a mentor/teacher, and each pair had been assigned a particular intervention. Somewhat to my delight, I'd drawn the method of letting my charge write what she wanted to write, whatever she could be persuaded to write, as long as she wrote.

The plan was to assess changes in both attitudes toward writing and improvements in the kind of "school writing" they'd have to do in college. What Kendra wanted to write involved appropriating the heroine of a fantasy series and setting her off on all kinds of rather violent adventures. "He actually said 'dumb?'" I asked.

"He said 'silly.' And 'childish.'"

"Childish" didn't sound like a word she would have generated on her own. "Maybe he doesn't realize," I said carefully, "that many writers do quite well for themselves as professionals by writing things that other people find entertaining. You talked about writing your own fantasy series one day. Or a graphic novel. You'd be in good company."

"He'd never believe anything I wrote could be any good."

"What does it matter what other people believe?" But I wished that remark back as soon as I said it. Of course it mattered. I pulled up the first reassuring, though obviously vacuous, script that came to hand. "What I mean is, what matters is what *you* believe about yourself."

She snatched up the sheets she'd brought with her today, slinging them across the table between us like scraps hurled to unseen pigs. "He says I can't even do this right. He says it doesn't make any sense. You think that, too, don't you? You think it isn't any good."

These were always the tough moments, not just with Kendra but with anyone whose writing a teacher was responding to. Somewhere lay a balance between stoking a person's self-worth, a fragile construction that so often gets tangled up with their sense of themselves as writers, and providing the truth that would help any writer grow. The truth was that what Kendra produced wasn't particularly "good" by any criteria, and from what I could see, not necessarily appreciated by the other writers she corresponded with. I'd seen her scraping for the stingiest "likes" on fan websites. My best me would help her locate herself in all that judgment, but that day such a noble effort was beyond me. I chickened out and temporized.

"'Good' is relative," I insisted. "It depends on where you are on the learning curve." This I did believe. "Here's what I want you to do for next time. Make a list of the writing things you think you're good at. Then pick one thing that you think you could improve on and be ready to tell me why you think you could do that one thing better. Tell me what's wrong with the way you're doing it. Then we'll see."

Was I interfering too much? What if what she *wanted* to write was nothing, since nothing she wrote could be any good? But no—for our study I had to keep her writing. I told myself all I was doing was giving her a way to persist.

She frowned, but she drew the scorned pages back to her, muttering something that sounded a lot like "I hate him." As usual, she sat frowning and hunched as we read the day's haul together. I took care not to wax too enthusiastic. She'd see through me. But she pounced on every hint of faint praise.

Down at the curb, I waved at the Latina housekeeper who often ferried her, fretting over the kinds of conflicts every writing teacher struggles with. *This is not a therapy project. It's about writing. Whether she really hates her father is not a variable I have been empowered to consider. But I wish he would keep his damn mouth shut.*

Would I have pressured Anna to write more like Stephen King?

"You're too critical of her," Eric had said. "She's just a kid. Quit trying to turn her into some kind of genius. Let her play with a goddamn doll if she wants to, not one of those boring 'intellectual' games."

"Maybe they're boring to you," I'd retorted. "She likes them. She wouldn't want to play them if she didn't like them."

He'd timed his parting shot as he always did, opening the kitchen door and stepping through it so I'd be left stewing over my unspoken answer: "You don't have the faintest idea what she likes," he sneered.

Looking back, I'd be thankful if all Anna had to fear from her father was a little disapproval of her writing. Whatever demands I made of her had not turned deadly. Somehow his had.

10

Later that Saturday I forced myself away from my so-far unproductive forays into Simone's past to read Kendra's begrudged pages. If only they didn't look so tepid and uninviting alongside the rather lurid worries I was trying to escape. I considered adding to my files of downloaded research on the motivations of reluctant writers. After all, I'd owe the team a comprehensive research article on my share of the study data. Grand ambitions. But when I sat down at the computer, all I could actually do was glower at my pictures of Eric and Celia and fret over how I could bull my way through Diana to Simone.

As too often, I lingered over Celia's cool, honed figure, stark in her whites and blacks, her face an implacable mask. Surely she'd been one of the mean girls in high school, like the ones who had hounded Corinne. A proxy for the villains Ms. Miller wanted to bring to justice. Maybe I could help do that. I could certainly try.

It had occurred to me that, come Monday, I could make some phone calls to teachers and coaches who had known Anna and pose some delicate questions about her social circles. The police said they had done that back when, and I had certainly put social media to work quizzing everyone I could think of on my own. But now my queries had a more concrete focus; I had actual names if I could discreetly deploy them. Maybe I'd find some trickle of information Raging Sarah would let me share with Russell. But how could I wait till Monday? I'd claw my heart to shreds sitting here.

I slapped off my computer, swept Kendra's papers aside. I wrestled out shorts, a polo and a windbreaker, and walking shoes. I stashed Alice (resistant little object), scored my car keys off their hook by the door, and headed for Town Lake.

Town Lake is a luminous plate of water laid crossways of the Austin city center, a capture of Texas's quiet-moving Colorado River (not the Grand Canyon one). Luxury hotels, expensive restaurants, and outdoor cafés on West César Chavez Street overlook a riverside green space through which threads a gentle walking path along which only some of us walk. Others jog, dance, progress through tranquil meditative moves. Obviously the path gets more use on a spring day like this than in winter or carbonized summer, but over the past few years I'd adopted a couple of favorite stretches where even in perfect weather the crowds were thinner. A lot of people wore headphones, but I liked the contemplative silence. I'd conceived my best article ideas in the extra oxygen of those stretches; maybe this April day would work its usual creative charms.

That day, as it turned out, I saw very little of the scene around me. My brain flung up detritus, mostly in the form of faces, and of course my daughter's face was one of those I saw. So many times I'd played games: what she would look like, how I would know her, if she suddenly appeared in a group of anonymous passersby like one of these? She would sweep her hair up like that girl's, wouldn't she? Paint her lips that girl's dare-me color, tilt her chin with that girl's look-at-me flare? These images weren't conscious inventions. They came to me as clearly as if they really were memories. Future memories. I claim there are such things.

Today, though, other faces shouldered in. Kendra's—I worried about her embattled ego, and whose job it was to rescue it. But of course, Corinne's face, and Simone's.

I did not know Simone, but I had seen her on campus with her mother. I had decided I wouldn't call Clauson down on her until I had no choice. I couldn't shake the distressing image: a young girl—like my own daughter?—trembling under a police interrogation. All for a simple lapse of good sense.

A toddler in denim overalls and sneakers with sparkling lights along the soles darted underfoot. His young mother bounded after him, shooting me an apologetic grimace as she crossed my path. I gave her an absent smile; I managed most days not to think of every mother I encountered as the person I was not but should have been.

And not to play that game of future memories, seeing in every teenaged girl's face a reminder of what I had lost.

Like the girl's face I found fixed on me as I rounded a curve in the trail.

Not a future memory. A past one. From an hour ago. I'd seen her on my computer when I was studying the new set of images Clauson had sent me, next to Corinne.

She'd have stood out in a crowd even if she hadn't shown up in Clauson's pictures: tall, lithe, a cascade of strawberry-tinted hair tied off her clear face with a glittery headband. She wore a flowery long-sleeved tunic over denim shorts with artfully frayed hems. In the pictures her regal white smile in her ivory features marked her the foremost of the court ladies. Now, turning her back on me abruptly, she took out a phone and bent over it as she cut a clean swath ahead of me through a trio of joggers appearing around the next bend.

This girl knew Corinne, she knew about that dagger. She had not made her way to a place I liked to walk for no reason. I went full Raging Sarah. I took off after her.

Her long stride made keeping up more of an aspiration than a goal. The path wasn't packed, but still I triggered indignant shouts in my hurry. I was close enough to see her when she broke her flight to exchange a quick message with another girl making her way along the trail toward us, a near-clone in clothes and carriage but dark-haired . . . Simone.

Over the blond girl's shoulder Simone saw me. She saw me see her. She wheeled and headed back the way she had come.

I did a couple of extemporaneous two-steps with people who blocked me as I picked up my pace. It was absolutely past odd that these two girls had turned up *just here*. Maybe they had been watching me long enough to know my habits. Or they could have followed me here.

The two girls parted, the blonde cutting right through a pair of dog-walkers and Simone darting left. Simone's misfortune was that I knew her name. "Simone!" She didn't turn. Her steps quickened. I closed on her, just another jogger, not at all pursuing a young woman who, twenty yards ahead, did look back. A twist awfully close to fear spasmed across her clear young face.

She turned away again, sleek dark ponytail bobbing. Still she didn't run. Instead she intercepted a man coming toward her. In walking shorts, a T-shirt, and over it an unbuttoned long-sleeved shirt, he looked close to my own thirty-five years. Like Simone, he had glossy dark hair, in his case, trim and disciplined. The smile on his neat tanned features, clearly one of greeting, crumpled to a frown of distress when Simone grabbed his wrist and tugged to drag him away as I gained.

I called again, "Simone!" The man shook free of her grip and looked back at me. Simone hauled harder; when he didn't follow, she skittered backward, away from me. But he came right at me, and I braced to meet him. "Who are you?" he demanded. "Why are you chasing my daughter? What is this about?"

His polished good looks were vaguely familiar. Had I seen him at functions with Diana? I drew myself up, carving words out of my panting. "My name is Sarah Crockett. I know Simone's mother from when I was faculty at UT."

He glanced over his shoulder at Simone, who bounced a few steps away, an antelope on the verge of pronging over the nearest horizon. He came back to me. "I repeat: what's this about?"

Boy, did I want to tell him what this was about. But more important, right now, was preventing him from calling 911. I forced myself down off my Raging Sarah high and made myself meet his gaze calmly. "Simone knows me. I've told her mother—Diana—about a problem that concerns her. Are you . . . ?" But he had no reason to answer my questions. "I assume you are her father. I'd be glad to tell you about the problem if we could go somewhere and talk."

The worry in his gaze deepened, digging creases around his eyes. "Honey," he said to Simone, "do you know this woman?"

"No." Simone plucked her glittery blue jacket more firmly around her. "She's lying."

Back to me once again came the man's troubled gaze. "I need to talk to my daughter. If you'll excuse us . . ." He took Simone's elbow and turned her as he started away.

Tackling him about the knees would earn me an assault charge. I called out, "Mr.—!" But of course his name might not be the same as Diana's. "Sir!" My shout jerked stares our way. I lowered my voice. At least he paused and listened. "Sir—I'm sorry, I don't know your name—but Simone knows about something that affects my personal safety." I was going to wear the shine off that dagger if I kept using it to gain a hearing. I fumbled in my belt pack, found an old receipt and a pen and scribbled. "I hope that you will talk to her and possibly to Diana." He frowned at the scrap of paper I offered. "My email. I'll be glad to meet with you and explain my concerns."

He gave a sharp nod. "Simone and I will discuss it." Simone fidgeted with a cascade of bright plastic bracelets, her brows, firm and straight like her father's, knifing down in dismay over dark, unmade-up eyes. Again her father took her elbow, turning her. I stood watching the man's broad back recede.

First impressions are tricky. I don't trust mine. I'd been wrong just last summer, when I misjudged Russell and what he wanted from me. But my first impression of Simone's father that day encouraged me. He'd been polite; he'd listened; of course he would want to talk to his daughter. A responsible man, a measured soul—a lot like

Russell, in fact. The sort of man who would confront hard truths about his daughter calmly.

In some ways that judgment turned out to be accurate. In others it was hopelessly wrong.

11

I might have headed home to wait for the ding of Simone's father's email landing in my inbox. But I'd had enough of dithering for a while.

Hey, I had made something like progress. I deserved some reward.

A true reward might have meant driving to the airport and buying a ticket to Santa Fe and Russell. But I needed to be here in Austin, primed and just seething with cunning, when Simone's father's message arrived.

So what reward should I claim? Definitely something special. Something I would usually deny myself. Like, I thought, a dinner in one of those swanky restaurants lining the riverfront on the thoroughfare above it, César Chavez.

I could afford it and I had earned it, facing down both of Simone's parents and Simone herself in the bargain, without losing my cool for more than the frenetic moments when I'd chased her and her friend. So I planted myself in the middle of the Town Lake human current, where I took out my phone, called up the restaurant possibilities, and picked one. That I wondered for even a second whether I was properly dressed marked me as hopelessly middle-class, but if I was, so be it. My money was good. I also snubbed those pernicious self-doubts when they asked whether a single woman would be looked down on as a likely inadequate tipper; I fixed that by wriggling past the frowning host at the place of my choice as I mouthed "bar." Soon I was deep in arguments with a tipsy also-unaccompanied woman on the stool beside me as to whether *Frasier* or *Seinfeld* was the better '90s sitcom. I came down on the side of *Frasier* not because of the aesthetic criteria I gave her but because I loved the way Niles's mouth made that lopsided "O" whenever he stumbled into one of Frasier's disastrous schemes. I drank two of a thing called a Blood Moon Valentine and went home to find an email from Nicholas Hudson on my machine.

———————

"I would like to take you up on your offer to discuss the situation you think Simone is involved in," he wrote. "Please let me know a good time, preferably tomorrow afternoon."

I parked myself on the balcony to metabolize the bourbon while I thought through my options. I discovered that I did not have spectacular hopes that Mr. Hudson would be able to tell me much. Simone's quick, defensive "She's lying" made me doubt Mom and Dad could coax the truth out of her any better than I could. There was always that threat I kept rejecting: scaring at least some facts out of her by turning her over to the police.

After all, she had secrets that clearly distressed her. Someone who could get answers should ask her what she had done that made her afraid of *me*. Someone like Raging Sarah, who wanted to slam into this girl as if she was a piñata, shove past this meticulous Mr. Hudson, who thought a civil conversation could shut her up—

Sheesh, what was this, a psychotic break? The bourbon, I guessed. The dregs made me want to call Russell. Their dirty alcohol glow said I should tell him about Ms. Miller. It said that he would not dismiss her claims as demented nonsense, the way I'd thought he would. The bourbon said he would reassure me that I had every right and reason to bore past all that family's defenses to the truth I deserved.

I went so far as to pull out my phone.

But the bourbon was lying. Of course he wouldn't say that. I could barely say it to myself, not when in front of me rose that girl's blanched face, the way she buried herself in her father's shadow. Not an image on a screen. A real girl, in trouble. What if somewhere, somehow, Anna had faced such a moment? I would not want her facing someone who was trying to figure out how to frighten her even more.

I had to squelch this urge to run to Russell. It wasn't fair to add to his worries when I'd resist his cautions anyway.

I sat in the dark in my glider, as usual brushed by the small April noises; it was too early for the locusts that would drum through the summer heat. I looked at my sleeping phone. A touch could bring Russell's face to me but it always took imagination to reach through the pixels and draw him close. The memory of our long slow strokes made me shiver even though the spring night was warm.

But suddenly with that message in my email waiting, I found myself hearing Raging Sarah's warning: that Russell would resist what it might take to find Anna, who was what *I* needed to make us whole. Some of "what it might take" might be dangerous, even crazy; what would he say then? From where I sat now that kind of resistance, however mild, looked like a rejection, a shearing off of the part of me where my only hopes for Anna still hung on. He'd want me to kill that stalwart, resolute Sarah that *I* had invented to sustain my hopes for Anna, so that the other one, the one he called his, would be the one that lived.

So I huddled in the dark with a burn that was both refusal and longing. I was not ready for that choice. My doubts foretold a growing stash of secrets between us, a cold landscape my anguish would not warm. A tract of silences and things not said that I would have to nurture even though what I really wanted to nurture was us.

I was not used to tears. I didn't immediately understand the warmth on my hand.

I wiped the tears on my shirttail. The bourbon, making me silly. It was a long way to any such crossroads. I stood, unsteadily, but not drunk, and made my way to my desktop, where I sat and wrote to Mr. Nicholas Hudson that I would be glad to meet him for coffee at three o'clock.

12

A less-inviting email confronted me over my Sunday oatmeal. "Sarah," Diana wrote, "I'm a bit concerned. I coaxed out of Simone that when she was at Town Lake with her father yesterday afternoon, she saw you and you pursued her. I'm trying to understand what is going on, but I don't think the situation will improve if my daughter feels threatened. I ask again that you give me a chance to learn what has happened. I assure you I don't take this lightly, and I will be in touch soon."

The flush that rose to my face had nothing to do with the heat of the oatmeal.

All right, I had pursued her. But "threatened"? I'd backed down in a most ladylike manner when her father faced me. But I did wonder. What would I have done if Mr. Hudson had not been there? I walked myself back through those heated moments. That I had recognized the line I must not cross reassured me. Apparently I didn't have that kind of meanness in me. I would not buy Anna's safety at another child's expense.

At least, not unless I had no choice . . .

I calmed myself by feeding Alice banana slices, a task that always requires a certain level of attention. I had to admit that the most discreet approach to Hudson would be to let Clauson handle him and any questions about his daughter's involvement in Corinne Miller's fate. But I had made my own judgment about Mr. Hudson, and that judgment said that if I asked nicely he could be an ally. Too soon to give him up to Clauson. By the time I left for my meeting with Hudson, I had conceded that Diana was right: the route to Simone was through her parents, and I didn't need to be urged to be careful. I wrote Diana coolly, "Thank you for letting me know your thoughts."

But her message raised another question. Should I meet with Simone's father without telling Diana? She might feel I'd broken some kind of promise. But I might learn things from him she wouldn't tell me or possibly didn't even know. So I dismissed that qualm. But as I crossed with my coffee to the table at Caffé Medici where he waited, another intruded. Diana hadn't witnessed my confrontation with her daughter and she'd bristled. He *had* witnessed it, and by golly, a parent was a parent. But he relieved me by saying in the most urbane manner possible, "Thank you for agreeing to meet with me."

I persuaded my mouth to loosen its clench. "You're welcome," I said urbanely back.

But he toyed with his cup, his clean-boned hands restless. He met my gaze without quite accepting it. "I should clarify right from the start. Diana and I are divorcing. Our lawyers are at work on the details. Since Simone is an only child, obviously it's been tough on her. More to the point, if there's some problem, Diana is not likely to tell me about it." He nodded at a question I was too urbane to ask. "Yes, it's that bad." He ran a quick tongue across his lips. "I am Simone's father. I need to know what's going on."

We had both come dressed business-casual-plus, me in dark slacks, a white blouse, and a tailored jacket, he in pressed jeans, a blue Oxford shirt, and a conservative sports coat, as if we both wanted to lead with our most civilized selves. I was surprised to find him so svelte and chiseled: I would have expected Diana to choose another academic, possibly a poet or linguist, with a Bohemian wardrobe and a lot more hair. This man, with his sleek dark waves tamed over his tanned temples, his Rolex peeping out from under his coat sleeve, had a cutout crispness that belonged in a boardroom. Probably the kind of man who wouldn't like having his time wasted. As for myself, I had zero time I wanted to waste. I said, "Did you talk to Simone?"

He raised a single brow. "More or less. She stuck to her claim that she didn't know you."

I pinned his gaze. "Do you believe her?"

He sighed. "No."

The slump in his voice reassured me. It signaled shared concern about what Simone might be hiding. I asked, "So she told you nothing?"

"I'm hoping you'll tell me whatever it is she can't."

Even if he had accepted that Simone might be the one lying, he wasn't yet on my side. Diplomacy had never been one of my strengths, but with more delicate face-offs like this one before me, I had better ramp up my skills. Or maybe it was my newfound cunning I had to perfect. "I don't know all that much, either. That was why I wanted to talk to her yesterday. But you were right. My plying her with questions isn't the best plan. Diana has asked me to give her time to get answers, and I certainly hope she does."

"Can I assume you're going to tell me, answers to what?"

I took a breath. For all his efforts to face facts, protecting his daughter would stay high on his list. "I'd like to ask a question that may possibly get me to some of those answers. Whose idea was it to go to Town Lake yesterday afternoon?"

He frowned. "Whose . . . ? Why?"

"Did you suggest that the two of you go?"

He sat back. "If you . . . I see. For what it's worth, I texted her about getting together, and she wrote back she had already agreed to meet some friends at Town Lake. I said could I catch up with her there, just for a little while, wouldn't intrude on her plans. She . . ." His face twisted as he processed the memory. "I knew she didn't really want me there, but it was something *I* wanted." He tapped his coffee cup on the table. "You think she went there because she thought she might see you?"

So little I could tell him that wasn't speculation. And it was far too soon to try a turn to Anna. "It looks as if Simone . . . knows something about . . . the events leading up to another girl's suicide." Again that dagger aimed at me came in handy to justify my intrusions. "And about a threat against me."

"A threat?"

Diana had known about Corinne. Did he? He went on, chasing the guesses I wished weren't all I had to give him. "Why would my daughter possibly want to threaten you?"

I deployed more diplomatic cunning. "I don't know that she has."

I described the dagger images, keeping my language undramatic. He flexed tense fingers on the edge of the table. "How did you get these pictures? One of these girls gave them to you?"

"No. A policeman did."

He stopped breathing for a second, his grip on the table going rigid. "And Simone was in these pictures?"

"Yes. I also heard her name attached to a social-media message I learned about."

He sank against the back of his chair, staring out the tall window beside us. "Oh."

A sound of damage, as if I'd chipped a brittle edge. I had learned last summer watching Russell's struggles with his daughter Tommy how the fate of a single child of divorcing parents could set off flames. "I haven't told the police about Simone."

His gaze came back to me slowly. For the first time I felt as if he really saw me. Really *wanted* to see me. But he rocked the chair back, balancing with his death grip on the table, as if he needed a new angle to work his way around what he saw.

"But you feel you should tell them," he said.

"I've been struggling with the decision, yes."

He snapped the chair forward again, visibly reclaiming his cool center. "Just to get this out in the open. Is there even the remotest possibility that any of this has anything to do with your personal history? I mean, you're not exactly invisible. There was some coverage of you during that case last summer. Some mention of some things you said when your daughter . . ." He turned a hand over. "A lot of people know who Sarah Crockett is."

I stopped my own fingers from clenching around my coffee cup. "Depends on what you mean by 'people.' Surely not all of Austin devoured the news about me last summer."

He moved a shoulder. "People in the UT English Department. Some people in administration. People who know people you know. I'm in two of those categories." He reached for his own cup but just twirled it. "I work at UT. In University Advancement. And as it happens, I know Eric Wyles."

We sat in silence. I hid my indiscreet hands in my lap. *Come on, cunning. Where are you?* After a moment I said, "In hopes that we can move forward, I will stipulate that to the best of my knowledge, there is no connection between my personal past and whatever is going on with these girls. But since I still don't know what's going on, 'to the best of my knowledge' is as far as I can go."

"Simone really was frightened of you," he said.

"I realize that. It perplexes me."

"You say she sent some kind of social-media message? About a suicide? The Miller girl?"

So he did know that much. I nodded. "Calling Corinne a name. To be clear, I don't know that she sent it. Anybody with access to her account could have sent it. Her running from me yesterday was my first real sign that she was involved at all."

His gaze went distant. I waited, congratulating myself that I had the self-control to let him sort out his intentions. I could not put them to use until I knew what they were.

At last he looked around, straightening briskly, his decision apparently made. "I'm going to ask something of you."

The last time a young woman's troubled father had asked something of me had led me into what turned out to be a precipitous vortex from which none of us—neither me nor Russell nor Tommy—had emerged unchanged. But I had come here ready to set off a vortex if I had to. I waited for him to go on.

"You're going to keep digging on this," he said. "What I read about you makes that pretty clear. Just remember that Diana's not going to tell me what's going on, and I would probably be naïve to expect Simone to tell me the whole story, either." He took his wallet from an inside jacket pocket and removed a business card. With a silver pen, he crossed out "Nicholas T. Hudson" and wrote "Nick." "All I ask is that if you see any sign that my daughter is in danger—physical, of course, but emotional as well—you'll let me know."

How clean, clear, firm that card was, how precise his handwritten name. I slid that promise into my own wallet. "Do you think she might be in danger?"

He looked at me hard. "Do you?"

"I think it's going to be tricky to sort out who's in danger until we know more about this situation."

He tried, then, to smile. It wasn't a smiling moment, and his face knew it. "I hope I'm not the source of any danger."

I gathered myself to leave, slipping my wallet with the card in it into a pocket. "I hope not, too."

13

At home I sat down to work through Kendra's efforts. She might as well have written nothing, for all the attention I paid the pages.

And as it happens, Nick Hudson had said, *I know Eric Wyles.*

I'd met that revelation with deliberate silence. No—determined silence. It was too soon to let him guess that my past with Eric might color my business with him. Really, why shouldn't Nick know Eric? He worked at the university; he'd surely attended various English-department functions while he was still with Diana, no doubt meeting both Eric and me. I didn't remember him, but receptions are swirls where you smile at a lot of strangers. Or he could have struck up a conversation with Eric in the men's room, then followed up on some mutual interest. Nothing sinister in that.

And after all, he was a father who cared about his daughter. Did he talk to Eric about Anna? Did he talk to Eric about my accusations? That possibility gave me a queasy turn. But why should I care? I'd wanted to shout those accusations from the rooftops. I'd quit promoting them because my lawyer said not to. But why not shout them now to this Nicholas Hudson . . . excuse me, Nick?

After all, he had said he already knew the essence. If his main source of information was last year's reporting, he was working with a skimpy and fairly innocuous account. But what if he'd learned more of me from Eric? It chilled me to think of myself sitting across from "Nick" while he mentally rehearsed all the awful things Eric had said about me.

If Hudson had asked outright, I would have had an answer. *The Sarah Crockett you heard about is pure invention. The mere mention of Eric's name won't make me go banshee. This is Sarah. This quiet, deliberative woman sitting here.*

The woman his daughter was afraid of.

Like Diana—and like me—he'd puzzled, why?

Exuding bourbon fumes on my way home from Town Lake last night, I'd cobbled together a theory. Some of those girls did know Anna. They knew as well about my negligence, my carelessness, the way I had let danger take her. I read my own fury at myself into their threat. As sobriety won, that scenario looked less credible. They had waited six years to bring their cryptic charges. But my guilt proposed that Corinne had recently told them some story that made me a target. I struggled to build these speculations into an explanation that the quiet, deliberative self I was crafting could share with my new friend Nick.

In search of that deliberative woman I focused on Kendra's quixotic paragraphing and rambunctious syntax. Ulp. She was writing about her father again. She'd given him a fictional name, and, in the illustrations she often included, a cloaked, wizardly persona, but I recognized her version of him. "'Prince Desmond,' he snarled. 'The maiden Esmarelda is not doing the work that has been assigned to her. She must be punished.'" Poor Esmarelda. She'd already been banished from about six places by various patriarchal disciplinarians. The child was always having to gather up her increasingly meager belongings and slope off to some other barren country where she would once again be found inadequate for her assigned role.

Sigh. Fathers and daughters. Did I invite them into my life? I hadn't had issues with my father. He hadn't been the most demonstrative of human beings, disciplined out of emotional bluster by his military career, but he'd been even-tempered and patient, bearing up well under what I read as his disappointment that I was not the womanly daughter he assumed he should want. I thought he worried that I might end up as a modern Emily Dickinson, bright but plain and alone. I'd worked not to add to his burden; I'd packed as many womanly virtues into my academic self as I could manage. It had been my far-more-rambunctious older sister who'd played a

Kendra-like irritant to him. "You were such a *good* girl," my sister diagnosed, and yes, I guess I was.

Maybe if I'd been less of a good girl, less well-trained in optimistic self-delusion, I wouldn't have married Everybody's-Golden-Boy Eric, to whom my father had taken quite a liking in their brief acquaintance before he died. Good womanly girls caught the good guys, that victory evidence they really were good and worthy, and for a short while, we all thought that catching Eric proved me worthy indeed.

———

That Sunday afternoon that deliberative side of me had been quietly deliberating about too many things to remember that she had to buy a functioning tube of mascara. The necessity reasserted itself: Sane Sarah had a social engagement that many people would call a *date*.

The word "date" hung over me like a light bulb on a fraying cord threatening to fall and shatter because of a conversation I'd had with Russell when he came to Austin over the holidays. A light-hearted dinner together, a few nights together, afternoons of Hill-Country hiking: a reminder of what hope was for.

Lying beside me in bed on his last night, Russell said, "There's one thing I wonder about that you never tell me when you write or call me."

At that point I was taking every moment as light-hearted. "No, I don't tell you Alice's latest curse words. That's for Instagram or Tik Tok."

He made a face. I knew enough about his social media accounts to know he didn't consult them for pleasure. They were where people he needed to keep track of for his job might post scraps he needed to know. "No," he said. "I mean you never tell me about stuff you're doing with friends."

"Oh." I snuggled into a warm place I got too little of. "The last person who wanted to know about my friends was one of those FBI agent who thought they might be suspects."

"So I can assume you do have some?"

In my head I started a somewhat shamefaced listing: our lab manager Gregory, my assistant Carmelo, Taneesha . . .

"That's taking a long time to come up with," he said.

"I get sunlight." A tiny bit of heat in my voice. "I'm not growing moss."

"And I wouldn't play some kind of jealous jerk," he went on as if the heat hadn't registered, "if once in a while you shared a drink with some guy you happen to know." He propped himself up on an elbow. "People need friends."

"You're not saying I should start *dating*?"

"Dating is an extreme way to put it." He readjusted the elbow. "No, I'm not talking about dating. I don't know. Join a book club. A garden club. A . . . what do people do to make friends these days?"

"Quilting?"

"With all due respect to quilters . . . my mother was one . . . I doubt it." He laughed.

"Maybe *you* should start dating." I toned the heat down by stroking the back of his neck, which I knew could make him shiver.

"I'm too busy."

"So you wall yourself up in your office?"

"Oh . . ." He got in his own strokes. "I do okay."

When my voice came back, I said, "But I'm serious. I mean . . ."

That was when the conversation tried to get away from us. What if the resolution he was waiting for from me never happened? One day *he* might be the one needing to fall back on social graces he shouldn't let go to seed. But I did not want to turn all that loose between us, not in one of the moments I could let myself be happy. If I found Anna I would never have to. "Okay. I'll go out for drinks if anyone is foolish enough to ask me. I'll go to concerts. I'll read what the book club is reading instead of student papers."

"I'll expect full reports in case I have to rush over and defend my boundaries." He didn't give me a chance to come up with a snappy retort to that.

———————

So that was how I ended up thinking I ought to invest in some mascara. I remembered the dating protocol. You cleaned up. You decorated. You preened. So I hiked around to the nearest CVS. Sheesh! Ten dollars for a tube the size of my little finger! I left the tube on the shelf and settled for my own version of decoration, a sparkly top and a cheery headband.

It was not as if I had not spent the five years before meeting Russell skulking in a convent. Here and there I really had tried to shed the moss. Sometimes, though, it seemed that over those years, whatever gods controlled such things had leaped out at even the faintest stirrings on my part to whisk the object of my interest away. This one turned out to be gay, that one in a committed relationship, that one too young, this one a difficult drinker . . . I didn't think of Russell as a more successful effort at dating. So many of our encounters hadn't been dates, they'd been struggles for survival, for both of us.

The beneficiary of all this angst was Kendra's former high-school English teacher, Bob Delacroix. I doubted that Russell would need to rush back to Austin to defend any boundaries against Bob. We had been thrown together on the research team, and we'd shared some laughs. Nothing wrong with shared laughter as a basis for that strictly friendly friendship I had agreed to pursue.

Bob reminded me of the athletic coach at my old middle school in Atlanta, a big guy with thinning pale hair who herded us kids around the sports compound with bluff and energetic goodwill. Bob knew of a place off Sixth that wasn't crowded and open on Sunday, where we ate juicy tacos that refused to hold together; the mess bothered him more than it did me, but he laughed when we both ruefully resorted to forks. He told me how he'd more or less stumbled into teaching English because it was the job open when his health had forced him to give up coaching (Ah! He *had* been a coach!); he'd taken grad courses in the UT program to bring him up to speed.

As I'd suspected, the grounds for more than a casual acquaintanceship were sketchy. Bob had come to Austin from St. Louis to coach at a school I recognized as prestigious and selective, where the kids were "awesome" compared to the remedial summer-school bunch, many of them Cresthill admits, he was putting up with now. I nodded politely through reports of kids' attraction to graphic novels rather than "real books." A discussion of his enjoyment of dirt-bike racing led us away from kids' universal failures; he let me talk a little about some Big-Bend hikes I had taken. I think he was as glad as I was to opt out of a late-evening Reggae jam at Maggie Mae's. At the lot where, arriving separately, we had parked several spaces apart from each other, we said stilted goodbyes.

Reaching my car in the lot beneath the I-35 overpass, I tossed my phone on the passenger seat and sat in darkness for a few minutes wondering if I'd made a dishonest use of this unsuspecting victim with whom even a prolonged friendship looked like work. All this ruminating made me slow to flip back the sun visor I'd left down earlier for my drive home in the darkness. And just slow enough deciding that I was being murdered that Bob drove off before he could hear me scream.

14

I certainly did scream, flinging myself out of my car at Indy-500 speed, beating at my hair, my shoulders, the air. Only when nothing pursued me into the circle of glare under the sentry light did I stop hyperventilating and flailing. My heart was pounding so hard I thought bits of it were popping up into my throat.

I finally recovered the presence of mind to look around. No one in sight, just the silent rows of cars. No sound but my car pinging that I should shut the door.

I said to no one, "What the fuck?"

My phone still lay in the passenger seat, and I'd long ago turned off the dome light to protect the car battery, so I could see very little in the shadowy interior. I inched forward. The weak parking-lot light fell on a scattering of flaky litter on the pavement beside the open door.

I peered down. God help me if some noxious chemical had rained down as I flipped the visor. I touched the mess with my toe.

Bird feathers. Gray with white flecks—mockingbird feathers, if I had to guess in the dim light.

I peered inside the car, reaching timidly for my phone. Sure enough, my flashlight showed the remains of a dead mockingbird.

I looked around again at the crowded lot. A couple appeared from the street level, laughing quietly. They climbed into a car a few rows over; if they saw me, they gave no sign.

Had I left my car window open while it was parked behind our house that afternoon? Yes; in fact, I had left it open more than once in the hot, fair weather of the last week. I circled my car, opened the passenger door, and pulled a tissue from a stash in the glove box, mentally toying with possibilities I knew were absurd as soon as I considered them. An open window wouldn't tempt a self-respecting bird to take up residence in the space between the visor and the windshield and hang around to die in the baking heat. A very sick bird? Well, maybe. I'd had no particular reason to walk around to the front of my car when I climbed in it, so the bird could have been there cooking for days.

Circling back, I bent to retrieve the still body. A scattering of feathers floated free as I snugged the tissue around it and picked it up. Beneath the tissue I felt something more solid than feathers. I peeled the tissue back. The fragile body was wrapped in a folded piece of paper bound by a rubber band.

I set the bird down on my car hood and pried the square of paper open, tilting it to the street light to read it. The note was handwritten, big loopy kid letters.

It said, "Quit accusing him."

———————

I used another tissue to dust off my car seat. I climbed in, closed the door, and locked it. I laid the bird on the passenger seat, gently. Sat there in the dark. Meditating once again on the wisdom of calling Lt. Clauson, and on the degree to which, given what I had just learned, I did not want to do that.

Don't you want to talk to me, sweet bird? Don't you have something to tell?

They probably assumed I'd see the bird and note whenever I got in my car. That I'd pulled it down on myself alone in the darkness and scared myself silly was a bonus I had no intention of ever admitting they had achieved.

I peered around the big lot again, thinking, *they're not standing across the street taking pictures, they came in our yard.*

But now I knew why I was a target.

The only "him" I'd ever accused, was accusing, was my ex-husband, Anna's father, Eric Wyles.

———————

At home, I bagged the bird and stored it in the freezer. The note I stuck to the outside of the door with a magnet, in full, badgering view.

I calmed myself by sitting down with notes for my next meeting with Kendra. Better than not sleeping. I wrote "planning strategies" across the top of a notebook page. Dutifully I brainstormed questions. Did she plan at all before writing? Outlines? Sketches? Had Bob or some teacher like him influenced how she planned . . .

They can get DNA from that note.

I made myself breathe again. *Calm down. What good would that do?*

It would tell the police if Simone had handled the paper. But to learn that, they would have to ask Diana for a sample of her daughter's DNA.

Sure. Like I could imagine the police asking for that when no crime had been committed, and Diana amiably acquiescing. That particular door snapped shut. But I kicked the one next to it open. I'd promised Diana that I would give her time to talk to her daughter, but the note had changed things.

Eric is involved. Somehow.

Eric is involved in a threat against children and against me.

Something Corinne knew about? Something Simone could explain?

I set down my pen, rose, and crossed to the fridge. I took the note into the bedroom and from the back of the top of the chest fished a small box. It was one of those wooden ones with the inlaid chips meant to look like ivory. Maybe it was old, and maybe they were. What it looked like didn't matter because I kept it high up atop that chest of drawers, pushed far back, where I couldn't see it. But not being able to see it hadn't kept it from creating a dense, cold center of gravity in the room.

It had been a gift from my sister. She named it my "Box of Hope." "Every day," she said, "I want you to put a piece of your hope in it.

When you put so much in that there's no room for more, I want you to take it some place and throw it off a cliff. Then buy yourself the nicest box you can find, and every day, I want you to put a little bit of NOW into it. Something you're doing *now*. Do you understand?"

I disobeyed her. Whenever she asked how my box was, I told her, "There's still room for more hope in it." So into it tonight went the note, such a tiny slip to hold so much promise. *Eric is involved with children. There are witnesses. I'll get him now.*

I shut the box on this excitement quickly, for fear all the hope I'd been saving so long would leak out into the dry, hungry air.

——————

For the millionth time, all chance of sleep somewhere off in another country, I opened the folder of pictures on my computer desktop to look at *him*.

I saw again all his threats last summer, so much bluster, raging at me and sneering at Russell because of our surveillance, a rant coming from somewhere visceral I had always called fear. Fear that one day I'd get the answers only he could provide. *What happened that day, when you went to pick her up at the Girls' Club and you say she wasn't there?* I imagined his lover Celia with him that day, the three of them together, a deadly combination. Eric knew what happened that day, and somehow, now, with the new tool at my disposal, surely I could force the answers out.

He didn't believe I would ever risk a fatal confrontation. He'd been banking on my fear of that final answer to keep me cowed all these years.

Do you know some teenaged girls, Eric? Apparently some know you.

Of course reality intruded: even now there was no easy route to his secrets. My case against him had been molding on Clauson's desk ever since I'd first handed it to him, and it would take more than some girls' stories to prod him to act. Eric, at bay, would give me his same snarling denial. Still, I had the note now, and Simone and her cooperative father. A route, I reminded myself glumly, that involved somehow worming answers out of children, a process I had every reason to "be careful" about.

So if this was a new key to useful information, where was the door it would fit?

He wasn't alone, you know. Not in the pictures, not on that fatal day. I sat forward and looked at Celia again.

How little I really knew about her. More than once in the year since I had first learned of her and had so timidly stalked her I had wondered whether she was a mother herself. Surely somewhere in any mother would be some awareness of, some empathy for, another mother's pain. I'd snorted dismissively: that ice elf? No space in that shriveled body for children. But now, I considered. There must be many dark turns in her six years with Eric I could be exploring. Was I missing a bet?

You probably laugh at me, I told her cold image. *But you know only the broken effigy Eric peddled to serve his ends. Maybe YOU should look closer. If your lot is tied to his, maybe you should be getting some answers for the questions I'll be asking of YOU.*

Brave talk. How could I move past brooding and act? If I squeezed all my anger into a knot inside my heart so tight it imploded, the shock waves would roar across whole landscapes and find her. I closed my eyes on her image and sent every bit of that rocketing energy her way.

But of course that was hopeless. I closed the desktop folder, even sorrow exhausted. Then as I braced to stand, the dark thing that was my raging alter ego touched my shoulder. *You've finally acted,* she whispered. *You've called her. She'll hear you. She'll answer.*

And by God, she did.

15

It took her only two days to answer the call.

Monday I had made myself follow up on the scheduling work Taneesha and I had done on Friday, as well as on an article I would summarize at our next research meeting Wednesday. I stubbornly seized time from these duties for my so-far-futile effort to locate either Corinne or Simone in Anna's past. I had placed calls to the elementary school where Anna had been nearing graduation, learning that one of her old teachers had retired but another was still on the faculty. I left my number for both. By Tuesday neither had responded. I found the still-active teacher, Ms. Ropp, on Facebook and posted a request to message her, assuming she would recognize my name and guess why I wanted to contact her. I decided to be patient, not to seem obsessive. People rightly feared too much passion these days.

So I was fully disgruntled Tuesday morning when I headed out for necessary errands—a trek down I-35 to a repair shop I used for my sunglasses and a stop at a nearby HEB. I realized just seconds out of the HEB parking lot that someone was following me. The three lefts to the repair shop showed me the red car a discreet distance back, too far for me to make out the emblem on the grill. When I pulled into a parking space at the shop, the car eased to the curb, still keeping a measured distance. When I emerged ten minutes later and drove off, it fell in behind me again.

Even if I had not been primed for this moment, a few test turns and changes of speed told me this wasn't just any old tail (assuming there is such a thing). This was provocative, in-your-face-bitch harassment. The driver sped up, whipped around corners after me, begging to be noticed. When I stopped so suddenly that the red car skidded up behind me, the linked Audi rings were unmistakable. *Ah, she answered your summons*, Raging Sarah said.

I eased my car forward, the Audi dropping back, then picking up the pursuit again. I was salivating for this confrontation, but how to take charge? I needed a place public enough that I could shout for help if necessary but not so public that raised voices and strong language—like the kind I might end up using—sent people to their phones to call the riot squad.

Nor did I want to alert lurking FBI agents. But no black SUVs appeared in my mirrors. I led us serenely to the Wal-Mart off 71.

I parked at the end of a row. The Audi pulled in, too, stopping some hundred yards away. I opened my car door.

The Audi whipped backward, spun, and took off.

"Coward!" I shouted. "What the hell is your problem?" The only answer was a squeal of tires.

Shit. Here I was, all fired up, but no fight. I could go home and print a picture of her and let Alice shred it. Or I could tame my pumping heart by doing something useful, like prepping for Kendra's session that afternoon.

Shaky, not so much with a sense of letdown as of heavy things still waiting to topple, I drove home, parked in my usual backyard spot, and lugged my various purchases upstairs. Alice was hanging sideways on her cage bars. Maybe it was a strange sense of balances shifting that made me uncomfortable about letting her out. I felt compelled to check the lock on the French doors to the balcony. As I stood there, the red Audi pulled up to the front curb below.

I opened the doors so she could see me. She could have picked me off with a single shot. She got out and looked up at me from behind huge sunglasses, her feet spread, her hands held out from the sides of her dark blue running suit as if she were the one in the line of fire.

Oh, this moment felt like a long time coming, a payoff for all those times I hadn't let myself accost her, had held myself back from the dangerous business of asking frightening questions and making demands. But I saw I hadn't adequately planned. Neither rage nor diplomacy would work in this situation. I hadn't perfected the requisite level of cunning. I needed something subtle . . . for example, being the adult in this situation, above foolishness like screaming across parking lots or screeching around corners. "I'll open the front door," I called down in my best Sane Sarah accents. "Please come in."

Then the faint vibrations as she climbed the stairs, out on the landing a tremor of breathing. I slipped my cell phone in my pocket, my keypad set on 911. Overdramatic? Maybe. But we were about to find ourselves in a small space crowded with a lot of demons. I opened the door.

"Sarah Crockett," Celia Monahan said.

The Sarah Crockett whose manners I was exhibiting nodded. "I'm putting on a pot of tea and I have pita and hummus. Please come in."

She blinked, opened her mouth, closed it. Well, I'd won that round, sort of, knocking her off balance. Already small and narrow, all bone and muscle in the jogging suit, she seemed to shrink a little as she faced me. She crossed her arms, arching her back as if taking her stand on the landing. "No, let's talk here."

I looked at my watch. "I have an appointment in two hours. In the meantime, I'm going to eat and do some paperwork. I'm inviting you to come in and eat with me." *Let's see how she likes being killed with kindness*, said my subtle, adult mojo. "If you'd rather stand here, you may do so until my appointment arrives. At that point, if you don't leave, I will call the police."

"This isn't a police matter."

"Not yet."

She uncrossed her arms, swiping at the dark hair slicked back to her buoyant ponytail. She looked like a more seasoned, bolder version of Simone. Her thin red mouth tightened. "I want you to know what being followed feels like," she said.

So she had finally reacted to the team of spies Russell and I had set on her. Maybe she suspected them of being in cahoots with the FBI, which was apparently sniffing around her contacts. As for me, I had been stalked by Simone and her accomplice at Town Lake on Saturday; I'd found a dead bird in my car; and when I climbed out of my car after arriving home on Sunday, I had felt the need to scrutinize my own backyard. We were both being pursued, weren't we? A kinship beyond the scintillating attentions of Eric—who'd have thought it? "I do know," I said politely. I gestured, said again, "Come in."

She hung there, possibly calculating whether she really wanted to poke her hand into a trap I might spring. Finally she edged in, turning slowly and examining the room.

But she spun back to me, wound up tight enough I could hear her gears spinning. "I'm sick of it," she snapped. "I said it's not a police matter, but if it has to be, it will be. I want it stopped."

I left her standing there and went into the kitchen. She pivoted to watch me over the counter. From her curtained corner Alice let out a supersonic shriek. Celia jumped and I allowed myself a tick of pleasure. "It's just a bird." I opened a cupboard. "I have coffee, if you'd prefer that."

"Did you hear me?"

I measured tea, chamomile for peace. She thought she would get to ask all the questions? "You'll have to tell me what it is I'm supposed to stop."

"Having me followed. Obviously."

"To stop it, I would have to know who's doing it."

"You do know."

Well, yes and no. "It will help if you tell me about it," I said.

She opened her mouth, but swallowed whatever she had meant to say. So I'd scored another tiny point, like picking up one of those energy packets in a computer game. She moved farther into the room, peering around more deliberately: my untidy, crowded bookshelves, my paper-littered desk, my couch draped with various clothes, the miscellaneous objects scattered around on tables and shelves, pretty much at random—all surely different from the hard, shiny lifestyle I'd intuited from the pictures Russell had sent me of her. She found her way back to face me. "Using children to harass me—that's just too much."

I was in the act of setting the kettle on the burner. She gave a sharp nod as I froze, the kettle suspended inches above the hissing flame. She said, "You didn't think I'd notice *that*?"

With great calm, I arranged two cups, sugar, and lemon slices on a tray. Eons later, the water boiled. I poured it into a ceramic pot. She swiveled to watch me carry the tray to the coffee table. I eased onto the sofa. Her arms had closed across her chest again.

By that time I had put words together. "Yes, I've had people investigating you," I said. "And I think you know why. The children—I assume you mean teenaged girls—that's something else. They're harassing me, too. It has something to do with Eric. They seem concerned that I'm a threat to him." I poured my tea, playing a calm little schoolmarm. "I'd like to be a threat to him but so far I haven't succeeded. I don't know why these girls care about me."

Uncertainty creased her frown. She chewed her lip for a second. "These kids . . . You don't know who they are?"

"I've been trying to find out," I told her. "One of them must know Eric. I don't know how they might know him. Do you?"

Again she clapped her mouth shut on an answer that must have popped up too quickly. She drifted the length of the room toward Alice's closed-off corner, deep among whatever demons had accompanied her here. I poured a second cup of tea. It steamed gently. She whipped back.

"I know what you think about Eric," she said. "You're wrong. You have no idea what Eric went through when Anna disappeared."

I caught that blow in my breastbone. "Eric did not privilege me with his emotions."

She only shrugged, sinking onto the arm of the sofa. She gave her slick head a shake, some of that carbon-steel tension leaking out. "I'm tired of people lurking and taking pictures, I guess thinking *I'm* somehow involved with what happened. It's got to stop."

I nudged the second cup toward her. She didn't take it. "Why don't you go to the police?"

"Like I said . . ." Another shrug.

Because you're involved in something you don't want the FBI poking into? I didn't ask that; better to let her wonder how much I knew. "That's your decision, then."

A swipe of her pony tail. "But it's ridiculous. Eric didn't do anything, I didn't do anything, and even if we did, how is following us around—what, six years later?—going to help?"

"I don't know yet," I said. "That's why I'm still doing it." I asked a question I was sure she hadn't yet truthfully answered. "Why did you come here today?"

"I told you, I was tired—"

"But our surveillance has been going on for nearly a year. Why now?"

She fiddled with her elbows for a long moment. Then she rose. "If there's something going on with Eric . . . but it's me these kids have been following. What could they think they've got on me?"

What indeed. I raised my brows.

She turned and walked to the French doors and back, sucking her lip in. "Those girls . . . you make it sound like you want to know what they're up to."

"Anyone who's being harassed would want to know why."

"So you'll try to find out?"

I answered the need I was hearing. "Probably, yes."

Again her frown tightened on some knot she was trying to tease out. Behind her guarded thoughts moved a barely smothered restlessness that I found myself wanting to read as sadness. She stiffened with some decision. "You have a piece of paper anywhere?"

Pieces of paper I had in spades. I handed her a notepad and a pen. She scribbled. "That's my cell. If I can tell you who they are and you find out why, you have to tell me. If you like that deal, text me yes or no. If I have anything for you, I'll text back."

I took the pad. Her handwriting was angular, firm. I tore off the sheet. It would fit in my box of hope nicely. She went to the door, turning back to me as she opened it, her dark brows slicing down.

"I think you should be more careful," she said over her shoulder. "You could hurt children."

I couldn't help a rush of indignation. "I would not hurt children."

She scoffed. "Just be more careful with other people's children than you were with your own."

She didn't slam the door because I grabbed it. I charged out but she moved fast, already halfway down the stairs. I caught myself on the third step. I still held the piece of paper she had given me with her number on it. In my fury I had wadded it, maybe past deciphering. I pivoted slowly, aware I might stumble because I was shaking, and went back inside where I could carefully flatten the paper. Even before she drove away she'd get the message. "Please send me as much as you can so I'll know what to be careful of."

16

Late that night a spring storm came through. I should be used to such blows, living in these parts as long as I had. But the past six years had taught me that even things tied down with heartstrings could be ripped away.

So I listened to the wind slamming against my bedroom window and the rain behind it, machine-gun rapid, big chunks of the heavens coming at me out of the dark. Then the lightning, ah, the lightning, hunting me with doomsday cracks of thunder. I wanted it over. Gone.

Then of course the wind fell, the pyrotechnics died, and the gutters sighed and gurgled. *I'll sleep now*, I thought.

But I didn't. Celia Monahan's thin dark shape slipped in and out of my mind's eye. She had a secret. Maybe many. She knew things. Even with no idea of what they were, I discovered that I feared for her and whatever private treasures she was holding onto. She was afraid *for* something. Someone. Some child she did, after all, have some tie to? But once I found out what she feared, I'd face both our dangers.

Into this restless fretting came a sound.

I sat up, in that tingling alertness probably only people who live alone can feel.

Again. From outside, at the back of the house, below the small balcony outside my bedroom. I eased my legs off the bed. Yes: low voices, urgent. Then silence. Then running footsteps, shallow and receding. I stood and peered out the bedroom window. Our cars sat peacefully under the backyard sentry light.

Burglars? Who in this house owned anything to attract burglars? Our computers? Computer thieves would have to start at Adela, who only owned a tablet, and I wasn't sure it worked.

True, burglars might find us an easy target: Adela and Larry and Wallace all slept at the front of the house; last year when we had midnight visitors, they'd all been slow to hear the back-porch mayhem I'd created. The noises that had disturbed me tonight were hushed ripples, unlikely to wake them up.

They came in our yard.

Those stupid girls—in our yard?

Oh, sigh. Not an impossibility, not at all. This disturbance was almost certainly my doing. Adela couldn't kick me out for attracting trouble since I owned my flat, but I'd rather spare her the kinds of trouble I seemed to incite. Whatever mischief I'd triggered, it was my job to stop it, hopefully before anyone else found out.

Still in darkness, I pulled a windbreaker over the T-shirt and shorts I slept in and slid into my clogs. Easing downstairs and along the hall past Adela's dark kitchen, I wondered if my stalkers had brought me more messages. Another cryptic note? Another sad little body? I paused at the door to the porch to listen, hand on the knob.

A creak. A sound I could convince myself was someone breathing. Another creak. Someone walking. Inside the outer screen door. On the porch.

We all had keys to the porch door that we'd upgraded after last summer's excitement. Maybe Larry and Wallace were coming home after a late outing and whispering so as not to disturb anyone. But the voices had been urgent, with a high whine behind them. Not men's voices. Girls'.

More creaking. Something clanked, probably one of Adela's potted succulents getting bonked. I distinctly heard a female hiss: "*Shit.*"

If I opened the door, the culprit would vanish. I knew from experience I couldn't catch up to young bodies fleeing into the night.

I snared the extra porch-door key from its hook in the kitchen and slipped back down the hall to the front door. I cracked the door cautiously, but nothing moved in the small front yard. I edged through the side gate in our picket fence to creep along the driveway, keeping close to the house. At the corner of the house, I paused. Nothing moved in the back yard, either. A faint scratch-scratch came from the dark porch to my right.

Last summer's visitor had been a harried young man who might have been dangerous. Were these girls dangerous? *This* girl, since from what I could hear, there was now only one.

Raging Sarah would have charged, bellowing. With Sane Sarah coaching, I eased clear of the shadow of the house, alongside the porch. Beyond the screen, on the porch, a hunched shape on hands and knees rocked back and forth over a patch of the floor. Her back to me, she didn't see me; I rounded the corner of the porch and faced the door. The screen beside the door hung loose, cut. She didn't react as I crept up the steps and slid the key into the lock. Only when I opened the door and entered did she jump up and spin.

"Shhhh!" I hissed. Too late. She fell back, shrieked, then leaped up, aiming for the cut place in the screen. I blocked her. She bolted right. I blocked that, too. I did not want to touch her. "Calm down," I said. "I'm not going to hurt you."

"I-I didn't—" she stammered. "It-it wasn't—"

The porch light flooded on and the hall door opened behind her. She shrieked again and dove so fast past me I would have had to grab her sweatshirt to stop her. She plunged through the torn screen, getting her feet under her as she hit the ground. I stood and watched her go.

"What in the world?" said Adela. Larry and Wallace crowded out behind her. Just like last summer, Wallace brandished a hammer.

"Oh, another kid wanting into my life," I said, wishing I could make the words come out lightly.

The three of them were staring at the floor at my feet. I looked down.

A large smear of black paint, probably from a spray can. A tipped-over bottle of soda. A wadded paint-stained cloth. The paint, muddled from scrubbing but readable, said, "Stop or Die!"

"She was trying to wash it out," I said.

"That'll take more than a little soda," said Wallace.

Adela glared down at the defaced floorboards. "Who in the world was it?"

I wished I didn't know. But it was all out of my hands now.

I sighed. "Her name is Simone."

17

“Kids in trouble smell me,” I said. “I give off some kind of odor. I don’t know, desperation? When they get desperate, I smell like home.”

We sat around Adela’s kitchen table. Wallace had laid the hammer on the table; now he sipped the hot chocolate Adela had set before us in her silent, unfussy way. We had a problem more complicated than installing a garbage disposal before us. I’d have preferred a bottle of wine to the hot chocolate. Maybe two.

“You should take to wearing perfume,” said Wallace. His auburn hair looked sleep-rumpled. “The police need to know.”

“I agree,” Larry said.

I’d seen this debate coming and had mentally slapped together my objections while Larry and Wallace inspected the dark yard for more possible damage and Adela warmed the milk for the chocolate. “I’ve talked to her mother. I promised her I wouldn’t call the police until she had a chance to find out for herself what was going on. I mean, the girl was probably caught up in some kind prank and she did come back to clean it up.” I caught Adela’s dense brown eyes, behind her thick glasses. She did not look at all understanding. “I’ll call her mother right now.”

At least I earned some silence. Wallace twirled his hot-chocolate cup. “So what is it you’re supposed to stop or die for?”

“I think it’s about Eric.” They’d never known Eric. He’d come to the flat only once, in the daytime when Larry and Wallace were at work and Adela at her book club. He’d come that day to threaten me. It gave Raging Sarah a rush to know she could inspire that much emotion. “I’m hoping Simone’s parents can help me figure out if there’s something going on with him.”

"Sounds to me," Larry said, leaning back in his chair so his long, pajama-clad legs would fit under the table, "as if some young woman somewhere has a crush on him."

"That would explain a lot," I said. "Whoever's involved in this thinks I'm out to hurt Eric. Which I am."

Adela stirred her "World's Best Grandma" cup. It had been a Mother's Day gift from her granddaughter, a teenager now. "Kids get themselves riled up, but they'll lose interest. Especially if they don't get away with their nonsense."

Wallace shrugged. "I don't know. These things can get out of hand."

It *had* gotten out of hand with Corinne Miller's suicide. But dragging in Corinne would complicate this already messy discussion: one troubled kid was plenty for my housemates to deal with in the middle of the night. Wallace pushed back from the table, snaring his hammer (I'd give a pretty penny to see him ever use it!). "If I were you, I'd tell Eric. Let him take some responsibility. After all, he could end up in trouble over something like this."

I almost said, "I hope so." But I no longer had much influence over who got into trouble and for what. "I'll have to think how to do that, since Eric and I don't usually communicate."

"A simple email," said Wallace. He took his cup to the sink to rinse it. "The girl's probably home in bed by now." He pushed the chair he had vacated back under the table. "Clean-up's going to cost. It'll probably have to be sanded. But like I said, Sarah—really, for the girl's sake—it's a matter for the police."

So I'd lost that argument. But Adela jumped in. "No point in getting the police out here at this hour." She pushed up, reaching for the other now-empty cups. "As long as she doesn't turn back up with more mischief. I'll call the police in the morning."

"Involving the police will certainly get her parents' attention," said Larry.

I propped my chin on my hand. The clock over the sink said one-thirty. It felt much later. Much too close to an unpleasant daybreak.

"Yeah," I said. "It sure will."

———————

Hauling myself upstairs reminded me that Celia Monahan had not returned my message. But the text was out there somewhere, a buzzing electronic gnat I hoped she wouldn't be able to swat off. Losing Simone to the police would make Celia my new lifeline. Without access to Simone's secrets, I'd have to double down on my search for hers. I should have tried harder to get her to trust me. She had no reason to think I would want to help her, my cheating husband's bit of stuff. And if she had been involved in Anna's disappearance, she had reasons to fear me as well.

To brace myself for my miserable wee-hours talk with Diana. I poured a glass of wine, a very small glass. Just to have something to twirl as I talked.

She must have entered my contact info into her phone because she answered, hoarse from waking, "My God, Sarah, it's two a.m. What in the world?"

"I'm really sorry." A major understatement. "There's something you need to know. First things first, is Simone home?"

"What do you . . . she's at a friend's. What's the matter?"

I spoke fast to get ahead of more questions. "It might be a good idea to check with the friend's parents. Simone was here. There was trouble. It looks as if she and some friends painted a, I guess you'd say threat, on our porch."

"She was where? At your house?"

"Yes. Less than an hour ago."

"You saw this?" Her tone took on an accusing tenor.

"I saw her, Diana. She ran away. I'd prefer to deal with it all tomorrow but I wanted to make sure she was somewhere safe."

"I'll call her."

"Yes. In the morning—"

She hung up.

If she wanted to know what was going to descend on her in the morning, let her ask me. Finally, as I begged for sleep to claim me, she texted: "They're both safe. I'll talk to her tomorrow."

Glad someone's safe, I thought.

——————

Then it was day, too soon, crisp and clear after the storm. No word from Diana. I had a nine o'clock meeting on campus with the research team, with just enough time to shower, dress, eat, and play with my bird. She crapped on my blouse and I had to change, leaving me even less time to make my meeting. I texted more hastily than I really wanted to: "I'm glad Simone is safe and I hope you will talk to her. There may be a cost to clean up the damage. That will be up to my housemates. I'll look forward to hearing from you." I changed "hope" to "assume." I did not mention police; I'd ask Adela to let me pay for the clean-up myself if that meant I could avoid them. But as I was stuffing my book bag to head downstairs to talk to Adela, she rang me. "The police said they'd send someone, but they didn't say when."

Damn. Too late. Fortunately Adela didn't know Diana's contact info so I could probably get to Diana first and warn her. "Call them back, give them my text number. If one of them happens to be a Lt. Clauson—"

"That pink fella."

I had to laugh. "Yes, that about describes him. Pink granite. If you talk to him, tell him to call me."

"I'll give them your number." She hung up.

Someday, I thought, I'd like Adela and Clauson to square off. I'd like to watch the physics of that collision from a safe spot, say, on Mars.

Downstairs Adela had patched the torn screen with duct tape. The black paint had dried hard and glossy. Yes, clean-up would cost. The drive to campus would give me time to decide what to tell Diana. I wished I could have kept my promise to let her handle her daughter. Surely she'd understand I'd had no choice.

I hadn't kept my commitment to Clauson, either. I hadn't told him about the dead bird or about Simone's connection to the cyberbullying girls. Up to now, though, I'd known only that Simone *might* have been involved. Now that I knew she *was* involved, it was time to quit veering around troublesome facts. Diana or no Diana, I should funnel what I knew straight to him.

Fatefully, that morning, I didn't pull out the main driveway toward the street in front of the house. Instead, hoping for less traffic, I squeezed the Corolla into the tiny alley behind the house so I could head over to Guadalupe. As always, I crept along that alley to avoid the various garbage cans strewn along it and the overgrown shrubbery trying to claw at my car doors. Russell and I had had quite a chase down this alley one dark night. My mind escaped into that adventure, Russell calling me Sundance—

Something jumped out in front of me, a dark blur across my windshield—there, then gone.

18

I stomped the brakes so hard the car actually bucked. My bag and yesterday's mail and my sunglasses all cascaded to the floor.

For a breathless instant I sat and trembled. I heard little yelps and realized I was making them. I opened and closed my fingers on handfuls of air, then stumbled out of the car.

I edged past a wet, clutching bush of some kind, holding onto the car for balance. I hadn't felt a thunk. I hadn't hit her. I couldn't have. By the time I reached the front fender, I was envisioning spewing blood, jutting bones. The sight of her sitting upright in the weeds beside the lane, staring at me, one hand twisting her pony tail, jarred loose a breath so fierce it threatened to turn me inside out. "Oh, my God. Are you all right?"

She scrunched even deeper into the overgrown verge, her eyes huge and sunken. She wore the same sweats I'd surprised her in last night. "You can't tell!" she wailed.

"Can't tell. . . ?" I put out a hand, but she didn't take it. She went on staring at me, tears welling. "Tell what, honey?" I crossed to her, kneeling. "How long have you been out here?" Her friend might have lied about her whereabouts. "Have you been here all night?"

"You can't tell," she said again. She drew her knees up, pushed to her feet. I rose with her, my hands hovering to help. She wheeled and grabbed my fingers. "Please, please."

"Are you hurt?"

"My mom'll kill me."

Thank God, no sign of blood. "Yeah, after she hugs you." My voice came out drier than I'd expected. "But I can't say as I would blame her."

"I'm okay," she said, calmer now. "I thought you were stopping."

"I did stop." It seemed important to get that clear. "Let's get in the car. I need to take you home."

She stepped back. "I'm not going home."

"Your mom thinks you're at your friend's house."

Her eyes widened. "Oh, God, you told her."

"I had to. I had to make sure you were safe."

She shook her head, no tears now, just throat muscles clenching. She still gripped my hand. "You have to tell her I didn't do it. It wasn't my fault."

I couldn't force her into the car. Nor could I make my meeting on time. I propped myself on the hood, grateful for the warm sunshine seeping into the alley. I took out my phone to call Diana. Simone said, "I didn't do it. Tell her! Please."

"So who did do it?"

"I can't tell you."

"Why not?"

"It's . . . they'd . . ." She shook her head, her usually glossy ponytail limp, dragging across her shoulders.

"Are you afraid of them?" I asked.

"No!"

Well, that was a lie. I balanced my phone in my hand. Maybe if she'd be straight with her mom, the whole police mess could be avoided. Her parents would settle with Adela and arrange for Simone to tell the authorities in charge of Corinne's case what she knew. My plan to dissect Simone to get at her story had been shoved to a back burner by the terrifying moment she jumped in front of my car. "Why can't you be truthful with your parents? You were trying to clean up the mess, so you won't be blamed for it. But they have a right to know that you've gotten in some kind of trouble."

"I'm not in trouble! I didn't do anything!"

"Well, yes, actually." I scrolled to my contacts for Diana's number. "You did and you are."

There'd been a risk that saying that would run her off. But apparently her need to win my cooperation overwhelmed the urge to flee. "Look," she said, suddenly intent and chilly, "it wasn't my idea to paint that, it's this girl I know, she has this thing about . . . him."

My fingers froze halfway to Diana's icon. "My ex-husband? Eric?"

"Yeah," she said, way too eager, "and she's kind of crazy about it. She wants you to stop saying he killed your daughter. She thinks he's *perfect!*" A sneer crept in under that adjective. "I can't tell you who it is because I don't want to get her in trouble. But if you'll just friend me on Facebook and message me that you know he didn't do it, I'll share that with her and she'll get over it. Then you can forget this, all this . . . this stuff ever happened. What's so hard about that?"

Ah. One of her friends, in the throes of a fascination with Eric, must have come across the stories about me from last year, and in her sixteen-year-old panic, Simone chose to believe that the accusations in those stories could be erased at will. Somewhere out there in her world were these friends she couldn't cross, and for her, that threat reigned. Were these the "friends" Corinne's mother said had killed her? Maybe Simone's foray into property damage would be a godsend if it made her spill those friends' names to someone who could ask hard questions. For example, were any of them once friends with a girl named Anna? I was telling myself this was not the time to ask that when my phone rang.

I hoped it might be somebody from the team, since the meeting would be about to start. No. Diana's number popped up on the screen.

She sounded breathless. "Sarah! Have you heard from Simone? She took off from her friend's house, no one knows where she's gone."

Her voice in the phone carried and at its echo Simone's bravado faded. She fidgeted, looking over her shoulder as if she'd decided flight was the better option and was scouting the exits. I sighed. "She's right here."

"There? At your house?"

"In the back driveway of my house." I told her what she hadn't asked. "She's okay." I offered the phone to Simone. "Will you please tell your mother why you're here?"

She took the phone. Risky, I know, to trust her with it. She might be more desperate than I thought. "Mom?" Her voice came out tentative at first, but it gained strength. "Yeah, yes, I know, but this lady is accusing me of something I didn't do and I had to tell her I didn't do it. She hit me with her car."

She glared at me, triumphant. It took effort, but I kept my lips clamped.

"Yeah . . . okay." She held out the phone. "She wants to talk to you."

I accepted it. Diana said, "Sarah? Seriously?"

"I didn't hit her." Probably I should be calling 911, to have the girl checked over before that charge grew some fangs. "She crossed in front of my car. Look, I wanted to wait to hear from you before taking any further action, but something's come up that means I—"

"I'm on my way to get her," said Diana, and hung up.

I ended the call, facing Simone. "She's coming to get you."

"I can get home." She tossed her head, bending to dust off the seat of her sweats.

"How you get home is between you and your mom." Time to bring down the hammer. "This whole thing has taken a really ugly turn. Property's been damaged and I'm not the only one who knows you're involved." She started to interrupt but I overrode her. "You've lied."

"I told you!" she said, a hot flare in her voice. "I didn't do anything!"

"Someone did. So when you talk to your mom, you might want to think about what you owe your friend."

I wasn't sure she heard me. She peered around, wheeling back and forth. I decided it really would be wise to show her on her feet, uninjured; I opened my phone camera and hit record.

Her eyes widened. "What are you doing?" It came out as a strangled gasp. She lurched toward me as if to grab the phone.

I hefted it overhead. "In case your mom is worried about what happened. No one will see it." Unless it became part of a court case. Her effort bounced her back and she stood there panting. "She will almost certainly expect you to be waiting out front. I'll back the car up so you can get by."

"I'm sorry, I'm sorry! I didn't mean to!" she cried, looking younger and more vulnerable by the second.

"Simone," I urged her, "please tell your mother everything."

She said nothing. I turned off the phone and put it deep in a pocket, then climbed in and put the car in reverse. To my relief, as I backed, she followed, and when I reached the yard and pulled to the side, she marched past, fiercely not looking at me. She rounded the corner of the house and started down the front driveway. I got out and climbed the porch steps, shooting one more self-preserving video before letting myself into the main hall. Adela's car hadn't been out back, so she hadn't witnessed this debacle. Just as well. If she realized that Simone had lurked in our bushes, she might march out to the curb and give Diana an impolitic earful about irresponsible parents and delinquent juveniles.

So I watched alone through the panes in the front door. Simone leaned against our picket fence. She took a phone out of her pocket and hunched over it, idly scuffing the sidewalk with her gold-laced running shoes. After a while, a dark green Mercedes pulled up. I retrieved my own phone, texted. "Diana, my housemate has told the police about last night. I'm sorry this has happened. I hoped to prevent it. I've asked Simone to be truthful with you."

Simone crossed to the car and got inside. I couldn't tell if my message got delivered before the Mercedes drove away.

19

I headed back outside to my car. My phone whistled: two texts. One from Bob, at the campus meeting I was supposed to be attending: "Where are you? You okay?" One from Celia Monahan.

Celia's contained no message, just an attachment. I replied to Bob, "Little emergency here, nothing big, taken care of. Sorry! I'll be there in ten."

Eleven, because I opened Celia's attachment. It was a spreadsheet, the file titled "Hang-gliding demo/clinic" and dated the previous fall. Exactly what Lt. Clauson had asked me to hunt for: a list of the girls in Corinne's social world who were connected to me. Connected through Eric.

The girls who had attended that hang-gliding demo included both Corinne and Simone.

———————

There's little so calming as an academic meeting where you respond to every contention with "You make an excellent point" or "That's a useful observation." Our discussion, on which I managed to focus, centered on learning more from our young writers about the ways their parents reacted to their writing projects. Perfect for my concerns about Kendra. Back home, I climbed the stairs, closed my door, and eased onto my sofa with a hair-nibbling parrot on my shoulder. Thought, *okay, Celia, let's see what we have wrought.*

She had sent me the list because she thought I might learn something from it. At least, so I surmised. The girls had been following her. Had they learned something about Celia and Eric? Had they just possibly remembered a girl named Anna they once knew with whom Celia was a special friend? Probably not. Celia would want to hide any such connection, not hand me the means for ferreting it out.

Did I have to take this list to Clauson, even though it was what he wanted? I had already betrayed my promises to Diana to keep the police out. Would I betray some similar promise to Celia if I gave Clauson the list?

It wasn't Raging Sarah poking my conscience. Some plain old common-sense gremlin was whispering: *Uh, Sarah, withholding evidence is a crime.*

Evidence of what? From what Clauson had said, another department handled situations like this one—presumably cyberbullying and other social indelicacies, only some of which were crimes. If there'd been no crime, how could I withhold evidence about one? Still, something had inspired Clauson not just to seek my help but also to warn me. Celia had warned me, too. Russell would surely have warned me. The warnings didn't scare me. They intrigued me. But Clauson's injunctions did remind me that, as a private citizen, I couldn't interrogate the girls or for that matter, Celia. A law-enforcement officer could do that. *Sorry, Celia.* I punched Clauson's number into my phone.

He was in. He didn't give me time to speak. "Yeah, Dr. Crockett. I'm still planning on doing something about the Monahan woman. It's on my list. I got paper work to get through, so thanks for now and goodbye."

I got in ahead of his hang-up click. "Forget worrying about Celia, Lieutenant. I talked to her myself yesterday."

Making him fall silent always gives me a tiny thrill of power. I caught the creak of his office chair. "So you stalked her after all."

Now a full pulse of power. "Celia came to me."

"Yeah. To tell you to stop Russell Pierce's goons from following her around."

Clauson and I never whiled away our moments together with small talk. I dove in.

"She came to me because teenaged girls had started hounding her and she thought I'd resorted to child labor," I said. "I assured her I hadn't and asked if she had any connection to a group of girls like that. Today she sent me a list of names. A roster for some sort of hang-gliding class Eric taught." He didn't interrupt. "Corinne's name is on it. It seems the girls might have a . . . well, an interest in Eric. If so, that explains their interest in me."

His silences didn't always mean I had overpowered him. He often came back fiercer. In this silence he audibly shuffled papers. Then: "You'll send us that list?"

"Absolutely. When can I expect to hear what you find out?"

"It's complicated. The first thing the unit on this case has to do is find some reason to think there's been a crime."

This news wasn't going into any file drawer. "These girls threatened me."

"I don't think you're in any immediate danger."

And here I'd thought he worried about me. "There has been a crime. Vandalism."

I envisioned his brows hiking. "Vandalism?"

I told him about the paint. "I asked Adela to have any officers she talked to call me. No one has yet but I assume they will." Or should I assume that they were at that moment interviewing Adela, who was telling them that I'd identified one of the young women? "The daughter of one my former university colleagues was part of the group. She came back to try to scrub up the paint and we caught her."

"You *caught* her?" He sounded as if I'd said we shot her.

"Well, I recognized her, but she ran away."

Now he'd be slouching back in his wooden swivel chair, rubbing his eyes. "When did you plan to tell me about this?"

"I have told you. I also told her mother."

"You protecting this kid for some reason?"

"She's made that pretty impossible."

Over the phone, a tense little tapping noise. A pen on the desk? "You know, Dr. Crockett, I thought I was just doing a colleague a favor on this thing with the Miller girl. Thought you might be able to figure out who doctored those photos from your contacts at the university or something. But somehow you've managed to make it about your daughter."

"Yes," I said quietly. "And in that case, we know a crime was committed."

His sigh rattled, as if he'd caught something in his throat he needed badly to get rid of. "Forward that list to me."

——————

I shut off the phone. There, I wouldn't be arrested for withholding evidence. Of course, there was still the dead bird in my freezer, the note with possible DNA, Ms. Miller's insinuations, the little scene in the back alley. But these weren't evidence of anything. No, I thought, pretty fierce myself, they were those open doors I could go through. I wasn't going to let Clauson shut them. Not yet.

A part of me pitied Clauson. He hadn't been in charge of my daughter's case, but he'd witnessed that ugly history, sometimes from far away and sometimes with only his desk to block it, across all six years. He was a professional—and a father. Failing to find a lost child had to ache. He knew, like I did, that Celia had sent me that file for a reason. He couldn't pretend he didn't want to know that reason. Even his hard little heart would shrink from another scar.

——————

Adela called to tell me that an officer—a polite young man "with all his hair shaved off"—had come and gone while I'd been at the meeting. He'd recorded Simone's name, taken pictures, accepted my contact info. Now Adela was headed out shopping, for a meat grinder, of all things. Not without reason, she'd decided she didn't trust any of the hamburger in any of the stores. "My mother ground our meat," she'd told me. "We knew how many cows were in it. For all we know, that store stuff could come from a thousand half-rotted old cows."

So the police had been prompt. That meant that the car I heard pulling up below when I opened the balcony doors after stashing Alice was surely Diana in her green Mercedes, come to condemn me for siccing the police on her precious daughter. Instead a sleek gun-metal-gray car slid up to the curb. Police come for more information? But Nick Hudson got out. Slammed the door with what looked like serious intent. Shoved his way through our gate. I went out to peer over the balcony railing. On the small porch below, he was leaning on my bell.

He was quick too, I thought. He must have already heard from Diana or from Simone herself about Simone's transgressions. Well, I'd set straight any tales either Diana or Simone might have told him. I punched the intercom. "I'll be right down."

When I opened the door to let him into the hall, I found him banging his fist against the door frame—slow, heartbeat blows. He stopped his clenched fist in mid-air at the sight of me. "Celia was here yesterday."

Celia here yesterday? This was the last thing in the world I'd expected him to say. He must have come from his office; he wore a dark, expensive-looking suit that broadened his chest and shoulders, a pale blue shirt, and a gold and blue tie. But something about the way his dark hair leaked over his forehead told me *something's broken here*.

"What did she talk about?" he demanded. "What did she tell you?"

"Tell me? About what?"

"She came here and talked to you. What did you talk about?"

I had to move the measured, responsible father I'd met before to a different side of my brain. "Excuse me, Mr. Hudson, but I don't have the faintest idea why you're asking about Celia. I didn't even know you knew her. She would be the best person to answer your questions. I suggest you direct them to her."

"I can't," he said. "She's dead."

In the burdened silence that fell, my phone rang. I took it out and glanced at it, relieved for an excuse to avoid his eyes long enough to figure out what my own face should be doing. It was Clauson.

"Is he there?" he demanded.

"Yes."

"Keep him there." He hung up.

20

I had to get Nick inside, make him sit down.

If I didn't, he was likely to collapse. He'd started trembling, faintly but enough to stir the air between us. He took a step toward me but caught himself on the door frame. "Who was that? Who was it? The police?"

I supposed I'd learn soon enough how Clauson had known Nick's destination. In the meantime, did the lieutenant assume I could physically detain the man? "Please," I said. "Come and tell me what happened. We can talk back here."

I turned from the door to the hallway that would take us past Adela's kitchen and into a little alcove off the porch where we often met with people we didn't want to invite into our homes. After a few steps I risked looking back. He was feeling his way along the wall in my wake. We made it to the alcove. To my relief, as I settled into a chair, he sank to the small, worn couch opposite me, burying his face in his hands. His shoulders began to shake. I waited for him to find his breath. Clauson or whoever he sent would be here any minute. I wanted Nick to talk to me first.

"She was . . . she was . . ." He lowered his hands, wiped them on his trousers. "Someone pushed her off her deck. She was lying on the rocks."

"You were at her house?" I took the jerk of his head for a nod. "You're sure she was dead?"

"I went down to her. Her eyes were open. Blood . . . from her ear. I picked up her arm. She must have been lying there a long time . . ."

"Did you call 911?"

He took a racking breath. "Why did she come here? What did she tell you?"

"So you called 911 and left?" That explained Clauson's command to keep him. "When did all this happen? Just now?"

"She told me she found out something from you she had to check out. She wouldn't tell me. It got her killed."

What had I told Celia that would prompt a murder? Only that the girls' surveillance wasn't my doing or Russell's. Was she afraid of someone else she thought might be behind it? The man the FBI was tracking? Did the girls, indeed, know secrets about her?

Maybe if I told him about Celia's list and how it implicated his daughter, the revelation might surprise something helpful out of him. But I didn't have that much cruelty in me. Not yet. "How did you know Celia?" I asked.

"Did you talk about something to do with Eric?"

Ah. Eric. He knew Eric. And if he knew Eric, he probably met Celia through him. But this grief wasn't the behavior of a friend of a friend, sympathy for an acquaintance's loss. I sorted through what to tell him. Anything I shared could end up looking like interference in a police investigation. "I know about Celia and Eric," I said.

"He killed her. I know he did."

I felt a surge of deep gratitude for the sudden yelp of my phone.

"We're outside," came Clauson's flat voice. "What's the situation?"

"We're talking quietly. If you come around back, I'll let you in."

"I'll have people out front, too," he said. The connection went.

"That's the police," said Nick.

He sprang up. I didn't. De-escalate. "They probably want to know why you left."

"I had to . . . I wasn't thinking." He pivoted to the porch door, tried to open it. His gaze took in the key hanging on the wall and he reached for it. I did nothing. Tackling this big guy wasn't on my agenda. As he unlocked the door and plunged through it, right across the black-painted message, I rose and followed. Beyond the screen, Clauson mounted the porch steps and rattled the outer door on his side. Nick stopped. His shoulders gave way. I edged past him and used my own key to unlock the porch door.

Two uniformed officers, stalwart guys with guns on their hips, pounded up the steps behind Clauson. "Nicholas Hudson?" Clauson said.

I knew what Nick saw: a stone monolith, squat, rosy-hued but implacable, blocking his path. Clauson produced his ID. "I need to ask you a few questions. In my office. You can come along quietly and willingly. Otherwise, I'll place you under arrest."

Nick squared himself, got his breath under control. "I need to call my attorney." He fumbled toward his coat pocket. And suddenly Nick and I were both looking at the barrels of two guns.

I couldn't help starting, flinching sideways. Nick looked at me, then back at the officers. He let his hands drop, mouth open in rueful comprehension. "Oh."

"Do you consent to a search?" Clauson asked.

"I don't . . . I'm not armed."

Clauson tilted his head. One of the officers stepped forward. Nick wilted, holding his arms out from his sides. "Look, I was upset. I didn't . . ." The officer patted him down briskly, removing the slim phone from his coat pocket and handing it to Clauson. Clauson studied the phone for a moment.

"May I speak to my attorney in private?" Nick asked.

After a second Clauson handed him the phone. He jerked his chin at the officers, who backed out onto the steps, letting the porch door close. Then he waved a hand at me, directing me back into the hall. As he followed me, he frowned at the stains on the porch floor. With the door closed, he pulled the flimsy window curtain aside so he could watch Nick through the panes. "What the hell was he doing coming here?"

"How did you know he did?"

"He waited just long enough to take off for the first 911 responder to spot him. A unit picked him up and called in this location, which naturally I recognized." He gave his mouth a wry twist he might have meant for a smile.

Did *I* need an attorney? "He knew that Celia came here yesterday. He seemed to think she'd told me something. I don't think he's aware of that list I told you about." Beyond the door, Nick paced in and out of view, phone pressed to his face, wiping his forehead with his free hand. "What happened to her? He said someone pushed her off her deck."

"So what did she tell you?"

"What I reported to you on the phone. About the girls following her and thinking I was involved." I considered. "She seemed to think I'd learn something from these girls, and if I did, she wanted me to tell her."

"Learn what?"

He was like a bulldog, jaws locked on a prey. "Whatever it is, I've hardly had time to learn it. How did Celia die?"

I didn't get a chance to find out whether he'd answer. A rap came at the door. From the other side, Nick said, "I'm ready, officer. My attorney will meet us at the station." He sounded flat, almost drugged, as if someone had turned off a switch. "I'll fully cooperate."

"Just one moment," Clauson called. With the door to the porch still closed, he jabbed a stubby finger at me.

"This isn't just a bunch of kids playing around any more," he said. "I don't know what the connection is between these girls and you and this woman, but every inch of my gut tells me there is one." I started to say, yes, I told you, Eric. But the finger, stabbing, stopped me. "Do. Not. Do. Anything. Without. Consulting. Me."

Here came the temptation to mouth off. But I reduced it to a tense nod. Out on the porch where Nick waited, Clauson pointed to the paint. "Don't let anybody touch that." The officers backed down into the yard, and with Clauson as backstop, they herded Nick out.

Behind them, I locked the porch door. Shit. I'd learned virtually nothing. The morning's cataclysms had left me in that familiar limbo where Clauson would tell me whatever he damn well wanted.

Hmmph. In my view, "do not do anything" covered too much territory to have any meaning. It certainly didn't cover half the things Raging Sarah was capable of.

21

Diana hadn't written back to report on her talk with her daughter. No real reason she should. I'd done right by my stars, even giving up a chance to shove on the door through which Simone had scuttled, but Diana might not consider me so noble, certainly not if she'd had a visit from a cop. I considered playing concerned colleague and calling. Asking, for example, if she'd talked to Simone's friends, hoping to hear a name or two on Celia's list.

But by the time I reached my landing I knew there was another call I had to make. So much had happened since I last talked to Russell—God, not even a week ago!—that the world we shared might belong to some fantasy universe. I had to contact him now because his team was damned efficient. I'd long realized they had police contacts; they would have told him about Celia. He was probably wondering why I hadn't already called.

I had to decide what he needed to know: about Nick, Ms. Miller, Corinne, Simone. As I settled with my phone, I found the answer painfully simple: for now, none of it. The morning's events had added complications to my search for new leads but I needed to keep all those doors open, ideally without having to wrestle for the right to take risks. Of course, Russell could possibly learn things I couldn't, or learn the same things faster, but once he did, would he do what needed doing? Only Raging Sarah could be trusted to do what needed doing, and for now, I had to leave things in her hands.

So in that combative mood I finally hit the icon. Best for now: find out and confirm what he already knew. His voice came almost before the first ring ended. "Sarah, thank God. I got a report about Celia. What's going on?"

I didn't like the alarm I heard in his snapped question. "For all anyone knows it was an accident. It looks like she fell."

"What does Clauson think?"

"I don't know. You know how he is. He'll tell me what he thinks I need to know when he's ready."

A silence too brief to contain the emotions I tried to read into it. When he came back his tone still sounded urgent. "We still don't know what was going on between Celia and this Franklin. Or how many people could get dragged in." He took a breath, his next words cracking a little. "Where is Eric in all this?"

We had agreed Eric was mine to deal with. "I haven't seen him. Clauson will probably talk to him."

"Excuse me." Judging from the quick bark, his alarm wasn't abating. "There's been a murder."

"Clauson hasn't—"

"He will. I know we said I wouldn't tell you what to do but I don't like this at all."

Thank God it wasn't FaceTime; he couldn't see me close my eyes. Whatever I didn't want to see was still there when I opened them. "Russell," I said, "I'm not in any danger. All I've been doing is searching for people who might have known Anna. I've talked to some of her classmates' parents. If it helps, I have no reason to believe that what happened to Celia has anything to do with me or Anna. I'm being careful, I swear."

"If I recall from not so long ago, your idea of being careful is plunging around trying to see what will crack."

"Nothing's cracked yet." I owed him notice of my ongoing determination. "But I sure hope something will."

His silence this time felt as if he had gone to a place where something was buried to see if it looked like it might still be breathing. He came back sounding tired. "You know I'll do what I can."

"You've already done far more than I would have ever thought to ask for."

"It's what you don't want to ask for that's . . ." I wasn't sure I could hear *him* breathing. "We'll leave it there. If I hear anything, I'll tell you. And if anything changes, you'll tell me."

Those last words weren't a question but I answered as if they were one. "Of course."

"Seriously. Be careful. I'll be here if you need me."

"I know that."

Our goodbyes left unspoken what we needed to be careful of.

———————

When we hung up, I sat down to email Diana. "I assume you got my text this morning," my much-worked-over message finally read. "I am truly sorry I wasn't able to let you deal with all this first. I hope you have been able to talk to Simone and that if there is something I need to know, you will tell me. Thank you for your understanding. Sincerely, Sarah."

A bit too groveling, probably. I had done nothing that required forgiveness. But I did feel bad for her whole family. Did she know about Celia, and that her husband had been the one to discover her body? If she did, she had plenty besides my moral failures to worry about.

All this angst had disrupted my own plans. I had stolen a few moments to expand my searches for links between Anna, age eleven, and Simone and Corinne. But the barriers between me and Simone's secrets now included not just her indignant mother and her strangely compromised father and a goddamn police force, but also the ire of my housemates, who had every right to resent the presence of vandals and police and even possible murderers on our very porch.

At least so far, I consoled myself, I had exhibited adult behavior. I had not yet screamed at anyone, even at Simone for lying. I rewarded myself with a sweaty foray down to our backyard garden. The sunny, cleared patch had originally been Adela's project, but as the guys and I began to help with watering and weeding, we shared in what bounty the Texas broil allowed. I yanked up insurgent grass blades and tossed them into the compost heap, checked the newly planted cabbages for caterpillars, and picked an early gush of sugar snap peas to take upstairs.

A Wednesday, not a Kendra day. I wished she was on deck; she'd have been perfect medicine for my restless mind. I needed to let go and give my subconscious a whack at all the rampaging possibilities piling up in my head.

Back upstairs, I took out lettuce I'd picked and washed yesterday. I tossed in pickled beets, pepper rings, my peas, and some olives and feta. I made myself carry my virtuous salad to the balcony and sat down. I made myself eat it. But lettuce and beets and olives do not soothe the savage breast, I can attest.

Because my subconscious couldn't whack past that one thing, so clearly high on Clauson's roster of forbidden actions, that I discovered I wanted desperately to do.

I wanted to look into Eric's eyes the day his lover died. I wanted to crawl the lines of his face, find the fractures, the abysses. I wanted to read there why Nick said he killed her. I wanted to see that he had.

Because if he had, finally, they would get him. At last.

It felt so close now, the skin on the back of my neck prickled: the finding out.

But I needed a script, to risk it, to get me through it. Didn't have one. *Was* I afraid? Of what he could make me face?

I thought, *waiting isn't cowardice, it's patience. When you go to him, be sure you're ready. Be armed.*

I got up from the dregs of my salad and delved deep in the freezer for a long-forbidden pint of mint-chocolate-chip ice cream and ate all of it. That helped a bit.

——————

I didn't really think I would find a script to confront Eric in the Perry-Castañeda Library at UT. No, I fled there in search of that other Sarah, the elusive sane one for whom decisions were a matter of logic and calm. I found hints of her deep in the stacks of bound journals on student writing from the 1920s and '30s, ruminations of theorists who spoke to a corner of the research in which I had a share. I found more of her in the UT Union, where chats with ex-colleagues I hadn't seen in ages let me laugh about a student who had introduced his pet snake to the writing center by spilling it out of his knapsack along with his lunch. I got filled in on the latest horrific upgrade of the course-management software as well as the trials of a colleague who'd let AI write the faculty-meeting minutes with interesting results. When my friends headed back to their offices, leaving me still sipping my coffee, my alter ego did prod me to check whether Celia's murder, if it was a murder, had made the news. Not yet. I looked to see whether Diana had answered my email—she hadn't. I finished the coffee, put away the phone, and headed for the crowded Union lobby—only to run smack into Diana, standing in the door.

She looked planted, as if she'd been there for some time. Her glare made no secret that I was its target. A white, tense line ringed her red lips. Her fingers tortured the strap of her satchel. "I am simply furious," she said.

I couldn't help a backward step. She slung the heavy bag to her other shoulder, almost grazing me with it. "You have damaged my daughter irretrievably. I cannot believe you acted so cavalierly. You know nothing of the circumstances, yet you exposed her to harassment by the police."

She had evidently skipped over my cowardly ascription of the police interference to my housemates. People on their way out edged past, some scowling at us for blocking the entrance. "I would really like to talk about this," I said, "but not in this entrance. Can we please go sit down?"

"Simone had nothing to do with any of this. Certainly not with Corinne Miller's death."

My voice wanted to shake. I tamed the tremor. "I'm going back in and sit down. You can join me if you want." I turned and reclaimed my table. After a moment she crossed to me. She put her bag on the table but didn't sit.

"I wasn't going to subject myself to this discussion until I'd conquered my anger," she said. "But when I saw you here I decided there was no reason to delay." *Her* voice didn't shake; it sliced. "Simone went to your house last night alone to undo the damage that others had done. Foolish, yes, but she's still a girl and girls can be foolish. She wanted to protect others. She had no part in what they did." Her makeup, always so aggressively applied, cracked across her cheeks like eroded sand.

In the middle of the harangue I found that I could think. I couldn't question her daughter, but I could question her. "Do you know a woman named Celia Monahan?"

Did she ever! So said her long, gulping breath. "I'm aware that she has a relationship with my ex-husband. But I do not know her personally. I understand she's also been involved with *your* ex-husband, who, you may not realize—"

She stopped, wetting her lips. She'd decided not to go someplace I urgently wanted to send her. "What about Eric?" I said at last.

"Nothing. Ms. Monahan has nothing to do with Simone."

"But my ex-husband does?"

She stared at me for a second, then leaned toward me, bracing her knuckles on the table.

"The reason I wanted to handle this in my own way is that my daughter has been told—she does not *know*, it's strictly hearsay—that your ex-husband has molested one or more of the young women in her social circle. Several of them, including Simone, under seventeen. What do you know about that?"

A chill rolled over me, almost glacial; the ability to think I had just celebrated went icy numb. My mouth must have dropped open as I looked up into Diana's gloating little smile.

"Being the recipient of this information has traumatized Simone," she went on, "and I needed time to understand how she was dealing with it. Now I won't have that time. She'll be forced to discuss it with police officers. Because you identified her and put her in this spot."

She straightened, righteous, giving her own meaning to my silence. She assumed, I guessed, that I could not produce an excuse adequate to the depravity of my sin.

"There has been damage done," she said, "and you are partly responsible. You must have known what kind of man he is, yet you said nothing. You have—"

"I have not said nothing. I have—"

"—a responsibility now, and you have a duty to act on it." She hoisted her bag and turned, but looked back. "Do not contact me or anyone in my family again."

———————

Conscious of so many staring people, I managed not to say *fucking bitch* aloud.

No mistaking Diana's intentions. She meant to shame me. I felt no shame. Surprise, fear, and yes, raging raw hunger for action—and a slow burn at the sheer injustice of it all.

I had said nothing? A simple Google search would have told her how much I had said.

Slowly, sitting there with my hands clasped, I struggled to back far enough off my anger to consider rationally this portentous news.

"Molested" could mean a lot of things, from inadvisable language to inappropriate groping to consensual sex with a minor to forcible rape. I had evidence, sitting in my freezer, so far shared with no one, that Simone's "social circle" had been inspired to really stupid behavior by some sort of melodrama in which Eric was involved. At least one of those girls was actively trying to shield him from attackers like me. At least one had apparently wanted to make life hard for Celia. Well, someone certainly had made her life hard. Was it too crazy to think her killer might be a jealous teenaged girl?

For Eric, of course, there was no excuse. Even if a teenager, male or female, leaps on top of you naked, you call the police, you call parents, you tell someone.

Perhaps he did tell someone. Celia. Or she found out. And what might a child molester do when his secret was threatened? Eliminate the source of the threat. Even if that threat was your lover.

Or a fragile young woman so distressed by what you had done to her that she couldn't go on living.

Or your own child.

The hands of my watch clicked toward six. The noise around me rose: chatter, laughter, scraping of chairs. Evening classes starting. The pain of Diana's unreasoning accusations receded. What loomed larger now was how I could use what Diana had told me to bring about what I wanted most in the world but had almost forgotten in the rush of demands from others: justice for my child.

22

Clauson's little cactus was still alive.

Every time I thought of Clauson, I remembered the little plant's dusty, cockeyed fingers groping skyward out of the plastic pot. In my mind's eye it called up all too clearly his monochrome, cluttered office, where I'd spent some often unpleasant moments the year before. The cactus was a gift, Clauson had confirmed, from the grinning blond boy whose pictures covered the filing cabinet beside the lieutenant's desk. The cactus *will* bloom one day, I thought. But I'd seen no sign of blooms last year, and none now.

And no sign that our prickly relationship was any closer to blooming. He slapped a manila file folder shut and shoved it to a corner, glancing pointedly at a wall clock as I settled across from him. Barely eight a.m. "Whatever you've got for me, make it quick. There's more than one death investigation in this town."

"Is that what it is, then? A death investigation? Celia could have fallen by accident?"

"We don't know yet. That's why it's called an investigation. Hudson tell you she fell?"

"He thought she'd been pushed."

Now a check of his watch. "So what've you got?"

Things to tell him. Things that might actually jar him out of the official rigidity that had so often stood between him and the steps I needed him to take. Steps that even Diana would want him to take if she could get over her fury. "Nick said Eric killed her. Did he say that to you?"

He sighed. After a second he sat forward. "You know I'm not going to blab to you about an ongoing investigation unless I think it would help the investigation. So how will me telling you what Hudson said help *us*?"

So I found myself in one of those rare moments when I had half a hope of surprising him. "I'll know whether Nick has already told you what his ex-wife just told me."

He turned a palm up, inviting me to lay my offering in it.

"Her daughter Simone," I said, "told her that Eric had molested one or more of the girls on that roster. Maybe even Corinne."

The open hand closed into a fist. He turned it over and rapped on the desk. Once. Twice. He sat back and shook his head. "You liked hearing that, didn't you?" he said.

I closed my eyes long enough for the blood heating my cheeks to settle back into its veins. "How high will I have to count before I risk responding to that?"

He ran a hand through his thin, pale hair. "It's a fact, though. You licked it right up, and you know it. Look, if he's involved, we'll deal with it. But we'd need pretty good evidence to charge him with murder based on what some kid said."

I sat wordless for yet another moment, counting really fast on my way to ten thousand. Finally I got my throat working. "An accusation of molestation is not something 'some kid said.'"

He shrugged. "Bad way to put it. But there's a long road between an accusation and proof, and an even longer road between that proof and proof of murder. But yeah, you told me something I didn't know, and as a matter of fact, as soon as you leave, I'll start the wheels turning to see what's been done about Hudson's daughter, find out what she knows." So they had pussyfooted around Simone, rich kid with touchy parents? He raised a finger as I opened my mouth. "Word of warning. We're dealing with a minor here, and third-hand information, if all you know is what her mother said she said. The only way I can justify questioning her is the possibility she knows something about a possible homicide. She'll show up with a clump of lawyers and what we get out of her will be what the lawyers tell her to say."

Since I'd already armed myself against that possibility, I gave my own shrug. "So I can trust that you're taking this seriously?"

"Yes, for the record, I am taking an accusation of molestation seriously."

I waited until I had risen to my feet and was close to the door before I nodded. "You mean you're taking it seriously—this time."

———————

I didn't leave him huffing in protest behind me. That's not his style. I did leave him shaking his head as he bent over the work on his desk.

He had, though, revealed something about his talk with Nick. Nick did not know about Simone's accusation against Eric. If he had, he would have bludgeoned Clauson with it, as I had.

What was more, Clauson had used the word "homicide."

When I reached my car in its space under the elevated lanes of I-35, I rolled down a window and sat. Odd how the groan of tires on the concrete spans above me could be soothing. The coarse sound blocked out the beat of my heart.

Little girls in love with Eric, sucked into his airy orbit, unsuspecting. Celia and I, their rivals, inspiring them to reckless jealousy . . .

I didn't know who was involved in this escapade, or how many. It could all be Simone's invention, for that matter. I had watched her lie.

An interrogation from Clauson wasn't going to sort her truths from her evasions or dig into what else she might know if the right person—maybe a lost girl's mother—asked. Maybe nothing could find that much truth in her. Her mother didn't seem all that willing to try.

As for me, for now I was shut out. Clauson wouldn't share what Simone confessed. God knew I couldn't touch her. That left only one person with the access and possibly the means to get at her secrets if someone told him what to ask. I sat there a restless half hour, convincing myself that the enormity of Diana's news gave Simone's father a right to know.

23

Half an hour later, in the rising heat of brilliant sunlight, I sat outside the Development Building, staring at Nick's parked car.

Its presence in the lot told me one important fact: he was not in jail. Nor was he sequestered in mourning. He was right here, in his office. Where I could get to him.

It was eight-fifty-five, on a Kendra day. Her appointment was not till four. Whatever I decided to do, I had a chance to get it done.

But my will resisted. I was going to add a major complication to the very real grief Nick had shown me. Justifications for that cruelty fluttered around me like fitful butterflies. None of them had landed by nine-sixteen when Nick came out of the building and crossed to his car.

He walked the way he had walked with police packed around him, as if whatever kept his body erect had collapsed around a cold cavity. His grief was not the same as mine, but I knew how deadening that empty space could be.

He got in the car, but, like me, just sat there. From my angle I couldn't see what he was doing. Lolling back? Slumping forward? As the seconds ticked by, piling up into minutes, my stomach began to clench.

"Oh, surely not," I said aloud. He couldn't be that distraught. I tried to recapture the look in his eyes yesterday when he'd come to me with news of Celia's death. Yes, distraught. Stunned. Most of all, I'd seen my own inability to console him mirrored. But I saw as well the even deeper desperation of a man whose road ahead had plunged into nothingness. My help would be feeble, but as I opened my car door to go offer it, his taillights flashed.

I slid back behind my wheel. His tires shrieked as his car lurched backward, then forward to the traffic light at the parking lot exit.

My body made its own decision to pull out after him. *He's going somewhere that has to do with Celia, and therefore has to do with me.*

He made a scorching right turn into a too-small gap between cars. I got a lucky break as the light changed. Then I was on my way—to what and why I had no idea. Driving just felt good: concrete and active. Doing something. So I drove.

Where were we going? He didn't know my car, so in city traffic I could risk a close tail. We made the U to take us south along the I-35 corridor, then a right across campus, so westward, for sure. Nick knew better than to choose the more southerly arteries that would have mired him in a logjam of traffic. Instead he opted for ritzy subdivisions and convolutions, roundabout-by-the-map but faster, that aimed us toward the Hill-Country crossroads of Bee Caves.

Tailing got harder. On rural Hill-Country roads the speed limit is usually 75, and believe me, no one drives any slower. Nick drove faster. Last summer I'd screamed through winding canyons with a sense of urgency at least as demanding as the frenzy that fueled him, but slaloming around curves beside cedar-choked abysses hadn't been fun then, and it wasn't now. He didn't seem to notice that the same car was sticking to him; he slowed through Bee Caves just enough that neither of us got arrested, then pressed on ever westward at the junction with Texas 71.

So it was going to take much of my day, this journey. Should I cancel Kendra? I'd have to watch the time and be ready to make that decision. Because now I knew we were going to Enchanted Rock.

Why not? Enchanted Rock is a *destination*. You'd understand if you'd experienced its powerful ability to suddenly Be There. Every time I'd found time to visit the State Natural Area, coming up from the south, I'd been startled anew when I reached the crucial rise and faced its sudden insistent presence on a featureless cedar-pocked plain. From this direction, north to south, I spun along after Nick across cattle-guards and past signs warning of loose livestock, and the huge bare dome of granite did not disappoint me: farther away, on a horizon, less assertive. But still impressively *there*.

It's a batholith, defined by the dictionary (or the Visitor Center, where in past visits I had read every placard) as a bald intrusion of igneous rock, usually granite. Stone Mountain in Georgia is another example, as is Half-Dome in Yosemite. What marks Enchanted Rock is the way it springs at you, four-hundred feet massive. Eroded slabs of granite on its surface apparently catch the wind and sing. I'd never heard them sing. Maybe Nick and Celia had.

How little I knew of their relationship. He loved her—God, yes. Love leaped out of his body language, out of the wrenching in his face. But had she loved him? I mentally screened those pictures Russell had sent me of her with Eric—two sleek bodies, whippets, joined in headlong abandon. Nick seemed so much more . . . well, grown up. But often people fell for their opposites, as I could painfully attest.

Even if the Rock wasn't part of Nick and Celia's past, it didn't surprise me that he'd come here. People seek out places of beauty, even the cruel beauty of naked rock, when they need solace or escape. But from the moments I'd watched him climb into his car, that other possibility had lingered. People had died here—accidentally? Deliberately? Was I being silly? Hadn't I decided that this was a sane, reasonable man?

Maybe those worries surfaced because just last year, Enchanted Rock had taken on a new, fatal connection for me. I couldn't think of it now without the reminder of the role it had played the day Russell's beautiful wife died.

If there was death at the Rock that day, I'd have to let Nick lead me to it. I dropped back to make sure I didn't pull in to the park gates too close on his heels. If my worries turned out to be unfounded, it would be so much better if he never knew I'd done this. Once in the sprawling lot, I stopped worrying about being spotted; even on a school day, the bright spring weather meant that the place was packed. People crowded around tables and tailgates and car trunks, applying sunblock and gathering water bottles. Nearby a troop of firm-bodied young rock climbers were stuffing their kit bags. Celia probably came to rock climb. And Eric? Had he dangled beside her from the sheer drops off the Rock's north side?

Had Nick?

I found a parking spot where he would be unlikely to see me, but close enough that I could see him. He didn't get out right away. Should I text Kendra? I had just taken my phone out when Nick emerged from his car.

I put the phone in my pocket, tucked my purse under the seat. I would deal with Kendra later. Whatever happened here, I wasn't rushing home until I'd seen it out.

He had shed his coat and tie and put on sunglasses. He had no hat, and as far as I could tell, only dress shoes for negotiating the Rock's slick face. I was glad for my own sunglasses and the little bit of traction I'd have with my everyday shoes.

At least, I assumed we'd be climbing. Sure enough, he made his way through the lot to the path etched through the boulder-cluttered base of the Rock. The water bottle I grabbed from my car was only half-full, but Nick had no water at all that I could see.

I tucked myself behind a clutch of climbers not too far behind him: a couple in their thirties in cycling outfits, a pair of teen-aged boys more engaged in shoving each other than making progress (why aren't you in school?), another lone woman, in shorts and a denim shirt, toting a backpack. The lower stretches of that climb deceive: moderately steep, requiring common sense pacing for all but the young boys, who soon gave up their tussles and bounded ahead. Nick, twenty yards beyond, ignored them as they scrambled past. He walked more slowly than my other companions, his gaze on the rough granite at his feet. Even if he had looked back, he wouldn't have noticed me among the throngs of hikers. Maybe he wouldn't have noticed anything.

It's a full thirty minutes before the Rock shows you what it's got. I'd read on the website that climbing it was equivalent to summiting a thirty- or forty-story building. Do tell. The hot, pink face tilts sharply; on some stretches, the slope is so steep you can actually brace your hands on the granite in front of you as you climb. Ahead of me Nick pressed on sternly, sometimes slipping and slewing loose rock downhill behind him. I let a bearded man with trekking poles pass me. Sweat built and dripped off my jaws.

I slipped between two big boulders to rest and drink. Above me, Nick's figure rose for a stride or two against the deep blue sky as he breasted the summit. Sweat pasted his white dress shirt to his shoulder blades; they rose and fell with his panting. Then he disappeared over the crest.

I hurried back to the path. The summit, I knew, leveled out into a small circular plain riddled with shallow solution pools. Beyond, the Rock fell off sheer to cactus and mesquite. Where he went from here, what he did now—I'd invested a good part of a day so far and some sweat equity to find out. I scrambled to the top.

He wasn't loitering. He was moving fast. Straight toward the not-so-distant precipice on the north side of the Rock.

He disappeared from view over the far rim. I began to run.

He came back into view, twenty feet below me, perched on the most precarious of slopes. Four hundred feet below him lay the spare Texas plain. Were there trees down there to break his fall? Couldn't remember. A figure popped up in my peripheral vision, a young guy in a tank top and a ball cap. He framed his mouth with his hands. "Hey! Buddy!" he shouted down to Nick. "Hey, that's dangerous!"

Nick didn't so much as flinch. He took a step closer to the edge. Loose scree puffed up under his feet. "Wait, wait, wait!" I shouted, stumbling toward him, my own feet skidding. "Wait! Nick!"

His head jerked around. He turned to look up, his sunglasses catching the blank blue of the sky. I thought he teetered. "Nick!" I shouted again.

I inched down the slope toward him. "I have something to tell you," I panted. Five feet from him, my footing gave and I sat down hard. Nick and I now stared at each other, our gazes level. His mouth fell open, from dismay or astonishment, no telling. I hadn't the faintest idea what to do next—other than get him away from that edge.

Above and behind me, I could feel a crowd gathering. A hot breeze ruffled Nick's dark hair. "This is a terrible place for a conversation," I said.

He looked past and above me. I risked a glance. Sure enough, gawkers spiked the skyline. His gaze came back to me as he pushed up the sunglasses. "What are you doing here?"

"I followed you," I admitted.

"Why?" He tilted his head, his frown bewildered.

"There's something you need to know." How could I lay out all my motives and worries sitting here mere feet from an oblivion he need take only a single step to choose? "I sat outside your office trying to make up my mind to go in and see you. But then when you came out and took off, I . . . I was scared."

"Scared?" He looked up at the crowd again, then around him. "I wasn't going to jump, if that's what you're suggesting."

"I am profoundly glad to hear that."

A rivulet of pebbles rolled by my right hand. I glanced up and back. A slight young woman in a Park Ranger uniform detached herself from the jagged line of spectators. "Everything okay down there?" she called.

I looked at Nick. He looked at her. “Yes,” he said.

“You’re in a restricted area,” she said. “That’s why we have these signs here.”

She pointed. Duh. I’d had my mind on other things besides signs. Apparently, so had Nick.

“It would be a good idea,” said the ranger, “to come on back up.”

Her calm order worked. Wordlessly, Nick climbed past me. I got to my feet with great care. A few steps beyond me, Nick looked back. “Do you need a hand?”

“No, I’m fine.” So to speak.

He waited for me, let me scramble up ahead of him. The ranger intercepted us, hands on her belt.

“People have fallen from there,” she said. “That’s why it’s restricted.”

It seemed polite to answer. “Yes.”

She frowned: stern mom, with reason. “I’m authorized to give citations. I’ll forgo that. But let’s don’t do this again.”

“No,” I said.

She looked at Nick. “Sir?”

He gave a short nod.

She stitched on an official smile. “Good. Have a nice—and safe—day.”

The onlookers parted, some with a twitch of let-down, as we reached them. Nick still trailed me. About halfway back across the summit, I planted myself in his path. “Can you give me ten minutes?”

He sighed, rubbed his neck. His face, fair-skinned despite the black hair and brows, had gone ruddy. “Is it about Celia?”

“Actually, it’s about Simone.”

He stared past me for a long moment, his jaw working. He rubbed the hints of dark hair above his unbuttoned shirt collar. My mind skipped to Celia. He was extraordinarily good-looking, this Nick Hudson, in a way completely different from Eric. Eric glistened. You spotted him on the side of the road and wondered what that shiny thing was. Nick . . . my first thought was you'd find him in a box in a toy store. All molded and polished and air-brushed.

Had Celia ever taken him off the shelf?

He crossed to a set of boulders and sank onto one, gestured me to a seat on the other. He stretched long legs out before him. "So tell me about Simone."

24

I scraped my hands against the rough stone I sat on. So many ways I hated having to tell him about Simone.

"Did Simone ever meet Celia?" I said.

He turned the opaque panes of his sunglasses on me. "I thought you had something to tell me, not ask."

A just accusation. "You wanted to know if my personal history had anything to do with this group of girls Simone seems to be involved with." Soon I'd have to slide the conversation toward Anna—surely he'd be willing to tell me what school Simone had attended—but that move could at least wait until his grief-driven sweat had started to dry. I pushed my own sunglasses up the bridge of my nose. "I told you that as far as I knew, it didn't. But now I suspect it does."

"Because of Celia?"

I had thought of him as one of those doors I could push through but the hard black sunglasses blocked me. "Simone and a few of her friends, including Corinne Miller, went to a hang-gliding demonstration Eric set up." He'd recognized Corinne's name when we talked before; he did not react to it now. "A good guess is that at least one of these girls developed a crush on Eric. If so, some of the girls decided to intimidate women who had some connection to Eric. I'm one of those women." I took a breath. Now for what I'd nearly slid off a mountain to tell him. "Simone told Diana that Eric had molested at least one of the girls."

"Molested." He picked the word up as if it were a small, ugly parasite he'd found crawling on him.

"You asked me to tell you if Simone seemed to be in any kind of danger. I couldn't tell from what Diana said what kind of danger she might be in." A hot breeze licked the sweat off my neck; his white shirt had started unsticking from his ribs. "Diana's angry that I didn't keep the police out of it. But the police had to know about the vandalism to our porch and Simone's involvement in that—"

"Vandalism? What kind?"

He hadn't had the bandwidth to notice the paint stain after finding Celia. I recounted what happened. "Diana says Simone just came to clean up what the other girls did."

He chewed on a corner of his lip, eyes narrowed. "Did you talk to Simone?"

"Briefly. She begged me not to tell anyone she was responsible for what the other girls did."

He tilted his head skyward, maybe consulting the heavens. "What else did you tell the police?"

Yes, everybody worried about the police. "They had to know what Diana said about Eric. But I don't know if any of it's true, so I don't know whether Simone is in any danger. But I thought you might want to find out."

"Celia didn't say anything about any of this?"

I told him about the hang-gliding roster Celia had sent me and the girls following us. "Celia thought I'd sent them. When I convinced her I hadn't, she sent me the hang-gliding roster, just an attachment, no explanation. Maybe she meant to follow up later." I shook my head. "It seems to be Simone who's made this charge."

He turned away, leaving me only a sliver of his attention. If there had been an opening there, it had closed.

"You thought I was going to kill myself, didn't you?" he said.

"I couldn't help remembering how you were yesterday."

He spun back to me. "Celia must have known. That's why he had to kill her." If he saw my shiver at the way our minds met, he ignored it. He jumped up. "Thank you for telling me this."

I shook my head. "Someone had to tell you." I stood too.

He took a step as if to walk away. But he turned back. The sunglasses blocked my view of his eyes, but the rest of his face told me what I'd see there. A deep seriousness, a commitment, that tightened his whole body. When he spoke, his voice was molded, careful, as if I were a wary animal he had to pacify.

"From what I read," he said, "I know that for a long time, you've wanted to bring Eric to justice. I want justice for Celia. And for my daughter, but above all, her safety. There's only one way to get all those things." He glanced away for a moment, but this time it seemed only to gather himself. "The two of us care more than the police ever will."

I nodded.

He said, "I want permission to stay in touch with you. And I want you to promise that whatever happens, whatever you learn, you'll tell me."

A cold and terrified joy swept over me, and over Raging Sarah. "Of course you may stay in touch," I said as quietly as I could. "Absolutely. But I can't talk to Simone, or to any of those girls."

"You can talk to Eric," he said.

Slowly I nodded. Just yesterday I had decided I wasn't adequately armed for combat with Eric. I had new weapons now, thanks to Nick's wife and daughter, but would that be enough? Nick must have sensed my hesitation. "You're the one who can get at him," he said urgently, as if I had protested. "The one he's afraid of." He looked at his watch. "You have my email. Contact me if you hear anything. Or if you need me." He touched me, a hand on my wrist. Just a touch, no passion. "Thank you. You have no idea."

I sat in the hot wind, watching him stride away.

——————

It didn't take the whole drive back to Austin for me to realize that I'd given a lot and received little. Nick was like Clauson: another man full of information who wouldn't tell me anything.

The frustration made my palms sweat. But beside it rode a stirring in the air around me.

You can talk to Eric. You can get at him. He's afraid of you.

I pulled off the road before turning east south of Llano. Sat there.

It will happen this time. With this man I will make it happen.

I was not alone any more.

25

By the time I pulled into my parking space at home, my sense of loneliness and hopelessness had resurfaced. I climbed my stairs sucking in the day's unfulfilled promises and encroaching dangers as if they'd replaced the very air.

Preparing mentally for Kendra's session didn't help. For all my academic interest in her progress, that afternoon I struggled to settle into workshop mode.

And her father Alex would pick that day to come along.

He climbed heavily behind her as I waited for them on the landing, looking puffier than I remembered. "Whew!" he said. "That's a workout. Keeps you fit, I bet."

"It helps." Just as getting normal words out helped with my immediate problem, sounding sane. "How are you doing?"

"Fine, just fine. It occurred to me I hadn't seen what Kendra's been up to for a while, so I thought I'd drop in."

Actually, parents "dropping in" unexpectedly didn't fit our research protocol, but on this day, in my harried state, I didn't relish a confrontation. Still . . . "You and Kendra both okay with your visit?"

"Yeah, sure," said Kendra, pushing in and dumping her notebook on our work table. "He can hang out. I don't care."

Alex rolled his eyes behind her back, as if the shrug that came with her words was just one of those teenaged things. As it well might be. But the possibility that it wasn't made this session one that would need to be managed—ideally by a facilitator in complete control of the situation. Which I was not.

"Let's sit down." That was safe enough. We all pulled out chairs. Alex tugged at the collar of his sport shirt as if still needing more air after his climb. He'd have had to take off work early to come here, I realized. He was worried about something. For better or worse, I needed to know what.

"Have you talked to Kendra recently about her project?" I asked him.

"A little. She tells me it's going fine."

Kendra ignored us, laying out her pages, her pen, pulling her water bottle out of her backpack and thunking it on the table. Alex clasped his hands, waited. Again, my turn.

"Have you read any of it?" I asked.

"Oh, no! Forbidden!" He threw his hands up in not-quite-mock horror. "But I guess I'm not supposed to, am I?"

"Not unless she invites you." I turned to Kendra. "As we've discussed, it's up to you."

She didn't look at us. "He can read it if he wants."

"Let's do this." I spoke quickly to ward off the awkward pause I felt coming. "You pick a section you want to work on, tell us what you want us to listen for, then read a little. Just a paragraph, if that's all you want to share."

There. That would limit her father's unsanctioned intrusion without making it a federal case.

Another shrug from Kendra. "Okay. Well. This part. This is part of what I wrote last night. I want to see if it's exciting enough."

She turned a much-scribbled-upon page and read. "The huge unicorn stallion ran straight at Sheth'nia. Fire came out of his nose. His hoofs stomped the ground. Sheth'nia turned to run but the fire from his nose burned her. She screamed."

I deliberately kept my shoulder to Alex, though I felt him shift in his chair. I mentally unfolded one of my gentle scripts. "A couple of things I hear as a reader. You use 'run' and 'ran'—sort of ordinary verbs. I wonder if they might be stronger, more interesting. Maybe more surprising words that would make the unicorn more vivid and Sheth'nia's efforts to escape more desperate."

She shrugged. She seemed to have brought a whole box of shrugs with her. "Sure." She made a quick note. "Okay."

"Any ideas?"

She wrinkled her nose. "I guess 'ran' could be 'charged.'"

"Could be."

"Ummmm. You want me to change it to that?"

"You know the answer to that question. You try out different possibilities and you decide."

Relief settled over me as I fell into my benign-coach mode. Thank goodness, I didn't have to grade her choices. When a reluctant writer like Kendra discovered that she had options that could make a difference, that was progress. She rewarded my self-discipline by reading two more paragraphs. I risked a couple more delicate prompts. "Seems to me you've done quite a bit of writing since our last session," I said as we wound up.

"It's not any good."

"Remember Anne Lamott?" We'd read Lamott together. "Shitty first drafts?"

"Yeah, I guess."

She pushed her chair back, stuffed her pack, then from the door looked back at Alex. She knew what would happen next. So did I. Sure enough, Alex lingered. "I'll be there in a minute, honey."

Her eyes narrowed.

"In just a second," he said.

She left us, jerking the door to behind her.

"What's the prognosis?" he said. "She getting anywhere?"

So many times we'd met with the parents, discussing the assessment measures we'd be using at the end of the project. Apparently Alex had absorbed nothing from these briefings. Could I get him through the door without sounding like a scold? "She's writing a lot now. She's enjoying it. I'm glad to see that."

"But that stuff—that's nonsense. What good will that do her in college? In a profession? Unicorns! Dragons! Shouldn't she be writing about real things?"

If "real things" were Kendra's only options, she wouldn't be writing at all. The need to explain again, now, on this day, exhausted me. "You know, we have a parents' meeting next week. That would be a good topic to go over—" I left out *again*, "—then."

"I just need to know she's getting somewhere." His soft jowls flushed with clear anguish. "I just worry about her, that's all."

"I know."

"So you think she's learning things?"

"Yes, I do."

He sighed, looked at his watch. "Well, I guess . . . her mom's home waiting. Wants to go out for pizza. I better get on."

So he left, possibly to grill Kendra about what she was learning, and receive another dose of "fines" and shrugs.

26

I moved that young woman's well-being to another day's set of problems. I sat down at my computer to dig into the problem that was always front and center for me.

Top of my head as I opened my cloud storage: was I being too respectful of Nick's feelings? There were so many questions he could answer if I could decide how and when to ask. The simplest, one I had been surfing after on my own for several days now: where did Simone go to school? I hadn't succeeded in worming that question into the morning's conversation; it was first on my list for talks to come. But between worries about Kendra and frustrations with Alex, a new idea for answering that question without Nick had edged in sideways, delivering a strategy I could exploit. If I knew for a fact my daughter and his had been in classes together, what a perfect segue into a larger conversation about other children who might have known Anna, talked to her, listened to her, comforted her when she cried.

So in my cloud account I opened the folder where I had long ago stored scans of all the pictures I had of my daughter. Among them, year after year of school pictures, neat rows of children lined up and instructed to smile. I had not looked for Corinne there; I doubted I could pinpoint the six- or seven- or eight-year-old face of a girl I had never met. But Simone's face filled my vision. Surely I would know her. I would find her and I would say to Nick Hudson, *I saw that Simone went to the same school Anna did . . .*

That was not how it worked at all.

For the second time in too few days my body broke my long-standing rules against crying. If Simone's face was among those I tried to inspect, the tears blurred it away. And there was more blocking me, not just tears but a fog of denial. It was bad enough that I had to search for her in the prehistory that was NamUs, the remains of what once was but now wasn't. This, too, was searching for what she had been, years ago, in the past. *No. I search for my child in the future. The face I will know is the one coming toward me, running toward my open arms.*

I would have to do this search when I could bear it. I put all the pictures away.

———————-

Note to interested parties: Do not lie down on your sofa at 10:30 at night and think you can distract yourself from current worries with an academic article on the interaction between cognitive processing and amygdala receptors. That is, do not engage in such a combination if you expect to stay awake past 10:45.

I woke up at 1:20 a.m., tossed aside the article printout on which I had intended to make insightful marginal notes, then staggered to my bedroom and found my bed by accident. And proceeded to wake up at 4:48 a.m.

My troubled sleep was Nick Hudson's fault. I'd fretted not only over the barrier he presented between me and Simone, but also over all he had withheld that I needed to know. For starters, what exactly had been the state of affairs between Nick and Celia? Did Simone know Celia? Could Simone have told Celia what she told her mother about Eric, leading Celia to a fatal confrontation? My anxiety to find out what Nick had kept from me made the pale hints of daybreak spill across me like cold creek water. Sleep? How?

I killed an hour showering, sorting through clothes in search of a professional "me" that lived in that closet somewhere, hand-feeding Alice on my shoulder since she insisted she would be forced to feed on my ear if I didn't, and opening and closing the balcony doors six times.

I killed a half hour eating breakfast. That made it 6:30.

Then I worried. Alice helped by flapping to the top of the bathroom curtains—from which I could only retrieve her by risking my life standing on the edge of the tub. She helped more by refusing to come down.

I wanted one thing. To know what happened to my daughter. Okay, two things. To know as well whether anything I could do now would help her. Even if that meant only burying her properly, in a place where bones would not be molested. Where I could kneel beside her, undisturbed.

Three men knew answers I needed. Clauson, Eric, and now, Nick.

Which one of them should I harass?

Eric? I would be so much better prepared for him if I had more information about the girls and this hang-gliding clinic. Oh, and about Celia, and who else might have loved her.

Clauson? He knew how to block me.

That left Nick.

The hell with his feelings. By eight a.m. that Friday morning, I was parking once more in his office lot.

———————

This time I got out, slammed the car door, and strode smartly toward the entrance, a tough chick invincible in her dark-suited armor, the mascara I had finally indulged in just the start of my war paint. The low heels on my shoes made a satisfying clank on the hard bureaucratic tiles as I turned down his hall.

What would coax the pain and fear and yes, anger out of him, a frontal assault or an end run? I opened his office door firmly—only to find—wouldn't you know it?—that he wasn't there.

"Are you expecting him soon?" I asked the young man behind a desk in the foyer.

"He usually gets in a little before nine. Would you like to make an appointment and come back?"

"No. I'll wait."

"There's coffee. Can I get you a cup?"

"Thanks, no." Another cup would only exacerbate my jitters. I headed for a chair against the wall, got out my Kindle, opened the latest *Research in the Teaching of English*, and pretended to read.

And so Nick found me when he arrived at ten to nine. He came to a full stop before me, the way you might if you discovered a bear in the middle of your hiking trail. Clearly he hadn't expected an invasion from me so soon. He shot a look at the young man, who gave me a freshly curious glance and said, "Couple of messages. I put them on your desk."

Nick turned back to me. "Please. Come in to my office." To the young man he said, "No interruptions, Jeremy." He let me precede him through the inner office door.

He had made up his mind about my invasion by the time he circled to the chair behind the wide desk and I settled into the institutional chair before it. A lot of what I was seeing, I decided, was a man who'd had little sleep adjusting to a new kind of day he would have to get used to, a day suddenly missing a crucial piece. I was just one more disorientation in that wobbly mix. He took off his suit jacket, draped it over his upholstered chair, ran his hands through his smooth dark crown of hair as if it had tried to erupt into cowlicks, and finally sat.

His office was the diametric opposite of Clauson's. I couldn't even figure out where I could deposit my bag without disturbing the ordered symmetry of the room. The polished desk held inbox, outbox—both empty—a blotter, and a pen set, its instruments arranged regimentally. His computer sat on a shelf at his elbow. No notepads, stacked papers, or scattered paperclips. The two pink message slips the young man had delivered stood out like desecrations. I looked for a picture of Simone, didn't find one. "I should have suggested this," he said. "I wasn't completely with it yesterday."

Setting my bag on the floor directly in front of me, I chose an end run. "If I understood you yesterday, you think we can help each other. But if I'm to be of help, I need to know more."

He sat, too upright, hands flat on the blotter. "What specifically do you need to know?"

So much for collaboration. He had found time to think about his relationship with Celia and decide what he ought to share. But I had come here to prod. "I learned of Eric's involvement with Celia this past year. It came out when a friend of mine found out that before my daughter disappeared, she'd been in a car Celia owned." I left out that Eric's semen had been found in that same car; one tangle at a time. "So I know that Eric and Celia had been involved since before Anna disappeared." I took a moment to mentally clarify where I hoped to take this. "But you seem involved with both Celia and Eric in ways that made you say Eric killed her. You seem to think that Eric might be guilty of what these girls accuse him of. I hope it's clear that because of Celia's . . . proximity . . . to my daughter, what you know about her matters to me."

He swiveled in his chair. "You're asking about me and Celia."

"Yes." For a start.

He considered his answer for a pile of seconds before he released it. "I guess you realized I was in love with her."

I nodded. "Yes."

"She was in love with Eric."

I nodded again, though his testimony proved nothing about who Celia loved

He tilted back in the chair, canted it to his right. There, overlooking a grass-edged walkway, was a tall window much more modern and more securely shut than my office windows in Tremaine. He invested several long moments in that window. Finally, he said, "It's hard to talk about her."

"I wouldn't ask if it wasn't vital to me."

He drummed tense fingers on the desk blotter. "She was in love with Eric and I did everything I could to change that. I told her Eric didn't love her. I don't think he did. She was starting to listen to me. He knew that."

"Did you know her six years ago, when Eric and I were still married, and before my daughter disappeared?"

He fiddled with one of the post notes on his blotter, made a decision. "Eric was cheating on you." His shoulders stiffened. Another rearrangement to the items on his blotter. "I didn't cheat on my wife. I started divorce proceedings as soon as I realized my feelings for Celia. I don't know if she knew Eric was married at the time."

"She knew my child." Anna had been in her car. The police would have said that proved nothing; she could have been there without ever meeting Celia many times. Still, in my view, her presence in that car supplied grounds for a reasonable question. "I was wondering . . . did you?"

He must have heard the sandpaper in my voice. His face changed. "Did I . . . ? Oh, meet your daughter. I'm sorry, I'm not dealing with this very well. I hadn't even—"

I was not to know what he hadn't even. The office door burst open. Diana stood there, spitting fire.

He leaped to his feet. I looked back and forth.

"What are you doing here?" she shot at me.

"Talking to Nick."

"What about?"

I crossed my arms, said nothing.

She pivoted to Nick. "You said you had to see me. What about?"

"We need to talk about Simone."

"What about her?"

"About what she told you about her friends."

Her gaze swung to me again. It took me a second to decide to get to my feet and hoist my bag to my shoulder. Nick said, "Don't go."

"This isn't any of her business," said Diana.

His whole demeanor had hardened. "I think it is."

"Nonsense." Diana snorted. "She's put Simone—and us—in an untenable position. She has nothing to say about this."

"What's untenable about it, Diana? Simone told you she might have knowledge about a potential crime. She might even be a victim. Were you going to keep this a secret from me?"

It didn't seem quite right to sit down again. But standing between them, I felt riddled by crossfire. At least his question had temporarily stymied Diana. Her mouth worked, an opening and closing wound. She found a constricted voice. "Nothing's going to come of it. Simone won't be seeing those girls any more."

"What *has* happened, Diana? What did she tell you?"

"It's all talk. Teenagers pretending. Simone doesn't need to be harassed by the police. She doesn't know anything about any crimes."

He wheeled to me. "What do you think?"

Count into the millions, Sarah. Couldn't. His deadly serious gaze wouldn't let me. "What Simone said has to be followed up. If there's any truth to it, other people might be in danger." Other people's children. Trusted in Eric's company. As Diana herself had pointed out to me just the other day.

"The police already know," Nick said.

"Yes." Diana's voice crackled. "*She* told them."

Fortunately my words came out level. "Yes. She did."

Diana ignored me, facing Nick across the desk. "My lawyer will go to the police station with us. He will speak for Simone. She knows absolutely nothing, just rumors. He will not let her be interrogated like a criminal. Traumatized. As you obviously would."

Nick shook his head; now it was the empty inbox that demanded repositioning. "Where is Simone now?"

"At home. Belinda is there."

"I need to see her."

"You can't."

He gave the inbox a shove that dislodged it six inches. "Excuse me, but I can."

Diana's right hand clenched around the strap of her bag, but her left, folded across her waist, trembled. She swallowed. "My lawyer will call you to set up a meeting."

"No lawyer." He stepped back, straightening. "If you won't have me at the house, you must go get her and bring her here."

"Ridiculous." She spun away.

"Sarah," he said sharply. "That police officer you're acquainted with—Clauson. Will you tell him that Dr. Cleveland is tampering with evidence? Since that's exactly what this is?"

Again his gaze held me. He wanted to know what kind of partner I was. Were the outcomes we wanted really the same? I'd have liked to give him a clear answer, but I couldn't have said in that moment what outcomes he wanted. Diana spared me. She froze with a hand on the doorknob, chin up at him. "You wouldn't."

"Your choice."

She glared at me. Speculation had edged into her eyes. He had called me Sarah. "I'll call you."

"By ten."

"I have to get home. That's too soon."

"By ten."

She gave a hitch of her shoulder. The move could have meant dismissal or surrender. She let herself out, slamming the door.

Once she had gone, Nick let out a heavy, deflating sigh. He sank slowly, now toying with items on his desktop like buildings in a tiny village where he would be enforcing the law. "Sorry about that."

"I'm not sure she knows about Celia's death." The death—as far as I knew still considered accidental—had not been front-page news.

He nodded, gaze distant. "Did you get the sense that the police would make talking to Simone a priority?"

"Actually, no. Lt. Clauson didn't seem especially excited by what I told him about Eric either—as a suspect in anything."

"I know that lawyer. By the time he gets through with Simone, she won't have a clue what she's supposed to say. Or what she should do."

There were gears here, lives turning and grinding against each other. I didn't want to put my hand into that machinery. But I had to, if I wanted what I said I did. "Did you ever meet my daughter/" I asked, this time more gently. "I thought maybe she and Simone might have gone to school together."

He looked up, searching for focus as if the change of subject had confused him. "I'm sorry, I didn't . . . Simone went to Benchmark. That would have been six . . . Did your daughter go there?"

Benchmark. A ritzy private school. Any chance of an environment like that for Anna had been precluded by Eric's spending on his business. I didn't know how Nick interpreted the deep sigh I gave as I answered. "No. It doesn't matter. What's important now is learning whether Eric has an alibi."

His gaze cleared. "Yes. That would be perfect."

I realigned the chair I'd dislodged when I rose with the exact center of the desk. "So you'll keep me posted about Simone and I'll see what I can learn about Eric."

His eyes might have been on me but his mind wasn't. "Simone is what matters. I'm grateful to you for helping me reach her."

"She is what matters. Our daughters are what matters." I turned to the door just slowly enough I hoped he could feel me thinking, *and don't forget that your part of the deal is to help me reach mine.*

27

Back home, I told myself that the research-team meeting coming up that Friday afternoon was a step in meaningful scholarship. That didn't make it any easier to shut down the questions only Eric could answer. Raging Sarah's questions. *Did you know about Nick? Was Celia playing you? Did she know Nick's daughter? What did Nick's daughter tell her about you?*

I had managed to get an answer to one important question. I believed Nick about Simone's school enrollment. Simone and Anna would not have crossed paths. At least not at school. Corinne almost certainly didn't go to Benchmark either. But there were rafts of other activities where the three girls could have stumbled across each other. Knowing what not to pursue felt oddly empowering. At least I knew more than I had at eight a.m.

But the moment was fast approaching when the research team would expect a report on my individual progress toward the collaborative publication our grant demanded. I plunged dutifully into collating my notes so I'd sound halfway coherent at the meeting. With one byte of mind-space I transferred my meeting notes from my desktop to my tablet. With the other half-million datalets I formulated a question that I directed to Alice, since she was the only one there to hear me: "What do I know now?"

I deduced from her fascination with her reflection in the computer screen that she was not listening.

"Narcissist," I told her. She pecked at her image. I felt compelled for the sake of my computer to remove her from its environs. I put her on my head. She walked down my hair, jumped off my shoulder, and goose-stepped into the kitchen.

I was reasonably sure I had put away anything she could damage or do damage with. "Fine. I'll talk to myself."

I knew a few things. I knew that Diana hated Nick, Nick loved Celia, Simone was in trouble, Eric might have done something I might be able to convict him of . . .

But what did I *need* to know?

That list filled out quickly. What did Simone know about Eric's relations with the girls and what could she prove? Who did Celia love? Did Eric think she loved Nick? Did Celia know or suspect what Eric might have done? Did Eric know about this tantalizing and so far invisible Franklin, whom the FBI had seen with Celia? Did Eric have that alibi?

And who killed her? Because I had decided, obviously with no evidence, that someone had.

A small fraction of those queries might have finally captured the interest of the local news. I clicked on the TV for the noon update. Water main break in Windsor Park. Okay, got it. Ongoing search for a public school superintendent. Got it. Had they mentioned the death of a fairly upscale local woman in the six minutes of the program I'd missed? But then:

"Police are investigating the death of Celia Monahan, a longtime Austin resident known for her contributions to local arts. Monahan's body was found Wednesday morning at her home in West Austin. Police have not released a cause of death."

On the screen flashed a picture of Celia standing before a banner advertising a charity she'd been involved with. The screen returned to the anchor, who shifted her gaze to the next teleprompter and moved on.

If other channels had carried the story, I'd missed it. On my phone I punched up the *Austin American-Statesman*. A search produced a paragraph that didn't add much. I learned that Monahan was formerly married to "financier" Richard Briscoe. A spokesperson for Mr. Briscoe, who was in Denmark on business, stated that Mr.

Briscoe was saddened to hear of Monahan's death but that they seldom communicated, in fact had not spoken in more than a year.

So now I knew a bit more about Celia's death. But not much more about her life. About what she cared about, gave her heart to. What secrets she might keep.

I thought about Celia's expensive toys, her flashy car. I put these together with a wealthy—possibly very wealthy—ex-husband. The words "pre-nup" and "settlement" popped into my mind.

As well as a new set of questions: Did Celia actually "work" at all her "consulting and advising"? If not, who supported her? Eric? Or did she support him?

Eric would be able to answer that, but would he? Unlikely. Would Nick?

My phone calendar reminded me harshly that my meeting impended. Slurping a hasty lunch smoothie, I stashed Alice, bagged my tablet, and double-checked to make sure I had my UT campus credentials; then, with my door opened and my feet on the landing, I discovered I must have subconsciously blocked the perfect person to ask.

Why was I reluctant to contact Russell for these dry facts? They fell well within the boundaries of our deal. By the time I reached my car I had mentally composed my questions. What could he learn about Celia's finances? About Eric's? I clicked on my phone to write.

But that wasn't what I found myself writing. Somewhere I must have been carrying around an accusation I hadn't answered: *be more careful with other people's children than you were with your own*. Children Celia had hurled into my arms as she stalked out my door. But whose children did she think me capable of wronging? Whose child would she *care* if I damaged? I typed into my phone, "Did Celia ever have a child?"

A question I should have asked *her*, I thought as I drove.

As well as another question on the heels of that one, almost making me slam into the car in front of me at a red light. Could this be Eric's child?

28

And yet I behaved very well at the meeting. Sitting in the lot a few minutes beforehand had let sanity reclaim me. Eric's child? With Celia? What was so unlikely about that? I needed to let that theory chill a little; I could do nothing about it now. But this was exactly the leverage that would help me face Eric. *No wonder you're not searching for OUR daughter. You're too busy playing World's Best Dad for HER daughter.* Because it was an endangered daughter I had endowed her with.

But where was Russell? What useless thing was he doing that he wasn't answering me? Behind my wheel I checked my phone as if some rogue toggle needed resetting to make it ring. Sane Sarah whispered, *be patient.* With a sigh, I bumbled out to do my professional duty, for which I was paid, I remembered. I set the tremulous ghost of the imagined child I had created out of nothing on one of the chairs along the conference-room wall behind me and bade it wait.

Pretending to be calm helped me display appropriate collegial manners; I even let myself be talked into a beer at the Union after we broke up. Bob wanted to buy my drink but I fended him off, gently, I hoped. During our chat a question arose about a controversial 1950s paper. The paper had appeared in an obscure rhetoric journal but had been anthologized in one of those hefty volumes that everyone felt obligated to buy but that ended up on an unreachable stack on a top shelf. Listening with mannerly politeness to the discussion, I realized, first, that the topic tied directly into my corner of the research project; second, that I only vaguely remembered the paper's complex argument; and third, that in my Cresthill office, I not only had the anthology that included the paper, I knew where the book was.

So, good-byes said, crossing the campus maze to my car with still no word from Russell, I found myself deeply courted by thoughts about that book, the paper that I could start writing if I had it, and the dense intellectual arguments I could bury myself in. Oh, that structured, well-crafted world called me, an island of sanity in my choppy universe. Somehow, with a full spring evening's daylight ahead and no word from Russell, I set off in a mentally untethered state in what turned out to be a fateful decision: I headed cross-town and up-town to lay my hands on that blasted book.

———————

The book was exactly where I expected, though heavier and harder to wrestle from its shelf. Still no Russell. I stood with the book in my hands long enough to realize that I wasn't up to any writing that night. Maybe a form of peace was what I'd come in search of. Nothing, I saw as I looked around me, could be more peace-inducing than bringing long-overdue order to my habitual office chaos. Raging Sarah complained that this was yet more shirking, but I ignored her and went to work

My office isn't dirty in the sense that dust bunnies and cobwebs have piled up in corners. Rather, every inch of space is so jammed full of papers, books, and journals that no self-respecting dust bunny would even think of trying to stake a claim. So cleaning meant creating a huge stack to keep, a less huge stack to send to the shredder, and a tiny stack to throw away or take home.

Choosing what went into each stack put a cork in Raging Sarah for a while.

———————

Come eight o'clock that evening, as dusk dimmed the generous light slanting in from the courtyard outside my big windows, I couldn't say the office was any cleaner. It was, however, differently arranged.

Whether I'd ever again be able to find all the things I relocated remained to be seen.

Surveying the new (dis)order I'd created, I finally felt I could be allowed to sit down. With the lights off, the little room was still and restful. Tucking myself into the comfortable chair in a niche behind a file cabinet, I realized that for the first time in days, I felt relatively safe. What, though, did I have to be afraid of? The physical danger stalking me could be reduced to a few teenaged girls playing out a fantasy. The other dangers I faced were ones I didn't really want to put a name to. They hung in the air, an impending sadness, as if opening the doors in my darkness would unleash heartache I hadn't intended for people I didn't know. Well, whatever was coming and to whom, my dark corner hid me for now.

But even in this haven a sharp little sting found me, a text from Russell's number. "Got your message. Sorry to be late getting back. I'll see what my people can find out."

Well, I couldn't expect instant answers. Had he wondered why I wanted to know? Would he ask? This time, no reason not to tell him. He wouldn't see Eric's child as our problem. I shouldn't, either, but I hadn't been able to banish her from the mental shelf where I'd stashed her. I closed my mind on her and wrote back to Russell, feigning patience, "Thanks!"

Dark fell, the campus lights tempered with moonlight as they cast bright squares across the office floor before me. It turned out I was every bit as tired as I had thought. Evidence in support of that thesis: I slept.

And jerked awake, I didn't know how much later. And thought, even as I struggled to consciousness, why "jerk"? Why did I feel as if a shock had roused me? What was wrong?

What was wrong was the shadow cast by the light from the windows on the floor scant feet from me. The shape of a man.

He was standing at the window. The window latches rattled. He was trying to get in.

The first cold rush of terror subsided almost as soon as I was aware of it. He couldn't get in. Just that winter Maintenance had refurbished those locks. If he broke the glass he'd set off an alarm. The chance that he posed any immediate danger to me was slight.

Especially since he couldn't see me, hidden as I was behind the tall files. All I could see of him was his silhouette. He looked big, apparently draped in something fairly voluminous, possibly a windbreaker or a cowled sweatshirt. It wasn't Eric. I knew every quiver of every muscle in his body. Or Nick; he lacked this man's hunched bulk. From the way the man's shadow twisted, his head angled downward, I concluded he was inspecting the window frame in the moonlight, possibly to see whether it would yield to tools.

He straightened and gave the windows another rattle. He turned sideways, unmoving, as if listening. If I had been alone there in the dark, I might have been content to sit there until he went away. Or call campus security. But Raging Sarah tolerated no such evasion. This predicament had given her an excuse to resurface. *You bought my silence with a promise to find out things. This guy wants into your office. Finding out why is a damn good start.*

Nonsense. I couldn't break through the window and slam him to the ground. My mind churned. No random vagrant would risk breaking in. Was he someone connected to Corinne? To Anna? To Celia . . . with whom I had had a private talk the day before someone killed her. In whom the FBI was interested, because she had had a conversation with a vaguely identified man . . .

I wanted to see this man's face.

If I confronted him through the window, first he'd be in shadow and then he'd bolt. Campus security might catch him. And identify him as my intruder—how? As I debated, his silhouette disappeared from the trapezoid of light.

Raging Sarah shoved my phone into my hand and snatched my office keys off my desk and flung me out into the hall.

The corridor was well-lit but empty, the students all in their night classes. I clattered past closed offices, pushed through the heavy entrance, and beat feet for the right-hand courtyard that separated Tremaine Hall from Argonne.

No one. I pivoted. The broad grassy quad sloping from the Social-Sciences buildings on my left toward Cresthill Avenue was dark, empty, though on the sidewalk across the quad were scattered figures, students coming and going from the dorms. I peered down the sidewalk in front of Tremaine and Argonne toward Cedar Street. A single tall male figure draped in that hoodie or windbreaker strolled downhill about a hundred yards distant. I broke into a trot in pursuit.

But what to do? Had he looked up Sarah Crockett on her campus faculty page? If so, he would know me. Should I care? After all, I seemed to be already on his radar. Even if he recognized me, he wouldn't attack me with students and pedestrians coming and going on the busy sidewalk. My job was to get a look at him. I broke into a run.

He turned left along the promenade at the foot of the quad. I timed my move to catch him in a bright space under a streetlight. I smacked into his shoulder from behind, hard enough to knock us both off balance. In what I hoped looked like an instinctive gesture, I grabbed his arm. He let out a startled "Hey!", jumping back.

"Oh, I am so sorry," I gushed, winching myself around to face him. To buy time, I brushed at his sleeve as if to dust off the marks of my impact. A windbreaker, not a sweatshirt. "I didn't see you turn."

He jerked away, swiping at the sleeve. I had only seconds for my look. Damn, no tattoos or obvious disfigurations. Just a doughy-faced, middle-aged man, with short brown hair on the verge of receding. "Did I hurt you?" I asked. "Are you okay?"

"Yeah, yeah," he said, not unpleasantly. He tugged the collar of the windbreaker to straighten it. His gaze flicked over me, impassive. No sign of recognition. "No big deal. Forget it." He sidestepped me and moved on.

I tagged along, all innocence, implanting hairline, set of ears, slant of eyebrows, in my mind's eye. In the dim light, I hadn't been able to make out the color of his eyes. One characteristic I'd noted: an unusually small, puckish nose in his wide, bland face. I was pretty sure I'd know him again.

He reached the southeast corner of the quad and turned to descend the steps. Before he went down, he pivoted and looked directly at me.

I kept my own gaze level and walked resolutely toward him, as if on my own business. As I approached, he clattered down the steps and crossed toward the nearby parking garage.

I strolled past the steps and on down the sidewalk. After a few yards, I glanced behind me. He had disappeared.

——————

Campus security sent a businesslike uniformed woman to inspect my windows. No sign of tampering. Her flashlight didn't reveal footprints in the short dry grass outside. "We could check for fingerprints. Did he wear gloves?"

"I honestly couldn't say." I had kept my heroics to myself. She took my fairly useless description. "The light was pretty dim," I said.

"We'll see about prints," she said without much enthusiasm. "We can't do much without more to go on. Possibly someone else saw him. Just keep an eye out in case he turns up again."

29

When I got home I shoved the book I'd gone to so much trouble to retrieve to a remote corner of my desk. My thoughts over that restless night did not venture near rhetorical theory. Instead they swirled around this child I had conjured. Would she look like Anna? Had Eric told her about Anna? Did she fly with him like Anna? I even named her: Christa. Celia's Christa. Saturday morning I woke from a dream of this creature in Anna's old bedroom, pawing through Anna's clothes.

My phone rang early, Clauson returning the call I'd left him. "Oh, I believe you saw someone. Definitely not Hudson or Wyles?"

"Definitely."

Who else is there? Maybe your friend Pierce?"

"Ha, ha." Clauson had never forgiven Russell for being innocent of murder. I hung up.

It took several cups of coffee to dispel Celia's Christa. *Whoever she is, wherever she is, she is not your enemy*. She would, after all, still be very young. *She isn't the danger you should be dealing with*, said my third cup of coffee. *Or the one with answers. Spend some of this energy on the guy who tried to break into your office last night*.

Occam's Razor, the theory that the simplest answer was probably the correct one, made him likely to be "George Franklin," the guy Russell had told me about, the one whose encounter with Celia had intrigued the FBI. Why imagine two menacing strangers instead of one? Whoever he was, what did he want with me? I had a theory. The man had been tailing Celia; he knew she had been to my home. He wanted to know what business she and I had with each other. He thought some clue in my office might reveal me as more than some staid university professor. Someone to whom Celia had entrusted damaging facts? Could he have been stalking me already? Would I be able to catch him at it if he was?

And what about the people stalking him? Now that I'd slammed into him on a public street when I could have easily skirted around him, would I turn up in a surveillance video at the FBI?

Alice shared her views in an electric morning whistle. "Yes, yes." I freed her, dodging her impatient flutter to the sofa, reaching absently for her dishes to clean them.

You should be scared. You should tell Russell about this man trying to break into your office.

I carried the crusted little objects to the kitchen. Dropped them into the sink and turned on the water, my actions automatic. Tell Russell? His alarm would grow sharper. He'd ask me to wait for the strangers on his team or at best Clauson to ask questions only I knew needed asking and to decide what I had a right to know.

For now I would wait for signs of immediate danger from my window man.

———————

Almost on cue the text I'd been waiting for from Russell came as I was talking myself out of a fourth cup of coffee. "Eight years ago Celia had a child with devastating congenital damage. A boy. The child died at three months. There's a death certificate on file in Travis County. I hope that proves useful."

Somehow I wasn't surprised. So maybe there had been buried sadness under the steel of Celia's bravado. Did Eric know about this child?

The text went on: "I hope you are doing all the things you want to be doing. I'll be in a meeting for a while but shoot me a text if there's anything more I can do." He attached a GIF of a guy in a suit sprawled in a chair with ZZZs overhead.

I didn't so much have more questions as speculations. Were Eric and Celia involved nine years ago when this child would have been conceived? Possibly but unlikely; Eric and I had still been clinging to the honeymoon phase. Nor did I think she'd had a child since then. A preschooler in their lives would have left a visible trace. Another dead child? Russell could probably find that out if I asked him. I almost started to text.

But I stopped, struck by thoughts of what I was really chasing. A child between them, his child, would be a new weapon in my longstanding siege. It would hit a brittle spot. But was I planning to sit and wait for Russell to supply me with this new power? More chasing ghosts around corners? More stretching the misery out?

Logic finally wormed through as it long ago should have: nothing Russell could do or tell me would provide the answers I wanted: he did not know those answers. Nor did Clauson. I could sit here for the rest of my life fending off the logical conclusion: if I wanted answers I shouldn't waste time on people who didn't know them. All I had to do was find in me, finally, the courage to confront the one who did.

30

The house where Eric and I lived sat on a cedar-packed hillside, its many southwest windows opening onto a deep canyon. In the days when I lived there, many a night I'd stared down at the firefly brilliance of other people's houses blinking up through the trees. This was the ritzy side of Austin, where people like the Crockett-Wyles balanced on the edge of space.

To reach it, you followed a winding drive along the canyon contour. The neighbors' homes blocked the canyon view. Most of the entrances to these homes were recessed, shielded from passersby by trees more substantial and respectable than the feral cedar. These people's need for privacy meant that I'd never been caught. Never been spotted slipping across their clotted front yards, dodging their motion sensors, sinking into the shadows in my black sweats and black cap.

Those had been Raging Sarah's sorties. I didn't boast of them, but I didn't disown them, any more than I disowned her. Watching Eric from the dark of that hillside had given the raging side of me a power I couldn't claim any other way.

It had been a while, though, since I'd come on such a mission. Last summer, Russell's summer, had filled so completely with lives—with life and death and other's people's hopes and wishes—that what Eric did in that big cold box chiseled into the wall of the canyon became—almost—a melodrama set in a dollhouse that I'd put away with other childish things.

I gave him the house. It was one of the three things he took from me. He took not only the house and the child but also the woman I thought I was. The woman who believed in herself, her professional competence, her value as a mother, her worth as someone to be loved. He had denied me all those selves. Maybe if that woman had survived his depredations, she could have fought for this space, could have dismissed its cries, its moans, its accusations, as so much creaking woodwork. Maybe she could have gone on to live a life Eric could not spoil.

But I fled and he took it. That he could deaden himself to all that anguish said something about him. Something, of course, I already knew.

My daughter disappeared on a day when he and I quarreled over breakfast in our aerie above the canyon. If her voice echoed for him now in the silence I'd left him, he somehow ignored it. Or maybe he silenced his guilt with the woman I had sometimes seen here with him. I could name her now.

I drove three doors down to the Marshalls' and turned around in their broad driveway. Then sat there, in shade at the opposite curb.

I had nurtured the oak by the flagstone walk through three summer droughts and two rough winters. Eric had planted the English ivy. "That ivy will kill the tree!" I told him. "Don't be stupid," he said. Now the sea of ivy was twisting up the tree, groping it, turning its limbs to stark black stobs where there should have been a green fullness. *I told him. I told him so.*

As I stalled there by the Marshalls' driveway, scraps of the language I was preparing—threats, warnings, intimations—flitted inside the car like trapped flies. But nothing settled. Even Raging Sarah had no idea what we were going to say.

———————

Eric did not open the front door at my ring. Instead he came out of the garage, its door trundling up as I turned at the sound. He stood there, Golden Boy in the afternoon sunlight, gently tousled, his flaxen hair wispy in the breeze. He wasted no energy on pleasantries. "What do you want?"

I'd rehearsed invective, but when had that worked? As for Celia's Christa, a threat backed only by my imagination, he'd laugh. But cunning said I had a real threat and told me to use it. "Where were you when Celia died?"

He shifted his car keys from hand to hand, came up the walk a step toward me. "What the fuck do you mean?"

"She came to see me. The next day somebody killed her. Was it because of something I told her? About you?"

He jammed the keys into a pocket, snorting. "Celia'd heard every one of your lies a thousand times over. Nothing *you* said would have made any difference to her."

I hadn't seen him close up for a year. I looked for signs of grief. But his face was locked, nothing escaping. So if he grieved for Celia, I was not allowed to know.

I did see age. I'd always thought of him as a young man. Now, I would have said, youngish. Fissures opening around his mouth, acid etchings in the tan of his throat.

"Our talk made her send me a list of names," I said. "Young girls' names."

I'd hoped for a flicker of guilty knowledge. His wheat-blond brows came together. "Excuse me?"

"Corinne Miller was on that list. And so was Simone Hudson. Unfortunately, I'm connected to both of them. And so are you."

He spread his hands, palms up, looking skyward as if to some sympathetic deity for relief from my madness. "What the hell are you talking about?"

So I'd achieved one goal I came for: I had shaken him up. He wasn't laughing, hadn't zoomed away with an obscene gesture. "The police talked to you, didn't they?"

He stuck the imploring hands in his pockets. I had the pleasure of seeing him flush. "You're using what happened to Celia to beat me up again, aren't you? Just like last summer. You tried to use her against me then, to feed your crazy ideas. It didn't work. If you've got something to say to me, say it, then fuck off."

A little late for Mr. Defiance. "Oh, I'm not denying that if I had some way to hurt you, I would. Right now I don't know what I can tell you because I don't know what the police shared with you. Maybe they've already told you everything."

His frown deepened. For the briefest of seconds his gaze shifted from me into an oblique space. I said, "I asked where you were because there's evidence you have a motive for killing her. I want to give you a chance, now, here, to stop me from thinking even for a heartbeat I can help pin her death on you."

Hands still in his pockets, he rocked back on the balls of his feet, exactly as he would have if I'd shoved him. He recovered, rebalanced. "Jesus Christ."

"So give it a try," I said.

He shook his head, turned toward the garage, but after a step looked back over his shoulder. "Get your buddy Clauson to tell you where I was. He won't? Won't they tell you stuff that's none of your business? Celia was . . . terrific. I didn't kill her. End of story. Now leave."

He disappeared into the garage. I stepped where I could see his vintage red Mustang, so like the one he'd owned—and dumped, hastily—when Anna vanished. He backed the car out with a jerk, then sat in the driveway a moment while the garage door shut. He lowered the window. "If you harass me, I will call the police on you. You know that."

I spread my hands. "So let's call them now."

He slammed the gear shift. The car jumped a foot backward, making me stumble into the ivy. Didn't horses jump like that when they sensed a rider's fear? We stared at each other. He'd always managed to deliver a punch at the end of our confrontations, but I had my own punch now. I sprang forward and caught the glass of his half-open window to land it. "Is it dead, too, your child with her?" But he just lurched hard into his paved turnaround, jolting me clear.

"Go peddle your lies to Clauson. He asked me about you and your buddy Hudson—"

"He's not my—"

"Ask him if he knows what his sweet little kid was up to." He gave another yank on the gear shift. "Ask him where *he* was when she died."

He barely missed smacking his big stone mailbox, the one the ivy was devouring, as he gunned the red car into the road.

I stood there wanting to shout after him loud enough for the whole neighborhood to hear it: *how many of those girls did you fuck?* But at least I had left a claw mark. He had driven off thinking of Nick. Nick and Celia. I almost laughed as I climbed into my car.

31

Down the street, Jenny Coronna worked in her yard. The Coronnas and their next-door neighbors, the Atkinsons, had gone sensibly xeriscape, planting drought-resistant yucca and cactus. I couldn't quite see what she was doing, except that it involved a wheelbarrow and a spate of kneeling.

If I'd stayed here, kept the house, what would I grow here now? Something less suffocating than Eric's ivy. Neighborhood children would have cavorted with hummingbirds among my flowers, gathered in my bright, spacious kitchen, chugged the sweet iced tea I made them, wolfed oatmeal cookies. They'd ask about the little girl in the picture. I'd tell them. I'd say, you must be so so careful. You must fear the ones you love.

Yes, I thought as I rolled down my car windows, Eric's anger meant that I'd knocked him off base. Looking for balance, he'd pivoted to Nick. Making him flounder had buoyed me. But he had raised new questions for me to digest.

Nick was on Clauson's list for the killing. And why not? They knew he was there. I could only vaguely envision Celia's house in West Austin from some of the pictures Russell had sent. I imagined Nick and Celia on the high deck over a rock garden, Celia demanding that he call Simone out for her lies about Eric. Nick would retort that he would not have his daughter subjected to such accusations. Then Celia: *If you don't take steps, I will.*

Would it have been tragically easy for that argument to carry them too close to the deck railing? How much carelessness would it have taken, or how much violence, for someone as lithe and quick as Celia to stumble? Was Nick capable of such carelessness, or such violence? I simply didn't know.

Eric had shrugged off my jab about the child. As I had expected. One thing I had learned: Eric didn't know what Celia and I had talked about. He had to wonder what she had told me about him.

And one other thing I'd accomplished: I'd set something new in motion. I could feel it. Like those big precariously balancing rocks you find in eroded canyons, Eric's world teetered on a delicate foundation, and I'd given it a shove.

Who would be standing under it when it fell?

———————

I reached home by ten-thirty, surprisingly calm since I'd just spent ten minutes in the company of the man who might have killed my daughter. Alice was raking her beak on her cage bars, presumably to express her disgust that I was over here and she was there. I ignored her. I had a mission now. My ability at last to face Eric, even with so little accomplished, had given me a new sense of my strength; with that came the resolve to open my stash of Anna's school pictures again.

I knew now from what Nick had told me that searching for Simone had been pointless. In contrast, while the search for Corinne among all those kids' faces might be as difficult as I had imagined, until someone convinced me I wouldn't find her, I had no excuse not to look. If Ms. Miller had been truthful, Corinne had known Anna, had possibly even been her confidante, and other children I might find among these old records might have known her as well. I would come to those pictures now hard-eyed, cold-eyed, with no tears.

I turned to photos of activities rather than the year-by-year pictures of Anna's classes where the rosters already told me that Corinne would not appear. One photo showed the cast of a school play in which Anna had played a leprechaun. Paired with cast shots was a sweep of the student audience, the faces of children in the first rows visible in the footlights. One of the teachers monitoring from the edge of the room was the retired teacher for whom I'd left a number. Had she been given my message? Come Monday I'd call and find out. Beside the various shots I tiled photos of Corinne from those Clauson had sent me. I swung back and forth between the two sets of faces, zooming, juxtaposing. I already knew to skip past Anna, three rows back, so that I could float above tears throughout my search.

Corinne's face was not among the ones I could make out. I pressed on. Around fourth grade, Anna had come to love science and began showing up in candid views of a school-wide science fair. To find Corinne if she was there, I started from the first posted images when she might have been present. These science-fair photos each showed fewer children, but the school's online newsletter stored a lot of shots. I settled down for a long slog. But early on, at a stagey image of kids miming interest in an electrical circuit, I stopped. Looked twice, then three times, at the girl in the embroidered white sweater. Looked really hard, at her and at Clauson's image file. I looked as well at the teacher with the encouraging smile beside her. The retired teacher. And in the next shot, which I raced to, that teacher was the cheerful mentor at Anna's side.

Come Monday, somehow, some way, that teacher, Ms. Vanhoven, would hear from me.

——————

Around noon I rose from my discovery for a tea break. But tea wasn't what I wanted. My perseverance deserved a reward. In all those years, I prided myself that I had not turned to serious drinking. Nor to Xanax, or Valium. Not even to the comforts of therapy. The fact was, I had not wanted my anger quenched by any narcotic. Still, this particular mid-day I had earned a glass of the velvety red wine I stashed for special occasions. I poured it. Just a fraction of a glass.

And the soft breeze that flitted over the balcony where I settled—I had earned that too. I should eat; would a call to a food-delivery service for something wonderfully greasy between bread slabs count as lunch? Even a Big Mac and a daytime TV game show would be more useful than rehearsing yet again my grievances against Eric. But I indulged in gaming out ways to bring him to account.

For example, could I find out if Eric was connected to this George Franklin? I had no evidence he had ever met the man. But Eric was Celia's lover. Wouldn't he track who she was seeing? Celia's relationship with Franklin had been serious enough to send Franklin to my office. Assuming the would-be intruder was Franklin. I had decided to trust Occam's Razor and believe he was.

Should I ask whether Russell's spies had their own mug shot of Franklin? No; for the moment I'd keep myself and whatever threat Franklin represented far apart in Russell's mind. That threat was still vague. He hadn't tried all that hard to get into my office, hadn't shown any interest in me when I so carefully almost knocked him down. Maybe if I sat tight he'd show up again. My job now was to find some way of staying sane until Monday, when I could track Ms. Vanhoven down.

I needn't have worried. That Saturday had already been eventful, but it had not finished giving a lot of people's lives a shake.

Like the driver of the white RAV4 that passed sedately in the street below. I didn't register the car until a scant few minutes later, when an identical white RAV4 eased past in the opposite direction, slower than the first.

I set the wine glass down on the balcony floor. I waited. My senses hissed *yes* when, for the third time, a white RAV4 inched back up the street.

In a cupboard by my glider was a pair of binoculars for watching the neighborhood birds. I snatched the binoculars out and aimed them at the car. The side windows were tinted but I could make out the face behind the windshield. I knew who it was.

The latest RAV4 manifestation turned the corner to my left. I stood. As always, opposing voices tugged on my choices. One ordered, *call Clauson. Let an officer ask the questions.* The other said, *and learn what?*

Raging Sarah is nothing if not inventive. She knew what to reach for in a high closet: an apparatus I'd been pestered into buying for a social event I preferred to pretend never happened. To my surprise I remembered how to use the contraption. I jogged downstairs, out the back through the porch, and edged around the corner of the house until I could see up and down the street.

Here the car came, slower still. I loped down the driveway, spun full-face, and splattered the looming grill with my paintball gun.

The RAV stopped with a lurch that must have bounced the driver off the seat. With one of those hybrid hums, the car shot backward. "Oh, hell, no," I said aloud, racing to draw abreast of the driver-side window. Some deity must have been watching, because just as the RAV accelerated in reverse to escape me, another car, a Civic, came around the corner and blocked it. My paintball gun brandished, I ran to the RAV driver's door, face-to-face with the girl inside.

The man in the Civic rolled down his window. "What's going on?"

I ignored him, rapped on the girl's window. She glared back at me: the girl I'd seen the day I encountered Nick and Simone at Town Lake.

The Civic man revved his car and pulled up alongside of us. "You could have caused an accident!" For a moment I worried he might think I was assaulting the girl. Even Raging Sarah wouldn't have smart answers for that one. But he hit the gas and roared past. I raised the gun and blasted the whole side of her car.

"Oh my God!" she shouted, loud enough I could hear her through the closed window. "Stop it! Oh my God!" I lifted the gun again, not sure how much paint I had left. She shoved the door open and scrambled out, pushing past me and surveying the damage. "Are you crazy? This is illegal! You're attacking me!"

I eased between her and the open car door. "It'll wash off. What do you want?"

"Oh my God!" She swiped at the paint, leaving parallel finger tracks. "My dad'll kill me."

I lowered the gun, stepped back from the car door. "Pull it around the back of the house. Tell me what you want and I'll help you wash it."

"What if it doesn't come off?"

"The sooner we hose it down, the better."

She watched me as I pointedly maneuvered so I could pull out my phone and click on her license plate. With a thunderous glower, she slid behind the wheel. She let me direct her into the driveway and into the space behind my Corolla in the back yard, where I knew we could reach a hose.

32

The paint sloughed off easily into supposedly biodegradable puddles. I gave her a towel from the trunk of my Corolla and studied her as she dried the hood. She hadn't bought those shorts, that halter top, those sandals, at Goodwill. Her hair, rose-streaked, captured light in a long pony tail.

I grabbed another rag and started polishing the windows. "So what's your name?"

She pursed her lips and scrubbed hard with the towel, shrugging.

"Don't be silly," I said. "I have your license number."

"How do you know it's my car?"

"The car your dad'll kill you over?"

She stopped scrubbing, straightened, kneaded the towel. Then she picked it up and folded it with a care that might have been an effort to create order in a situation she'd lost control of. "You can't tell anybody about this."

This teenage social circle was awash in things I couldn't tell anyone.

"You have to promise," she said.

"Can't. Until I know what kind of secret you want me to keep."

She flung the folded towel on the hood and faced me. "You have to help me get him!" she said.

Ten bucks said I knew who she meant by "him." This was the precariously balanced rock of Eric's life falling, and I was directly in its path. I retrieved the wet towels and laid them across my car roof to dry. "What do you want to get him for?"

She looked down at the drenched grass at her feet, as if she'd dropped something but couldn't remember what. She pulled her pony tail tighter. "I don't . . . it isn't . . ."

"Were you here the other night? With Simone?"

"That was just . . . That was stupid. Now that . . . now . . ." She gathered her breath, hands raking her hair and disrupting its perfect shimmer. "He raped me!"

The words hung before me like flung embers. I opened my mouth, closed it. She floundered on in a voice thick with choked sobs. "I just went there to talk to him and he dragged me in and pushed me down. He ripped my clothes off and held his hand over my mouth so I couldn't scream." She rubbed at her eyes with the backs of her wrists, the sobs turning to hisses. "He said I wanted it. He said I deserved it. He said he would . . . I would . . ." Her face quivered, flushed now. "You know how awful he is."

I managed to convert the *holy shit* that tried to escape me into acceptable commiseration. "Oh dear."

"You have to believe me," she wailed.

My mind raced, stacking duty against a sick exhilaration. With effort I fended off that dirty, distracting joy. "Have you told anyone? Your parents? Did you call the police?" The prim training from campus workshops on sexual misconduct deserted me. "Can I take you to a doctor?" I remembered to ask. "Call someone?"

She took a big hiccupping breath. "It's too late now. They wouldn't believe me."

"Of course they would."

"Oh, sure. They'd say I asked for it. That I was a slut."

The sobs still quavered beneath her words. So did a riptide of anger. But of course she was angry. Who wouldn't be? Yet her anger played on me with a force I didn't like. This door was one I'd waited a long time to open, but I was finding it hard to charge through it. "Honey, how old are you?"

"I'm seventeen," she said sharply. "You can't tell unless I say you can."

"There are legal obligations—"

"No, there's not. I'm old enough now." Anguish flooded back.

"I don't care if you're a hundred. Rape is rape. You can't handle this by yourself."

"We have to *get* him." She spat it. "You'll know how."

I crossed to the porch steps and sat down, more aware than I liked of the black paint still staining the boards behind me, the message warning me to stop accusing Eric of violence toward children. Her gaze still on me, she slumped against her car, picking at a cuticle, scratching her arm.

"When did this happen?" I asked.

"Yesterday. Last night. I just went there to talk to him."

"About what?"

"You don't believe me, either."

"Whether I believe you or not doesn't matter. You've told me about a serious crime. This is not a secret I can keep."

Her fair skin with its creamy tan flushed even deeper. A muscle throbbed in her jaw.

"Then forget it," she said. "I was lying. If you tell, I'll say you made it up."

"Why can't you tell?"

"I thought I could tell *you*. That's why I came here. I hoped I'd see you and get to talk to you. I thought you would believe me. You would care."

My mind began strained gymnastics: *she's here, she came of her own free will, you didn't violate your orders from Clauson—so use her. What does she know?* She was troubled. But escaping an assault would be troubling. What could I ask that would help us? She came close enough that I could see the spark of an aged knowledge that did not belong in those young eyes.

"He did that to your daughter, too, didn't he?" she said with a cold passion. "They would finally get him for that."

So much anger. And danger. But for whom? "Anybody know you were going there?"

"No."

"Has he ever called you? Texted? Messaged? Is there a record on your phone?"

She shook her head, the long flaxen hair swinging. "I took all that off my phone. I didn't want anybody to know."

"Know what?"

She wheeled back to her car, spinning to face me. Tears had finally broken free. "That I was so fucking stupid. To trust him! To not know what he would do! Oh, God."

The scenarios were all too likely. The girls in the group Simone and this young woman belonged to might well have competed for Eric's attention. I could imagine this one boasting that she'd won an assignation that many of them craved. She would have gone not expecting trouble. She would have gone so that she could revel in her ability to claim hours of his time. If he'd turned her away, as any decent man would, no problem. Her friends need never know he'd rejected her. On the other hand, if he'd laughed in her face . . .

An ancient instinct said reassure her somehow. Embrace her, hold her, protect her. But anything I could fight off already had her. "It's hard to know what to do without proof," I said.

"I know! I have no proof. That's why I came to you."

I thought about Eric's volatility, the rages that could explode. But even when I considered what must have happened with Anna, I honestly hadn't envisioned anything this reckless and brazen. I'd always imagined his depredations as insidious, incremental, testing how far he could go without getting caught. Yet the strain of Celia's death, police pressing for an alibi . . . people did slip over the edge.

I rose, picking up my paintball paraphernalia. "If you hoped I had some sort of proof, I'm sorry to disappoint you. I'll have to think about this."

"But you can help! You can say—"

"No. I have to think."

She swiped at her damp cheeks. "Please, please, don't tell anyone I came here."

"If you don't go soon, my downstairs neighbor will see you when she gets home from her church group." I gathered the damp towels. "If you want me to help you, it would help if I knew your name."

It took her a second to answer. "Peyton."

"Peyton what?"

A sideways flick of her gaze. "Peyton Finch."

"Okay, Peyton Finch." I came down on the syllables firmly. "Do you have your phone?"

A dumb question. "Yes."

"Get it, please."

She opened the passenger door and came up with a slick little rectangle. "I know your email at—"

"No. Don't contact me at the university. Enter this number." I waited while she typed. "Text me there," I said.

"You'll text me?"

"When I get the number. Peyton, seriously, if you want me to arrange for a doctor—"

She shook her head, wedging the phone in a tight pocket. "I just want to get him."

"We'll see."

She circled the RAV4, and got in. She backed out carefully, then stopped beside me and lowered the passenger window. "Please. Don't tell anyone."

I said nothing. She sat staring at me for a long moment. At last she eased around and drove on out to the street.

33

The RAV's hum receded, my distress giving way to a familiar frustration. I had been told a lot, but I hadn't learned much.

Except for one important thing.

I climbed the stairs quickly. Fumbled a folder out of a drawer. On top lay my printout of the list Celia had sent me: the girls in Eric's hang-gliding class.

Yep. Peyton. Not Peyton Finch. Peyton Eckstrom.

The list didn't supply addresses. Yet possession of another name meant another tiny step in my search. Especially since, from the looks of it, Peyton was the one whose crush on Eric had led to the threat on me.

Had her infatuation played any role in Corinne's death? I let myself out on the balcony. A risk, settling onto my glider. Creatures on the prowl could spot me there. But I needed fresh air to judge how the land tilted before I could plan my next step.

My efforts to link Corinne to Anna would have to wait until Monday when I could track down that teacher. Meanwhile this Peyton lead had a black-hole gravity to it. But finding out meant negotiating shaky legal ground. If Peyton was a student at Cresthill, possibly taking some of our dual-credit classes, my course would be clear. As a "Responsible Employee," I was charged with reporting any such incident to the Title IX Coordinator. But a quick look at the Registrar's records, which I could access as an administrator, showed she wasn't enrolled in any programs at Cresthill.

So what was my duty? She'd said she was seventeen. If she really was seventeen, and my relationship to her was that of a private citizen, I had no duty to report.

But, said my vacillating mind, assault was a crime. Did I not have an obligation to report *that*?

Except, of course, she'd specifically instructed me not to.

That left me with a packet of ugly information. How I handled it could help her, or do her irreparable harm. I stifled Raging Sarah, who trod impatiently on my delicate conscience. And yes, part of what stormed back and forth across my conscience was my own convoluted motivation. What she'd told me felt like a found ring of power laid in my path by some helpful wizard. When I handed that gift to Clauson, I would hand him the power.

The longer I sat there, the more the gift dissolved to acid in my hands.

——————

I expected Clauson's phone to go to voice mail, but he picked up. He didn't sound surprised at my call. He must have grown used to me invading his space at my own leisure, like on a Saturday afternoon, no doubt a time he had set aside to catch up on his always voluminous files. "Just can't stay away, professor? Sure, if you got to, come on in."

When I arrived he pushed away from his computer and swiveled. He looked paler than usual. Yep, too much desk work. I settled into the chair I'd come to know pretty well.

He raised his brows.

"Have you told Eric about Simone's accusations?" I asked.

One of his hard little smiles crossed his face. "That's part of an ongoing investigation. You know that."

I shrugged. Raging Sarah and I weren't constrained by his investigations. "Does he admit knowing the girls on that list?"

He leaned back and laced his fingers over his barrel-shaped belly. "Look. I know why you want this information and why you think you deserve it. I wish I could get you to believe that when I learn something that I think affects you—"

"Everything about Eric affects me."

He flexed and unflexed his fingers, then rubbed at a scratch on his chair arm. He studied it, not me. "Let me ask *you* this. Do you have any reason to believe that any of these girls on this list were harassing Wyles?"

An old game of his: getting more out of me than I ever got out of him. "Harassing Eric, rather than me or Celia? How?"

"Oh, I don't know. Calling his phone, leaving notes on his car, following him around, following Celia—like you said—since that hang-gliding thing."

"Isn't the issue here what *he* did?"

"You think any of these girls might have been dumb enough to go to his place?"

We considered each other. "Let me guess," I said. "He claims one of them did, but he told her not to be an idiot and sent her packing."

"You think there's any chance of that?"

I shifted in my chair. Tried to see over, under, around, Eric's latest wall of plausible denial. "Those accusations, what Simone told her mother. You said you were going to talk to Simone. What did she say?"

He shook his head. "You know better than that."

Not for the first time dealing with this man, I wished I could lift his desk and tip it over on him so he'd have to beg me to drag him out. "Hmmm. Lawyer with her. That doesn't surprise me. Her mother thinks telling people it's just a bunch of gossip will keep Simone safe."

"What *you* told me was hearsay." He bore down on his next words, delivering more than his standard closed-mouth rebuff. "If we want to tie Wyles to this death investigation, we will need more than that."

I eased to the edge of the chair. "Where was Eric when Celia died?"

His hands went out again, this time in an arc of supplication. "As it turns out, you could find that on Google. He was at a conference in

San Antonio. The American Aerodynamics Association conference. He shows up on the presenter list."

"He was there all weekend?"

"We're following up on it. How can I convince you of that?"

He wanted my patience. But I'd been patient for nearly forever. "I do believe you're following up. But you have to follow up a lot of directions. For me, there's only one direction."

"But I can't put all of our eggs into your basket."

Last summer he'd paid a price when he put his eggs into his own basket instead of mine. "Here's what I do know," I said. "People are in danger here, and I have an obligation, even it's not a legal one. I'm going to learn all I can about what happened to those girls and Celia. I won't keep anything from you, but I won't wait for your permission to ask questions or follow up on things I find out."

He clamped down on his lower lip. Folded his arms.

"Three things," he said. "One, I will arrest you if you obstruct our investigation in any way, or if you put anyone—including yourself—in danger in any way."

"Fair enough."

"Two. You could get hurt. You and some of the other people you put at risk by digging into this."

Damn, he was channeling Russell. "I am aware of that responsibility."

"Three. Sarah . . . if by some unlikely chance Eric Wyles is not guilty, not of your daughter's disappearance, not of these girls' accusations, not of Celia Monahan's death, your . . . single-mindedness could be making it easier for the real criminal to get away."

I willed myself not to blink. Again I bit back, *yes, we both know all about letting the real criminal get away*. Again I leaned forward, as far into his space at the desk would let me. "That other criminal, if he or she exists, is your business. Eric is mine."

We sat in that suspended space for long moments. Then he shifted, sighed, scratched the back of his neck. "God help us. Look, I have some stuff I'm in the middle of—"

He was not going to dismiss me that easily. Not when for once I had a hook he'd have to do some fancy wriggling to slither off of. I put both hands on his desk and pushed up, looming over him and all the stuff he was in the middle of. "The girl who went to see him to tell him she loved him came to my house. She told me he raped her."

"Oh, she did?"

Heat shot up the back of my neck. I slapped the desk, jarring loose one of his paper towers. "Sexist dismissals are not what these young women deserve."

He looked at me steadily. "You believe her?"

I opened my mouth. Closed it. Tried again. "I have no idea whether to believe her. But someone should actively consider the possibility that she's telling the truth."

"What's her name?"

"She said she was seventeen, so I'm already telling you more than I'm obligated to."

"So if you think I don't need to know, don't tell me." He reached for a folder.

This made at least the seventh time in our acquaintance that I mentally called him a bastard. "She said her name was Peyton Finch. But there's a Peyton Eckstrom on the hang-gliding list."

He pushed up, too, sticking the folder under his arm. "Fine. Another one whose lawyer will tell me what she doesn't know."

I wheeled for the door, most of me shaking. I had not quite made my escape when he called, "Just remember those three things."

——————

I spent more hours than I cared to admit that Saturday resisting the urge to introduce Clauson's three things to a bottle of wine.

It was only four o'clock. Any such plan would render me useless for the remainder of the day.

But I wanted to be useless. Oblivious. I had vacillated outside the police station on 8th Street, thinking about all the venues within walking distance where oblivion was for sale.

I am able to report that I resisted my unhealthy impulse. I took myself home, hauled out the muddled pages of the tangled argument my share of our research project was weaving itself into, and in that small universe was not useless for a while.

After dark I did pour some wine and let it lead me where I realized that I'd recently resisted going, to NamUs, the government database of the as-yet-unfound. I couldn't shake the illusion that the digital souls I'd so often walked among in that database noticed my visits and mourned when I stayed away very long. But I had grown tired of lifting the lids of virtual coffins only to find possible answers again and again rotted away to pixelated dust. My heart wanted to turn toward the living, Someone out there knew something and could tell me. The bodies that had moved into my world stood whole before me, beckoning. Or so my heart said.

I logged out of NamUs with a whispered *I'm sorry*. I Googled "American Aerodynamics Conference," and there it was. My ex-husband was named on a one-forty-five p.m. panel the day his lover died.

Bummer. Sleep showed no signs of claiming me. I poked among all the potentially revealing steps I had not yet taken. I had not heard from Nick since the scene with Diana in his office. His silence might mean that he wasn't ready to discuss so intimate a crisis with me. Now on top of Simone's claim was the story from this girl Peyton. How much did Nick know? What would he do with what he did know? Talking to him took on an outsized priority. I called the number he'd given me, got voice mail. Said, "I have a lot to tell you." Sat up with the TV chattering but he didn't call.

I won't say I slept. I walked among the crypts of NamUs, gathering delicate bones one by one from the graves as I passed them, until at last I had enough to build a whole child.

34

The next morning passed in a messy whirl. Scattered bits of research. A rare Sunday session with Kendra, in which I learned that one of her wizards had developed a cruel streak he had not exhibited before. The unusually lively way she described him—"tall but blubbery," "stomping around and getting in people's way"—made him sound an awful lot like a stand-in for her dad.

I considered burying myself once more in Anna's school pictures, but I could not bring myself to face those rows of faces when they had already told me the one thing I cared about. Corinne had certainly known Anna. But maybe only to speak to? Or to share scary secrets with? How could I get a dead girl to talk?

I fretted that Nick still hadn't called. I'd decided to hold off telling him about Peyton until I knew what Clauson planned. But if we were partners in the effort to bring Eric to justice, I owed him the news of Eric's alibi. Had Nick ever encountered this George Franklin? I finally gave in and picked up the phone to call him, only to berate myself for acting like a thwarted lover. Give him time to pick his own knots apart, like whether Diana would even let him talk to Simone.

I caught myself watching the street from behind my closed windows, alert for loiterers, whether in creeping cars or on foot. This man I thought was Franklin—had I been too casual about his interest in me? Would he be the next to stalk me? Would I be able to spot him? When I began imagining shadowy figures lurking behind the lamppost on the corner, I knew I had to get out of there.

Libraries usually distracted me so snarls of ideas could unravel. But I had just spotted a review of a new exhibit at a favorite Sixth-Street gallery. A roomful of paintings is also conducive to creative meditation. So I scarfed down a sandwich, dusted myself off, and went.

———

A sign at the door said, “Please be courteous to our other patrons. Turn off your cell phone.”

I am apparently only a moderately courteous person. I set my phone to “vibrate.” I had barely exposed my needy nerves to a few of the helpfully diverting paintings when the phone shivered in my hands.

“Where are you?” Nick wrote. I confessed that I had abandoned our mission. He was not sympathetic. He wrote back, “Meet me outside in ten.”

I tripped out into the scalding sun. No denying that having a co-conspirator buoyed me. Even a co-conspirator who, like Eric, was under investigation for murder. Nick came up the sidewalk in a jerky hurry, in a lightweight zippered top, sleek jeans, and trainers. Even from a distance, I could feel his impatience. He had been so hard and sure with Diana. Now he approached me as if he knew he had to rush forward but couldn’t figure out where.

“Eric was presenting at a conference in San An,” he said, looking around as if invisible pedestrians might edge up and listen, “but he didn’t register for the conference until ten minutes before his session. He was here in Austin the whole morning Celia was killed.”

Well, he’d upstaged my thunder. Still, my heart jumped at the details he’d added. “How did you learn that?”

His face flushed with his own excitement, darker than mine, with a low current to it. “Let’s get coffee or something.” He gestured. “That bakery down there is okay.”

We took an outside table. I settled across from him with an iced coffee. “Eric must realize his alibi won’t hold up. He’s not stupid.”

“Oh, he’s probably got a raft of stories about all the things he did in San An that day. With all sorts of witnesses who’ll say they saw him where when.” His voice hardened. “I’m going to find out.”

"How?" I couldn't imagine Nick trekking around San An, badgering store clerks.

"I know a guy who was at that conference. Works for a space-program start-up." The excitement jittered through him. "I asked if he saw Eric there and he said, yeah, he bumped into him at the registration table. In a hurry because he was late." He took out his phone. "I'll text you his number. He'll probably be willing talk to you, maybe even the police. After all, you're the one who—"

His phone rang. "Excuse me." He glared impatiently at the number as he tapped to answer. His voice quickened. "What?" I was pretty sure the other voice, percolating through the phone, was Diana's. "Jeez! How could you have let that happen? . . . Sheesh, of course I will . . . You don't know anything? She didn't say anything? Nothing?" He picked up his coffee, his gaze passing distractedly over my face. "I have stuff to do . . . Yes, of course it's more important. I'll call you back."

He ended the call. Suddenly seemed to notice me still sitting there.

"Simone's missing," he said.

"Oh, no!"

"She took off, took a bunch of clothes and some credit cards. Some cash, too."

I shelved all the news I had piled up to tell him. "The cards will give you a way to track her. Her phone, too."

"They'll tell us where *they* were, not where *she* is." He jumped up as if about to race away, but then spun back to me. "Are you doing anything? Will you come with me to find her?"

I tried to list all the steps I should be taking instead. Like what? "How do you think I can help?"

"I just think . . . maybe, I don't know, I need a witness."

I waffled. Did what Simone was up to have anything to do with Eric? With Celia? With me? But of course it did. Everything did. "Let's go."

———————

We zoomed off in his Prius, cutting over to Lamar and up to 15th, making holes in traffic if it didn't part for us. I resisted the urge to grab the overhead handle. "Where are we going?"

"I think she might be with one of her friends."

With Simone's safety at stake, I could make no case for holding back about Peyton. Besides, I'd told Clauson, and Clauson and I weren't *de facto* partners. "Is one of her friends named Peyton?"

"Peyton Eckstrom." He glanced at me. "You know her?"

Personally I preferred that he keep his eyes on the Nissan we were roaring up on. "She came to my house." Still, I hesitated. He was in a bomb-throwing mood and I didn't like handing him a detonator. But if we really were partners . . . "She claims Eric attacked her. His story is that she showed up at his place to tell him she loved him and he told her to get lost. Unfortunately, she probably can't prove anything."

"But you believed her?"

"It doesn't sound like Eric, attacking someone who could so easily tell on him, but then he's had a stressful couple of days."

He literally drove the car sideways into a slot in the next lane that was at least a foot too small, then over again when we passed the car we'd been stuck behind. I covered my gasp with a cough.

We survived long enough to reach our destination, a big, newish construction tucked in among late Victorians. I closed my eyes just a second to savor the fact that the car was no longer moving and I was alive. When I opened them, Nick had already jumped out and circled to my side. I got out. "This is Peyton's. Her mother's probably here."

I hoped so. I didn't like the visible tic in the muscles of his jaw. When we reached the narrow porch, he stepped back, hands on his hips, his dark hair falling over his forehead. The door opened on a tall blond woman in capris and a loose Oxford shirt, gold glinting at her throat and on her wrists.

"Why, Nick! Hello!" But her gaze found me and clouded. I wondered whether I looked like what we used to call a truant officer. "What's the matter? Is something wrong?"

"Simone had an argument with her mother and stormed off." Other than ignoring her pleasant greeting, Nick sounded cordial. "I thought Peyton might have heard from her. Do you mind if we ask?"

The cloud didn't lift, but the woman brightened it with a practiced smile. She held out a hand to me. "I'm Lydia Eckstrom, Peyton's mother."

I took it. "Oh, sorry," said Nick. "This is Sarah Crockett." Who would he tell her I was? "She's a friend."

Lydia nodded at me, the smile turning bland. Facing Nick, she replaced the smile with a frown. "I haven't seen Simone, but I'll ask Peyton." She hesitated the briefest of moments. "Would you like to come in while I check with her?"

"Thank you," said Nick. "I'm sorry to barge in like this. It's just . . . I'm concerned."

"My goodness, yes." Lydia led us across a foyer, then through double doors into a formal living room whose shadowy stiffness gave the impression it was seldom used. "Please have a seat. I'll be right back."

She let herself out. Neither of us sat. Nick paced. "She'll lie to her mother. We've got to see her."

I suspected she'd lie to us, too, especially if we charged her like a pair of pit bulls. Yet . . . if I thought she stood between me and news of Anna—

I caught a flicker of motion through the wide front window. I jumped up, impulsively grabbed his arm, then pushed past him, back out into the foyer and out the front door.

He followed. Peyton, already halfway down the driveway, must have heard us coming. She looked over her shoulder, quickened her steps, then began to jog. I wanted to bolt after her but caution stopped me. I didn't dare touch her. But Nick plowed past me as Peyton reached the street. She broke into a run. So I had to run. I had to be between them when he caught her. I called out, "Nick, don't!"

But he outpaced Peyton, wheeled and blocked her. She spun away from him to find me right behind her. "You told, didn't you?" she spat at me.

Nick's gaze flicked back down the quiet street. I followed it. Peyton's mother hurried toward us. I had no time to think. I said, "Yes. And it seems I'm going to get a chance to tell your mother now."

Blood raced to her cheeks. Then her gaze went cold. "Josephine's at three," she said. "I have something to tell you."

Nick looked from Peyton to me and back again. "Where's Simone?" he said.

Hard to tell whether Peyton would have answered. She set her mouth as Lydia reached us. "Peyton, honey. I thought you were upstairs. What are you doing out here?"

Peyton knew exactly what face to present to her mother. "I was going to Ron's. He wants to hang out."

Lydia started to speak, but cut her gaze to Nick and then to me. She smoothed her tone. "Mr. Hudson came to see if you'd heard anything from Simone this morning."

"No. Was I supposed to?"

I could feel Nick breathing. When he spoke his words seemed carefully paced. "Peyton, she's taken off somewhere and I was hoping she'd contacted you."

"Nope. Sorry."

He raised a brow, not letting her gaze go. "If you hear from her, will you let your mother know?"

Peyton shrugged. "Sure."

She took a step up the street. "Peyton, honey," said her mom. "I don't think this is a good time to go to Ron's." She took Peyton's hand. "Go back to the house."

"But it's just—"

Her mother's chin dipped. Peyton sighed and turned. As she trudged, abused victim, back up the pavement, she looked back once. At me.

"Nick, is there something I need to know?" Lydia asked.

I didn't know how much she'd seen and heard and I doubted he knew either. He shook his head. "It's just that I'm worried about Simone."

"If we do hear something, of course we'll immediately let you know."

She waited. The taut line of Nick's shoulders didn't quite soften. "Thanks. I'd appreciate it." He stretched an arm behind me. I let him steer me past her. She smiled at me brightly. "It was nice meeting you, Sarah," she said.

———————

"Well, that was awkward," I said as we wound out of the neighborhood.

His mind wasn't on social *faux pas*. "Peyton has something to tell us."

To tell me, I mentally corrected. He drove more slowly now, almost as if he had decided to let chance guide us. I breathed gratefully. He shot me a glance. "So Josephine's. Do you think she'll show?"

The restaurant Peyton had named was more sophisticated than I would have expected. "She believed my threat."

More silence. Then, "She knows something about Simone. I need to be there."

An unsettling prospect, Nick and Peyton together. "Do you have any more ideas about where to find Simone?"

He nodded. "I know a place where she sometimes meets friends."

I checked my watch. Not quite an hour before Peyton had said to meet her. "How far is this place?"

"Not far." He still thrummed with an anguished current. Maybe he did need a witness. A collaborator in jail would be useless. He took a turn back toward Lamar. "I still think Simone would have contacted Peyton. But I don't think Peyton would have sneaked her into the house, or anything like that."

"I wonder whether Lydia knows what Peyton's been up to."

"Do I know what Simone's been up to?"

Anna dropped into my mind, a thin shape, not the way she usually visited me, but foggy, a girl who had slipped past the limits of my vision. "If my daughter were here, a teenager building her own life, I'd probably be asking the same thing."

He didn't answer. Even on Sunday afternoon traffic piled up around us, coagulating at lights. I decided to make these moments useful. "Did Simone know Celia?" I asked.

"She met her." He sighed. A long silence. So much for useful answers. But then he thumped the wheel. "She said, 'Are you going to marry her?' It was at a time when Celia wasn't seeing much of me. I said, 'Probably not.' That seemed to calm her. I was trying to figure out what was going on with me and Celia, so I didn't push the issue with Simone."

His revelations turned my mind from Simone to Celia and these two men. Celia wouldn't be the first woman to string two men along. I was beginning to think that Nick was the second choice, the spare.

At a busy intersection we pulled into a strip mall. The corner store was a chain pizza joint and game room. "How would Simone have gotten here?" I asked. "This is a long way to come."

"She has a credit card and she knows how to call Uber. Or somebody gave her a ride." He twisted to face me. "Would you come in with me?"

Forty minutes now to meet Peyton. Surely if Simone was here we'd know quickly. I followed him in.

35

Games and pizza. I remembered that allure. Local hangouts before there was such a place as Instagram. So kids still found their way to places like this. We entered a big, echoing room, silent on a Sunday. But not completely deserted: two boys hunched over a digital game table in one of the many booths, the zings of their plays and a shout of victory puncturing the early-afternoon calm. But I would bet that most evenings the space would fill with crackling electronics and the high young laughter of people like Peyton and Simone.

No Simone now. Along one wall stretched a long soda-shop counter. Behind it, a short, rotund man with a shiny bald scalp looked up from fiddling with a flavored-slush dispenser. "Howdy. What can I do ya for?"

I hung back a few feet as Nick crossed to the counter. "I think my daughter Simone Hudson likes to come here and I wondered if she'd been by today."

The query locked up something in the man's expression. He pursed his lips, squinting. "Don't think I know that name. Lotta kids come in and out."

I understood his reluctance. Even if he had seen Simone, knew her, he could be stepping into someone else's troubles if he put two strangers on her trail.

He turned back to the machine. Nick's hands, at his sides, closed into fists. I reached for his elbow, thinking there was nothing for us here. But just as I made contact, one of the boys in the booth said, "Simone left with that jerk Bailey Jaspers." Then the same voice, louder: "What the fuck!"

Nick and I turned. The boys glared at each other across the table. I was pretty sure the one on the left, closest to us, was the one who had spoken. The other one cut his gaze at us, then back to his comrade. A warning kick under the table? The one who had spoken became intimately focused on the table before him. Nick crossed.

"How long ago?" he asked.

The boy went on staring at the table. He rapped an icon under the glass, a little harder than touch screens usually required. "Don't remember. After lunch sometime."

"We just saw them for a minute," said the other boy, his brown eyes determinedly candid. "We don't know her all that well."

There was a history here, one the second boy did not want us involved in. Nick's hands were clenching again. "Mind telling us your names?"

"What for?" said the second boy. "We don't know nothing."

I said to Nick's back, "I need to get to my meeting." I stifled what I was thinking: *This isn't the time or place.*

He looked back at me, then at the boys. He extracted a card and set it on the table. A crack almost too thin to hear fractured his voice. "I'm not sure where Simone is and I'm concerned about her. That's my home contact information. If you hear anything you think I need to know, please get in touch."

The boy looked at the card, but didn't pick it up. After a second he gave a noncommittal nod.

Nick wheeled. For a second I thought he'd forgotten I was standing there. But he stopped short of pushing past me and stepped aside so I could precede him. I beelined for the door. "Thank you," Nick said with careful cordiality to the man behind the counter.

"No problem," said the man.

Outside Nick opened the passenger door but held it. "I know Bailey Jaspers."

"If you want to go find him, I can get an Uber to go meet Peyton."

He frowned, his solemn gaze searching inward. "Peyton also knows Bailey."

"Is Bailey a danger?"

His hands worked on the doorframe. "I'd rather she would be with him than with Peyton."

From Peyton's calculating gaze as I negotiated with her on the street, I had an inkling of what he meant. "What do you want me to do?"

He slid into the driver's seat, gripped the wheel as if it might veer toward a ditch on its own. His phone rang. He answered, "Jesus. Honey, where are you? Your mom and I have been worried sick . . . what? What friend?"

He looked up at me blankly, listening. He spoke again, harshly. "That's not okay. I need to know where you are right now."

A long pause that made his grimace more painful by the second. "How long?" Under his dark hair his fair skin was ashen. More listening. "Simone, if you're not there when I get there, I will have the police show up at the Jaspers'. You don't want that, do you? You think Mr. and Ms. Jaspers will . . ." The grimace tightened ferociously. "You'd better be."

He smacked the phone on the console. I said, "What?"

"She says she's with some friend on her way to the Jaspers'. She wouldn't tell me where she is now. Says she'll be at the Jaspers' in an hour." He punched the ignition button. "We'll just see what little Bailey and his friends are up to."

The heat coming off him was making *me* sweat. "Nick . . . I don't think it's a good idea to go to these people's house like this."

"Like how?" He glared at me. "How am I supposed to go? All handshakes and smiles?"

I didn't want to unleash him on Peyton, either. But something had to supply the time to calm him. "You said you don't know where she is now. You have an hour. Let's go meet Peyton. She might tell us something about what happened between the girls and Eric. Like you said, about Simone."

He looked as if he'd forgotten Peyton. "You want me to come with you?"

"It's better than spending the half hour sitting in these Jaspers people's driveway. I mean, you'd have to take me back to my car anyway."

He was breathing so hard I wasn't sure he heard me. But he took a long slow gulp. "All right. We'll go meet Peyton."

"Hopefully have a reasonable conversation. Learn something."

"Yeah, I'll try to fucking behave myself," he said.

——————

Fortunately, the restaurant wasn't crowded, not at that time on a Sunday. We found a patio table and got out our phones. Nick spoke into his, wasting no breath on preambles. "I'm picking her up at Bailey Jaspers'." He listened. "I'd think you'd know these kids better than I do."

I focused on the screen in my hand. It had occurred to me we could learn something about Simone's and Peyton's circles by scrolling the pizza-place Facebook page.

Nick said into the phone, "We did that. She said she hadn't heard from her . . . I didn't have a Taser to torture it out of her. Call Lydia if you have to." A sigh. "If she calls you in the next half hour, for God's sake, call me."

He punched off his phone. I held up mine. "Look what I found."

We waded through images posted on Instagram and Facebook. Simone was tagged in several, her dark eyes crinkled above her sunny smiles. So were Peyton Eckstrom and Bailey Jaspers. Bailey was a stocky redhead with what looked like a good-natured grin. And there, crunched in among them all, was Corinne. I hunted the tiny image for signs of her coming fate. But she smiled easily at the camera, an arm around Peyton. They were all hooked together that way, all for one and one for all. Behind Corinne was another young man who looked a little older than the others, with flaxen-gold hair and wide-set eyes, a lot like Peyton. He grinned into the shot with his hands on Corinne's shoulders. I scrolled. Another shot lower down, again tagged with Corinne, named him: Cole Eckstrom. Peyton's brother? Yes, I could see that. Tall self-possession. "Do you know Peyton's brother?" I asked Nick.

He frowned. "I didn't know she had one. He must be in college."

I scrolled more but the young man didn't turn up again. "Interesting that both times he's close to Corinne."

"It could have been the same night."

"The dates are different, but that could just be when the pictures were posted." I looked closer. "These posts were Peyton's."

Nick's gaze had left the phone. "There she is."

The last two times I'd seen Peyton, she'd been flustered, caught off guard. This time she'd had a chance to work on the person she wanted us to see. Sleek in textured dark jeans, a layered white blouse, and elaborate sandals, Peyton crossed toward us as if we were meeting to discuss a corporate merger. A long-strapped white-leather purse swung from her shoulder. They all had looks, these upper-middle-class white girls I'd found myself in the midst of, but she was the one who would turn heads.

Still, her effort at sophisticated nonchalance seemed lost on Nick. He returned her radiant smile with a chilly frown as he held out a chair. She slung the purse on the chair back and turned to the table, but he cut off her silky moves to arrange herself. "What do you have to tell us?" he snapped.

She took a cool moment to look us over. I struggled to envision her sneaking onto our porch at midnight, spray-painting a crude warning. Maybe she'd sent stooges on that errand, girls who looked up to her, maybe even championed and protected her. After her appraising once-over, she faced me, her voice smooth in the subdued atmosphere. "So who have you told?"

Young as she was, she made me choose my words with care. "I've told the police. They're investigating a suspicious death that may involve Eric and they needed to know what you said."

She blinked. "Whose death?"

"Celia Monahan's."

A waiter walked into this strained moment. With that luminous smile, Peyton asked for a diet soda. The waiter left. Peyton twisted quickly to unzip the white purse. She took out a tube of lip gloss, slightly scented with cherry; she applied the gloss, then returned the tube to the purse. She looked back up at me, every movement as deliberate as strokes in a painting. A long blink. "I didn't know."

Kids her age probably didn't watch the news. So she truly might not have heard about Celia. "The police know you were following her around."

A faint hitch in her voice betrayed her, the lines of her careful grown-up image blurring. "We didn't hurt anybody."

"Corinne got hurt."

"Corinne!" A burst of theatrics cracked her composure. "I didn't have anything to do with Corinne." She jerked the purse strap onto her shoulder. "I didn't come here to be accused of stuff."

"So what did you come here for?" Nick said.

She gave a little jump that twisted her around to face him. "Eric didn't know everything about that woman. He thought she loved him. But I know things about her he doesn't."

Nick waited, so still he might have been made of painted china. He barely glanced up when the diet soda arrived.

"You can tell Eric," Peyton hissed, picking up the glass, "that Celia has a secret lover. She goes to him every day."

My first thought was that she had seen Celia rendezvousing with Nick. But in that case, she'd have recognized him. "Who?" I asked.

She sucked her lips in. Her gaze went from audacious to veiled. "I don't think I'm going to tell you that."

Nick stared at her so intently, so rigidly, that I thought that if I thumped him, he'd shatter. I wasn't sure what he was thinking, but my own mind had taken a speculative turn. Franklin? "Peyton, Celia Monahan died under suspicious circumstances. It may turn out to be murder. Now you have given me new information that might have some bearing on her death. I have no choice but to share it with the police."

Another blink. Those long blinks seemed conscious, an effort to reset the space between us. I toughened my voice. "I think it would be a very good idea if you went home right now and told your parents what you've been doing, what happened, what you know or don't know. They'll be able to decide how to help you deal with the police."

We all sat for a long moment. She set the glass own, drew a line in the condensation with a coral-tipped finger. "I'll just say I made it up."

"If you truly think that's the best solution."

She tugged on the strap of her bag, twisted it. Nick said, "Why did Simone go with Bailey Jaspers?"

"Who?"

"Bailey Jaspers."

"Oh." She reduced Bailey Jaspers to a cool shrug. "He's just a guy I see sometimes at school. I have no idea what he's doing with Simone."

A knot was forming in my chest. We'd needed to learn what Peyton could tell us, but to get it, we were taking immense responsibility for the well-being of this girl. What should I do, what could I do, about her parents? Diana hadn't believed me when I told her what her child was doing; would they?

What bothered me even more was my own focus: not on what she needed, no; on what her news about Eric and about Celia meant to *me*. Celia had a secret lover. She betrayed Eric. What could I do with this news? *Grill her*, said Raging Sarah. As always it took effort to slap a muzzle on Raging Sarah. I slid my chair back.

"Peyton," I said, "I know you know some things about me and about Eric. You know that what I've accused him of is serious, and so is your accusation. I mean what I said, you must talk to your parents. I hope that you—and they—will give the police any information that might have any bearing on any of this." I stood, for that brief moment feeling taller than she was. "Thank you for coming."

She slammed her chair back and rose to face me. "You!" Her color rose. Nick jumped up between us, looking back and forth. "You can stop him by believing me and by making the police believe me. Instead you're calling me a liar. You must love him, too, don't you? Well, he molested Corinne and that's why she killed herself, if you really want to know." She cast a glance at a few discreetly cocked heads at nearby tables. When she spun back to me, slinging her bag to her shoulder, she was archly smiling. "I can't wait to talk to the police. I can't wait to tell them how you've *protected* him."

She strode off, her cool grace curdled to fury. Nick looked at me. "That's heartbreaking," he said.

To my relief he sounded calmer. Now I was the one whose heart was racing. "She's caught up in emotions she doesn't understand."

For the briefest moment his hand brushed my wrist. "You did the right thing, telling her to talk to her parents."

The touch left no marks. For that I was thankful. Our partnership could not have handled more turmoil. We were burdened with enough.

36

The drive to this Bailey Jaspers' felt very long.

I didn't share Nick's faith that Simone would keep the appointment she'd committed to. "If Simone's at this boy's house and she decides she doesn't want to go home with you, she'll hide when she sees your car."

He chewed his upper lip. "She said she'd be here."

"Still, I'd suggest not parking right in front of the house."

"Hopefully his parents will be there."

Our luck wasn't in. No parents to keep things civilized.

Instead, when we climbed up the steep drive to the sprawling house on an almost vertical lot with a view over Lake Austin, the teenaged boy I recognized from the Facebook pages opened the door to our rings. If Simone was there, she'd had plenty of time to head out the back: a highly visible doorbell camera had recorded our approach. The boy—Bailey—blocked the door with his chunky teen-aged body, his sun-streaked auburn hair falling into clear brown eyes under assertive brows. "Simone changed her mind. She doesn't want to talk to you."

"She's here, then." If Nick felt relief, it didn't drain the tension from his body.

"Yeah, but you can't come in." The brown eyes flicked to me, held for a second. I thought, *he knows who I am*. He turned back to Nick. "I'll give her a message."

"Bailey, she's still sixteen, she's a minor," said Nick. There was no yield in his voice. "Your parents can explain to you the legal ramifications of preventing me from seeing her. For example, sheltering a runaway. Are they home?"

Bailey's youth betrayed him. He stepped back, then pushed forward again, gripping the door hard. "She's okay. She's here because she wants to be. We're not making her stay."

"We?" Nick said.

Shadows moved behind Bailey. A taller figure stepped into the space over the boy's shoulder and took the door from him, opening it wider: an older, blond young man, early twenties, his striking resemblance to Peyton even clearer than in the Facebook posts. He said, "What seems to be the trouble here?"

I don't often use the expression "What balls!", but I did so then, under my breath. Cole Eckstrom knew perfectly well what the trouble was. The way he eased Bailey aside, as if we grown-ups could come to a rational understanding, just plain rubbed me wrong.

But I bit back my hmmpf of indignation. Nick said, "You're Peyton's brother, that right?"

The young man appraised him coolly. "Cole Eckstrom. I assume you're Simone's father." He held out his hand.

Nick didn't take it. Cole withdrew it with a casual shrug. "Tell you what," he said cheerfully. "Wait here a second. Hang in there, Bailey." He disappeared into the shadows beyond the door.

Bailey eyed us, clinging to the door as if it needed his support. "She's okay," he said again.

Nick clamped his lips together, rocking back on his heels, chest out. Bailey glanced nervously over his shoulder at a sound behind him, then opened the door wide.

In the hallway beyond, Simone stood in the arch of Cole's arm, crying, a hand on her mouth, the other arm folded across her waist. Nick strode right into the house, forcing Bailey out of his path. It took Cole the briefest of seconds to step aside. Nick wrapped Simone in his arms, rocking her gently. He spoke to her, but I couldn't make out his words.

"I assure you," Cole said with that air of commanding everything around him, "she's been perfectly safe here. Perfectly okay." He touched the back of her pony tail.

Nick swung her away, giving her no chance to protest. "Let's go, honey. You don't have to go to Mom's right now. We'll go to the apartment." He ushered her toward me. "Do you have everything? Your purse? Your phone?"

She shook her head. "I'll get her stuff," said Bailey hurriedly. He darted into a side room and returned with a small blue-leather bag. Simone took it, fumbling. I stepped out of the way. Bailey looked back at Cole, who gave another expressionless shrug.

Simone didn't resist as her father guided her down the driveway and around the curve to where we'd left the car. She slid into the front seat, grappling with her seatbelt; I let myself into the back behind her. She twisted and stared over her shoulder as if she hadn't seen me until then, and maybe she hadn't. Her father climbed behind the wheel and she spun to him. "What's she doing here?"

——————

It was an unpleasant drive home.

Simone telegraphed her utter disapproval of my presence by staring rigidly ahead, ignoring her father when he gave her long, worried glances. He waited until we'd almost reached the lot where I'd left my car before he spoke to her. "Are you hungry?" She shook her head. He reached toward her but she tucked her hands into her armpits. "What happened, honey? Did you have a fight with your mom?"

She shook her head again, with a withering glance back at me. "We'll talk later, okay?" Nick said.

When he pulled up beside my car near the gallery where our odyssey had started and I opened my door to get out, he draped an arm on the seat back behind Simone and said, "Thank you. The support meant a lot."

Back at home, I settled cross-legged on the couch as if I could calm myself by faking meditation. No meditative mood ensued.

Instead, I considered grumpily what I had done to make Simone so sullen. Okay, right, tattling. I had sicced the police on her. I pondered. Tattling, withholding evidence. Which was the graver sin?

I'd already decided that whether or not I believed Peyton had no bearing on my duty to report what she'd told us at the restaurant to Clauson. I left a message on his voice mail, telling him I had learned new things he might want to know. New things about Celia, I carefully clarified, since she was the one he was investigating—as usual, not Eric. But sitting there alone with the information, I turned it over and over in my mind. Had Peyton seen this lover? Had she seen Celia and, say, Franklin, in an intimate situation? Or maybe Peyton was reporting Celia's doctor or her therapist or the fitness coach she went to every day.

I still hadn't pumped Nick on my speculations about how Celia lived. She couldn't possibly live off Eric; the Eric I knew was profligate to a fault. The possibility of another man in the woodwork, this mysterious Franklin or whoever, offered answers. She was young and attractive. Why not?

I gave up sitting cross-legged; my feet had gone to sleep. I avoided the wine cabinet, heating water for chamomile tea. Taking down a mug took me past the refrigerator. Where many women my age would have tacked up photos of their children, I had posted photos of Eric and Celia that Russell had sent me. Among them was one of Celia by herself, climbing from her Audi before a house fronted by a low sandstone wall.

I stood with mug in hand considering her slim figure sharp against the wall, with a wide residential street beyond her. I thought, *hmmmm.*

I poured my hot water, dunked in my infuser, and crossed to my computer. I called up the Eric-and-Celia photo files.

My vague memory hadn't misled me. Of the eight shots in my collection of Celia alone, three others showed her in front of that wall, in one case stepping through a breach onto a driveway. Another showed her bent over her phone on the street before the wall, walking toward the driveway opening, the house itself beyond her. I went through the full set of photos. None with Celia and Eric together could be construed as anywhere near that house or that wall.

The house was nothing extraordinary: two-story, a half-moon driveway rounding up before tall, dark-tinted windows under wide eaves blocking the Texas sun. Scraggy but graceful scrub oaks provided meager shade. A few yuccas and some bristly grass completed the tidy landscaping. To the left was a single-car garage. The stone wall, almost chest-high and a bit imposing, was the only distinguishing feature. It gave the house a barricaded, forbidding look.

Suddenly I wanted nothing more than to find this house where the cameras had caught Celia in some solitary haunting. But how? The photos from Russell's team had date stamps but no locations; it had occurred to me to wonder what he thought Raging Sarah might do with information like that. I shot him an email with the relevant dates, as no-big-deal as I could make it, asking if he had the GPS data for those pictures. But hitting "send" didn't calm me. I wanted to find that place. Go to it. Now.

37

I had thrown my share of tantrums over the way technology consumed and controlled and disappointed us. But that day it didn't let me down. I bent over the four relevant photos: one from across the wide, two-lane street showed a number beside the front door. Zooming in blurred the resolution so that I couldn't be sure if the number was 4366 or 4368. I scoured the shots that showed the streets, hoping for a visible sign. No luck.

I turned to my maps app and pulled up the full digital map of Austin overlaid with the boundaries and names of its sections and outlying appendages. I typed 4366 into the search box.

Good girl, little app. The number produced a short list of hits, street addresses beginning with 4366. The first two were in Round Rock, a community northwest of Austin. So the app understood it was Austin I was interested in. The others ranged from someplace in Oklahoma to Nevada to Boston. I hadn't spent much time in Round Rock, but from what I remembered, its leafy residential neighborhoods were possibles. I wrote down the addresses, then tried 4368.

This time my haul included two addresses closer to town. I plugged the first into the search box. Not that far from me, in Hyde Park, but the house I was after didn't fit the Hyde Park I knew. I tried the second address, 4368 Woodridge Avenue. Clicked on the street-view thumbnail. And there it was.

The neighborhood lay just beyond the curve of the river in a municipality attached to the greater Austin sprawl. In the online pictures, dated three years before the dates on my Celia pictures, the roof of a silver SUV was visible above the wall. A spin of my view showed a small park a few doors down on the other side of the street. The images confirmed my first impression: the wall discouraged anyone who might want to stroll up and knock on the door.

I was plotting my route to the house when I jumped at the chirp of my phone.

It was Clauson. I'd left a message, planning to tell him about Peyton and her claim about Celia's secret lover. He must value my various revelations more than he let on, at least enough to return my calls.

Technically, I now had even more news for him. But if I told him about this place Celia regularly went without Eric, he'd order me not to go there.

If I didn't tell him, I'd be obstructing his investigation.

I let Clauson's call go to voice mail. Maybe there was a benign word to replace "obstructing" if the obstruction didn't go on too long.

———————

At the house I drove past slowly. Not too slowly. My encounter with Peyton had alerted me to how suspicious creeping back and forth on a quiet street could look.

Only one or two cars passed me on the peaceful residential boulevard. I turned around in a side street a couple of blocks farther on and pulled up to the curb on the opposite side of the road.

The house did indeed set itself off from its neighbors, not just with its wall but also with a privacy fence framing it on both sides. I stepped out of my car so I could peer over the wall at heavy shutters bordering big dark windows on either side of a dark-painted double door. The garage door to the left of the house was closed. The only departure from the photos was a For-Sale-By-Owner sign beside the driveway breach in the wall.

I photographed the sign. No telling how long it had been there. If the house was connected to Celia, it might be recent. Very recent. *Your lover falls to her death so you decide to get out of Dodge?*

I settled into my car seat, wishing it reclined far enough to hide me. I concocted lies for Clauson. I'd been . . . somewhere? . . . when he called. Driving? I'd passed this house by accident, recognized it from the photos . . .

Another half hour or so surely wouldn't add more than a month or two to my time in the slammer. Maybe the stars would align in that half hour and I'd see this lover. Maybe I'd recognize the man who'd tried to break into my office. Find out whether Peyton had been at least partially right.

But no such good fortune prevailed. After forty minutes I could feel Clauson's cold hand on my neck and hear the door of my jail cell clanking. I reached to start the car.

My phone chirped. A text. From Russell.

"The address you wanted is 4368 Woodridge," he wrote, fortunately not asking why I was asking. If he knew I was lurking here in full stalking mode, he'd surely tell me to call in Clauson. "I'm sending a couple of more recent photos of the location you might find useful. Hope they help."

Bazinga. Two of the three new pics showed a man climbing from a low-slung slate-blue car in front of the garage. In the third, he stood just inside the wall with Celia, their heads close.

These had date stamps from the week before her death and before Clauson showed me the dagger photos. I wrote back a quick "Thank you!"

I zoomed in, getting a good look at the guy. Not my intruder: this man was in his early thirties, I'd guess, slender, more "cute" than handsome, with strong cheekbones, a full mouth, and tousled hair on the amber side. He wore a taupe shirt, fashionable slacks, and from what I could see, sandals without socks. He wore a heavy gold watch but, as best I could tell, no wedding band.

On the whole he was more nondescript than Eric, more off-the-male-model-shelf, and less controlling of the space around him than Nick. I studied the picture that included Celia. I couldn't call the relationship it showed intimate, but she was certainly interested in whatever he had to say.

My phone rang. Clauson again. Damn.

For lack of any more excuse for delaying, I answered. He snapped, "Where the hell are you?"

How did the man know? Did my phone tell him? I made what seemed like the only feasible decision. "I'm sitting outside 4368 Woodridge in Rollingwood, hoping to get a look at the guy who presumably lives here."

"What the hell for?"

"I've been told he's another of Celia's lovers."

"By whom?"

"Got ten minutes?" I asked.

———

There were no laws against Nick and me getting information from Peyton; we'd been legitimately searching for Simone. So all Clauson could do was snarl like a dog guarding a bone. I suspected that if and when he needed Simone and Peyton to talk, he'd have ways of making it happen. But when I asked whether Celia's death had been officially declared a homicide, he snapped, "When we know, you'll see it on the news."

Grrr. I needed to hang up before I said what I was on the verge of saying.

"You'll send me those pictures. All of them," he said.

"Sure."

"And by the way, professor, this girl's dad you're running around with, I'd be careful. From what you've told me, it sounds as if the two of you are taking a lot on yourselves."

"Thank you for the advice," I said. And punched "end call" hard.

Fifteen minutes before, I'd been ready to call it a day, for now at least, and head home. But "running around with"? I folded my arms and glared across the street as if by sheer will power I could levitate it off its foundations and shed light on what slimy things lived underneath. I was still sitting there, concocting lines for knocking on a stranger's door so late on a Sunday, when the guy saved me from myself by coming home.

He pulled into the driveway, stopping before the closed garage. The blue car was a low-slung sporty model whose make I couldn't distinguish in the fading light. He climbed out, a computer case over one shoulder; the garage door trundled open, and he disappeared inside. As the door wound shut behind him, I made out a sports coat over a light-colored shirt, no tie.

My hand was on my door handle, my weight shifted for a sprint across the street. But before I could open the door, a big black car purred up the road and pulled to the curb almost directly opposite me. I didn't recognize either of the two bulky, dark-suited men who climbed out and marched past the wall to the recessed front door. Within seconds the door opened. I sat forward to see. The men offered up small card-sized cases I couldn't help interpreting as folds for badges. The man in the house opened the door wider. They all went inside.

Something else I would see on the news? Or did the FBI have their own cable channel to which people like me couldn't subscribe?

After barely ten minutes, the two men emerged. The young man watching them from the doorway actually waved in farewell.

I wound my hands around the steering wheel to keep from beating on it. What had the FBI asked him? What lines had he fed them? I hadn't pried my fingers loose when, instead of getting into the black car, the driver crossed the street, directly to me.

He stopped beside my window and made a circular motion with a finger. I clamped my teeth on the inappropriate comments wanting their freedom and let the window down.

"Are you Sarah Crockett?" he said.

I nodded.

He put his meaty hands on my door, on my open window, and leaned toward me. "Dr. Crockett, you need to go on home."

"It's a public street."

"There's a statute against stalking."

"I'm not stalking. This is the first time I've ever been here."

"Don't make it a habit."

This wasn't the FBI. This was Clauson inviting me to picture the inside of a cell.

"All right, I won't," I said. I made myself add, "Thank you."

He sighed and straightened. "The lieutenant said he'd call you in the morning."

I wanted to say, "Oh, goody." Instead I said, "Good."

He waited until I started the car, stepping back to let me ease into the sparse traffic. How did they know I planned to drive around the block and pull up to get the license number off the sporty car the guy had been driving? They followed me all the way home.

38

That evening, the TV news gave me six seconds on Celia. "Police are still calling this tragedy a death investigation." The Internet gave me nothing. I scrolled to Nick's number, ending up in voice mail. I said, "Call me. I've got news."

I curled into a tight ball on my couch, repeating and repeating what I would say—or rather, what Raging Sarah would say—to Clauson. *You owe me. You've had my child's case for six years. Now you've got a murder. I've given you information about that murder. You owe me. You owe me for the six years you've done nothing, and for what I've given you.*

That's how it piled up, spasms of anger spiked with some very bad words.

No telling how long I might have lain there if I hadn't left my wicker kitchen chair too close to the counter. Will I never learn? "Good Alice, good Alice," she was saying, with ominous little clicks between her words. I staggered upright and wove toward the sounds. I had long ago learned not to leave dangerous objects or unsafe foods on most surfaces, so I didn't fear for her safety as much as for my newly purchased store of fruit.

As well I might. "Bad Alice!" But she couldn't be blamed for locating a beautifully ripe banana laid right across her path. Or rather, three of them. She'd apparently been checking to see which one was sweetest. It seemed they must all be equally sweet, given the egalitarian destruction she'd wrought. When I invited her onto my sleeve to ride back to her cage, she scorned me. Only when I carried the bowl across the room could I lure her with a slimy pre-chewed piece of fruit. I shut the door on her a bit reluctantly. I'd been glad of the interruption.

I sat down at the computer for a dogged return to what so far had been a futile effort to find a link between Anna and any of the girls. Ms. Vanhoven—Audrey—did not seem to have an online presence.

Searches had not produced her on Facebook, Instagram, Tik Tok, LinkedIn, or anywhere else I knew to look. Various apps assured me they could connect me to her for twenty-five dollars. I even tried several, learning of Audrey Vanhovens in Colorado and Vancouver but not, so far, in Austin. Could I be spelling her name wrong?

Why didn't Nick call? I hoped his evening with Simone had gone peacefully. Nothing I could do to help unless he asked.

I pushed away from the computer and tried to get my head around it all. Two girls, Corinne and Simone, driven to despair. My own remembered angst at being excluded from the beautiful, popular cliques had not driven me to such extremes. Not that I could really look to my own experiences for answers. I'd been pretty far out on the fringes, a female nerd, more interested in books than in dressing up. And I hadn't had the funds to wear the chic outfits and the boutique shoes. Simone, though, was a sleek contender, circling the inner sanctum. The reminders of failure would sting in that rarefied space. Especially since it was already laced with her quarreling parents' pain.

That night, exhausted by my helplessness, I finally slept. I woke fairly late Monday from a dream that the police had come to take me away for thinking disobedient thoughts, only to find that the shriek in my ears was only Alice's siren imitation. I freed her and cleaned her cage, managed to force down some oatmeal and some rescued banana. It was ten when the phone rang.

I jumped for it. Not Nick. Clauson. Oh, yeah, I'd been promised a call.

"You okay there, professor?" he asked.

"Depends," I said. Fractured sleep didn't improve my temper.

"You'll hear it on the news. We're upgrading the investigation to a homicide."

I could have told him they would. "Why?"

"The news will have the information we can release."

I traced a circle on the breakfast table with a tense finger. Beyond Peyton's claim, the details of our search for Nick's daughter were not mine to share. I focused on what I knew was connected to Celia's death and now, officially, her murder. "Maybe you have some news for me about that house?"

He sighed. "I'm telling you this so maybe you'll mind your own business. Nobody there's likely to be a murderer. Or to know anything about the murder."

"In the pictures—"

"You mean the ones you haven't sent me?"

"Yeah, you'll see she went there an awful lot to be visiting a casual acquaintance."

"So when I get them, I guess I can check, right?"

"Sorry, I've been . . ." Worrying about a girl in trouble. "This guy who lives in that house. Did you ask if he knows Eric?"

"I didn't ask him anything. I'll look at the full report."

"And did anyone ask him when he put the house up for sale?"

A silence. "What does that have to do with anything?"

"Be interesting if it was the morning he found out about the murder." I indulged in a moment of tart silence. "Wouldn't it?"

"Oh, yeah. The Sarah Crockett imagination."

The overwrought Sarah Crockett imagination that had already uncovered more about Celia Monahan than he had. "The last time we pitted my imagination against your logic, who won?"

I had a few such small, sweet moments. Paper rustling, chair creaking. "If you harass this guy, it'll be stalking."

"You're the one I'm going to be harassing," I said, and hung up.

———————

I had texted Nick after hanging up on Clauson. A terse answer. *Hanging in there. Will call.* A clear message freeing me to go about our business on my own. Now, in the buzz of my new find, I decided to postpone my pursuit of Audrey Vanhoven until I saw where this Celia's-lover lead took me, an assignment that would take me back to 4368 Woodridge. And might require a dye job. Or a wig.

Yesterday I'd done some basic research, searching online For-Sale-by-Owner sites. And found it. The real-estate listing first appeared the day after Celia died. So it had been posted the morning of her fall. The day of Eric's conference. To which he barely arrived on time.

Had I provoked Clauson into doing the same search? If so, maybe, just maybe, he'd take my discovery of the house more seriously once he saw that date. Maybe he'd already ordered detectives back there. Maybe they'd be watching for me, reporting my transgressions. No point in a wig they'd see right through.

I did take the precaution of parking just past the little park that lay across the street. The road had picked up a bit of Monday morning traffic. No official-looking cars among the few nudged along the curbs.

I mimed a meandering stroll down a pebbled walkway into the park. Today it was occupied. Two women sat on a bench facing a scattering of playground equipment, their backs to me. A man in a blue windbreaker and gray ball cap sat on a second bench across from them, elbows on knees. Two boys, five or so, and a younger girl clambered on the gym equipment, their shrill shouts reaching me across a stretch of sparse grass.

So I couldn't station myself in the park. Or wander around for long. If the police showed up, they'd ask these people if they'd noticed anyone suspicious. Like nondescript brown-haired female loiterers such as myself.

Hands in my jeans pockets, I sauntered a few steps farther along the sidewalk, pretending to study the FSBO sign outside 4368. The threesome might take me for a buyer interested in the house. But the women focused on the man, whose hunched, attentive posture made me wonder what kind of urgent goods he was selling. The women, in contrast, looked stiff, almost leaning away from the man.

I edged onto the park grass, but couldn't overhear the conversation. Even at the distance, though, I could tell the women weren't nannies. One had sleek straight hair pulled back at the base of her neck, the kind of blond that takes maintenance, and the other wore a shorter chestnut do nicely puffed into a slick helmet, a chic scarf around her neck.

Though I couldn't see much of his face, the man didn't look like a drug dealer or a panhandler. What then was worrying the women? Blondie glanced away from the conversation at a shriek from one of the boys, who perched atop the sliding board in what looked to be an unwise position, but she turned back to the man, locking into whatever he was saying. The man reached up to adjust his ball cap. And then I knew.

And had one sane choice. Back the hell out of there and call the police.

I groped for my phone, hit Clauson's speed dial number, putting the phone to my ear. My motion must have caught the man's eye. He looked up, his gaze snagging on mine. Even at the distance, I saw his eyes narrow, his mouth tighten. He knew me, too.

It was the man who'd peered into my office window that night.

His gaze slid back to the women. Redhead cut a glance over her shoulder at me, frowning. The man flashed her a smile. I got Clauson's voice mail. "I'm at the house on Woodridge. The man who tried to break into Tremaine is here. Send someone."

The man stood. He didn't look at me. He smiled at the women again. He touched the brim of the ball cap and turned to cut across the grass toward the street, away from me.

I moved. My angle would intercept him before he reached the curb. Surely he'd run. But no. He just glanced at me and kept walking. I felt the women's gazes at my back. "You!" I said to the man, a quick jog getting me in front of him. "Why were you trying to break into my office? What are you doing here?"

He stopped, giving me the gentlest, most bewildered of smiles. "Excuse me?"

I should call 911. And tell them what? "You tried to break into my office in Tremaine Hall on the Cresthill campus last week. I saw you. I'd know you anywhere."

And I would. His most discernible features, now that I saw him in daylight, were still the puglike nose but also eyebrows thin enough to be drawn on and a broad flat mouth that opened on a hedge of uneven lower teeth in his dry smile. The hat covered his hair; all I could note were the slightly graying temples. It was not a menacing face, just immobile, the only touch of life the quick snap of small, searching brown eyes.

"You've mistaken me for someone else," he said. So mild. The eyes darted to the women, and the smile took on a twist of pity. "I'm sure you don't mean to be making a false accusation. Now if you'll excuse me . . ."

He stepped past me. I swiveled. Damn. No police racing up to help me. Raging Sarah grabbed his windbreaker sleeve.

He looked down at her hand where it twisted in the cloth.

"Take your hand off me," he said.

Raging Sarah didn't. "I called the police."

He looked past me at the women. I didn't look around at them. His gaze came back to me. I said, "You're George Franklin. You know about Celia."

The eyebrows shot up. "Miss . . . Whoever. I don't know anyone named Celia. Your . . ." he looked at my hand again, "assault won't persuade me that I do."

I let go of the sleeve, Raging Sarah surrendering. But not entirely. "I know about the FBI. They investigate missing children. What do you know about that?"

His hard little eyes barely shifting from me, he pulled a phone from a pocket and tapped. Was *he* calling 911 now? I hoped so. But he said, with a flat smile, "If you called the police, they should be here any minute, correct?"

"Any minute." I pulled out my own phone. It was maddeningly inert.

"I'm going to walk to the next corner to meet a car that's coming for me," he said. "If the police arrive before it does, please point me out. If they don't, you'll have to excuse me. I have a full day ahead."

Again he looked past me toward the woman, then turned.

My hands—Raging Sarah's—grappled toward him, but they closed on air. He had barely covered the hundred yards to the corner when a massive Lincoln pulled up and stopped. "Have a nice day," he said as he opened the passenger-side door and folded himself in.

39

I stood trembling. My helpless rage was still smoking when I finally let myself turn around.

The women were staring. They had their phones out, their children clutched to them. I took a step toward them. They shrank back.

"You were here last night," the blond woman said.

I found my voice. "Yes."

"With police," said the redhead.

"Yes."

"Who are you?" the blonde said.

I glanced back at the house. It sat silent, windows shadowed, door closed. Had these women made their own 911 calls? I turned to their hostile frowns. "My name is Sarah Crockett." How to reassure them, win them? "A woman was murdered. I know she had a connection to this house. She also had a connection to something vitally important to me." I had the child card as well as my trusty dagger card, but I would not spend them until I had to. "That man tried to break into my office. I need to know who he is and what he has to do with this house."

The women looked at each other. "I told you so," Redhead said.

I folded my shoulders in to look nonthreatening. "If you know anything, you could be a big help to me."

Blondie drew her children even closer. Redhead anchored the other boy close with a grip on his wrist. Blondie said, "So you don't know that man?"

"I was hoping you knew."

A pregnant shared glance. The blonde tossed her shiny hair. "He wanted to know all about the house, too."

I took another step. This time they didn't cower. "Do you mind telling me what there is to know?"

"Well . . ." began the redhead.

"We don't know anything," the blonde supplied.

Over my shoulder the house still held onto its secrets, walled in. "I saw the young man last night. Do you know who he is?"

The redhead gestured toward the bench where the man I thought was Franklin had sat. "*That* man was trying to scare us. He acted like he was official and there could be a danger to local children and we should be watching what was going on." She nodded toward the blonde. "Donna finally asked him if he was police. He didn't exactly say no."

"Are you police?" Donna—the blonde—asked.

I extracted pictures from my jeans pocket. Celia and Eric at an art show, Celia and Eric wheeling their bikes across the river greenbelt, Celia and Eric hoisting pints at a sidewalk brewery. "Six years ago, someone took my daughter from me. For six years, the police have been trying to find out who. So far, the only one who's learned anything at all is me." I held out the pictures across the still-wide distance between us. "Have you seen *this* man?"

Redhead wanted to see the pictures. With her wide-eyed child still clamped to her side, she edged away from her companion toward me, tilting her head as she drew close. "It looks like the realtor," she said.

"The realtor?"

Donna hiked her pale brows. The redhead took the pictures from me. "I'm not kidding. That looks for all the world like the man who helped Brendan put out the For-Sale sign the other day."

I quieted my hands, crushing them together. Redhead offered the pictures to Donna, who shook her head. "I didn't see that."

"I'm almost certain," the redhead said.

My breath had caught somewhere behind my lungs. "What day?"

"The day she got killed. You know, that morning. I did think it was odd."

I let the pent-up breath out slowly. "If the police should ask you—"

"Seriously, Gail, this isn't a good idea at all," Donna said.

A hint of a flush rose in her friend's face. But she held on to the pictures.

"We really don't know anything about this," Donna said. She turned to Gail. "You certainly don't want to have to testify in a murder trial or something. At least not without talking it over with Doug. At least not till we know what's going on."

"Well . . ."

Donna turned to me. "What did you say your name was?"

"Sarah Crockett."

"I think we should Google all this." Donna's kids had busied themselves in the grass at her feet. "Jeffrey, Katelyn. Time to go."

"I'm making soldiers," said the boy, offering a leaf impaled with a twig.

"You can make soldiers at home. Let's go."

"Really," said Gail, "if I did see someone connected with a murder, I think I should tell the police about it. Of course, if I had to *swear*—"

"Jeffrey!" said Donna. "Put those leaves down. Now."

She took an arm and lifted the boy to his feet. The little girl stayed sitting, picking up her own leaves. By the time Donna reached for her hand, she had a crumbly collection.

"I think you better talk to Doug," Donna said to Gail. She turned to me.

"There's definitely something going on. First that man, and now you. And Brendan, who moved in here out of nowhere and who everybody barely knows. At first I thought he was just busy with whatever he does, he certainly doesn't seem to be keeping regular hours like he's working, he could be doing *anything*." She hooked an arm around the boy, dusted the little girl's hands. "And her. Yeah, I saw that on TV. Coming and going, most of the time at night when he's not even there." She herded the children before her toward the sidewalk. "So I just think we ought to be careful." She looked back one last time. "I'm sorry about your daughter," she said.

"Oh, I am, too." Gail peered down distractedly at her son, who was offering a handful of dirt for her inspection. "I see, honey. In a minute." She waved the picture. "Can I keep these?"

"Yes. Of course."

"If I can . . . I don't know. I definitely should talk to my husband."

"Yes."

"Let's leave the dirt here," she told her little boy. "You can play with it some more tomorrow." Her smile to me was rueful. "Must be nice to get so much fun out of so little." I nodded choppily. For a second she hesitated, as if she thought she ought to reach out and touch me. "I hope it turns out okay. So terrible."

"Yes. It is."

She rose. As she took a step to leave, she stopped. A marked police car pulled up to the curb. She looked back at me, eyes widening. The uniformed officers, a man and a woman, emerged. The woman advanced toward us. "Dr. Crockett?"

"Yes." Oh, sigh. Not again.

"The lieutenant sent us to get you." Her questioning gaze flicked to Gail, back to me. "Should I tell him you're coming?"

I crossed toward her, leaving Gail watching. *Am I ever*, I breathed.

40

This time we didn't chat in his office. This time he stood over me in an interrogation room.

I sat primly, waiting. He sighed. "You can't keep doing this."

Every time I saw this man, an unbidden word ran through my mind: *work*. This man worked. He spent himself daily. Sometimes what he worked at gave him no pleasure. As now. He knew I needed something his work could not give me. I saw the ache in him, a helpless hurt inside.

I couldn't spare pity. "I was on a public street, in a public space, talking to people who were willing to talk to me. If these actions are crimes, please arrest me. Then my legal options will be clear."

He ran a thick hand over his pink face. "I don't want to arrest you. I'm worried you're going to make me." He jerked out the chair opposite me, plunked into it. "Every acquaintance Monahan had won't end up being a suspect. You need evidence tying that house or that guy who lives there to the murder."

"I have evidence," I said.

I reminded him about the man I'd seen at my office, about seeing him at the house, and filled him in on the man's intimations and probing with Donna and Gail. I reported as well on the mysterious "Brendan" who lived there. About Celia coming there when Brendan was absent, and at night. About Eric, late to his prestigious conference because he was hammering in a For-Sale sign.

He put a hand to his chin, tapped his pinched mouth with a forefinger. "You showed this woman Eric's picture? That contaminates her testimony. She's primed to identify him."

"You would never in a million years have thought to call in Brendan's neighbors to see a line-up with Eric's picture in it."

He dipped his head. I took the dip for a nod.

I thought of offering some kind of reconciliation, an acknowledgement that I was getting places he was not because I could afford a single-minded focus on this one case when for him it was one duty among many. But the fact was, I was running down information because I knew who to chase. I'd been offering that knowledge for six years.

He pushed back to his feet again, with a low grunt, as if standing took effort. "We'll take this all into account."

"Either he killed her," I persisted, looking up at him, "or someone told him something had happened while he was on his way to the conference. Either way, he delayed taking off for San Antonio to do things he considered urgent. Maybe he went by her home. Maybe someone there talked to him or saw him." I rose to face him. Apparently I was free to do so. "I'm going to check public records to see who owns that house."

"Public records will tell you that guy Brendan owns it. Brendan Brightwell."

"And did you ask him why he's selling all of a sudden? After what, six months?"

His face twitched in exasperation. "Maybe he doesn't like Texas weather."

We faced each other across the table. I felt as weary as he looked. "You won't help me," I said.

He spun away, veered back, thumbs in his waistband, fingers dug into his palms. "Dr. Crockett, if you are right about Eric Wyles, one day a piece of information will surface and we will know it. The expression 'smoking gun' means something." He raised a hand to block interruption. "Maybe this woman's claim about seeing Wyles will pan out. But I don't know yet, and neither do you."

"So you'll talk to her?"

"We'll look into it."

"You can't risk a yes?"

"Anything I tell you is a risk."

So there we stood, that thick wall still and always between us. I picked up my bag. "Are you waiting for me to tell you when the next person gets murdered?"

His lips tightened. He crossed to the door and opened it. "Just don't let it be you."

———————

It was well past three. I hadn't even thought to be hungry. No time now to stop for food, comforting or otherwise. Kendra and I were meeting at the Flawn Academic Center, once the undergraduate library on the University of Texas campus, now a state-of-the-art digital-resource and research lab. She'd been reading up on "writing stuff" and she wanted me to vet some books she might check out online.

Since her willingness to spend time looking for books on writing provided a data point on her progress as a "willing" writer, I needed more excuse than my morning's adventures to break our appointment. So I gobbled a half-smashed cheeseburger dripping with ketchup behind my steering wheel and mimed "chipper" and "attentive" when she joined me at a study station.

She logged in using her account as a research participant. The titles she called up on the online catalogue didn't surprise me: the canon of "how to write well." "They look boring as shit," she said. "But that's what I got when I put in, 'learn to write.'"

They hadn't been boring to me when I'd encountered them at just about her age. But then I'd been in love with words and eager to tame them. Kendra was just starting to discover that she could manner words if never quite domesticate them. It had just begun to occur to her that the "likes" she craved for her fan-fiction could be earned.

"Maybe you don't need to go there just yet," I suggested, since no one needed to hone their prose *à la The Elements of Style* until they'd produced a good bit of it. Kendra needed inspiration, not discipline. "You like Stephen King, don't you? You know he's written some books on writing."

"No shit."

"Let's look him up."

We downloaded King's most popular book on writing to her account. She lolled back in the none-to-comfortable chair and scrolled through some opening pages while I dug out my laptop to surf fan-fiction blogs. I wanted to know more about some of the models Kendra had been following. "I'm going to refill my water bottle," I told her. "I'll be right back."

I headed for the water fountain across the room. And stopped. Curled into a chair directly in my path, staring straight at me, was Simone.

Yesterday she'd gone home in the protection of her father. How had she landed here?

Her direct gaze told me this was no chance meeting. She lowered her feet to the floor and straightened. She wore pink shorts and pink plastic sandals and a pink-flowered blouse over a halter, her hair pinned back in pink-sequined barrettes, for all the world an impossibly innocent youngster out for a giggly afternoon at the mall. Except for her face. Its fault lines were as jagged as shattered glass.

I sat to face her. "Does your mother know you're here?"

She arched her back to sit taller. "No."

My first instinct was to grab my phone and call Nick. But I'd left the phone back at the table with Kendra.

"It's inappropriate for me to talk with you, Simone, without your parents knowing."

Defiance surfaced. "Are you a pervert or something?"

A tart answer died on my tongue. "How did you find me here?"

"We followed you." She brushed the question off. "It's easy. You drive slow."

"We?"

"Me and a friend."

"Peyton?"

A ghost trailed behind her dark eyes, so quickly only someone on the lookout would have detected it. "No. Someone you don't know."

I glanced back at Kendra. She seemed sucked into the computer. I rotated my empty water bottle in my fingers like one of those crazy eight balls. No good moves floated up.

"I'm going to call your father and tell him you're here," I said.

She jumped as if she'd been snagged from above by an invisible hook. "No. I came to talk to you."

I leaned toward her. "Simone, I can't keep your secrets. I wish I could. But too much is at stake. People have—"

"They died. I know."

"The police are trying to figure out what's—"

She jumped to her feet so abruptly the space between us seemed to sway. "Forget it. I was stupid." She squeezed out past her chair and the table. I wanted to catch her in my hands the way you'd clutch at a snowflake blowing past. But she moved quickly. "You'll never prove I was even here."

I pivoted as she left me. Fortunately Kendra still bent to her screen. so I wouldn't have to explain who I'd been talking to. I probably would have said "another student." I definitely would not have said "a friend."

——————

Kendra and I picked two books and two writing blog sites for her to explore. Sitting beside her, I struggled with my frustrations. I wasn't surprised at the signs that Simone had some sort of deeply painful secret, some confidence she both wanted to spill and wanted her listeners to conceal. She had picked me for this compromised role. Whatever she wanted to hand me, I'd felt I couldn't let her. Maybe it was no great loss. Nothing these girls had told me so far had inspired the police to action. *I* had acted, but futilely so far.

Kendra's dad picked her up on the corner of Guadalupe and 24th, leaving me to my own sorry devices. I headed toward my car in the growing spring heat. All I couldn't resolve chased me: my aggravation with Clauson, my worries about Simone, my heat-seeking rancor aimed at the smoking target that was Eric. Eeny-meeny-meiny-moe. Run down Eric, haunt the Woodridge house, call Diana. As I settled behind the wheel, I called Nick.

His hello came out faintly wary. I asked, "Do you have a minute?"

"What's up?"

"Have you talked to Simone today?"

"This morning. She wanted to go to her mother's so I took her. She seemed okay, quiet but I guess pretty much herself. Why?"

"She wasn't at her mother's a half hour ago. She was at the Flawn Center at UT." I pictured Simone's haggard face. "She said she had followed me there. She seemed to want to talk to me."

From his end of the call came silence. It was easy to intuit what went on behind that silence. I felt a twinge of fear for Diana. Oh, surely that was silly. Nick wasn't violent. I wished he would say something that would convince me he wasn't violent. "I'll call you back," he said at last, and hung up.

41

When I arrived home, a construction-company truck was pulling out of the driveway. I climbed onto the back porch to find that the black paint had been sanded off the planks. I had left a blank check with Adela. "This mess is about me," I'd said when I gave her the check. "Let me take care of it." She hadn't argued much, as she shouldn't. And in any case, the whole incident only cost me $258.65.

"Well, that's that for the time being," Adela said as I entered the hall.

For the time being. I smiled away the delicate sting of those words. I'd already been twice as much trouble in her life as Larry and Wallace put together. Luckily for me, she didn't know, in this case, how much more trouble we were all still in the middle of.

Upstairs, I unloaded my bag but not my frustrations. What, oh what, had Simone wanted to tell me? What was Nick doing? Were the police questioning Eric, or the elusive Brendan or red-haired Gail? Maybe my only shot at getting any answers was to stage a séance.

Apparently I would need a séance to summon Ms. Vanhoven. It was too late today to contact the school offices about her. I had paid less attention to Ms. Ropp, the teacher still on staff. She had not turned up in any of the pictures I had searched, at least not in a shape I recognized. But she'd been a part of Anna's life, and surely of Corinne's. I'd already found her on Facebook, had sent her a request to message her that she hadn't answered. Now I thumbed down her personal page, past her family, her hobbies, her travels. No images of students, perhaps wisely. I decided to try a friend request and had just logged it in when my phone rang.

Nick! No. A 212 number. New York.

I don't pick up strange numbers. Especially at seven p.m. It would be eight in New York. The number screamed robocall.

The phone rang itself out. If they wanted me, they knew how to use voice mail. And so they did.

"Ms. Crockett, my name is Dabney Mulligan. I'm an attorney representing Mr. Richard Briscoe, who was formerly married to Ms. Celia Monahan. I'll be in Austin tomorrow and I would very much like to talk to you, preferably in person. Could you please return this call at your earliest convenience? Thank you."

I had not yet pursued my curiosity as to how Celia supported her flamboyant lifestyle, not to mention Eric's. But when somebody gets killed, money's not an uncommon motive. Money could tie her to her ex—a "financier." I recalled reading that the ex seldom communicated with Celia. Why was his attorney calling me?

Well, that question might actually get answered. I pushed "call."

———————

Dabney Mulligan asked to meet me around five Tuesday at her hotel in the Domain. That meant I woke up restlessly on Tuesday morning with a long wait before I could find out exactly what she wanted with me.

Of course the Woodridge house lured me. But prudence said to defer my next claim on Clauson's forgiveness. Fortunately an email arrived to remind me to upload my draft of our research-paper introduction by the end of the week.

My adventures meant I hadn't started on that assignment; anyway, in my own research work, I wrote intros last. You really needed to do the work before you knew what you wanted readers to think you did. Yet, sharing our ideas for the intro might help us hone the wording of our question. It felt good to think about learning and human achievement instead of death for a change.

But death interceded, more or less. I'd been working barely a minute when I was interrupted by the damn phone.

This one an Austin number. What was the term for that, "spoofing"? When a spammer made the call look like it came from a neighbor? But I had sent too many pleas into the ether not to be hopeful when I risked answering. The woman's voice in my ear asked, "Is this Sarah Crockett?" and I quickly said, "Yes."

"This is Tilda Ropp. I saw your friend request and realized I hadn't responded to the message you left at school."

In my agitation I hit the space bar on my Word doc about twenty-five times. "Yes! Thank you for calling!"

"I'm assuming this is about your daughter. I can't think of any other connection. I know from my records that you met with me routinely when she was my student, like all parents." A slight hesitation. "At least you did. I don't clearly remember Mr. . . ."

"Wyles."

The reserve in her voice didn't surprise me. "Is there anything specific you want to ask?"

Why, yes, specifically, did my daughter tell you who was about to abduct her? That wouldn't do, but if I hoped to use this gift I couldn't tiptoe around. "I did want to ask if you also knew Corinne Miller."

"Oh, we-e-ll." She sighed. "That's another sadness. At least . . ." I let her find her way out of the sentence. "I was very sorry about Anna. I think everyone was."

"Thank you." Some of the teachers had sent notes but I couldn't remember if she was among them.

"I don't remember Corinne well," she went on. "I don't remember that she and Anna were particularly close. Was that what you wanted to know?"

"They were in the same class level—"

"I don't remember that. We had some pod activities where they might have interacted." She gave another sigh. "I don't think I'm supplying what you want to know."

She was a mother. I could feel it. She knew what a mother would care about. "Do you remember anything odd about Anna in those last weeks?" I asked.

Another long *w-e-ell*. I waited.

"She was always a cheerful girl. Center of a lot of happy little circles. But I do think, for a time before she . . . disappeared, I thought I was hearing her voice less often, and maybe it was a little less, oh, bouncy. But I have no real proof of that." A bit of sharpness surfaced. "If I can be plain, I attributed what I was sensing to the impending divorce."

She'd opened one of my door. "Did she mention that?"

"Not . . . no."

I did not want to scare her off. But I wanted this. "Did she ever talk about her father?"

The sharpness persisted. "I know something about your interest, Dr. Crockett. There was some news coverage. And the police did ask many of us about this." I heard the breath she took. "I can tell you specifically, no, Anna never discussed issues involving her father with me."

She'd hear my breath as well. "You have been very candid, and very kind."

Her voice softened. "I'm sorry. I know 'kind' is not enough."

When did it become so easy to cry? I had to wait to speak. "I do understand you answered all these questions, but may I leave you with this one request? If you think of anything Anna said or did that would shed any light on what she was experiencing—" Any connection with Corinne, for example. "—will you let me know?"

"I thought through that as soon as I saw your name. This is the best I can offer."

"I'm grateful you remembered her."

"I'm glad to remember her. She was a lovely child."

———————

I barely got myself human again in time to meet this lawyer at five o'clock.

———————

Dabney Mulligan reminded me a little of Diana. She was trimmer, tailored, even a bit corseted in her sleek navy suit. But she gave that same impression of having seized the space she occupied as a right, and that space pushed against everything around her, including me.

I had found her on LinkedIn. She fit neatly into the mold of a prosperous business attorney. Briscoe's firm was listed on her firm's website as one of its prestigious accounts. She had an easily located personal web page as well as accounts on several chat sites, where she mainly nattered about various corporate achievements, with here and there mention of a cat. I saw no sign of kids.

In the hotel café she settled comfortably across from me. "Thank you for agreeing to meet me. Hope you didn't mind the drive. I have another meeting here at seven, so your coming is a great help to me."

Our coffee came in cool white cups that gave me a handle to hold onto. "What can I do for you?"

She smiled, then sipped. The smile wasn't meant to soften anything.

"We know you were having Ms. Monahan followed," she said.

So many people seemed to care about what I was doing. "Was I?"

"At one point, Ms. Monahan thought Mr. Briscoe was responsible for what she termed 'harassment.' We responded to her request for an injunction by finding out who actually was surveiling her." The smile, just a pinch at the corners of her mouth, showed no teeth. "We knew that Ms. Monahan had an ongoing relationship with your ex-husband, whom you suspect of being involved in the disappearance of your daughter." The slightest pause. "Please let me say how sorry I am for your loss."

As if I could not "let" her say that? "It's hard to see what I can tell you that you can't find out for yourself."

She ran a finger around the rim of her cup, the nail deep red. She changed her expression, almost like scraping off a layer of paint.

"Ms. Monahan—Celia—received a divorce settlement from Mr. Briscoe. But the settlement was controlled by certain terms that Ms. Monahan had consented to. Now that she is dead, the disposition of the settlement is also subject to those terms. So far, as you can imagine, with the police so unforthcoming about what happened, we haven't been able to access any of her personal information. We can't verify that the terms have been observed, or that they will be." The finger circled again, then stopped. "We're gathering information from people who knew her so that we'll be able to properly direct our inquiries." Tap, tap on the cup handle. "Mr. Briscoe has a valid legal interest in her estate. I assure you his intentions are good."

The way she used Celia's name distressed me. As if she'd won it from me in a game. "Really, I didn't know her at all."

"Not many people did. She was very reserved." Mulligan sat back, her fingers now at work on the linen napkin beside her saucer. "I understand that you're concerned you might get caught up in a murder investigation. But that certainly is not my intention. So . . ." She went still, holding my gaze. "Let me ask you this, which I hope you'll feel able to answer. Have you seen any evidence that Celia was involved with a child?"

Evidence? Of "involvement"? An echo of my own speculations about Celia's hints that day of our talk? Surely this woman knew of the dead boy. But that was long past. I hadn't fully bought Eric's rebuff of my question about a possible child between him and Celia, but Celia's ex-husband could have no legitimate interest in any other man's child, even Eric's. I saw no reason to invite him into my own investigations, such as they were. I decided that since Mulligan was a lawyer, I need answer only the question she had actually asked me. I shook my head. "No."

Mulligan managed her mouth. "If you do see any such involvement, even the slightest hint, we would greatly appreciate it if you would let us know."

My curiosity gave way to unexpected indignation. Up went my defenses—for Celia. And any child she might be "involved with." "Here's what you need to know about me," I said. "I am extremely sensitive to the fate of children. I won't do anything that I think might subject a child to harm in any way."

"We don't—"

"You and Mr. Briscoe should decide what you can tell me that will convince me that, in fact, your intentions are good."

After a long moment, she nodded. "Fair enough."

She signaled the waiter, air-scribbling *check*. From an inner jacket pocket, she extracted a card. I took it. Vivicheck, Wavell, and Smythers. A Park Avenue address. She gave the waiter twice the price of our coffee and waved away his offer of change. "We, too, care about danger to children. So if there's anything you'd be comfortable sharing, with the understanding that you'd be protecting a child, not harming one, please, get in touch."

Leaving, she breasted the quiet room like a solid object cutting through waves. I remained fidgeting with my lukewarm coffee, mulling over this latest news.

Celia had been hiding things; of that I'd long been certain. From Eric? Definitely from Nick. And from her ex-husband. Why not?

Did this Briscoe know about my child? His lawyer had. What did he want to know that I could tell him? Did he know about the secret house—could it have been a *safe* house?—on Woodridge?

42

My meeting with Mulligan ended at the time of day when people getting off work headed for their gyms, their jogs, their bike rides, their waiting suppers. Before us all stretched a long late-spring evening, full of promise for those whose minds had not been dragged into cold depths by the weight of one word: *child*.

I wove through the cloister of hotels toward my car, wondering, how old did a boy or girl have to be before you no longer referred to them as a "child"? Last summer, Tommy Pierce had been eighteen, college age, but she had still belonged to some cohort I defined as children because of their call on me. Russell and I had never dwelled on definitions. Tommy and Anna were our children, age no determiner. What definition of "child" was this Dabney Mulligan using? The child I most cared about would be seventeen by now.

By the time I slipped behind the wheel, my mind had veered toward Celia and then past her to the child Russell had told me she had lost. Despite Eric's scorn, was she bound up with another? But if not Eric's, whose?

Was the secret house somehow connected? I'd had no chance to ask Nick whether he knew about Celia's visits there. Maybe he knew all about it, maybe it was an investment Celia had made and had wanted to give up. Maybe the gold-haired man Gail had seen was not Eric, the decision to place that sign that particular morning purely coincidental. Maybe, maybe, maybe. I headed homeward, thinking, *why doesn't Nick call?*

———————

I had persuaded myself to work on my intro draft when the phone interrupted again, around nine. Nick? No, but I recognized the number. I let voice mail pick up Diana's cold voice.

"Hopefully you will get this message promptly," she said. "My ex-husband is sitting in his car in front of my house. He has been there for the past hour. If he is not persuaded to abandon this behavior within the next thirty minutes, I will have no recourse but to subject my home, my child, and him to the intervention of the police."

——————

I'd once been to Diana's for a reception. I had no problem remembering the natural stone house set among the Tudor cottages; solar flares scattered through her elaborate landscaping illuminated a narrow front porch and a gravel sweep of driveway. There was no sign of Nick.

I turned around at a corner. This was not a neighborhood where you could sit at the curb in the dark making a phone call. I drove to where I could pull into a parking lot and take out my phone. If he didn't answer—

"She let her go to a goddamn movie!" came his outburst in my ear. "She's only been home a day from running to those idiots, and she lets her out of her sight!"

"Diana—"

"She called you, huh?" An unintelligible background rattling. "You didn't go, did you?"

"Well, I—"

"Don't worry, I'm back at my place. Behaving myself. Drinking bourbon. Fortunately I have a full bottle."

"I don't need you in jail, Nick."

"I'd rather be in jail than doing nothing. The police are doing what? Blowing this whole thing off?"

I hadn't been to his place. Maybe I should go there, lay a soothing hand on his shoulder. It was late, the nail salon in the strip mall where I sat turning its lights off. Maybe words would calm him.

Or maybe lies would? Or euphemistic misrepresentations? "They're following up. They may have leads we don't know about."

Now scraping, and a change in the breathing I could hear through the phone. "I'm sorry. I just want . . ." A slam, a smack, something hard landing. "He killed her. She found out he was molesting girls and he killed her to shut her up. Am I the only one who gets that?"

I couldn't argue; that had been one of my own theories. But there was something going on here that I didn't like encouraging. Possibly I could steer him to some of the facts we ought to be sharing. "I'm wondering if you might hear from Mr. Briscoe."

"Briscoe? What does that have to do with anything?"

"If he knows about you, he might think you know something about Celia. About what happened."

The unmistakable clink of ice dropped into a glass. "He lives in New York and she never saw him. I don't see what he had to do with us."

Us as in Nick and Celia. "What about her finances? Was he involved in that?"

"I didn't ask about her finances. Nothing to do with us."

"A lawyer for Briscoe met with me, wanting to know if I'd uncovered any connection between Celia and a child."

"A what? A lawyer?" Thankfully I didn't have to define "child" for him. "Jesus. Eric . . . could they have . . . ?"

"I did think of that."

"But you don't know if . . . ?"

"No, I don't."

"Look, that bit from Peyton about a secret lover, that's bullshit, if that's where you're going"

He needed grounding in truths even if they weren't soothing. "There's a house, Nick, where she goes without Eric. Sometimes at night." I wasn't sure I should give him the address; what would he do with that information? But how else to prove that the house existed? "4368 Woodridge. It's owned by a guy named Brendan Brightwell. I thought you might know about him. And an older man I've seen at the house, a guy named George Franklin. I've been wanting to ask you about all this because I thought she might have mentioned some of it to you."

A lot going on in the silence that followed. All the things Celia hadn't mentioned?

"Look," he said, brisk now. "I have things I have to do. I'll call you tomorrow."

"Please be careful," I said, the irony ringing in my ears as I said it. "Don't do anything rash."

"Really. Tomorrow. I'll call."

"I would appreciate it. Before you do anything. We have a lot to process."

"I'll call."

I sat with the silent phone for a long minute, trying to decide what I had accomplished. I knew too much now of what I wished I didn't have to know, and still far too little of what I wished I did.

43

Whatever Nick planned, he didn't do that night, because by Wednesday morning I'd heard nothing. No calls from Clauson, from Diana. Maybe he was sleeping off his rage.

Had he told Diana about Simone's visit to me at UT? That was certainly something she should know. True, Diana was the one who had stoked the hostility between us, practically forcing me into my alliance with Nick. Would she ever realize that what Simone was doing might be worth warning *me* about?

But the emails I started to her didn't want to finish. Finally I convinced myself that it was Nick's job —and right—to tell her about the UT trip. Let her take care of her own business for once. I'd take care of mine, which included making use of her husband and her daughter. Her daughter versus my daughter? Her daughter be damned.

It was a leap from that acid pronouncement to my virtuous fruit-and-oatmeal breakfast. Alice attached herself to my earlobe. Try eating oatmeal with a small but solidly built parrot clinging to your face.

"Syrup," she said. Actually, I didn't know what she said. It was just a word she flung out sometimes that sounded like "syrup." Maybe, I thought, somewhere there's a secret parrot dictionary where parrot parents could look up all those untranslated little sounds and know what their birds really thought.

I had needed such a dictionary for my other parent role as well, the one that had ended before I learned its hacks. A lexicon that told me what "nothing" and "I dunno" and "sort of" really signified.

Anna knew about her dad and Celia but never told me. She went places with them and never told me. Did they demand she keep their secret or did she choose to keep it herself?

A spoonful of oatmeal halfway to my mouth, I dropped it into the bowl and pushed away the food. I detached Alice and set her far away on the sofa. I didn't want her to feel me shaking. Birds react to others' pain.

———————

The Woodridge house was silent.

If I didn't want to get arrested, what was I doing here?

Taking my mind off Anna by doing one of the few things I could for her. That was what.

I'd parked far down the street on the opposite side from the house, maneuvering to face against traffic so I could see anything that happened there. I didn't know where Gail and Donna lived, whether they'd pass me sitting in my car if they ventured to the park. It wasn't a day for a park outing, light rain shouldering through in quick bouts.

I'd called the school about Ms. Vanhoven, and of course was told in annoyingly reasonable tones that it was not their fault if she had not called. Attempts to worm out more information about how I might find her earned me a "Sorry we can't help" and a dead line. On top of all those other dead ends to come to terms with: Nick's histrionics, Clauson's apathy, Diana's disapproval. Dealing with those ongoing frustrations was pointless. This house was all I had.

It was around ten. The mysterious Brendan had surely gone wherever he went. The house, all the houses, stayed closed, silent. It had occurred to me that I could just call the number on the FSBO sign and make an appointment to see inside. But the secrets I was here to learn wouldn't emerge in a real-estate visit. Slumped in my seat at curbside, I might just find out who came here, what they did, what they took away.

Raging Sarah stomped around in my head like a kid who had been sent to her room. I muffled her thumps by Googling. From the looks of it, Richard Briscoe was what everyone so far said he was. He owned his own investment firm, serving a "select" clientele; he employed half a dozen stylish young men and women with august titles and arcane financial specializations. His extravagance of choice, I learned, was sailing . . . er, more like yachting. The company website featured his adventure the previous summer, crossing the Gulf of Mexico from Cancún to the Virgin Islands with his wife Sutton and two young sons. In his pictures he was exquisitely clean-cut, even more sculpted than Nick, dare I say "plastic"? Sutton appeared to be blonde, what an AI might render if you gave it the prompt "chic."

I returned to the images of Briscoe's strapping little boys. Five? Six? If the child Dabney was seeking was a second child Briscoe had had with Celia before their divorce, it would be older than these. Naturally, if it existed, Briscoe would want to find it. Why hadn't Russell's surveillance detected the child? Could it be also dead, and hidden from Briscoe? I searched for some read of how long it had been since he split with Celia. The police probably knew. They'd surely be digging into everything about her . . . wouldn't they?

Then why weren't they here, doing what I was doing? Where was the stakeout to learn who "Brendan" was, what he had to do with Celia, whether and why Eric had been to this house?

They could be here, well-hidden. Other cars sat along the curbs; I couldn't see inside. But then, I told myself, a decent stakeout would be hard to detect.

———————

I had just looked up, remembering that I should be watching the house and not Google, when a flicker of motion caught my eye.

A dark-clad figure was crossing the street in front of me from the vicinity of the park toward the house.

I'd been around him long enough to recognize his brisk walk, the jut of his jaw, the tilt of his shoulders, even without the somber suit, white shirt, and tie.

Nick.

He strode past the wall into the front yard.

I didn't know whether to race to stop him or celebrate. Yes, giving him the address had been a risk. I chose to sit still, watching. Someone was finally breaching that fortress. Someone who, from what I'd seen last night, was angling to get in big trouble. Why stop him when there was a chance he might find something out?

I climbed out, undecided, mist settling on my light jacket. I tugged my baseball cap down on my forehead and edged up the street. I stuck to my side, slinking into the park to stay out of sight.

I craned to peer across the street and over the wall, but didn't see him. I checked my watch. How long should I wait? If no one was home, would Nick try to break in? Three minutes. Four and a half. I watched traffic for a chance to cross. But before I could move, two figures emerged from the shadowed front door, their heads and shoulders visible over the wall. One backed away, the other stalked forward. The one backing away, surprise, surprise, was Nick.

Nick backed into the driveway. The other man followed. He wore a cap pulled down over his ears against the rain and a stylish, unbuttoned canvas jacket and jeans. I'd had only those few glimpses of Brendan, but I was sure it was he. His hands dug into the jacket pockets, holding them away from his body at an angle that worried me.

I slunk deeper into the park. With his back to me, Nick couldn't see me, and Brendan appeared fixed on Nick. I edged behind a spindly oak. I didn't want Brendan to spot me and tie me to Nick; that would compromise any chance I might have of dealing with him on my own. All the same, if Nick needed help, I should be there to give it. I mentally urged Nick to get the hell out of there.

But he'd planted himself squarely in the driveway. Brendan took a jab of a step toward him. Nick backed again, stopped. Neither man spoke. In this halting way Nick made it to the street. Brendan stopped ten feet from him. From the shelter of the park, I was close enough to hear Nick say, "This isn't the end of this."

Brendan gestured with the hand in the right jacket pocket. "Go. Go on."

"It's a public street."

Brendan shrugged. "You got ten minutes before I call the police."

He turned and strode back down the driveway. Nick stood unmoving. I debated. If he planned to wait for the police to come and remove him, I would be safer and drier if I watched from my car.

So I headed back down the street, apparently not even on Nick's radar. A few spaces up from my car on the house side of the street sat a dark-blue Lexus, a dim figure behind the wheel. Hah. Maybe the police were doing their job after all.

I drew abreast of the car. Fancy wheels for a lowly policeman. Wipers came on, clearing the windshield. The driver's pale face, visible enough at the few yards between us, didn't turn toward me; he stared steadfastly at Nick.

It wasn't a cop. It was Franklin. Or the man I'd decided was Franklin. The man who'd tried to break into my office. Who'd sneered at me right here just two days ago. Who'd quizzed Donna and Gail.

44

I looked quickly away, kept my pace even so I wouldn't attract his gaze.

Even if this wasn't Franklin, he was someone connected to Celia. Why else would he show up—twice—at this house? My car was parked four lengths behind his, aimed the same direction as his, across the street. A couple of cars purred past as I reached my spot. I had missed my chance to read the front license plate; maybe I could get close enough to catch the number from behind. Up the street, Nick still stood in front of the house at the curb, arms crossed, feet apart, the thin drizzle plastering his dark hair. I shivered in the mist, water dripping off the bill of my cap, and climbed behind my wheel.

Finally Nick backed up a couple of steps, wiped his face with a sleeve, then headed up the street. I lost sight of him, but then the Prius I recognized as his pulled into the roadway ahead.

Behind it, the watching man's dark-blue Lexus pulled out.

I wanted that license number off the Lexus. I also worried that Nick hadn't had his fill of trouble. When we were searching for Simone, he'd said he needed a witness. From what I'd just seen, he needed one now.

So, not letting myself think of all the trouble *I* could get into, I eased out on the Lexus man's tail.

Following my prey through urban traffic wasn't like following Nick through open country, especially since this guy might have spied on me and would know my car. The first part wasn't so hard, with Nick ahead, then the Lexus, then me, several lengths back on the broad residential street, hoping we'd come to a traffic light so I could coast up and read the plate before the Lexus man saw me. Both cars I was tailing got caught behind a left-turning driver, but before I could close on my prey, the lane cleared and the two cars rolled on.

Nick had no reason to think he was being followed; he would probably go back to his apartment or to his office. The man behind him would learn who he was but little else. I could warn Nick later. For now I needed to keep up until we reached a light.

But Nick thwarted me, turning a sharp left. Without signaling, the Lexus braked hard and turned, too. I had to sit out oncoming traffic. By the time I could make the turn, I could still see the Lexus, but a slew of residential curves had cut off my view of Nick. Then a car shot out of a side street in front of me, of course slowing to a crawl when I most needed to hurry. *Please, Nick, turn on Bee Caves, back toward campus.* Yes: far ahead, a black Prius turned left at the light.

The Lexus and I followed; our little parade wound through the scattered businesses toward Mopac. The riffle of mid-day traffic forced me to make several leaps on yellow to keep up. Nick didn't take Mopac, his fastest way to campus. Instead, with the Lexus several lengths back and me chugging along in cautious tandem, he led us through Zilker Park via Barton Springs.

This part of the drive was bucolic, open spaces stretching on both sides. The moderate traffic let me drop back a bit, still with a chance to read the license plate at a traffic light as we neared downtown.

But Nick had picked up speed, his mind probably on Celia, on Brendan, on Simone. On all the things, named and unnamed, he *had to do*. So he probably missed a pedestrian stoplight flashing as he neared it. I slowed automatically; so did the Lexus. Nick tore across the crossing, forcing a jogger to jump back.

And from behind me, siren blaring, roared an Austin cop.

Beyond the Lexus, Nick obediently eased over, the cop sliding to the curb behind him with lights ablaze. I slowed, too, closing on the Lexus. As I drew even with Nick, he looked past the cop at his window and straight at me.

I gave him the briefest glance. There ahead, closer than I'd expected, was the Lexus. I fed gas. I had to risk being detected. I had to get the number off that plate.

But ahead, too quickly, loomed the Lamar intersection, cars piling up at the traffic light. Beyond the light, heavy traffic raced in both directions. If he turned into that rush, I'd lose him. Turn he did, left on an arrow. Behind him, I screeched through on yellow in time to see him, up ahead, veer into a left-turn lane.

I gritted my teeth. Follow him to a confrontation? Why not? He knew me, probably knew all along I was behind him. He wouldn't murder me in broad daylight. Would he? The Lexus turned. A car ahead of me made the yellow. I chickened out as the light turned red and traffic flooded the oncoming lanes.

Down the street to my left, the Lexus disappeared into a parking garage.

The light changed and I turned, stringing together a daisy chain of "damns." Following someone capable of violence down a public street was one thing. Tailing him into a cavernous, probably deserted garage was another. The garage seemed to be attached to apartment buildings. People would be coming and going. I nosed into the ramp, took the ticket, and chugged into the dim, cool space.

My phone rang.

I risked a glance. Nick.

On my right was a row of empty spaces marked "Reserved." I eased into one, hitting the answer icon.

"What the heck is going on?" Nick said. "Were you following me?"

"I was following a guy who was following you. The one I told you about, the guy who tried to break into my office and who turned up at that house. He was there, in his car. He took off after you when you left."

"A guy."

"A man who apparently knew Celia." I'd leave discussion of the FBI to a less hectic moment.

"Where are you?"

"I followed him into a parking garage off Lamar. I can see the exit, so he's here somewhere. I want his license number so I'll know who he is."

"I know where you mean. I'm only a minute away. Stay there."

I shut off the phone and reconnoitered. If the Lexus came down to the nearby exit, I'd need some sharp and highly visible maneuvering to get behind it. Could I post myself on foot near the exit, where I could read the plate as he passed? I was still debating when Nick rolled through the entrance and parked on my right.

He climbed out and looked around, then bent to the window I buzzed down. "This guy, what was he doing?"

"Watching the house. Watching you."

He straightened. Again reconnoitering. "What was he driving?"

"A dark-blue Lexus."

"Yeah, I saw that." He looked at his watch. "How long have you been sitting here?"

"Five minutes? Six?"

"Here's what I think. There's a second exit to this garage, on the next street. If he knew you were behind him, he'll have taken off already. If he didn't know, he'll have parked. In either case, there's no point in guarding this exit. We can drive around and see if we spot the car."

"Did you learn anything at the house?"

He shuffled restlessly. "Only that that guy has a hair trigger. And I mean literally. He came after me with a gun."

"You just knocked on the door, right? You weren't trying to break in?"

An answer I was probably better off not getting. He spun away, opened his car door. "Let's look for this other guy. Leave your car here. I'll drive."

I slid in beside Nick and he backed out into the ascending ramp. "You watch right and I'll watch left," he said.

We threaded our way through the switchbacks of parking levels. The rows of parked cars sat abandoned, no one coming or going. "So who do you think this guy is?" Nick asked.

"I don't really know. I saw him outside my office window one night, trying to open it, when I was there alone doing some cleaning. He took off when I spotted him."

"You think he's dangerous?"

"I don't think he wants to abduct me, nothing like that." At least I hoped not. "He must think I know something about Celia."

"Like what?"

"No idea. If we find him, I'll ask." We passed a Lexus, but it was the wrong model. "Anyway, he has your license number. He knows who *you* are."

Nick's fist tightened on the wheel. "Good."

We reached the top level and wound our way back down. We saw another Lexus, this one the right color and model; I got out to check, but spotted a florist's logo on the front door.

I sighed. "I have to tell Clauson about this."

"About what?"

"Definitely about the drama with the gun."

He drove the next stretch in silence. I didn't like that silence. Were we still being honest? We negotiated the last switchback toward the Reserved space where I'd left my car. Hopefully there'd be no ticket on the windshield. A silver Honda puttered up the ramp toward us, the first activity I'd seen. "You do need to be careful," I said.

He stopped the car and looked at me.

"Sarah," he said, "I want to bring Eric to justice. I thought that was what you wanted."

"Yes."

"Then you have to let me do it. Don't chase around after everything I do."

The current in his tone was not soothing. "Just stay out of jail, please." I got out, and walked around the front of my car.

And stopped.

Something—someone—had flattened my right front tire.

45

Nick got out. We both stared.

"Maybe you ran over something," he said. "You didn't feel the flat while you were driving?"

""No. How did he get past us to do this?"

He knelt by the tire, running his fingers over the deflated tread. "Do you have a spare? I can change it."

"No, no, I'll call that roadside service I pay so much for."

"I'll stay here with you."

"Thanks." I laughed grimly. "At least if someone comes along to reprimand me for parking in a reserved space, I'll have an excuse."

He pulled his car in beside mine, out of the way of the couple of cars that drove in while we waited. We leaned on our car hoods.

"Let's say it was this guy," Nick said.

"Yes, let's."

"He's sending a message."

"Yes."

"He saw you and he wants you to know it."

"Yes, that was why he was so easy to follow. He let me." I rubbed my hands together. "Let me interpret: if I want to play this game, fine, but he can do damage."

He looked away, then back at me, a crease between his brows. "That place you live, is it safe?"

Nick, of all people, worrying about my safety. "Yes. Fortified."

"I agree, you have to tell that lieutenant about this."

I hoped the extent of my relief at that remark didn't show. He was basically sane, I reassured myself. Saner even than I was, in the long run. "I'll call him when I get home."

———————

Nick waited for the tire man with me. Kendra was due at three, and it was nearly then before the auto-club guy chugged in. He moved fast, though, replacing the flat with my donut. "Can you see a nail or anything?" I asked.

"Not right off." He spun the tire. "I'll check when I take it back to the shop."

"Thank you, yes. I've got an appointment, so I'll have to pick it up later this afternoon."

He chugged off in his big truck. Nick slid into his car. "I'm heading back to work. Will you let me know what the police say?"

"Of course."

So we drove off sedately. Was he sobered by this whiff of danger? Was I? Maybe a little. But I was grimly amazed to learn from the morning's adventures that I was running around with someone more reckless than me.

———

Kendra dropped her notebooks between us, frowning. "Are you okay? You look frazzled."

A perfect word, frazzled. "I've had a kind of hectic day. Had a flat. That's never fun."

"Did you get it fixed?"

"I have to pick up the tire in a bit."

We were elbow to elbow at our work station, my kitchen table. She'd brought a much-thumbed notebook, one I hadn't seen yet. But she set it aside, handed me some sheets with a few crossed-out passages and scribbled notes. "I don't know what to do with this stuff."

It was work we'd examined at our previous meeting. She'd read it aloud, we'd talked, she'd made a few unenthusiastic marks, a couple of emphatic Xs across whole paragraphs—and apparently nothing else since.

One of those awkward teaching moments that needed bridging. But that flat tire had robbed me of any creative response. Fortunately I had my collection of scripts. "Are you having problems with this section?" I asked benignly, like a good little Turing machine.

She threw down the colored pen she'd taken out of her binder. "It's just stupid. I don't know why I wrote it. It's just stuff I did when I thought I had to write *something*."

Thinking about her writing, what she said about it, how she felt about it, pulled me back into a sane space. "Sometimes when you can make yourself just write *something*, things happen." Nothing had happened here, though. "What else did you write this week?"

She could have sighed and scrunched her face and said "Nothing." But she reached for that other notebook she had brought and flung it open. "I did do this stuff on that other story. You remember, about the evil wizard. I did a lot on that."

Oh, yes, the one I decided she'd written her father into. "Why don't you read me some?"

The upshot of her narrative was that the evil wizard had met his comeuppance in especially gruesome, graphically recounted ways. In fact, she'd drawn him in the margins, eviscerated, bleeding, her sketches kin to images of medieval inquisitions I'd encountered in histories I'd read. The maiden who'd been the wizard's victim delivered the *coup de grâce*, laughing maniacally. Kendra looked up after narratively kicking the oozing body a few more times, her faced flushed; she sucked in her lips and turned away from my gaze.

"Very descriptive," I said.

She crimped a page corner. "You liked it?"

"It's certainly vivid writing. The maiden really hates this guy."

She ran a hand over the page, softly it seemed to me. "It's just a *story*. I wanted it to be exciting."

That it had been so exciting to her worried me a little. But we were there to talk about stories. "It's some of the most evocative writing you've done. My question is, where does it take you? With the wizard dead, are all of Esmarelda's problems over? Is the story over?" Not just questions to keep her writing until the end of the study. No, real writers' questions. "What is she going to do now?"

She turned to a blank page and stared at it. "I don't know. I'll have to think about it."

"If you don't want to be finished, think about all the things his death doesn't solve."

She shut the notebook, leaned back. "It doesn't solve anything."

She would give me only her profile. I thought, she's angry. Or was she? She grabbed up the pages we'd looked at earlier. When she pushed them at me, she curled her arm and hand and elbow onto the table, making a barrier. "Tell me what I should do with this junk."

So we took up our familiar battle, her rush to be told what to do, my insistence that she was the writer, the one to decide. We worked through to an agreement. She would do *something* with the hated pages, good, bad, or indifferent, before our next meeting. She had done her own driving that day, and I saw her down to her car.

Then I sat back down at the table and thought about anger. About Kendra's outsized anger. At someone.

When the evil wizard appeared, always verbally beating on poor Esmarelda, I'd hypothesized he represented Kendra's father, with his constant carping that she wasn't showing enough progress, that her struggles as a writer marked her as stupid. How did that dynamic play out at home, with no teacherly interventions? Did his nagging warrant such an overwrought execution? So much glee in gore?

Or . . .

Reading the pages had loosed some fierce emotion. Left her scared at the dark twists of her own imagination?

Or . . .

How easily the thought wormed in: *she has some reason to want to brutalize him, punish him. Reduce him to mass of spilled guts on the page.*

I didn't build a dike between me and that thought. I watched it seep around my consciousness, on the edge of my vision. I hoped fervently it would stay on the margins. I had enough frightened young women on my mind.

46

The car-repair place found a puncture in my tire. "Ran over something sharp, it looks like. Not a nail. Maybe a piece of metal. That happens sometimes. Missed the sidewall, so I got it fixed."

I couldn't feel completely relieved. If the Lexus man did flatten the tire to send me a message, a puncture would have been his method of choice. A sharp poke, say with a handy pocket knife, was quicker than letting air out through a valve.

Could he have done that? I didn't have a spare tire on which to test my hypothesis. But I couldn't ask the mechanic if he thought someone might have been trying to threaten me.

At home, I called Clauson's number. Yet again, voice mail. But I'd concluded over the months I'd known Clauson that messages were forwarded automatically to his cell. "Things have happened. Please call me."

To my surprise, my phone rang almost right away. Road noise hissed in the background. He must be driving, maybe with his windows down in the spring weather. He'd have a hands-free connection. "So what now?"

"I was hoping that woman—Gail—"

"You said you had something for me."

Many somethings, but how could I extract payment in return? "Did you ask her about that man who quizzed them about the house? I saw him there today."

So gratifying to make him have to think before he answered. "So you were there today?"

"So was Nick. We didn't go together, he was there when I got there." I'd sorted through how to spend my spycraft most wisely. "Nick said Travis showed him a gun."

He came back faster this time. "So what was Nick doing?"

"I don't know. He'd gone to the door. I couldn't see." I hurried us on past Nick. "The man who tried to break into my office and who quizzed those women—he was sitting in his car watching the house. A dark-blue Lexus. I never got close enough to get the license." I didn't tell him about the flat tire; he'd dismiss the damage as coincidence. "Did you at least ask Eric if he knew him?"

"And describe him how?"

From vague sounds I interpreted as a motor dying, I gathered his car had stopped. Rustling noises followed. I sighed. If he hung up, I wouldn't get another chance soon. Should I bring up the FBI, the can of worms Russell had let me look into? If Clauson knew about that investigation, yet again he'd shut me out. "You did talk to Eric?"

"If we place Eric at that house, we'll deal with it," he said.

So no one had ID'd him. "He categorically denied being there?"

Now he sighed. "You need to start taking the fact that these people have lawyers into account."

Aha. Eric had issued a denial. My exasperation at Clauson wanted to bleed into resentment. I stopped it. Clauson was doing what he had to do. Like Nick. Like me. "I do have one more thing you need to know." I recounted my conversation with Dabney Mulligan. Yet again I had the small satisfaction of knowing I'd brought him news.

"Do you have this woman's number?" he asked.

I gave it to him, along with her LinkedIn info. "She said Briscoe has a legitimate interest in Celia's finances." The thump of a door closing. He was out of the car and I was about to lose him. "Money could be a motive. I wonder what Eric's legitimate interests are."

Again he took longer to answer than I'd expected. "Look, I appreciate what you've told me. I've already told you, be more careful. Be careful around Nick Hudson."

"Nick isn't the one who's dangerous."

A series of indiscriminate sounds. Walking up a sidewalk? Fumbling for keys? For answers? "Look," he said, surrender in his voice, "I know you hope it's Wyles we—"

"I don't *hope*. You've just never told me why it can't be."

Now I was sure I could hear a door creaking. "No," he said. "You hope. And you know you do."

He closed a door on me, yet again.

———————

In the hour that followed, the hour it took me to short-circuit my frustration, my sense of helplessness, my flaming rage, I did something I had done once before without knowing exactly how. All I knew for sure was that I screamed into the void at Eric: *you think they'll never believe me? You'll always have answers that prove how innocent you are? Well, I'm the one you'd better convince with those answers. Let's hear them.*

And to my utter, stunned amazement, he answered, just as Celia had.

47

But it really was very odd.

I'd dragged my mind off Eric by reviewing my research-intro draft when a text pinged. Fishing for the phone under a stack of papers, I considered the short list of people who might text. I hadn't heard from Russell since those last dry facts he'd sent me. No one had told him about my forays into danger, so maybe we could have a quiet conversation. But the snippet in the message box read, "It's Eric call me please at this # it's urgent."

I stared down at the message. Did I really have the power to summon the people on whom my sanity depended? The message was even more remarkable in that, in the six years since I lost Anna, Eric had never before called or texted. He had never before used the word "please" in any context I could remember. And never had he thought anything I wanted or cared about "urgent."

Now something *he* wanted was "urgent." La-di-dah.

I decided to let him stew a little. I hoped whatever his need was, it burned.

To occupy myself, I dug more into the possible haunts of the elusive Ms. Vanhoven, who might have witnessed the last days between my sweet ex-husband and my child. If I couldn't reach her through the school, where else might I unearth her? What did teachers do when they retired? Why, I thought, they volunteered! They ran after-school programs and book drives, served as museum docents. I tracked these ideas through newspaper archives and Facebook pages, waiting until enough time had passed to demonstrate my indifference to his purported crisis. At last I hit "call."

Of course I got his voice mail. "I'm doing as you asked, Eric," I told it. "If you have something to communicate, you may certainly call back or text."

I set the phone on the coffee table and crossed to Alice's cage, wondering what mental illness it would signify if I cleaned her cage twice in five hours. Surely the detritus for the morning's seed ball needed attention. Surely there were no circumstances under which cleanliness would not be a good—

The phone rang. I answered. My sane, calm voice amazed me. "Yes, Eric. What do you want?"

Never in six years had he whispered in my presence. Now his voice came quick and low. "I have to see you."

"Excuse me?"

"Listen." It was as if a high-voltage wire connected us, thrumming. "I'm being followed. If I'm seen talking to you, you might end up being followed."

I came up with five or six reasons to interrupt him. *I hope the police are following you. When did you ever care what happened to me? Why should I care what's happening to you* . . . I closed my throat against it all.

"There's an ultralight fair at Lago Vista on Lake Travis tomorrow. Do you know where that is?"

"Vaguely."

"You can look it up. But listen. There's a road that turns off toward a little park. There's a shelter there. Leave your car in the main parking lot and if you're clean walk to that shelter at eleven o'clock."

I said nothing. He said, "Do you understand?"

Still I said nothing.

"Sarah," he said.

"You can't possibly think I'm going to do this."

"I have something to tell you that you're going to want to hear."

"Tell me now."

"No." Then, after a burdened pause, "Please."

I stared at the glittery face of the phone, as if it were mimicking living emotions, trying to make me think a human being was on the other end. But this could not be a real human I was hearing.

This must be a bot taught some human manners. Human Eric would never plead.

"Will you answer if I call this number?" I asked.

"When will you call me?"

"When I'm ready." I hung up.

———————

I never really doubted that I would go.

This was exactly the kind of risk that, if reported to my official and unofficial advisers, would call down orders to desist. But I'd waited a long time for whatever was about to happen. Nothing was going to stop it from happening to me.

I called Eric back. He said, "I hope it goes without saying you need to come alone. And tell no one."

"Excuse me. I'm going to leave a message with a friend telling her where I'm going and why. If she doesn't hear back within an hour, she will call the police."

"She won't have to."

"Good."

"Sarah, you're not the one in danger."

"Eleven," I said.

"Yes. Please."

———————

I found Ms. Vanhoven. She made the mistake of getting her picture in the paper collecting canned food for a group called Austin Gathers for God. Their next event, for which she was listed as "Going," was two days away, a clothes drive at a school on Bee Caves Road.

Just possibly after my Thursday meeting with Eric I wouldn't need Ms. Vanhoven. I wouldn't need Nick or Simone or even Celia.

Eric claimed to be desperate about something. I couldn't wait to find out what it was.

———————

As I tucked myself into the battered little shelter on the hillside above Lake Travis, I saw why Eric had chosen this site. At late morning on a weekday, a park engineered for boat launches was deserted. Few boaters would venture to the shelter, and picnickers were at work or school. I could monitor the walk back to the parking lot where I'd left my car but people arriving at that lot would not be able to see me.

I'd taken my usual amateur precautions to decide whether I was being followed. If so, I hadn't detected my tail. Eric had claimed that *he* was being followed. By whom? The Lexus man/Franklin? Maybe Franklin had spotted Eric when he made one of his clandestine visits to Brendan at the house.

The question was why the guy—Franklin?—was interested in any of us. Me, Nick, the house, Eric—our link to him had to be Celia. My connection was most tenuous, a couple of degrees of separation. I replayed my theory: he thought she'd told me something that would incriminate him—or possibly expose him to the FBI. That flat tire might be a warning to think twice before I revealed it. Well and good, if I could figure out what he thought I knew.

I settled onto a bench in the shelter. Possibly the dangerous thing I knew was that the Lexus man existed. If I hadn't seen him at my office, if I hadn't seen him at the house those two times, he'd be a lurker, invisibly watching all of us. I took a shivery look around me, but if he had tracked me here, he stayed out of sight.

Eric, Nick, and I shared a second link besides Celia and Franklin: the girls. Peyton's claim about Celia's secret lover linked her to the house. Was the Lexus man also connected to the girls? But how would he know about them? I couldn't suppress a sharp hitch under my rib cage at an unwelcome conclusion. *He could have learned about them by stalking me*.

Sheesh. Franklin. The FBI and missing children. Teenaged girls. Just drama? Or another danger to worry about?

All that had to be for later. My worry now was to make use of this unexpected gift from Eric. After all, Eric was the one who *knew*.

From where I sat, I could see ultralights flowering gently as they rose above the trees. One, then two, three, their insect bodies diaphanous and quietly gaudy, their motors purring. I'd never begrudged Eric his love for these machines—had I? I wasn't terrified of heights, but I didn't like them. Hadn't liked the feeling of absolute nothingness below and around me the few times I tried one of his toys.

Had I been too quick to dismiss his disappointment that I wouldn't share his passion? Did he think that when we were married he could convert me? Had he ever really cared whether I ventured into that free-floating world with him? *And with Anna?* I really didn't know.

When I saw him trekking toward me up the slope from the far side of the shelter, I dismissed those questions. I folded my hands on my knees and waited with an inquisitor's chill in my heart.

48

But that day he threw me off kilter, the way he stopped when he saw me, a distance between us that was his doing, not mine. Not that he'd ever wanted a connection, but this holding back was different. Maybe I had finally made him afraid.

He'd dressed for the gaiety of the air-show exhibition, in cycling tights and a bright blue shell that showed off his stark athlete's body. Oh, I remembered that body, its edges like strata in rock. His muscles flexed as he looked over his shoulder, then crossed the last few steps into the shelter to frown down at me.

"You weren't followed?" he asked.

I let a shoulder rise and fall.

He looked around again, then back at me. "I've asked you before to leave me alone. I'm asking again. There's more at stake than you know."

Asking? I thought, remembering his spitting demands last summer when I'd succeeded at sending the police to his doorstep. I sat still.

"I know you don't care about me," he said. "There are other people involved. People who could get hurt. And if you get me arrested, they *will* get hurt." He set his shoulders against a corner column and slid down it, crouching, so that now I looked down on him. "I'm not lying. You have to leave me alone."

Same old shit: *you're beating up on poor innocent me.* The splint of ice inside me hardened. I thought of Corinne, of Simone. I did not let my mind slide toward Anna. I stood and walked out past him into the sun.

He sprang to his feet behind me. *I am alone here with a man who has killed, maybe more than once. He will finally betray his guilt, and this is how.* The surge of that certainty, of finally knowing, overwhelmed even the faintest spasm of fear. I turned to face him; if ever I was one-hundred percent Raging Sarah, it was then. Whether my body won or lost would not matter. I would *know*. And found that he had stopped again, beyond an invisible field that he could not seem to cross.

"Celia had a secret," he said from beyond that distance. "I'm responsible for it now. It affects someone . . . who's . . . who can't . . . who's helpless without me. You have to stop siccing the police on me. You have to get them off my case."

My gut said, *give me a break*. But Celia did have secrets, more than I'd discovered, many that even Clauson couldn't tell me. Against my best judgment, I couldn't convince myself he was lying. That felt extremely odd.

But I had secrets, too. What Gail had told me, for example. And my knowledge that his alibi was flimsy. I spoke for the first time. "What are you asking me to do?"

"You told the police I was at some house you're obsessed about. The day Celia was killed."

So that was it. Trying to worm it out of me, what I'd learned. "I told the police you had been seen there that day."

"You saw me?"

"Of course not. I didn't know that house existed then."

"Then who?"

I shook my head. "Ask the police that."

The muscles bunched beneath his slick tunic. This was the kind of moment when his anger would translate into a physical tension he could barely contain. He had always throttled it, but there had been close calls. He shut his eyes, breathed in and out. I waited. When he opened his eyes again he had flattened the anger out of his face in a way I'd never seen before.

"I never touched those girls," he said. "That Eckstrom girl had a schoolgirl crush. I rejected her and pissed her off. I don't know how I'm supposed to convince you of that, but it's true."

"If you're innocent, there won't be any proof against you, will there? Your lawyers can handle it. That's their job, not mine."

He closed his eyes again, as if the sight of me was more than he could manage. He opened them, wiped his mouth with a hand that did not look steady to me.

"I know the police tell you everything," he said, "so sooner or later you'll know this. But I'm going to tell you now before they figure it out because there's some hope you'll see I'm being honest." He dropped his hands to his sides again, rubbing thumbs and fingers against each other. "You can even go tell the police the minute you leave here. Save them some time."

I waited.

"I'm the beneficiary of Celia's trust."

I didn't know what effect he hoped for, but he sure got one. "You're what?"

"Her money—her divorce settlement with Briscoe—it's going to be mine."

"You inherited her whole estate?"

"Yes. That and some other money she made on her own."

"But . . ." I could only shake my head. I said, not expecting to hear myself say it, "You wouldn't kill her for money."

"I didn't kill her."

"Why you? Doesn't she have anyone else?"

"No one she could trust."

"She trusted *you?*"

"Yes."

"Yes," I echoed, almost numbly. "The police will be interested in this."

"Sarah." His voice intensified. "She knew I would take care of something important to her. I can't tell you what, or the police, or anyone. But it's important. You'd think it was important, too, if you knew."

"I know about the dead child," I said.

That made him jump. "Who told you?"

"It's public record."

Some of the alarm drained from his features. "That's history. This is not about that."

"Briscoe is looking for a child. His lawyer came to see me."

"Briscoe has nothing to do with us."

The second "us" Briscoe had nothing to do with. "Briscoe's after her money," I told him. "When he finds out about this, he might be the next person who thinks you killed her."

"Yeah," he said bitterly. "I get it. You can't let go. I'm 'it' for you. Well, fuck that."

His hard shrug turned him back into the old defiant Eric. "There seem to be a lot of people you're 'it' for," I told him. "If it's not Briscoe, who's been following you?"

"Maybe your new boyfriend, Nick Hudson."

I shrugged. "Yeah, Nick. Did Celia sleep with him?"

"No, she did not."

A sharp denial. Trusting her mattered. "But she kept stringing him on?"

He raked his hair back. "He was the one who kept hanging around."

"Nick thinks you killed Celia because she found out you'd molested his daughter. It might be wise to share what you know of him, if not with me, with someone."

His shrug was more denial. "Hudson can think what he wants. That has nothing to do with what I'm asking. I'm just telling you, you keep hounding me, you can hurt people here."

"I want to hurt people. I want to hurt the people who hurt Anna."

He threw his hands up. "God, Sarah. Do what you have to. Don't give a shit who you hurt."

He wheeled to storm off. A familiar conclusion to our exchanges. "Or was it that man?" I said to his back. "This man who's been staking out the house on Woodridge. Is he connected to your big secret? Is he the one following you?"

He pivoted. On his heel. "Man?"

I described him. Clauson was right, the details were vague. Should have been useless. But Eric's gaze froze.

I said, "You know who he is."

"Where did you see him?"

"He tried to break into my office. Then I saw him twice at the house."

He came toward me. I felt no menace. He said, "He knows who you are?"

"Yes."

"And you talked to him?"

"Briefly."

"About what?"

"About why he was interested in me."

Another abortive half-turn away. "What did he say?"

"Denied any interest in me or the house."

He came back to me, hands groping at something he couldn't get hold of. "Stay away from him . . . No. If you see him again, call me. Text."

"Who is he?"

"I can't . . ." For a moment I thought he was going to touch my arm. "Just swear you'll tell me if you see him."

"I can't swear—"

"Please."

There it was again, that alien word.

"You loved her, didn't you?" I said.

For the briefest moment, he did not seem sure which "her" I meant. He nodded. "Yes."

He'd always been a good actor, luring Anna out of my life, blinding me to so much. Why would he be less skilled at deception now? I surprised myself by sighing. "Regardless of whether I believe you or not, it's all gone too far for me to undo. Clauson will find out your alibi won't hold up. He may move slowly, but he'll get there. And yes, I do have to tell him. I can't keep this from the police."

He stretched both hands, the way he might if he meant to embrace me. "Sarah. I know what you want but I can't give that to you. If I could, I would."

A moment of silence unlike any I could remember ever having passed between us. We were like people just meeting who had been told rough things about each other and were waiting to see what to believe.

"People will die," he said finally.

"More people," I managed.

"Yes, more people," he said as he turned away.

49

I drove to the department. Clauson wasn't in. This was not for voice mail; I settled in to wait.

An officer on duty must have alerted the lieutenant because in less than a half hour he came through the front doors and planted himself, the whole solid block of him. "Well?"

"Not here."

He jerked his chin and wheeled. In his office, he kicked a chair out for me and circled to his own. Not gracious. As he sat, he raised his brows.

I told him about Celia's estate.

He said, "Why didn't he tell me this himself?"

"He thinks . . ." Of course, I didn't know what Eric thought. "*I* think it's possible he's trying to manipulate me. This business of someone else getting hurt, that's the kind of thing he knows I'd be a sucker for." My hands worked each other indecisively. "That thing from that Mulligan woman, that lawyer, about a child . . ."

"You really would be a sucker for that."

That remark deserved a retort I couldn't spare the time to give it. "Yes, Eric knew hinting about an endangered child would get me. I think that was what he was doing, but what child? Any child he was using against me would be one *he* knew about. But I don't think he knew about my talk with the Mulligan woman until I told him." I had not told Clauson about the dead child because it seemed likely he already knew. But so much had not been laid on the table. Time finally to fix that. "Did Celia have a child?"

He nudged one of his ubiquitous folders. Gave a pointedly huge sigh. "For the millionth time, when I can tell you things, I will."

His rules. His sacred ongoing-investigation rules. Last summer, more than once, he'd broken those rules. But it had taken lives at stake to make him do it. Like the lives he was toying with now.

"Here's the right answer to that question. Celia had a child. A boy. It had congenital defects. It died."

He chewed something out of sight behind his lips. "Yes. But so what?"

So what? For a moment I shared Eric's frustration. "Then what child is Eric using to sucker me? What child are Mulligan and Briscoe searching for?"

He looked deeply tired, trapped in all that paper. "When you find out, I'm sure you'll tell me."

Goddamn it. "Well, here's something someone ought to tell you. That man who tried to break into my office, and I saw at the house—Eric knows who he is. He asked me to call or text if the guy turns up again."

He rubbed an eye wearily, rocking the chair back.

"I asked your help when those pictures turned up," he said. "I should have known what I was doing. Every time I can't tell you something, you try to find out for yourself."

Sane Sarah took hold of my shoulders. I steadied my voice.

"Celia, Nick, the Mulligan woman, that man, now Eric—I didn't seek out any of that information. It came to me. I have brought it directly to you each time."

"You miss my point." He leaned over the desk, knuckles planted among the piled-up folders. "I already tried to tell you. Someone's going to get hurt. Maybe you."

I stood. "Here's the millionth and one times *I've* tried to tell this to *you*. Someone *was* hurt. And I am *being* hurt. Every day, every minute, every second, that my daughter is still out there. And you will not tell me what you are doing to stop that pain."

He spoke to the desktop. Gave me only the pink shine on the balding top of his head.

"Nothing that I could tell you right now would stop it," he quietly. He looked at me from under his sandy eyebrows. "We're both going to have to live with that for a while."

———————

So I lived with it. For a while.

Russell answered my first ring.

"I want to come there," I said.

He got it instantly. "What's wrong?"

"Just for tonight. Now. I have a meeting tomorrow. But I can get the flights there and back."

"I'm not in Santa Fe. I'm in Vancouver. What's wrong?"

If I went I would tell him.

"Has something happened?" he asked.

Many somethings. And telling him, handing it all over to him, would be another something. A surrender.

"I'm looking up the flights for you," he said.

"Vancouver . . . oh, well. I wouldn't be able . . . the meeting is important."

"As important as why you called me?"

That I did tell him, but left out the explanation. "Yes."

50

Friday morning I headed to UT for my meeting, holding on with both hands to my role as the stable, professional woman I had to keep on being, not some hysterical woman who would flee weeping to a man's arms. A woman braced in herself, owning her future, accepting, yes, what she had to live with for a while.

Russell had called me back. "I'm sorry," I blathered. "I was just frustrated. I'm trying to get Clauson to focus on Eric but I can't."

"For the murder?"

"I think he should be looked at. Celia knew something."

He took a beat, maybe to strip the frustration from his voice. "If there's anything there, Clauson will find it. He's not stupid."

"They all think I'm nuts."

"You aren't."

I created the laugh I needed. "Not yet."

He didn't want to let go of it. I could tell by the silence before he said, "Keep me posted."

"Of course," did not seem like the answer I owed him, but it was the one I had.

———

By the end of the meeting I felt sure I was still the person my daughter would want to come back to. As we gathered our belongings, a text came. Nick.

"Where are you?"

"In the Cactus."

"Meet me in the Goldsmith courtyard. It's important."

"I'm on my way to—"

"It's important. Please. Now."

———

The slim fountain wasn't running; the day was gray, unusually chill, which perhaps explained why students weren't lounging on the courtyard benches. He stood, hands fisted in his pockets, staring at me as I chose a bench for myself.

Rage hardened the set of his shoulders. "That . . . monster came to my office."

"Peyton? She came to you?"

"Right through the door," he snapped. "All dressed up like she was on a job interview. Like a queen."

Yes, I could seen Peyton parading into his office, chic white bag over her shoulder.

"She said he molested Simone." He forced breath past the words. "No, assaulted her. Just short of actual rape."

In some corner of my mind I'd been prepared for this moment. But not prepared enough. That day at Josephine House, Nick had taken in Peyton's claims against Eric with a cold cunning, as if scheming to put her pain to use. There was nothing cold now about the way his restless hands worked each other over. I sorted through a rush of gut reactions in search of the least harmful. "You haven't talked to Simone?"

He twisted his fingers together. "I wanted . . . I had to get my head straight first. I have to find some way to control . . ." He struck his left fist against his thigh, staring into the space between us as if black things moved there. "But too much self-control is a betrayal of my daughter. I need action." His voice hardened. "*He* knows what he did. Someone should make him confess."

"Nick . . ."

He started, as if I'd just reminded him of his name. He ran a hand over his face. "I've been dreading talking to Simone. But I have to. How she reacts, that'll tell me something." He breathed deep, shaking his head as if to chase off the black shapes squirreling through it. "Do you think there's some chance, some grain of a chance, that Peyton lied?"

"I don't know." My own voice cracked with the effort to contain my feelings. "I want to believe her. That's what worries me."

If he had heard what I said he sliced past it. "He has to pay for what he did."

But now *I* wasn't listening. "If Peyton is lying, then Eric is telling the truth. If he is, our case against him falls apart."

He walked past me three steps, then back, stopping to stand over me. "He's not telling the truth."

But I was thinking, *our case*. The one Clauson had told me I hoped for. If Peyton was lying, that hope collapsed. *No*, my heart said. I wouldn't let it. "Even if he didn't rape Simone, we could still get him for *something*. He could have egged her on, or tried his luck with the other girls."

"The way Peyton tells it, he didn't just 'try his luck' with Simone."

What I did hear then was his building fury. I thought about that day in the Flawn Center, short days ago, when Simone decided not to tell me whatever she came to say. Something she was so afraid to tell her father that I, an enemy, had seemed a safer choice? Had I counted all the dangers she was facing? What if what she could give her father wasn't what he wanted? "Are you sure it's a good idea for you to talk to Simone?"

He snorted. "Who else? Her mother?"

"Maybe a counselor?"

"I don't want people poking at her. Strangers. We have to deal with this ourselves."

We? Nick and her mother? Or Nick and me? "I don't think you should talk to her when you're angry."

He chewed his lip. "Like there's some other way I'm going to be."

Had I created what was coming? "Whatever she tells you, stop and *think* afterward. Tell someone. Tell *me*."

He crossed the small yard, taking in that plea from a mental distance. "You can't back out on me, Sarah. We need each other." After a second he nodded as if I'd answered. "I'll keep you posted on what I'm doing. But it may not be what you think I should."

"Nick . . ."

He turned and entered the building at the end of the courtyard, on his way back to his own professional masquerade.

———————

I was glad I hadn't told him about Celia's child, about Eric's inheritance, Eric's claim that he was nobly engaged in something for Celia. All that news seemed best stored out of his reach for now. Back in my lonely, quiet Cresthill office I worked through my drab notes from the morning meeting. But an uninvited certainty slithered up against me as I thought about Nick and *our case*.

I *did* want those girls to have suffered, if their pain was what it took. I knew I should be able to banish that feeling. But I could not close the door that was Nick.

51

My quiet sojourn in my office would have needed to be a lot longer and more cleansing to prepare me for what happened next.

It started with a text that caught me when I got home. I was surprised to find that though the number was Kendra's, the message came from her dad. "We need to cancel today. Thanks."

Pretty terse. Something wrong? I texted back, "No problem." I was actually glad for a breather but also puzzled. They'd never before cancelled at the last minute. "I'll see Kendra on Tuesday."

An answering text: "Probably need to cancel that, too."

Damn. Were they abandoning the study? I had seen no sign Kendra wanted to end her visits. Was Dad stepping in?

The question presented a delicate situation. Of course they could drop out, no reason required. Such freedom was integral to all institutionally sanctioned research. In any university study, the faintest whiff of coercion was the gravest of sins. Safest might be to let the issue ride. If Kendra wanted me to know what was going on, she'd tell me. Yet . . . we'd grown a relationship, and I'd developed a commitment. I wrote, "I hope you'll let me know if something's wrong."

I'd barely hit send when the phone rang. It was Dad.

"I've decided we probably need to have a conversation," he said, his tone pinging between anxiety and challenge. "Would you have a half hour if I happened by now?"

———————

So Sane Sarah had to do some cleanup in her emotional cupboard, making space in all the chaos for whatever lay ahead. Mr. Fuller might arrive with some sort of accusation—teachers were supremely vulnerable to all kinds of claims about hurt egos, mishandled sensitivities, demolished dreams, and other even more unforgivable misdeeds. In keeping with protocol, I'd recorded my Kendra sessions. They'd been low-key; my years of stolid teaching ordinariness would surely shield me.

I'd had a hard time setting aside the image of Mr. Fuller as the evil wizard in Kendra's stories. My own experience as a parent had ended prematurely; most of what I knew of kids and families grew from interactions with young people like Kendra when I encountered them as students. From those exchanges I knew something about the pain of young adulthood in an unwelcoming world. All the same, Kendra's unhappiness with her father had struck me as excessive. "Abuse" was so much on my mind that it infected my reaction to her stories. A painful dilemma: Kendra was my student. If I saw even the slightest hint of an inappropriate relationship, I'd have a duty to report.

But I opened the door to find a deeply flustered man on my landing, his eyes red-rimmed behind his pale-framed glasses, hands working worriedly on his trousers. I almost wanted to hug him, not call the police.

"Thanks for making time for this," he said as I waved him inside.

He seemed unsure what to do with the chair I edged toward him. "Can I get you tea or coffee?" I asked. "Water?"

"No, thank you." He dabbed at his full lips with the back of a shaky hand. "I don't know what's going on except that it has something to do with Kendra's writing." He wriggled to the edge of the chair, then sat stiffly. "She burned all her papers. On the desk in my study. Fortunately in a trash can, but it charred some spreadsheet printouts I was working on."

The pain of that report drew visible sweat on his broad, pale forehead. "My God," I said, but so softly I barely heard myself. "Is she all right?"

"Minor burns. But we had our doctors admit her to the hospital, which she immediately tried to run away from. Dr. Crockett. What in tarnation has been going on here?"

Going on here with you was of course implied, but the implication didn't feel hostile. The question seemed rather to leak from a well of despair. I folded my hands in my most stable-professional manner, as much to steady myself as to reassure him. "Did you talk to her?"

"If getting 'Nothing, nothing, nothing' is talking."

Where was the heart of this? "Did she ever let you read anything she wrote?"

He shook his head. "You remember how she acted about that the last time I was here. It was pretty obvious she didn't want me to read anything."

"I got that sense as well." So many complexities, too raw to share. "You'll remember, from the information sessions about the study, students can decide whether third parties get to read what they write. That rule governs what I can tell you about her work."

He blinked. Stiffened still more. "You mean you won't tell me what this is all about?"

"I doubt I know what it's all about." I hoped my reply didn't sound flippant. "An important part of the protocol—for the study and for teaching writing—is to focus on the text, not the person. Of course, writing is always personal, and sometimes it's cathartic. But teachers have to tread carefully into emotional territory. We're not therapists."

"I didn't say you were." He had loosened the leash on his hostility. "But you can't tell me there wasn't some clue to what she was thinking in her writing. I . . . we . . . her mother and I deserve to know what was going on with her here."

I suppressed the sigh that wanted to escape me. "I remember that you did get to read a little of her wizards-and-princesses stories."

"I told you, she should have been writing something different."

No, we had never settled the question of what her writing was worth. But he needed my patience. "My role this term isn't to teach her what to write or how. The single outcome we want to measure is her attitude toward writing."

"I'd say her attitude toward writing is pretty bad."

I didn't completely catch my sigh this time. "Yes, it does sound as if something connected to her writing has upset her."

He shifted with renewed energy. "What's the point of making her think that everything she spills out is perfect, especially when it's a bunch of nonsense, in my book?"

I risked a question that I didn't want him to read as the judgment it probably was. "Have you discussed how you feel about her writing with her?"

His next shift in the chair might have been called squirming. "What difference does it make, since she won't listen? I mean, that's part of the problem. I mean, going nuts like that, just because I didn't 'appreciate'—" he made air quotes, "—her crazy stories. That's not good."

"No, it's not." For the second time that day, I found myself dealing with an emotional need above my pay grade. "Maybe a counselor?"

"If it's about her writing—"

"Someone with training in family relationships should decide whether it's about her writing." I avoided full eye contact as I considered the options. "I can talk to my colleagues—"

"I don't want every Tom, Dick, and Harry knowing about this." He threw his hands up. "Look, I don't care about your colleagues or your damned study. I care about my little girl!"

Every note in that howl rang true. But I had few ways to help. "I do know that I'm not qualified to counsel her, and even if she were to resume the study, I couldn't tell you what she said or wrote."

"Useless." He stood, towering.

"I wish I could help you more."

He snorted. "You've done enough, thank you." He shoved the chair back and wove around it toward the door.

"Mr. Fuller," I said, hoping I had enough bark in my voice to stop him, "whatever you and Kendra want, please tell her I care about her. And I would like to know how she is."

His face softened minutely. He eased the door open rather than wrenching it. "I'll let you know what we decide. Probably won't be doing any more writing. At least, not that kind of writing."

I had my own opinion about that. I just nodded.

He nodded back. "Good day."

His steps receded. At least in this case I hadn't made any egregious breaches, ethical or otherwise. What devastated me most was my sense that I owed more to Kendra. Her involvement in the study had clearly triggered some crisis in her relationship with her father. Possibly her writing had opened a vein on the heartache of many thwarted moments. I hated seeing her go away with that grief still fermenting. I hated seeing her go at all.

He left me, though, with a disorienting sense that I hadn't had two separate conversations about fathers and daughters that day, but two scripts of the story they shared. Fathers struggling to see over walls where creatures with teeth were consuming their children, monsters they couldn't conquer until they could give them names.

Fathers who might themselves be the monsters they feared.

Her father's ire said I wouldn't be welcomed if I dropped in on Kendra for a visit. Were they watching her text messages? Still, I wrote her, "Hope you're doing better. Thinking of you." If by any chance she got the text, she would know that I hadn't shrugged off whatever turmoil had driven her to her rebellious act.

52

Saturday: two blue lines under the date on my calendar.

1. Lunch with Taneesha
2. Ms. Vanhoven

Taneesha and I had planned the lunch long ago, before mysterious daggers and frightened girls. Before Ms. Miller. Before I had ever dreamed of hunting down Ms. V.

With Ms. V's face planted firmly before me from the old pictures, I considered cancelling the lunch. But another face intruded: Kendra's. Lunch with Taneesha would give me something these recent weeks weren't supplying much of, a chance to ask a straight question and get a straight answer: what would Taneesha have done?

"Not a damn thing different," she said.

I made myself snare a dolma. Feeding my body in the middle of all these crises felt like an indulgence. "The whole thing just seems unfinished."

"I don't think a situation like this will ever be 'finished.' It's not like smacking a soccer ball into the goal."

Strictly speaking, sharing confidential information about a participant in the study was breaking protocol. But Taneesha did not know Kendra or the identities of any other students in the study. We were discussing some faceless person, totally in the abstract, in fact talking more about my anguish than about Kendra herself.

"What this looks like from here," she said, spearing an olive, "is people with a lot of anger who don't know what they're angry at. Or whom. They need to be angry at *something*. Dad chose you."

"I've been thinking his daughter is angry at him. It's a fairly reasonable hypothesis. Even if—I mean, I have no evidence of anything tangible, so it's not like I have anything to report beyond my write-ups for the team. But you could label his . . . his dismissal, his trashing, of the writing she wants to do as abuse."

She nodded quietly. "You could make that case."

"But I wonder if part of her is angry at herself for not doing or *being* what he so clearly wants."

Her gaze ventured past me, into considerations she didn't share. "Also not an unreasonable theory." She fingered her glass of cold Egyptian coffee. "Anger can be good if it finds the right target. Sometimes I think . . ." She lifted the glass but didn't sip it. "Sometimes not letting yourself be angry when you should be does its own kind of harm."

Behind her thoughtful gaze was a space our professional relationship did not invite me to enter. "Thank you for listening to all this. I just hate . . ."

"Don't beat yourself up about it. You did exactly what you had to."

We moved on to more pleasant topics. At least, I thought, the little spurts of anger I'd felt at Mr. Fuller's insinuations had sputtered into sorrow. My anger at Eric had better not dissolve so quickly. I was not done with it. It knew its targets. One of them waited for me in a school parking lot on Bee Caves.

———

By the time I reached the parking lot where Austin Gathers for God had set up its clothes drive, I had strapped down that righteous anger. An elderly woman might well have innocently forgotten to return my call. In the lot, women sat behind a table under a tent awning, a sign announcing "Drop Off Donations Here." A fair number of people were lined up with bulging bags and bundles. Volunteers stocked sorted clothing onto racks marked with colored tags. Even after refreshing my memory from my phone's file of pictures, I had to look twice among these volunteers to find my target: a sixty-something in a flowered blouse and capris. I did not remember her as so tiny, so drawn, the cheerful vitality I recalled somehow depleted. Okay, I thought, she has cancer. Or some wasting sickness. Or some sin on her mind.

She spotted me right away. She seemed to shrink even more, bending her neck and, I thought, almost crouching, as if to slink into hiding behind the rack of clothes.

I moved fast before she could disappear altogether, pursuing her around the end of the rack past women arranging blouses on hangers. "Ms. Vanhoven! May I speak with you?"

As a teacher she would know that "may" instead of "can" granted her the right to give permission. She did not. Cornered against a wall of jeans and trousers, she faced me, blinking through petite gold-framed glasses. Her mouth thinned as she squeezed the words out. "I'm sorry, Ms. Crockett. I have nothing to say to you."

So she *had* deliberately ignored the messages I had sent her through the school. I made myself breathe past the urge to unholster my returning fury. "I know you taught my daughter," I said with admirable calm over the collection of kids' T-shirts behind which she had sidled. "I thought you might remember something about her last days at school."

That seemed to be harder for her to hear than for me to say. Her lined face blanched under her graying hair. She looked around frantically. A man nearby wearing a badge of some sort appeared to notice her tension. I struggled to make my gritted smile look harmless. "Can't you talk to me?" I asked.

She went staunch, reminding me painfully of Ms. Miller. "The police asked all this. There was nothing to tell them."

"I have a couple of new questions. Can I just ask?"

Her chin went up, her mouth soured. "I will not be involved in a police investigation. Your daughter was an ordinary student. I remember nothing about her. I told the police that. They will have it recorded somewhere."

"Did you know Corinne Miller?" I asked.

That did it. She wheeled and wove through the racks past the donation table and into the tent.

"You knew her," I called to that vanishing figure. "You knew them both."

More people nearby looked toward me, frowning. My smile had started to feel like a seizure. I turned my back on the disapproving stares and maneuvered where I could see the back of the tent and the sidewalk beyond it. This was not finished. Ms. Vanhoven could not hide forever. So many people I'd wanted to grab and shake until I rattled their teeth out. Was jail at last the price for answers? By God, if that was the only answer—

My phone rang.

Eric.

"Come get your goddamned boyfriend. Before I blow his head off."

53

I roared through Lost Creek toward Eric's house. Nick's car sat at the curb around a curve. I screeched in behind it. Yet again, no Nick. Then I saw him, swaying in Eric's driveway, in his office clothes, his hands now the ones in gunslinger position. Fortunately empty. The fingers rigid and jutting, like white rakes.

No sign of Eric, either, the door closed. I wasn't sure Nick saw me. I called to him from the street. His neck jerked as if he'd been slapped. He looked around, in his eyes that bottomless pain.

I inched toward him. "This is not a good idea." Sane Sarah had been saying that kind of thing an awful lot lately. "Please. Let's go somewhere and talk."

Body stiff, he twisted his neck to glare at me. "What did you do, come to protect him? Keep me off him?" he accused.

"He said he would . . ." Unwise to talk of shooting. To talk of what, then? Danger? He was oblivious. I edged close behind him and timidly set my hands on his shoulders. He feinted sideways. I jumped into his path to face him. "Listen to me. Listen. Let's go. Please."

"He . . . he . . ." His breaths did not want to settle into words.

"Please, Nick," I said again. How to move him? "Where is Simone? Is she all right?"

Maybe his daughter's name reached him. He stepped backward, arms sinking to his sides. I put a hand on his chest—still risky, but I needed more than words. He yanked at his twisted tie, wiped his palms on his jacket. I propelled him backward an inch at a time. I didn't dare look to see if Eric had emerged to smirk at our withdrawal. "Let's go to my car," I said.

Shakily, we found our way to the street. At my car, he put a hand on the hood and leaned for a moment. I opened the passenger door. Waited. After a moment, he climbed in.

I scrambled behind the wheel and got us out of there.

———————

I could have taken him to his office even though it was Saturday, but I didn't want to take him to any public place. For one thing, he looked half drunk. His coat was rucked up where he'd yanked at it, his white shirt loose and askew. His hair pinwheeled in all directions. As I drove, he raked a hand through it but he couldn't swipe away the mayhem of his grief.

I took us out to a restaurant near the subdivision entrance, parked in the shade. Rolled down the windows for all the good it did. There was heat both outside the car and inside it, his heat. The smoke off my own turmoil added to the mix. If he had gone to the house to attack Eric, he had a reason. Only one reason counted. With the engine off, I turned to him. "Where is Simone?"

He sighed, fingers digging the skin of his jaw as if he wasn't sure there was still solid bone beneath it. "At her mother's."

"Did you talk to her there?"

"No, at my apartment. She has a room there."

"So what did she say?"

He faced me, the angle of seat and door behind him. "Not . . . what I needed to hear."

"Let's don't fuck around." I hoped my curse would reach him. "Tell me what she said."

He shook his head, breathed hard. "I tried to bring it up gently. That I wanted to help. That her mother and I needed to know. That was as far as I got."

A brittle dread stirred in me. I sank into a quiet huddle, prepped myself for a wait.

He sighed again, mouth opening and closing. "She screamed I should leave her alone. She 'hadn't done anything.'" He curled fingers in air quotes. "I said I didn't think she had. Then why couldn't I just leave her alone? I told her that seeing her upset like that made me think something bad had happened. She said, oh, yes, something happened." He scraped his right hand along the open window frame. "She said, it's too late. I said, did something happen with Mr. . . ." He laughed, an arid cough. "I called him Mr. Wyles. She said, with Eric, you mean."

"Oh." Or rather, *oh, God.*

"I asked her, I said, he's too old for you to call him Eric." His words tumbling. "She said, his name is Eric. I said, okay then, what happened with Eric? She said, nothing. I said, you're not acting like it's nothing. She said, Are you accusing me of lying? I said, how can I help if you won't tell. She said, you want me to tell you he raped me so you can beat him up because Celia was fucking him and not you."

Words tumbling like debris in a mudslide. He was trembling. So was I.

"Maybe she's frightened," I said. "Putting up walls."

"She's trying to protect him."

"What makes you think that?"

He pushed up straight, bracing on the seat back and car door. "I said—I guess I got loud—what the hell happened! Did he touch you? Did you have sex with him?"

I tried to keep the blanch out of my face. Would I have handled such a scene with my own daughter any better? Would she have asked this of me one day?

"She said, yes, I had sex, but you're not going to know all the sordid details because I'm not going to tell you. She said, it's none of your business who I have sex with."

He was breathing as if he'd been racing uphill. I opened and closed my hands on the steering wheel.

"She ran in her room," he said. "I stopped her from slamming the door. I pulled a chair over and sat in the doorway and blocked it." He tugged his tie loose. "She called her mother. I jumped up to go take away her phone. But I . . ."

Changed his mind, I hoped. Didn't touch his daughter.

"I told Diana that if anything happened to her while she was at Diana's, I'd go to court to get her. Naturally Diana just . . ." He waved his hand. "I guess you'd call it a laugh."

I looked for sense in his reporting. "So you don't really know—"

"Isn't it obvious?" His voice found new energy. "She was angry with me, over the divorce, over Celia. What better way to punish me than to take Celia's place?"

I bit my lip, hating the grim sense it made.

"And Eric loved it," he said, louder. "Paying me back because Celia cared about me."

A sense of Celia's presence, the feeling that she had eased in between us, kept me silent for a moment. Then I said carefully, "Celia's out of it now. Did you talk to Eric?'

"Through the door crack. The fucking coward."

"What did he say about Simone?"

"What would you expect? That he never touched her. Then he said that she was trouble. That I should take better care of her. I told him—" He rubbed his knuckles across his mouth. "Like you did of yours?"

I had to hold my breath for a moment. Celia on my landing as she started down my stairway: *Like you did of yours*.

"She had sex with someone," he said. "If it was some kid at school, why the drama? She knows I'd be mad, but she knows I'd make sure she was taken care of. But this . . . this is . . ." He found it. "Rape."

My fear for Nick was building. Fear for the risks he seemed willing to take. Again I wanted to channel Russell: *be careful*. We wanted to get Eric. Why let our anger goad us into tactics that would not work? But of course Russell knew "be careful" would have been useless if my daughter had come to me with such a story. No common sense in the world could have pounded caution into me.

But now it was not my daughter. For now, I could think. We couldn't browbeat Simone, couldn't drag her by her hair to the police and make her talk. But we had to get her story. Without it, all we could offer the police were our secondhand claims.

———————

I took Nick back to where he'd left his Prius, near the turn toward Eric's house. "I didn't want him bolting," he said.

"I doubt he has any intention of bolting." My remark came out dry. I adjusted my sunglasses, kept the engine running. He pushed his door open. "What are you going to do?" I asked.

"Go home. Drink."

"Nick—"

"Really, Sarah. I don't know."

His anguish, deflated and lost, dismayed me. I didn't know what I was going to do, either. "Please let it settle for the moment," I said. "Something will come to us."

"Lots of things come to me." He climbed out, unsteady. "For the moment, yeah, I'll let them sort themselves out."

I ached to see him climb in his car and go. Confronting Eric had not soothed him. In fact, the humiliation of being dragged off by a testy schoolmarm was probably just now sinking in.

I followed him at a carefully calibrated distance back down 360. It crossed my mind to keep following him. But I didn't. All that heat needed air around it. For both of us.

54

I parked in my usual space behind the house and tried to sort out the events I had just lived through. They stoked my worry the way the oxygen from an open window turns embers to flames.

Part of my worry was my own conduct. So many cautions and warnings I'd bestowed on Nick! What irony, when every word of my wise counsel was haunted by the sight of Ms. Vanhoven fleeing into that tent. What had I been about to do? Scare her? Oh, more than scare her. I wouldn't have gotten off with a warning. I'd have been face down on the concrete with my hands wrenched behind my back.

Well, I thought, I'd have been able to tell my daughter, *that was how much I cared about you.*

I hoped Nick would not have to say that to Simone, one day when she was able to listen and he had found his way back to words.

A night and a day ahead before I could do anything more about Ms. Vanhoven. I was about to heave my stressed-out self from the car when a text chimed.

From Simone.

"I have to talk to you."

I stared at the message. Yet again, it was clear Simone had something she wanted to tell someone, and clear that she had picked me. Of course I'd be willing to listen. But Simone was not free to wander around talking to whomever she chose.

Especially not people her mother considered miscreants. "Aren't you at your mother's?" I wrote back at last.

A short wait. "Yes. I came down to the basement. You can come in the side door."

A broken moment when my two alter-egos gave opposite orders. One side shrieked, *get the lead out! She's sitting there waiting to tell you what she knows!* But my sane self couldn't cram into the tiny space of a text all the reasons that plan was a non-starter. "Please call me."

Quickly. "No she'll hear me you have to come."

Like Diana wouldn't hear us talking in the basement. "No. I'd be trespassing."

"You have to. I'll be here. Come now."

"No. Tell your mother. She can help."

No answer. I set the phone on the dashboard and waited unmoving as if the act of getting up and walking into the house would break a cord between us. She didn't text back.

Finally I headed upstairs, trying to squeeze reassurance out of the inert phone. What was happening to her? Should I take a chance and rush to her? Was I letting her down? Alice squawked some kind of word as I entered. "Yeah, everybody wants to jabber." I sank to the sofa, set the phone on the coffee table, and stared at it. After minutes that should have been seconds, I made the only decision conscience and caution allowed me. I called Diana.

I decided not to read too much into the fact that she didn't answer when her phone showed her who was calling. "I thought you should know that Simone just texted me asking to talk to me. She definitely didn't want you to know. I have no idea what she wants to tell me. I thought that . . ." The sensible voice I'd manufactured failed me. "It seems important that you know."

There. I'd been wise.

Of course, being wise didn't equate to being calm. I fetched Alice, played upside-down parrot mechanically as we paced together, prowling into the kitchen where we did nothing, back out to the living room where we did nothing. We finally stopped at the French doors, looking down at the curb where over the past two years so many people had pulled up bringing me things I did and didn't want to hear. Russell, for one. Nick. Eric. Clauson. Peyton, too, in her SUV.

Supposing Simone did have something to tell me. Something she couldn't say to her mom or dad.

I should have gone. By now I'd know.

To still my fermenting brain, I booted my computer to stab at notes on my conversation with Kendra's father. I made a little progress, the afternoon waning. But as our neighbors' sentry lights bloomed in the street outside, my mind wandered yet again.

Nick, desperately in love with Celia, and battered by his daughter's resentment of that love. Surely he could unlove, with Celia gone. Unlove, maybe, but not unhate the man he thought had killed her. Could hate and rage tear Eric down? Again and again I came back to my certainty that we had no other weapon. Rage might sabotage us, but so often it had kept us going. Rage could break him. It might even break Ms. Vanhoven, deployed smartly. Rage, unlike love or pity, did things . . .

Alice said, "Car."

I swear she did. Maybe not. Maybe she said bar or far or dar or tar . . .

I got up and crossed. Yes, car. White RAV, at the curb.

———————

Peyton sashayed toward me up the stairs to my landing, regal and sure of herself: like Nick had said, a queen.

I blocked the door before she reached the top step. She tilted her head back, looked up. She eyed my white-knuckled grip on the door. "What's the matter? Are you afraid of me?"

I lifted a shoulder, surprised at how little pity I had to give her. Yet again, I had a hard time thinking of her as barely more than a child. "This has gotten too weird. If you want to see me, let's sit down with your parents. And record what gets said."

"My God." She tossed that polished head. "You'd think I had a disease or something. You're the one who's weird. Defending that pervert. He's got Simone so crazy she's making up all kinds of crazy stuff."

Did she know about the texts Simone had just sent? Had she been waiting for me alongside Simone in Diana's basement? "You and I can't have a private conversation." I edged back into the room. "I'm closing the door now. Have your parents call me."

She took the last step in a rush, got a hand on the door so I would have to shove her back to close it. "You have to listen to me. He molested Celia's little boy."

In spite of myself, I froze.

Her eyes flashed. That is not a metaphor. I saw their glow expand at her victory in the dim light. Or maybe it wasn't triumph. It could have been determination. Maybe even fear.

"A little disabled boy," she said, breathless, as if she knew she had only seconds to reach me. "He couldn't defend himself."

I tried not to sway, tried to stand still and regal in my own right. "This sounds like information for the police."

"So tell them," she said. "They'll believe *you*."

Oh, I'd be telling them, all right.

"Where is the boy?" I asked.

"What's the point in telling you? You won't do anything."

I wanted her out of there so I could pretend she had never been there, delivering this bombshell. In the same sweep of thought, I wanted to drag her in and choke out what she knew. I shook my head, more at my own indecision than at her.

She lunged into the space my silence gave her. "You still love him, don't you? Even if you know what he does to the boy."

I clung to the door for balance. "If you really want to protect this boy, stop playing games."

But I might as well have thrown up a hand to stop a striking snake. "You really aren't going to do anything, are you?" The twist of her young, clean lips—not a smile, no, but a torsion—registered a grim satisfaction. "You're going to let him keep doing what he . . . what he does." She came closer, still pressing the door open. "You know he's capable of hurting children, don't you, Ms. Crockett? Aren't you going to do something about that?"

"I'm going to ask you to call a police lieutenant I know and talk to him in my hearing. Or I'm going to shut this door. That is what I'm going to do."

"Some stupid cop?"

She made the mistake of drawing her hand back for her dismissive shrug. I shut the door.

And stood there beating my fists at nothing, my breaths coming so loud I couldn't hear whether she left or still lingered outside. Helplessness overwhelmed me. Fury gasping and thrashing because it didn't know where to go. Yes, I would tell Clauson. Yes, he could ask Eric about this child; Eric would find some perverse reason to stay silent. Clauson would file this story with all the others, to be "investigated" at some distant time, someday.

I crossed to the balcony doors and pushed out for the air I desperately needed. Below me, she was still there, sitting in her car, the dome light on. Looked as if she was texting. I found the calmness to think about *her*. Where did her ugliness come from? Some deep terror with no outlet? Fear that she couldn't live up to what her team of worshippers believed?

I was about to close the doors on all that speculation when I saw the Lexus. Parked on a shadowy shoulder down to the left below me, close to the corner of the street.

How did Peyton know about the boy unless someone who did know about him told her?

Someone keeping an eye on her? Who drove a dark Lexus.

A lot of people drove a Lexus. But no one on my street.

I grabbed my phone and bag and keys and bolted for the stairs. I didn't pretend I had any idea what I was doing. Whatever I thought of her, she was still a child. I fairly leaped off the porch, flung my car door open and myself inside. I backed over one of Adela's pea seedlings in my haste, and pulled into the driveway where I could see them pass me.

But I was too late. Both cars were gone.

55

A lot of hours slumped by. Some people probably slept in those hours. I was not one of them.

Sunday morning came. Simone stayed silent. If Nick had caused World War III, I felt privileged not to know. Kendra had not responded to my text.

I went on puzzling over Ms. Vanhoven. What was she afraid of? Was she where my energy should focus? Would it be worth going to jail if I could make her talk? I didn't know where she lived but there were other Austin Gathers events on their calendar. *I'll be a ghost in the paths she travels, until she begs to pay my price.*

I wasted energy stewing over whether to tell Clauson about Peyton's claims, and decided that he'd already stored everything I could tell him in his wretched files. His non-answers to my questions meant that he knew about the boy, whether he was alive or dead, whether he was really disabled, maybe even where he was. Did he know whether the child's care was the reason Celia had left her trust to Eric? If he didn't know any of that, it wasn't because I hadn't pointed him toward those revelations. No more nagging. For now, I wouldn't elaborate on anything.

More important was whether I had a duty to Peyton. I couldn't persuade myself that the Lexus driver wasn't Franklin. Why was he interested in her? My imagination produced some scary prospects. If the driver of that car was the FBI's Franklin, Eric's dangerous Franklin, maybe "duty" was too mild a word for what I ought to do.

So an Internet search: how many Lydia Eckstroms were there? The internet introduced me to quite a few but none in my neck of the woods. Asking Nick for a number would have forced me to tell him things I would rather he didn't know. In fact, a phone call didn't feel like the right choice for this duty. The day we searched for

Simone, Nick had been driving, but I had no trouble making my way back to where Peyton's family lived.

I climbed out in the peaceful upscale neighborhood and made my way up the walk past meticulous landscaping I hadn't even noticed that first time. On the small front porch, a camera doorbell watched me ring. Either the Eckstroms decided not to answer or they were not at home.

Well, it was right around dinnertime on a Sunday, and people did go on outings on nice Sunday afternoons. Accosting the Eckstroms in person on their return was not a good plan. Still, I hung out at their curb for an hour, my A.C. blasting. At some point the neighbors would start wondering. I returned to the porch and the sullen camera. "Ms. Eckstrom," I said. "I met you when I came here with Nick Hudson that day when we were looking for Simone. I'd really like to talk with you about something important." I gave my number. "Please call."

Sensibly back at home, I finished a draft of my conversation with Kendra's father for our committee to review. Would the committee see anything worrisome? If they did, at least the decision whether to act would be out of my hands.

That left me far too much of an afternoon in which I could come up with nothing useful. Lydia had not called. I wasn't about to roam the streets for a chance to spot Ms. V walking her dog. I thought of haunting the Woodridge house. But my gut told me that whatever had happened there was over. Brendan, whoever he was, knew he and his house were on the police radar, and Eric wasn't alarmed by my interest in the house. In my mind's labyrinthine turnings, the house, for a time, had been a hiding place for the child. That was why Celia had gone there, alone, at night. Not for a lover. For love.

In the afternoon, desperate to get out of that labyrinth, I drove out to Pedernales Falls. As I entered the park, a text from an unfamiliar number flashed on my Bluetooth screen. I let the car's sedate e-voice read it. "Ms. Crockett," said the voice sweetly, "I have been talking to my daughter Peyton and I am instructing you to stay away from my family. If you continue to harass my daughter I will get an injunction against you. Please do not communicate with me or anyone in my family in any way."

Hmmph. *You think I have unpleasant news about your daughter? Wait till you hear from the FBI.* True, my fears were pure speculation; Peyton might not be in any danger. Still, the girl had blundered into territory I'd have wanted to yank my daughter out of. I had been angry at Diana's stubborn blindness. This time I was just sad.

For a long time I watched happy children run shrieking across the spectacular Pedernales River rocks. My own daughter would be too old for such wilding now. She'd be like the teens I saw perched shoulder to shoulder on a boulder, despite the amazing landscape around them bent over their phones.

———————

I came to before daybreak Monday after another bad night, plagued by dreams of cleaning up some kind of debris that bred and cloned and multiplied faster than I could grab it to throw it out. Futility dreams. Sarah-doing-nothing dreams. In the desperate search for some step toward finding Anna I could accomplish, I once again imagined scouring Austin for Ms. Vanhoven and running her down with my car.

Attending to my neglected parrot took up a tiny chunk of the morning. I tried to teach her to say "Aristotle." She said a lot of other things, including "Real smart, Sarah," complete with my usual sarcastic spin. One more failure to cap off a string of failures, a long list of things Sarah had decided she couldn't do.

After eating something that involved a spoon, I made a list, not to my surprise of things I shouldn't do. Do not call Nick. Do not call Clauson. Do not obsess over what was happening to Simone or what might happen to Peyton. They were not my daughters. I beat my way toward positivity by adding to my list a commitment to some long-delayed research, not for the study but for my own intellectual development and the prestige that would come from displaying that development in the journals of my field. When Anna came home she would find me making so much money we could live in a castle. Ahead lay a whole day when I could bring that castle closer, if I could figure out how.

Into my list crept the thought that I had given up too easily on Ms. Miller. Unlike Ms. V, she had confessed, even if unwillingly, that she *knew*. But it would take a different level of cruelty to terrify her as I had thought of terrifying Ms. Vanhoven. The prospect of using her loss for my triumph turned my insides to a swamp.

I put her away for later. If all else failed.

Before waxing my floors or binge-watching *Cheers* (the Diane ones) came the idea of returning to Anna's school pictures, and that was what I eventually did. I had let up on my search after finding Corinne's image, but why? Anna had been surrounded by other children, any one of whom she could have told secrets. Among their parents might be at least one willing to help bring my daughter back from the dead.

So I catalogued the faces, the ones the photos captured and the ones I remembered. Sometimes I had only a first name, but my archived rosters helped. I forgot lunch, almost forgot Alice, which meant removing her from the keyboard by force. Previously I hadn't paid much attention to the boys at the school, thinking Anna was more likely to confide in girlfriends. This time I let the school-paper pages lead me to that year's football team, gawky youngsters hunched in their shoulder pads. I swiped to capture the names in the caption. And stopped.

Student coaches Petey Gostoff and Toby Walsh. Boys who were involved in an incident two years before Anna's disappearance. They claimed to have seen a man in a car who was stalking a fifth-grade girl on her way home from school. It wasn't like I had forgotten them. But I'd been fixated on Eric and when I didn't recognize the pictures of the suspects the police showed me, I had filed the old, unsolved case in a far corner of my mind. Would I recognize Franklin if I could see those pictures again?

It was nearly five. Clauson did not answer his phone. I told his voicemail what I wanted. I suppose what I really wanted was to admit that the third of the Three Things he told me to remember had taken on unwelcome power: *what if your fixation on Eric all these years lets the real guy get away?*

If I thought he would call right back, all cooperation, I was mistaken. I scoured the Internet, hunted for contact information for Petey and Toby, for news of follow-up on the case. My failure began to sober me: was I seriously replacing Eric with this Franklin, who had just now popped up on everybody's screens? Fantasy to think that his face might have been one of those I'd glanced at and dismissed so long ago. It was vastly more logical to assume that he had appeared on our radar because he was working for that lawyer and Celia's ex-husband, hunting for this mysterious child of Celia's, who, if Peyton was right, was very much still alive. He might have been the one to tell Peyton the child existed, and now was following her because he thought her surveillance of Celia had given her hints as to where the child was. None of that had anything to do with Anna or me.

I stopped with an eight-year-old newspaper archive open. What was I saying? Of course it did.

Because it had to do with Eric. Eric knew who Franklin was, what connected him to Celia, who he threatened and why. It all had to do with Eric. Everything about Eric had to do with Anna. And so, with me.

So why was I flailing around after eight-year-old archives when I could go to Eric and ask?

Easy. Because he'd deny it all, bluff past it all, and what could I do any different this time than all the others to make him tell the truth?

Well . . .

Of course I could do something different. I'd always been able to do something different. I just hadn't really wanted those answers enough. All that bit about "Raging Sarah"? She was a fiction. I was Helpless Sarah. Helplessness would let me live forever never knowing. F-o-o-r-e-e-v-v-v-e-e-r. I watched that word stretch out before me, a lifetime that at last I saw I could not bear living, could not bear eternal damnation all around me for the things I could not, no, would not, do.

Like now, when someone should be doing something about girls being followed by men in cars.

I got up from my kitchen table, went to my desk, unlocked a drawer, and took out my little gun.

56

His garage door was closed. It hadn't occurred to me in my rush that he might not be home. His charmed life had been disrupted of late, so he might be off at a lawyer's, or destroying evidence, or he might be at a warehouse somewhere, assembling one of his precious flying machines. But as I climbed out onto his driveway in the late afternoon sunlight, the little .38 heavy for its size in my jacket pocket, the garage door rose with its subtle creak. The Mustang, backup lights flaring, raced directly backward toward my car.

Not quite the confrontation I had braced for, but it had its own excitement. He lurched to a stop inches from my bumper, bounding out, shouting. "My God, Sarah! What the hell! Get out of the way!"

So many exclamation points in those utterances. I planted my feet, crossed my arms. A front-line assault with hidden backup. "I know that Celia's child is alive."

I waited for the usual flood of indignant curses. Instead, he looked at his car, sitting there humming. At my car. At me. "Not now . . . There's . . ." He threw up his hands, scattering his search for words. He shoved me aside and to my astonishment wrenched open my driver's-side door and leaped in.

"What the—!" If I shot up anything, it wouldn't be my car. I squirreled between his body and the wheel, blocking his left arm and reaching for his right hand as he pulled out the key. He twisted to shove me back, pushing at my face with the hand with the key in it, and as the hand met my face I bit down hard. He yelped and as he let the key fall I reached down and snared it, scrambling backwards onto my feet and digging out my phone.

He plunged toward me just as the 911 dispatcher answered. "What's your emergency?"

"Assault!" I screamed.

He froze, backed away, fists curling. "For God's sakes, no police," he hissed. "I'll tell you everything."

"I'm sorry," I told the phone between gulps, "nothing, I'm fine, a misunderstanding." I pressed End Call but backed farther, the phone at my ear. "They'll call back." He'd never before actually attacked me, but I was glad I still had 911 on the keypad. "So what's this 'everything'?"

His jaw moved. Teeth grinding? He used to do that at my obtuseness. "They're trying to abduct Ben."

Ben? Celia's little boy? Finally materializing? "They?"

His phone rang. He jerked it from the pocket of his sweatshirt. "Yeah?" I ducked my own phone into my pocket where the gun was, finger still on the call button. Eric's face contorted as he listened. "Yeah," he said again. "Coming. Don't. Unless you absolutely have to." He stuck the phone back in his pocket. "Sarah, I have to go."

I didn't move. "She left you the money to take care of . . . Ben?"

"I have to go."

"To hide him from his father?"

He raked his hair back. Didn't clear the stain from his face. "Ben is . . ."

"I know. Disabled. Peyton told me."

He looked around at my car, at his car, at me, as if he could rearrange us with some sort of mental levitation. "Not now. I'll tell you later."

"The faster you talk the faster the car moves. Why was she hiding the child?"

More shifting of his gaze at the sources of his frustration. His jaw jerked again. "Briscoe wanted her to abort. A vegetable, he called him."

The Mulligan woman, her questions about a child connected to Celia. "But she didn't. There was some kind of settlement with conditions. Did that have anything to do with the child?"

He wheeled toward my car and for a second I thought he might try to push it bodily out of the drive. "Yeah," he snapped back at me. "He made putting the kid in an institution a condition of the divorce settlement. Celia said it would just mean a slower death."

I saw, partly. "So she told him it was dead to get her settlement."

"To get her divorce and keep him out of some hellhole. And it's not 'it.' It's 'him.'"

"Wouldn't Briscoe have demanded a death certificate?" He didn't answer, turned impatiently to his own car, still sitting there running. "It looks as if Briscoe no longer thinks the boy is dead," I said.

He came back to me, shoulders tightening. "You're not going to move your car."

"You haven't answered my questions." My phone rang, the 911 dispatcher. "We have your location. Do you require services?"

"No, I'm with my ex-husband but for now it's settled. I'll keep a finger on the keypad." I hung up again. "They might just send somebody so you better talk faster. Is Briscoe the villain, or this Franklin guy?"

He took a jab of a step toward me. I backed up. His phone rang. He pivoted away as he listened, clawing the back of his neck. "Yeah . . . I can't, a crazy woman has me blocked, yeah, her car in my driveway. She won't move it. Yeah, ASAP." He pocketed the phone, took out a key fob. He clicked off the still-running Mustang; behind him the garage door ground shut. "I don't have time for this, Sarah. Brendan's coming. Take your self-righteous shit and practice it on someone else."

How long did I have? I took a step farther back and pulled out the gun.

His laugh came out sharp but fissured. "Seriously?"

I steadied the gun with both hands.

He raised a brow. "I could take that thing away from you in a heartbeat."

"Not before I fire."

He grunted. "Your hand is shaking."

Yeah, from my galloping heartbeat. "That should worry you. Talk."

He gave a slow, heavy shake of his head. "Fine, I'll talk, somebody ought to. You have no idea what you're dealing with. Franklin, or so he calls himself at the moment, he worked for Briscoe, white-collar bullshit. Then he started using Briscoe and it all blew up." He looked past me, tilting his head, but there was no sound of a car yet. "Franklin knew about the fight over Ben. He also knew how to get fake documents. Like death certificates, yeah. He started blackmailing Celia, threatening to tell Briscoe Ben was alive. She stayed a step ahead of him. Until . . ." He shrugged. "He got her. Like he could get you."

My sweat was making the gun slippery. "If you think he killed her, call the police."

"They'll drag in Briscoe."

"Well, gee, he's the father."

"Yeah, he had a test done for the custody threat." He raked his hair back again, with the exasperated roll of his eyes he always used to shut me up. "But that doesn't mean it's the kid he cares about. I don't know what Franklin wants or what he has on Briscoe. But if Franklin gets Ben, he'll set a price on him for Briscoe, maybe not just money. Maybe he'll want something Briscoe won't pay."

It was my voice, not my hands, I had to keep from shaking. "Of course he'll . . . if he doesn't? Pay whatever Franklin is asking?"

"Grow up, Sarah. People all over the world pay good money every day to get their . . . hands . . . on a child."

I heard myself make a noise. "Like someone paid for ours?"

He sighed, not the condescending sigh I was used to. A bruised sound, from his gut.

"I'm sorry about Anna," he said, "I always have been. I know what it's like to lose a child. But for the last time, I can't give you the answers you're after. The hell with trying to convince you." He took another step up the driveway, but instead of coming toward me, he swung wide. I wheeled to track him, aiming, as he drew even. We faced each other for the space of a breath. A car purred around the curb, the one I'd seen at the Woodridge house. Eric nodded at the gun pointed at him. "You'll have to shoot me to stop me from doing the one thing she asked me for."

The car pulled into the driveway. Eric waited through my second of decision before he crossed and slid in beside the driver. I watched with the gun metal burning my fingers as the car backed into the street, revved, and disappeared.

57

I had at least one answer. About myself, anyway.

I jammed the useless gun in my pocket, whipped around to my car, jumped in. Roared backward into the street. No way I was going to sit here, blind to so much. But at the turn onto 360, I stopped. Which way?

Fifty-fifty. I turned right, out of the Hill Country and toward the river. But no sign of the little car in the inevitable traffic jams.

As if I could follow the car in that kind of traffic even if I'd spotted it. I drove back to Eric's; not sure why. The red Mustang still sat in the driveway, the replacement for the one he'd managed to keep out of the police dragnet for years. I pulled in behind it as the streetlights began to flicker, listening to our old neighborhood rustling softly, reminding me of other times. Of how Eric had slipped from my wonderful husband to a perplexing worry to this black hole now opening before me, sucking in more lifetimes of spirit and commitment than I had to lose.

And now he was shaking up my categories again. Where should I file him? Should I move him from child-molester/child-killer to . . . what? Not concerned father. Not faithful lover. The past few moments had definitely nudged Eric into an indeterminate corner of my moral space.

How little I really knew. This child I had never seen: had Eric really sworn to care for him forever? *That* Eric? *My* Eric? I just couldn't find Eric where I'd always stored him. But then, I'd never seen Eric in love.

What about this Briscoe? Desperate father or fiendish villain? As for this Franklin, how could I check what Eric had said? Eric was just one of the people with a claim on Ben. Assuming there was such a child and Ben was his real name.

I toyed with actions. Going home and leaving these villains to their crimes was not an option. If nothing else, there was the possible danger to Peyton. I was sure she knew where this Ben was. She could be leading this George Franklin to him. When he found Ben, what uses would he have for her?

Her parents wouldn't help me find her. Would they listen to Clauson? But what could he tell them? That a lady he knew thought she might be in danger. On what evidence? Oh, that there was this bad guy named George Franklin, and this little boy, Ben, and this plot to abduct him and what did that have to do with Peyton and where was all this happening and you must be mistaken, our daughter is with friends . . .

Maybe I should try to find Nick. How would he take this new information? Maybe together we could . . . we might . . .

Nick wouldn't know any better than I did where Peyton was, where this boy was, where Eric had gone.

As I turned onto Mopac, the visions floated before me. A child lost where there were people worse than Eric. Calling for her mother. In the dark.

————

I was fretting at a stoplight when my phone pinged. A text.

Once more it was Simone.

I pulled into a parking lot to read it. "Please I have to see u my fathers going to kill eric. Please."

My fingers fumbled out. "Where are you?"

"At your house please don't tell."

"Go home. Tell your mother."

She did not reply.

————

I parked in my usual space. Sat breathing. Waiting.

Of course she had gone home to her mother. Of course she would make a sensible decision like that.

But of course, no, she was not in the least sensible but despairing, just as I was sure Anna had been, wrung with secrets she did not dare tell her mother, frantic to take hold of any hand offered, even by a stranger, that might pull her out of the dark. It was my hand she reached for because I knew the worst of her, and a place where you have no more secrets is the safest place to be. I could not be shocked at what she had said. Which was why she had picked me to say it to. So it made sense to accept that she was nearby, somewhere, waiting. I texted, "Are you here?"

After a few minutes I got out. Let her see me if she was watching.

She appeared. A pale shape in the mouth of our alley. In jeans and a sweatshirt. As she stepped forward, the dim light shone on a jumble of puppies on the sweatshirt. So some kids were still young. My daughter might remain forever in that stage.

We watched each other for a moment. "Let's go on the porch," I said.

She looked past me at the house. "Someone will see us."

"Yes, I'm going to tell Adela you're here. I want witnesses."

She turned on the balls of her feet, as if she might bolt. She didn't. She didn't move toward the house either.

"This is serious," I said. "If you're telling the truth."

"It's true. I told him some things . . he believed me. Now because of what I said he's going to find him and kill him. It's all my fault."

Her dark eyes were Nick's eyes, alive with a steadfast aim. "Go on, up on the porch," I said.

She shook her head, her taut young face furrowed. "It just made me so mad, him saying all that about me. I thought, if he wants to believe that, let him. I didn't know he would . . . It's all my fault, I just wanted to hurt him." She waved her hands.

I didn't summon Adela. The connection between Simone and me was so frail a witness would wreck it. I waited for her to climb the steps and choose the chair that made her feel most safe. As she sat, she twisted her fingers into a knot only a magician would be able to undo. "So what you told your dad . . . wasn't true?"

She nodded.

Belief pulled in all sorts of contradictory directions. Maybe what she told her dad was true or Eric's denial was true or just possibly, in some devastating surrender, she had consented to sex. Had she been, in that long-standing mean-girl parlance, a slut?

But belief in what she told me asked me to choose between my two Erics, one who could molest children or one who could rescue them. I tested every step toward her. "What exactly did Eric do?"

"Eric didn't do anything to me. I never even went to his house."

She drew a shuddering breath.

"And now my dad thinks he did and he came to my room today and tried to make me say where he was so he could go kill him." She slung her head back and forth, tears catching the silver lamplight. "I thought you would know where my dad is. He'll listen to you."

I pushed away the dire pictures she conjured. Nick's rage. Its scattershot aim.

"All he wanted was to be with that woman." Her voice trembled. "He didn't care about me."

The question I had to ask was brutal.

"Did Eric rape Peyton?" I said.

She floundered for a moment. Her gaze came back to me, hardening and darkening. "I can't talk about Peyton. You'll have to ask her."

"Where is she?"

"How should I know?" She found a well of rebellion. "I'm not listening to Peyton ever again. She's so stupid. She thinks this guy she's gone off with is going to take her to Hollywood or somewhere to be a movie star or something. That's so dumb."

"Gone . . . gone off?" I might have stammered. "She's with him?"

Simone's mouth set. "I can't—"

The damn phone rang.

Diana.

"It's your mother," I said.

A fierce shiver. "They track my phone. She thinks she can find out everything about me from it." A grim satisfaction. "She can't."

Diana's voice slapped me across the distance. "Let me speak to my daughter."

I offered Simone the phone. She shook her head.

"Never mind," said Diana. "I'm coming for her."

"We're talking."

"I will be there in five minutes." She hung up.

I looked at Simone. "Your mother's coming to get you."

She shook her head at something hard and bright.

"Please," I said. "Tell me what I have to know. Who is this guy Peyton's with?"

"I can't . . ."

"Can't what?"

"They'll . . . Peyton will . . ."

I pressed. We had so few moments. "Who is 'they'?"

"Don't you know where my father is?"

My nails dug into my palms. Out there, Eric on one quest, Nick on another, and Simone and I—I took a deep breath to keep me in the present. "No, we have to find him." I took out my phone, hit Nick's number icon. We both watched it go to voice mail. "Nick, I'm here with Simone. She's worried about you. Please call."

We sat. Wasting precious seconds.

"You know where Eric is," she said. "You should call him."

She was wrong that I knew where he was but right that I should call him. I punched his icon, said to his voice mail, "Simone says Nick is looking for you. She's worried about what he might do. Please call."

More wasted time.

"You want my father to kill him," she said.

The pulse in my throat lurched. As if, for a moment, the part of me that had sought exactly that kind of vengeance stirred in a dark mental corner. The part that had finally decided to risk whatever it took to free our daughter from our ugly past. "Nonsense." Even to me my protest sounded feeble. "Of course not."

She ignored me. "You want me to say he raped her. You've wanted to think he did that from the start." She pulled back into her chair, away from me. "That he hurt us. Well, he didn't. We all lied. Peyton was so . . . *pissed* because he . . ." Her stoniness broke. She clutched at the chair arms. "I don't know what he did to your daughter. But he didn't do anything to us."

My voice came out in the most meager possible protest. "My daughter—"

"I don't know anything about that. None of us did."

She sat forward again, her words urgent.

"I thought you could help me. It'll be my fault."

I closed my eyes, opened them to a stare both frightened and furious, the tears now a solid glaze.

"You said Peyton is with this man—"

"Peyton's with that weird guy—"

"The weird guy is after a little boy that I think is Celia's, and Eric is trying to protect him." For the first time, those words did not sound fantastic. "Peyton knows where the little boy is and the weird guy will go there with her or follow her. And Eric is after the weird guy. So if we can find Peyton, maybe we can find Eric. If we can find Eric, we can find your father. Is Peyton's number on your phone?"

She jerked sideways, headlights pouring around the corner of the house. She got to her feet. The car stopped in the driveway. Beyond the headlight glare a figure emerging. Diana's voice. "Simone! Where is my daughter? *Simone*."

"Don't run away," I hissed. "Don't make us have to look for you."

Her gaze cut between me and the approaching bulk of her mother, materializing out of the headlight glare.

"Tell me the number," I said.

"Simone!" Diana's summons boomed toward us, strident. "Come here. Now."

Simone reached into a pocket of her sweat pants. She held out her phone.

I took it. Diana reached the bottom of the steps. "I'm calling the police."

Simone stumbled away from me. "I'm *coming*." She blundered out the screen door, stalked past her mother. I went to the door. Diana faced me.

"I've told you," she said.

I said nothing.

"Next time I will have you arrested," she said.

I wanted her gone. I had a phone call to make.

58

Diana's car murmur faded. Glow from our neighbors' security poles lit the tops of the bushes lining the yard. I took out Simone's phone. At my touch it flashed to light in the semi-darkness. I found her contacts list. Pd, Per, Pey . . .

I was bringing my thumb down on "Peyton" when my own phone rang. Not Eric or Nick or Clauson or Russell. A strange number. I had no time for robocalls. No sooner had I let it go to voice mail than a number I did know flashed on the screen.

Eric.

He'd had no use for me on his hero mission. Unlikely he'd reassessed my value. But if he hadn't lied, where he was was where Ben was, and probably Peyton. I swiped to open the call.

He was breathless. "They got him. They broke in, took him. That Peyton kid was with them. In a van. Don't you have her number? You can find out where she is."

Standing there holding the link to Peyton, I tried to imagine the boy Eric was hiding from his father. Profoundly disabled. With a wheelchair? And here I loitered, wrestling with the remains of the raging half of me that wanted to tear off into the night. I had no reason to think that my feeble actions would make any difference to that child. To any of them—Simone, Peyton, my own daughter, or for that matter, Nick. As before, I told Eric, "Call the police."

Silences like the one that met me had always led to a remark, an insult, a challenge, once he cornered me where I had fled to escape. This time he said, "If you won't help me with this, say so now."

That plea found me. "I don't know what I can do, or who I'll be helping. I have to think this out."

"I don't have time for thinking."

"If I had a fast answer, I'd give it."

"You don't believe me."

"I'm not used to believing you."

The phone almost vibrated with the rush of his anger, lost and spewing. "To hurt me, you'd let this kid die. Or worse. And you'd hurt those girls, too, if you thought they'd get you to me."

If only Simone hadn't just said that. If only my conscience hadn't just said that.

"I don't have time for this," he snapped, and hung up.

The phone kept on glowing. I turned it off. Simone's had gone dark as well. The two phones in hand, I headed back toward the house. What could I say to Peyton to win her so she would tell me where she was and with whom? What could I do with what she told me? I had just reached the back porch when Simone's phone pinged. My heart caught. Peyton. I opened the text.

They're hurting this little boy don't call my mother call your dad come get me 459 wonston st

"Cold sweat" is not an expression. It slaps your shoulder blades with an acid frost.

So Peyton was finding out what she'd sold herself to.

My indecision lasted only seconds. Hadn't I banished Helpless Sarah? Wasn't Raging Sarah rebuilding herself spark by spark? What I did next wouldn't save Anna but there were people alive and waiting right here before me. I didn't even have to do any searching. I had the address right here in my hand.

I punched the voice-message icon on Simone's phone. "We're coming." That didn't seem adequate. "Hang on." What baloney. Nothing else to say.

I'd left my purse in my car, money, keys, ID, a few of the things I'd need to save a life. Like the gun.

I needed a better brand of courage than the fake grit it had offered. No time to race upstairs and store it. Beside the porch were upended buckets for our summer gardening. I hid it under the nearest one.

I dove behind the wheel, typed the address into my phone. As I reached for the ignition, a text flashed. Not Eric. That strange number. My app showed the first line of the message. "This is Audrey Vanhoven," said the text.

This was not seconds, it was one of those forever minutes. I sat with the text before me. It took a deliberate and conscious willing of every muscle and sinew my hand to close it and call 911.

"I want to report a child abduction," I said. I gave the address from Peyton's message. "Please contact Lt. Sander Clauson."

"Are you at this address?" asked the dispatcher.

"Not yet. I'm on my way."

——————

I aimed for the alley. The phone was searching for the address, hadn't found it. I reached the corner and swiveled into traffic. People alive and waiting, at least I hoped so. "Please hurry," I said into the phone.

"Wait for the officers to arrive," said the dispatcher. "Are you armed?"

"No."

"Don't act on your own. Stay on the line. Your call will be acted on."

What I could do on my own was call Peyton's parents. Their number might be on Simone's phone. But I was driving too fast, too erratically, to scroll through Simone's contacts. That would have to wait until I found myself wherever I was going. "Fine, I'll stay on the line."

My phone still hadn't found the address. I tried just the odd street name. That it found. Peyton could have mistyped the street number in her hurry. I set my phone with its live link to the police in the holder on my dash, its map bright in the dark.

Wonston was farther away than I'd figured, in a newish neighborhood east of I-35. By the phone, fifteen minutes. The phone detoured me through convoluted streets, I guess to save me five seconds. Still no word from my 911 contact. I emerged at last onto a straight shot, from the looks of my phone directions. Simone's phone pinged. Hoping I'd keep to my lane by instinct, I looked down.

From Peyton again. "459 Winston."

No other message.

She might be sending these pleas in stolen moments, fearful they'd take the phone from her. Maybe they had already, and this new address was a lie.

No way I could know. No way I could trust.

I veered into a parking lot, opened the map app on Simone's phone, and plugged in the new address.

The phone found this one. A long sweeping drive in the opposite direction, northwest.

On my phone 911 crackled. "Are you on the line? The address you—"

"I know. Typo. I have a new one." I gave it. "The girl sending these could be in trouble."

"I'll relay that," the voice said. "Keep the line open." The voice went away.

I started off in the new direction, toward I-35 to catch 183. Eric and possibly this Brendan might have seen where the van carrying Peyton had gone. If they'd followed it, they might catch up before the police could get there. They might be close enough to act *now*.

Especially if they knew the exact address. Which I hadn't told them yet.

Bottom line: if the police didn't make it in time, the sacrifice I had made would be worthless. Little old me wasn't going to rescue these two endangered children on my own. If the children were both real, and really in danger, they needed Eric and maybe this Brendan.

Never in a million years had I imagined turning to Eric for help.

I dropped the police connection and punched the icon for Eric on my phone.

59

Eric answered right away. His voice barked from a place in him I didn't remember. "What?"

"Did you follow Peyton?"

"We lost her. We're—"

"I know where she is. The police are coming." I spilled the second address Peyton had sent. "I'm going there now."

Silence. Then another bark. "That's not the right address."

"Yes. She sent it. I'll explain—"

Metallic rattles in the background. "Not Winston. Winson."

"But that's—"

"It was one of Celia's places. She had houses where she kept meds and stuff if she had to move Ben in a hurry. Franklin must have taken a key when he killed her." A voice in the near distance, a door slamming. "You stay out of this. Don't tell the police." He hung up.

I had missed my chance to stay out. I loaded the new address into Simone's phone. Back where I had just come from. I did a risky U. Damn, I hadn't called the police back. No more stopping. But then my phone rang. The dispatcher. "Ms. Crockett? There's no apparent disturbance—"

"I gave you another wrong address. I'm sorry." So what if she thought I was an idiot. "It was a text. I misread it." I gave her the correction.

"I'll relay the new address," she said, dripping disapproval. "We're transferring you to a less urgent connection—"

I flung the phone down with the woman still talking; I needed both hands for swerving around the truck ahead. Now the police would have to come from the far side of town. Or pull in cars they had closer, not likely since my emergency had dropped several notches in their queue.

I sliced across the bow of a big SUV to avoid getting stuck in a turn lane, took the light on yellow. By chance, I wasn't that far from Winson. It turned out to be a dark street of smallish houses, some with lights shining behind curtains. Street numbers on front-doors and porch frames were hard to read. Cars sat in some driveways, others at the curb. Other houses had garages. Not a dump, not squalid, but deeply quiet, in the dark menacing. I slowed, searching for house numbers. Not every house had one. Two thirty-five. Four fifty-nine would be farther down, far from the bustling traffic, in deepening shadows. Three eighty-one. Four twenty-three. Four forty-seven. These houses were closer together, no lights now.

There *was* a four fifty-nine. Sitting by itself at a dead end, a silent, sagging little house with an empty narrow driveway leading to darkness beyond. Even in the shadows I could make out the unkempt yard, weeds scraggling against the foundation. Hard to tell if there were curtains in the windows. There was certainly no light.

I let my car idle at the curb. Turned off my headlights. Sat and shook. I could have called Ms. V instead of giving up my own hopes up for nothing. The police would arrive. For nothing. Like me all fired up to rescue people who were dying somewhere else.

Would texting Peyton help? Could she tell me where she was?

If she was free, maybe. If she was alive.

The text app on Simone's phone was still open. The messages I'd received from Peyton earlier had slid higher on the phone. I scrolled up above them, then back down. I wrote, "Where are you?" and hit send. But a name in one of the messages I'd zoomed past had flagged me. I scrolled back. Sent tonight. Six-twelve. Simone to Peyton: *I have to tell my dad it was Cole.*

Cole?

Peyton had written back, *u do u die.*

Cole. A tall, slender, auburn-haired figure with an arm on Simone's shoulders that day Nick and I stood in Bailey Jaspers' doorway. Peyton's brother. *What seems to be the trouble here?*

Not cold sweat this time. A deep sadness. So much heartache for so many, when a little truth could have saved so much.

Maybe I was jumping to conclusions. Maybe it wasn't as simple as my imagination wanted to make it. Maybe—

A noise. A car engine, faint but disrupting, from somewhere behind the house. I jumped. Oh yeah, I sat alone on a dark street in front of a house where I'd just summoned the police to stop bad things.

A light on in the house? I blinked frantically. Yes, in a front room. In a brief flash before a yank closed the curtains, my gaze cleared on a wash of pink and white and a shimmering white-gold glow.

Peyton.

Don't act on your own. Don't rush into dangerous situations. Didn't I learn that last year? Apparently not.

Should have brought the gun, I thought grimly. What for, to terrorize Peyton? Oh, right.

My breath tight in my chest, I eased silently out of my car and crept up uneven stepping stones through a grabbing fringe of unmowed brambles. I found the brass doorknob; anyone on the other side would see it twist if I turned it. Was I ready? Not hardly. I took a breath and tried it. Locked.

Freeing that breath and fighting to control the next one, I inched along the wall past a hedge of dead, dried, alarmingly noisy bushes. Vertical metal bars blocked the window. The flimsy curtain gaped at the edge and I peered through.

She was alone, hunched on a sagging dark sofa shoved up against the bare wall to the right. A floor lamp cast a dim glow across her; her back was twisted to me as she peered down a dark hallway leading toward the rear of the house. The pink was her pastel sweats, the shimmer her pale hair wound high on her head in a messy spray. No sign of her phone.

She shifted to rise, seemed to crumple, sank again, hands pleating the sweat pants. I tapped on the glass.

She jumped, yelping loud enough I heard her through the window. She pressed a hand to her mouth and half-rose, then slumped again, eyes wide and searching. "It's Sarah Crockett," I said, as loud as I dared. "Open the door."

She pushed up and crossed unsteadily toward me. She shoved the curtain aside. On her wan face a red blotch, on her lip the start of swelling. "I can't, it's a key lock."

"Try the window."

"It's got bars." Her voice shook. She looked over her shoulder. "They'll be back. Call the police."

"I did. They're coming."

Then we both jumped. A gunshot, I was certain. From behind the house.

"Oh, God," she said, both hands at her mouth now.

Maybe the gunshot would draw neighbors. Or scare them into bunkers. "Where's the boy?"

She gestured toward the dark hallway.

"Go get him." I tested one of the bars. Corrosion flaked off in my hand. I wrenched against the grip of the flaking, splintery window sill.

"He's all hooked up. They said if the thing goes off he'll die. I'm supposed to watch—"

"Go get him." I pulled harder. The bar broke loose at the bottom. A light flashed in the hallway behind her. I pulled really hard. The bar came free. At least a weapon. She could worm through, if she just would. But she turned toward the hallway and cried out.

If my heart could have cried out like that, it would have. Eric stood there in the glow at the edge of the light. He thrust something that glittered toward Peyton. I made out his order: "Open the door."

Bless her, she moved fast, grabbing the key from him and slipping out of my line of sight toward the door. Eric shot me a glance. "Go start your car," he said more than loud enough for me to hear. He disappeared into what must have been a doorway off the hall. Peyton pushed the front door open. I glanced back at a sudden clatter on the sidewalk behind me. Another shout from my heart: *Police!* I turned. Not police. Nick.

Nick in a windbreaker with one hand in a pocket, his hair raked into a tumult of spikes. His eyes so bright that even in the dark they sparked. I braced but he shoved me against the door frame hard enough to jar out a yell. He looked around wildly. "Where is Simone?"

"Not here, I have her phone—"

"Where is *he?*"

"Nick, there's no time—"

Eric stepped back out into the hallway, just visible in the light. Nick went rigid. "You bastard." The words sprang out with his spit.

Eric said nothing. He disappeared into the dark. Running? "Nick." I grabbed his bicep, shook him. "Nick, listen." Nick barged toward the hallway, dragging me, elbowing Peyton. "Nick. Nick. He's rescuing Celia's child."

He twisted around, hands raised to shove me off him. I caught them. "*Celia's child.*" I came down on the words, angry, hard.

He froze in my grasp, stared blankly, panting, gulping something too thick to swallow. "Celia didn't . . ."

"Yes," I said. "She did."

He wheeled to Peyton. "Where? You're lying. Where's this . . ." The word didn't want to break out of him. He spun, searching around wildly.

"Right here," Eric said.

He burst out of the hallway, the dark curled shape against his shoulder, fetal in its limpness. To my amazement he thrust his burden onto Nick. Nick staggered against me and I reached past him to stop the child from falling, but somehow Nick's body obeyed some instinct that had survived his rage. His arms found the small body, the child's head against his shoulder. Beyond us Eric was moving. "Help me grab some of this stuff from the bedroom," he told Peyton. Numbly she stumbled toward him. Nick stood paralyzed cradling the comatose child.

"We've got to put him in my car," I told him. "Hurry." I took his arm to tug him. A clatter from the hallway. Eric was backing out toward me, pulling Peyton with him. Beyond him George Franklin, in a dark pullover and ball cap, a gun in his right hand. With his left he reached for Peyton's arm and for a moment she hung there, a prize between Eric and Franklin. "Go!" Eric told me over his shoulder. Franklin pulled Peyton across his body, the gun to her temple. Eric let go, edging away.

"Nick!" I said wildly, tugging. "Come on!" Suddenly I found my own arms full of warm, breathing child. He weighed nothing, more a wish than a body. I wheeled toward the door, thinking, *if only one of us can survive*. I looked back at Nick long enough to see the unmistakable black L of a gun in his hand.

I saw but didn't sort out then what I saw, Franklin's gaze shifting toward Nick, Eric diving, Nick firing. This time I didn't consciously name the crack as a gunshot, the horrific echo in the small space where those bodies fought. Then where Franklin had been the dark empty hall and above it all a wail I didn't identify as a siren until the dark-suited figures surged past me, one of them slamming me with my treasure against the wall. When I found air again, Eric and Nick stood in the door of the hallway with their hands skyward, Peyton before them, her hands outstretched, imploring, “Don’t shoot, they’re saving me, don’t shoot.”

60

So much to sort out in the long night that followed: one cop hustling me outside with my slumped burden; glimpses over my shoulder of Peyton huddling in a corner; Eric and Nick splayed with their hands against the wall. I wished I could tell Eric I was sorry. He'd wanted to keep the boy away from Briscoe. I found myself wishing he had.

More cars, more sirens, stark lights, and a whole phalanx of stiff-uniformed bodies charging past. A taut-jawed young man stopped among the grasping brambles to ask my name. Where was my ID? Whose kid is this, this your kid? That shook me out of the trance where I was still struggling to understand what had happened. "He's Celia Monahan's child."

Taut-jaw stared blankly, as if neither the name nor the word "child" made sense. "He needs some kind of treatment," I told him. "That man in there will know."

He took me by the arm, child and all, and dragged me to a police car. For a moment I thought he was going to take the child from me. Luckily for him an ambulance was the next bellowing vehicle racing up the street. He did not put me in the car until a patient-looking EMT crossed and held out his arms and I surrendered. "He needs some kind of treatment," I repeated. "A man in there will know."

Taut-jaw did a quick pat-down, taking Simone's phone, before guiding me into the car. So there I sat, locked in, through much more madhouse coming and going, lights blazing from the house now, neighbors and gawkers suddenly emboldened to plug the street. Some small pieces I put together through guesswork. That tableau: Eric and Nick hands overhead, Peyton pleading, the officers in TV defense poses, rigid. *Nick had a gun.* That was why the police shot people. But for Peyton, they would have shot Eric and Nick.

The cops remembered me after a bit, for all the good it did them. I said I wanted my lawyer (as if I had one). I said either my lawyer or Lt. Clauson. I got a couple of grunts in reply.

It had to be the tracking app in the phone that had led Nick to me. He must have thought Simone was racing to Eric. I had moved him far down on my list of people who might have killed Celia. He was first and foremost a father. I had watched him hold that child, even if only for moments. I knew now that if he had found his daughter among us, he would have gathered her to him like he had the child.

After many more bits of a bit, the police-car door opened. "I fucking told you," Clauson said.

It wasn't the first time he had sat with me in a police car after an act of violence. Then he had sat in the front looking back. Now he wedged his bulk in beside me. "Start talking," he said.

He'd have deduced a lot from my odyssey in the 911 records. "Not a whole lot to tell."

"We're not gonna play that same game we played last year. Talk."

I had used my time to sort out what I knew and what I shouldn't. "Whatever Eric told you I will probably agree with."

"So now he's your hero?"

"I don't know who was the hero. It was all a blur."

One of his heaviest sighs. "Did you know this Franklin guy?"

"I told you all about him. He tried to break into my office. I told you Eric knew him. I thought maybe *you* knew him. I heard he'd been seen with Celia."

"You heard."

"Yes. I heard."

He took a long time to breathe, wheezing a little, like a man being worn down. He probably didn't mean to let go of what he said next, you know, ongoing investigation. "Your boy Nick thinks he killed him."

Well, he'd come wanting to kill someone. "Franklin? Is he dead?"

Clauson groaned, belly deep. "Your door at your place lock good?"

"Yes. Why?"

He got out. He waved overhead. A uniformed officer appeared out of the hubbub. "Follow this one home. Make sure she gets inside. Stay outside her place until I call you." To me, leaning down, he said. "A full statement tomorrow."

"They took Simone's phone. It knows more than I do."

He grunted wearily. "I'll get it. Go home and work on your priorities a while."

———————

Morning came. I knew because there was a sunrise. Sort of: a dreary day, like old laundry. The cop guarded my house until after I had forced down coffee; he got at least one earful from Adela, whom I saw bent to his window in her bathrobe as the light rose. Wallace, I learned when I went down to steal Adela's print copy of the paper, had inspected the cop with binoculars. "God, he's a cutie. Get his name?"

"Don't remember my own name," I said.

I waited until the cop left to slip downstairs to fish my little gun out from under the bucket. Back upstairs, I locked it in the drawer where it belonged, then opened a voice mail from Nick. "They let me call. I'll be out later today. Can we meet?"

I was still sunk in my Xanax-fueled sleep, too lost in dreams about rooms full of students waiting for me to grade their papers. In the dream I couldn't find any of their names in my gradebook, though I flipped hundreds of pages. I stared at the innocent phone. Could we meet? I had to think about what for.

Around noon, which I decided was the hour he might reasonably have expected me to sleep till, I sent a text. "I need a few days. I'll be in touch."

About that same time I called Ms. Vanhoven. She didn't answer. I left a voice mail. "I was in the middle of an emergency. Please. I can arrange to meet you. Please call."

———————

The local news reported the bare bones of an "altercation involving gunfire" on Winson, no mention of names. The noon newscast was equally barren; no comment from police. If they freed Nick, would they free Eric? I thought of texting him but didn't know who was in charge of his phone. When my phone next rang at two, it wasn't Nick, it wasn't Ms. Vanhoven, it was an invitation to a police-station appearance. Whatever Clauson's fears for me the night before, they had apparently abated. No sign of an escort on my drive downtown.

At least the sworn recital of selected facts and garbled observations I provided that day was more truthful than the statement I had signed last summer. This time, Clauson already knew most of what I had to say. I didn't see him. I recounted to strangers Simone's terrors about her father's intentions and Eric's pleas to me that afternoon at his house; I included his claims about his ties to the boy and his fears for him. I even reported my attempts to warn Peyton's parents, my own fear for the girl and her foolishness. The statement taker was a mild fifty-year-old whose taut jaw, if he'd ever had one, had been swallowed by flesh long ago.

At least he was patient and non-committal. He asked why I had had Simone's phone; he only grunted when I said that she had given it to me so I could find her father. Let Nick explain the panic that had driven his daughter to me.

"We were worried about your safety last night," he told me as he stood for my dismissal. "We think the person of concern is no longer in this jurisdiction. All the same, we're arranging a heightened presence in your neighborhood for the time being. You might alert your neighbors so they won't be alarmed."

"Is Eric here? Or Nick?"

"Sorry," he said, with an effort at hardening his jaw line. "I don't have that information."

"Or the girl? Peyton? Is she okay?"

"No information, I'm afraid."

At least the land of "no information" was the one I was used to. I said "Thank you anyway" with a minimum of snark.

It was Peyton who haunted me on my weary way to the street. She'd had so much to deal with, with only a teenager's resources. My adult resources had barely been enough.

I did not mention her brother Cole. They had Simone's phone, they had Simone, they had Peyton. For God's sake, let them find out at least one thing on their own.

61

Reaching my car meant braving the downtown midday furnace. I had traded hopes of word from Ms. V for a fantasy of a cool silent place where I could collapse and sleep. That wish gave way to the realization that I did, after all, have responsibilities beyond my obsessions. It must have been years since I wondered whether Kendra was okay.

So on my way back to the car lot I broke stride and dug out my phone. Kendra might even have responded to my message. Bent over the phone, I made my shaky way to my car—and looked up to find Eric leaning on the hood.

We'd been here before, he and I had, me coming out of the police station, Eric waiting. Then, I'd had Russell at my shoulder. No one here with me now.

But this was not the snarling man who'd confronted me that day. Now he looked scraped to bone, the gilt melted. I put my phone away. The possibility that he might be innocent had created a new reality for me to live in. For so long my faith in his guilt had been a guiding beacon I could stay fixed on, dictating the paths of my search. With that faith gone, the biggest and brightest of my open doors toward Anna had slammed shut. Now, in the new darkness, I had a whole uncharted universe to search. That day last year, confronting him in this same parking lot, I'd demanded, "What do you want?" Now I wished I had someone to tell me what I wanted. I finally said, "Is Ben okay?"

He ran a hand through his still-evanescent hair. He lifted a shoulder. Didn't speak.

I shoved my hands in my pockets, edged closer, a feral core in me still distrusting. "Did they charge you with anything?"

He squinted into sunlight that did him no favors. "I actually have you to thank that they didn't. They knew from your 911 calls why I was there."

"What happens now? About Ben?"

"My lawyers are meeting Briscoe's lawyers."

So Briscoe did want his son. It sounded like Eric meant to fight to keep him. "Any news on what happened to Franklin? I guess he got away?"

A weary shrug. "Hudson got a shot off. If he hit him, they didn't tell me. Apparently he had a car waiting. When the cops finally got around to looking behind the house, he was gone."

"I heard a shot before you came in. I thought *you* killed someone."

"That was his goon shooting at me. I was driving Brendan's pickup and he hit it." His teeth worked in his jaw for a moment. "I took care of the guy, but I didn't kill him. When they looked for him, he'd disappeared, too."

"Was Brendan there? Did they hurt him?"

He shook his head. "He went to the Woodridge house to get stuff we thought we might need."

"So they're looking for Franklin?"

"They won't tell me, but I think I'm no longer their main person of interest in Celia's murder." His hands sought out his own pockets, in the same pants he wore last night, stained and chafed, I saw now, from some sort of battle. "Hudson got his lawyer, too, so we weren't detained."

I wanted to sit down. On the curb if I had to. I was so close to achieving what I had to make him do. I wanted him to open his mind, let me into those last weeks six years ago, those days and hours, when he'd had our daughter in his care. If he hadn't hurt her, he'd let her wander close to someone who had. My voice came out stronger than I'd expected. "May I buy you a cup of coffee?"

He rubbed a place on his wrist where a bruise, maybe from the night before, was turning colors. "Are you asking for permission? Isn't that what 'may I?' instead of 'can I?' means?"

"I guess I am, then."

"We need to talk anyway. So sure."

———————

On the short walk to a coffee shop on Red River we shared gems like "Hot, isn't it?" "Yes. Going to get worse soon." "Yes." He drank half his coffee before I'd even completely sat down.

But I felt hurried, these moments precious. As if he'd come to me under a spell that would wear off and return us both to the inferno we'd shared for so long. I allowed myself a sip of my coffee. "Did Anna ever meet Franklin?" I said.

He reached into a pocket and pulled out an envelope.

This maelstrom had started with an envelope that had made me sit unbreathing, sure Clauson had brought me news of Anna. Now here was another envelope; at the sight of it I couldn't help imagining disaster just as I had that first day. I stretched a hand with every nerve braced for the picture of my daughter's body I was sure I would find inside.

But my eyes had to work to focus. The hand itself failed to do mundane hand things, like pick the envelope up.

"It's not that," Eric said.

I drew my hand back. Looked at him. His features blurred in the fog filling my eyes.

"I'm sorry, I should have told you," he said. "I thought that, too, when I found it."

"Yes." My voice came out faint.

He picked up the envelope, slid open the flap, then laid it before me again. It contained a color photograph. A picture taken from the awkward slant of a surveillance image. A girl and a man.

The girl was Anna. The man holding her arm—forcefully, pulling—looked like Franklin. He was dragging her toward a car.

I knew the car. We'd found it the summer before, Russell had. A white Volvo. Russell found out who owned it. That was when I first heard the name Celia Monahan.

My fingers started to twist the photo. Eric took an edge, removed it from my grip. He set it beside him. "Yes, it shows what you think it does."

A choking breath. "But . . . how?"

"Four sets of people were spying on Celia," he said. "Most women would have turned into paranoid blobs of jelly. Not her. She confronted them." His mouth closed hard for a moment. "It got her killed."

Celia certainly confronted me. She'd focused on the girls, but the mind behind the intense dark eyes had been fixed on me, working hard. "Yes. Russell was watching both of you." But of course: Briscoe and Mulligan and their ilk as well, looking for Ben. "If Franklin wasn't working for Briscoe, yes, with me that made four."

"Like I told you, I don't know what's going on between Franklin and Briscoe. Celia didn't know for sure, either, even though for a while back then Franklin hung around pretending to be a pal. All she knew was that Franklin worked for Briscoe, then he didn't."

"You told me Franklin got the fake death certificate for Ben."

"Yeah, he had that hold over her. But she had to trust him." He sighed. "She was wrong."

"Maybe it was sex he was after."

"Yeah, maybe she let him think that. Keeping Ben safe . . . as you can probably imagine, she would have done whatever she could."

What would I have sold to keep my child safe if she had still been in my life the way Ben was in hers? "This picture? She took it?"

"Briscoe's people took it, years ago, obviously. Thinking they could catch her with Ben."

"Then he gave her a copy? Why?"

He steepled his hands with a kind of academic precision. "This last year Briscoe somehow found out for sure Ben was alive. Franklin must have told him. Briscoe told her that if she didn't give up Ben he'd hand the photo over to the police and tell them whatever dirt they had on Franklin, she was mixed up in too."

A lot now I figured out for myself. Celia understanding at last what she had in fact been mixed up in when she gave Franklin her trust. That day on her deck, had she been wildly reckless, meeting Franklin alone to call out his betrayal of her and the horrors the picture laid at his door? Or had she planned a different confrontation that had taken an uncontrollable turn? Eric went on with preoccupied speculations, as much to himself as to me. "I don't know if she actually told Franklin she had the picture. Even if she did, he may not know I have it."

Or that I have also seen it, I thought.

I did not tell him my own conclusion: how Franklin had learned that Ben was alive. Those girls and their silly, dangerous games. Sashaying in and out of Franklin's field of vision as he spied on Celia, leading him almost certainly to the safe house. I shuddered at my own speculation, about this strange man and his interest in all these pretty, salable creatures so close at hand.

But I didn't want to lay that complication before Eric, not with so much else between us. "The police—"

"I haven't shown this to the police."

"But . . . where did you find it?" New doubt broke my voice. "She showed it to you?" My throat tightened with the questions I wished I didn't have to ask him. *Have you had it for six years now? Have you known what it shows all along?*

I didn't have to make that charge; he surely heard it in the ever-present whispers of our past. He shook his head in abrupt denial. "I never saw it until this morning. We kept a lot of Ben's equipment in the house on Woodridge, including a couple of his wheelchairs. One of them had a pocket in the back where we used to leave notes, communicate with each other and with Brendan when he was keeping Ben. I didn't know if that was the wheelchair Franklin took last night or if it was still in the safe house, so I went there to look." He touched the envelope. "This was there."

Not a claim I could dispute. "The police need this."

A sharper headshake. "They know about Franklin, probably more than we do. Giving this to them just takes it out of our hands."

I, for whom passing gifts to the police had so often left my hands empty, said, "Takes what out of whose hands?"

He tapped the sheet as if to nail it to the table. "I can find this for the police any time I want. The moment will come."

"But you've shown it to me."

Our eyes met. Ten, twenty, thirty pulses in the muscles of his throat.

"You made my life hell," he said. "All your accusations, all your following. Having me tailed, photographed. Siccing those kids on me, and on her. No, I didn't always react calmly. Celia and I talked about why you did all that."

My throat must have moved, too. Eric and Celia, ensconced in one of their exotic nooks, discussing me. He rubbed his neck and sighed.

"Celia knew what you were feeling. She left a note with this picture, how she had struggled with what to do with this, considering the danger it meant to Ben. She made her own choice about Franklin but left what to tell you to me. When I found it this morning, I didn't want to give it to you either. I knew you wouldn't trust me." He scraped a hand across his features as if smoothing off ragged edges. "But I know what you went through. What it feels like as a parent to lose a child. I've always known. I just couldn't do anything about it until now."

I touched the picture. He reached as if to claim it. Stopped, the fingers curling into his palm.

"You owe me, too," he said. "For the hell you caused me. You owe me the time I need."

"Time? For Ben?"

"Time to decide what to do."

"Ben is safe," I said.

"I don't know that."

"Anna isn't."

A struggling sigh now, at the weight of a mass he knew was heavy because he'd lifted it so many times before. "Six years, Sarah."

"I can count."

"They don't . . . They can't . . . It's been too long. Can't we just let this go?"

I spread my hand over the picture.

"I have to tell the police you have this," I said.

He sprang up at me, his old impulsive fury. Caught the edge of the table and pulled himself back down. "If you want to know what happened to *our* daughter—" He slapped the picture so hard I jerked my hand back, "—this can tell us. If you will fucking let me look." He leaned over the table, no longer bullying. Asking. A new role he didn't do well at playing. "Just this once, goddamn it, for just a little while, can you please get off your self-righteous high horse? For once just give me the benefit of the doubt!"

He'd already worked one miracle: making me sit here wanting to believe him. "What can you do that the police can't?" I spent the bad card. "That Russell can't?"

The name didn't faze him. "Russell is not her father. He was not there when . . . all this started. I am and I was." A half sneer whose provenance I remembered. "Your buddy Clauson isn't and wasn't either. You've seen proof of that."

"Time," I said, unmoved, "will bring you closer to the day when you may have to choose between saving Anna and saving Ben."

He leaned closer. "What if I can save both of them?"

It was like trying to read one of those dense tomes I'd been trained to study. The ones where in one breath a writer seduces you with a coherent story and in the next rips the story you've bought into apart. He had never believed Anna was alive. Seconds ago he had played his old callous mantra, *it's been too long*. And now he claimed he could save her . . . to keep me from running to my buddy Clauson with news of leads he wanted for some purpose of his own? Or did he think he could get me to use my contacts with Clauson and even with Russell to help him save Ben?

I sat back, waited to get my heart rate within finite limits. "Whatever you're keeping from me, if it will help you find our daughter, use it. But of course I want a copy. By tomorrow." He didn't try to break my gaze as I put heat behind it: "I'll wait a week."

"Not long enough."

"Too long."

"Two weeks. Please."

There was that "please" again. "All right. Two weeks. But you're on the clock."

62

He sent me my copy. I scanned it, then folded it small enough to stuff into that box of hope my sister gave me. It filled the box to overflowing.

Ms. Vanhoven did not call.

———————

The next morning I was teaching myself forbearance by editing my summary of my meeting with Kendra's father when Nick sent a second text. "May I come by?"

"Yes, you may," I wrote.

As I expected, he kept his appointment to the second. For the first time I saw his perfectly tailored suit and blinding white shirt as armor. I was glad for that armor. I didn't want him naked, in any sense of the word, in what felt like a new life.

"You were right." He sat precariously on the arm of the chair. "It was Peyton's brother all along."

I'd read the texts on Simone's phone that night in such a daze of panic that I wondered if I'd imagined them. "Then you've talked to Simone?"

"Yes. But first I had to talk to Diana." He rubbed his hands on his smoothly creased trousers. "As you can imagine, that was hard."

"Has Cole admitted to anything?"

I'd seen Nick's gaze go dark before, but I'd never caught that hard luster in his gaze. "I'm the only one filing a charge against him. None of the other parents . . ." He lifted his hands. Seemed to push against a weight holding them down.

For Peyton's parents, this had to be a terrible trial. But if I hadn't seen that text, would anyone have ever mentioned Cole? Would Simone have finally named him? "What is Peyton saying?"

He shifted, very unNicklike, a sloppy reassessment of the space he occupied. “I haven’t talked to her. Lawyers won’t let me. I should tell you that the police questioned Simone.”

From what I remembered of her that night, I envisioned the new self Simone would find in Clauson’s presence. A strong, regal creature, chin up, lips tight. Celia came to mind, the two of them blending. “Were you there?”

“Yes, with our lawyer. But he said she could tell the truth.” Another repositioning. He seemed, like me, not to understand how physics worked in his new surroundings. “They wanted to know more about Celia than about Cole. About me, what I knew about her. What Simone saw. What the girls saw when they were following her. Simone saw that guy Franklin. Met him. He bought them ice cream.”

I made a sound. Nick’s gaze fixed on me. “I’m sorry,” I said. “I just thought . . .” I couldn’t finish. My mind had shown me my daughter, much younger, sitting in the clean, bright ice-cream shop not far from our home and reaching for something cold and sweet in a man’s hand.

“Peyton was the only one who liked him,” I said.

Maybe Anna had liked him. Trusted him because he was her dad’s friend’s friend.

“The reason I came,” Nick said.

I dragged myself briskly out of that freezing place. “I appreciate your letting me know what’s happening.”

“Well, yes. I wanted to do that. But I wanted to say how grateful I am to you. If it hadn’t been for you, Simone might have been dragged off by this . . . this monster.” He sighed. “Diana will see what she owes you, in time.”

Those quiet words told me that for him as for me, the world we’d shared so intensely had ended. I was grateful for that. I had a new journey ahead where Nick did not belong. "Simone is what should matter."

"She is what matters." He rose, shaking himself. Adjusting the rigid suit to perfect it. "I'm going to Diana's to pick her up now."

I thought then, chastened, of all I would not have learned had Nick not loved a woman who did not love him back. What I would have lost if his love for Celia had not driven Simone to me with her fears. "I want to know everything about Simone. About how she does. Her future."

"Oh," he said, drawing himself tall as if to lay a sword before me, "I'll make sure you do."

———————

I swear I felt my next visit coming, a tiny change of balance, one of those shifts I had started to recognize. I'd spent the evening working at my computer on my Kendra problem and thought I had stood up too quickly or that the ancient floor of my third-story apartment had tilted. There was no "may I?" attached to this visit, no request for permission. So I didn't get to grant that permission, or even decide if I could.

The disturbance was Russell, in a circle of streetlight below me, leaning against the door of the car he'd parked at the curb, looking up.

He did have to ask permission to climb the stairs. I pressed the buzzer to let him in.

There are many ways to describe what many women would have been feeling as they listened for his footsteps. A lover come from afar when she was most in need of his presence. Instead, I thought, *I'm not ready for this.*

I thought that he probably wasn't ready either, but had come all the same. So much that had happened to us had descended when we didn't have the luxury of preparing. Those times, we had grasped each other's hand and pushed on.

In so many important ways he was the same man I had been so thankful to see at this door all those good and bad times. Our recent talks, phone and video, had let me lose sight of the solidity of him, how he seemed to take up space where, without him, there would have been a hole in my world. In fact, there had been such a hole; I'd been so wrapped up in the events of the past few days that even the thought of him had faded. Now here he was, just like the last time I'd seen him on the chat screen, still with his close-sheared, almost military haircut, his quietly informal jacket and polo and jeans. In the flesh, at my door, he brought back to life that familiar hardness inside him that was warm.

What was different was the way he stopped in the doorway instead of entering, bracing a hand on the frame. He looked as if he had arrived in a strange new country, one, I thought, we had invented and now needed to invent a language for.

No rules for that language came to me as I stepped back to give him room. Nor did he speak as he removed the satchel on his shoulder, and set it on the chair that stood at right angles to my sofa. That had often been his chair. He did not sit. He opened the satchel and reached inside. He turned to me where I had backed up to the sofa and set a folder of papers on the coffee table. "This," he said, "is an archive of every text and email you and I have exchanged in the past year."

After a moment I sat. I did not touch the papers. He moved the satchel from the chair and settled in it, leaning toward me with his hands clasped and elbows on his knees.

"I brought it," he said, "because I want you to fill in all the parts that aren't there."

It turned out I understood our new language better than I thought. "Did Clauson call you?"

"No, but he didn't need to. I got enough of a report about what happened the other night to surmise what he could have told me." He tapped the folder. "This archive says nothing about it. Not one word of what led up to it, all the risks you've taken along the way. The other thing missing is any intrusion on my part. Any breach of our agreement." He fingered the edge of one of the sheets but did not look away from me.

Like that moment when I had taken out that gun with Eric, this moment had been coming. Perhaps, I thought, if we had not let ourselves be separated by so much space and time. If I had moved to New Mexico for example, giving up the stability and independence of my Cresthill position, we might have had this conversation, or many like it, long ago.

But I saw now that that life of shared physical space, had I lived it, would have been a distraction from this thing I had to finish. His very presence now, the solid insistence of his body, was a distraction, an interruption I had to attend to when my attention wanted to go to whatever it was that Eric was doing to save our daughter and his lover's child. In search of a future that only finding Anna could give us, I sat waiting to see this moment out at far as he would make it go.

My heart wasn't galloping as it had as I held the gun on Eric. It was deadly still.

"What would you do," I said, thinking of that picture in my Hope box, "if you knew that at this very minute I am breaking the law."

In his second of pensive silence, it was all there.

"I would have to know the situation," he said. "Until I did, I couldn't make a judgment. Any judgment." He shook his head with a ferocity I hadn't seen since before he was cleared of murder. "What matters to me is what that would mean to you. For you. The consequences for you."

"What I care about," I said, "is the consequence for Anna."

For the first time his gaze left me. When he turned back to me something braced and hard had begun to fray.

"Yes," he said. "I know that for you Anna is paramount. I see that. For me, Sarah, and I think you know this, Anna is . . ." He spread his hands.

I touched the sheaf of papers, as if I could make them a concrete connection between us. "We didn't talk about this enough," I said.

"Yes, we should have talked it out from the beginning. Are we talking now?"

"We said," I told him, "that I had to resolve this. It isn't resolved."

"We were in love. Are we still?"

My hands snared each other, didn't still the tremor. I asked the question I had run from since Clauson brought me those pictures. "Does our love depend on what I am able to resolve?"

He pushed upright. We sat far apart for that long moment.

"I can't compete with her," he said.

He laid his hand down beside mine close enough I could feel its heat.

"I can make it happen," he said fiercely. "We can make it happen. I have people on the ground who can find out things, you've seen that."

"Yes, I've been very grateful."

He slid the folder to him. "So what do I need to know to make it happen?" He flipped the pages. "All the blanks here, what goes there?"

I shook my head. "I made a promise."

If he had left then, I would have understood.

But he moved my hand gently from the folder, lifted it, and smoothed its edges. "I also have good lawyers. I think you're going to need them."

"Yes, probably," I said.

———————

He left me in the early morning. We did what love gave us license to do, but so could many other emotions, surely the need to hold each other ahead of unknowable loss. It was a seized spate of touching and breathing, rich reminders of what was there to dream of, and also a quiet and shared violence, gravity that comingled objects when so much conspired to drive them apart. I had met him when we were alone and I found, tasting memory in his sweat, what loneliness felt like, and I did hope we were still in love.

63

About three days later, I received three gifts.

One was an email from Clauson. A first. He had always preferred face-to-face or the phone. But the journey we had shared since last summer had taken hard turns and maybe his rigid habits had bent as well.

"We're releasing this to the press tomorrow, so I'm giving you a heads up." In that flat statement, an unexpected acknowledgment that he knew how much weight, for me, any news would carry. "We are asking for information on the whereabouts of Aldous Trent, aka George Franklin and a couple of other pseudonyms, in connection with the murder of Celia Monahan."

"No warrant?" I shot back. A warrant for his arrest would have been icing.

He responded quickly. "We're not the only ones looking for him. We'll ask for anyone with information to come forward. I'm assuming you don't have any such information, or you would have come forward by now."

I gritted my teeth. No, he hadn't unbent, he'd just found new ways to make his devotion to protocol needle. Next time I saw him, and I would, I would have to keep my hands in my pockets to avoid a charge of assault.

More information, though, in the reply to my terse "Yes." "We won't make any public mention of Benjamin Monahan's involvement in the events of Monday night. If you feel you have to disclose what you know about those issues, I hope you'll reconsider. As you know, there's ongoing litigation about the little boy's future. I'd like to keep that separate from police business as much as possible. I'm sure you'll understand."

I not only gritted my teeth, I ground them. Instead of the bland assent he might expect from a well-bred lady, I wrote, "Thank you for your instructions about the proper response to a child's suffering. They are most valuable. Sincerely, Sarah Crockett." Dr. Crockett to you.

To my surprise, about half an hour later he wrote back again.

"It seems to me we've never held back from giving each other instructions. Just so you know, sometimes I do listen to yours."

———————

The next was not really a gift but a penance, paid to me and not some god. Ms. Vanhoven wrote.

A long text, time-stamped five a.m.

"My conscience won't let up. I have to do this. Corinne told me about a man who tried to get Anna into his car. Anna wouldn't. Corinne's father had to take Anna home. I thought it was Anna's father, your husband, a custody battle. I didn't want to get involved. So I didn't report when I absolutely should have. I never asked Anna. That part, dealing with children's confidences, was always tricky for me. I never knew what to believe or who I'd get in trouble if I told. Corinne couldn't tell me what the man looked like, so at this late date, this won't help much. But now I have told you. I have nothing more to say."

The terse "Thank you" I wrote back was a dam on my fury. *He bought them ice cream*. Franklin, his appearance so different from Eric's: if she had told, described this would-be abductor, someone would have followed up.

We were following up now, following, I was sure, a ghost.

———————

The last gift was a packet. From Kendra.

Inside the mailer was a binder-clipped stack of typed pages, a hand-written note on top.

"Dear Dr. Crockett, thank you for your message. I'm sorry I didn't answer. I felt bad about what happened. It wasn't anything you did.

"I've worked on this some. I don't know if it's any better. Please don't think you have to try to fix it. Probably nobody can!"

A drawing of a smiley, in purple ink.

"I'm not as mad at my dad now. We're doing therapy together. He just wants the best for me. He just doesn't know what that is. But I guess I don't either, so it doesn't seem to do much good staying so mad.

"You taught me a lot about writing, even if I didn't know it. Thanks."

I read the pages that afternoon. They were not the same pages I remembered. The differences were subtle; it was still her language. But there'd been an uptick in that mysterious quality that my students called "flow." The wizard was still cruel, he still got his comeuppance. At the end, in a sequence never before submitted, Esmarelda claimed some of the wizard's tools and made them her own.

That Kendra was up and about and capable of such a mailing lowered the temperature on the crackle of alarm that I had been in the act of reporting in my research-study files. Shared therapy made it less likely that her anger at Alex was evidence of abuse. To me he had seemed benign but clumsy, a micromanaging parent whose idea of the best for his child did not take the child's own will into account. Possibly therapy might help him to a generous reading of Kendra's stories, in which, at some point, he might see what my non-expert theory suggested: that Kendra's plots fed off an age-old and often quite successful formula that contrasts a dastardly villain with an innocent and ultimately triumphant prey. And her tales followed as well, I thought, an equally time-honored pattern, in which writers of histories and novels and memoirs—not just authors but also writers of mental narratives—create villains to blame for problems, maybe even problems of their own making, that they cannot resolve.

As can sometimes happen, that literary judgment delivered a swift clap of understanding. I'd written my own self-serving story in that tradition of villains, my dastardly villain a creature I could blame for what had been done to me, what I was doing to myself, what had been done to my child.

The story had been so much clearer, so much more energizing, than the story I faced about Eric and me now.

Oh, he wasn't "innocent," but God knew I wasn't, either. There were a gracious many charges I had to answer about how we took care of our child. So much I had missed, so much I hadn't done, so many questions unasked, anger misdirected, suspicions turned to convictions. I was still angry: for his lies, for his omissions, for all the times he told me I was debasing myself with crazy hope. For his betrayal now, our daughter for this other. But I'd given him a pointy cap and painted him dark because I so desperately needed someone who had done this, who could undo it, if only I could find the right counter-spell.

One day, I thought, my daughter, will come back alive and she will write stories. Will she let her father and me read them? Who will we be in them? In the story I had been writing, I had cast Anna as Esmarelda: the powerless harried victim, not triumphant, but waiting for my love to rescue her from a rain of blows. If she did come back, would she take charge of her own story? Would she be content to play Esmarelda? Would she even care if I thought what she wrote was any good?

THE END of Book 2

If you enjoyed this book, please LEAVE A REVIEW at the retailer of your choice.

For news of Book 3

in

The Sarah Crockett Mysteries

AMONG THE LOST CHILDREN

VISIT MY WEBSITE

https://www.virginiasanderson.com

OR SIGN UP AT

VIRGINIA'S BOOKS[1]

1. https://virginiasanderson.com/newsletter-sign-up

ACKNOWLEDGMENTS

Many wise, patient and generous people have helped Sarah look for her lost daughter over the years. The first book in the series, *Among the Bones*, began its life in my brief years in Texas, and it was there that my valued friends and University of Texas graduate-program colleagues first met Sarah and where she set down roots. When I moved to Indiana to begin my teaching career, I was fortunate to find new willing readers. I spent many a Sunday afternoon with the Green River Writers, especially in the capable company of founder Mary (Ernie) O'Dell and colleague Deanna Hopper, who kept Sarah on track through revision after revision—and still does, month after patient month—letting Sarah and me know when we veer off course. I want to give a special remembrance to one of my most demanding Green River critique partners, the late Charles (Chuck) Suddeth; I learned to pay attention when Chuck drew a line across my text and wrote in firm black letters, "YOUR STORY STARTS HERE." At Indiana University Southeast, where I passed seventeen rewarding years, I tormented my librarian/teacher colleagues Nancy Totten and Teresa Reynolds with ongoing requests for readings. Not only did these beleaguered souls gift me with their time but also helped me craft Sarah's life as a dedicated writing teacher and administrator in a small, vibrant university where students bring so many hopes and needs. I owe much, as well, to the many generous members of the Internet Writing Workshop, who helped open up Sarah's story to its many quieter themes. Finally, and above all, in uncountable ways, I owe SR and WBS, who know who they are.

ABOUT ME

I am a native of Atlanta, Georgia, where I spent my teenage years wanting to ride horses and be a writer, pretty much in that order. For twenty years I lived in Tampa, Florida, where I taught horseback riding and accumulated the material for my horse-racing mystery/suspense novels: *King of the Roses,* St. Martin's Press (about life and death at the Kentucky Derby), and *Blood Lies,* Bantam/Doubleday (murder in the Bluegrass). Regaining my rights, I self-published slightly edited versions of these books, and, in 2023, I published *Three Strides Out: A Horse Show Novel of Suspense,* drawing on my years of riding and showing hunters and jumpers.

The Sarah Crockett Mysteries grew out of another facet of my life: my five blissful years as a PhD student in English at the University of Texas at Austin. There, many years ago, I created a character deep in pursuit of a vital goal: finding out what had happened to her missing child. The first book in the series, *Among the Bones*, begins Sarah's journey toward that goal; Book 2, *Among the Lies*, is the next step down that dangerous road.

I happily returned to the Austin of today to research what had become of the city in which I spent such wonderful years. Austinites will be aghast at my many errors. I apologize out front and beg forgiveness. I hope people will feel free to tell me what needs fixing. One miracle of self-publishing is that you can correct your mistakes!

Today I live in Southern Indiana, where for many years I taught college writing at Indiana University Southeast, a regional campus of Indiana University. My old horse Paddy is retired now, enjoying his new life of standing around and eating hay. After years of a full pet menagerie, I am down to one cat, Peep, and some nesting bluebirds who accept my supervision skeptically, to say the least. I am working on a new horse-showing mystery and diving into Book 3 of Sarah's story.

Please stop by my website, https://www.virginiasanderson.com[1]
to order and sign up for news of my books.

1. http://www.virginiasanderson.com

www.ingramcontent.com/pod-product-compliance
Lightning Source LLC
LaVergne TN
LVHW010636110826
845149LV00014B/2851
9780997576894